DAUGHTER

OF

ETHERON

BRANDON YOUNG

DAUGHTER OF ETHERON

The Saga of the Magicus Eye

Book One

Printed in Australia

ISBN 978-0-6480794-1-5

Second Edition, June 2017

For the reader,

CHAPTER ONE

THE COIN IS TOSSED

The galaxy moves in patterns. What came before will come again, and the sins of men now carved in stone will return to taint the hearts of those who rule today.

Elenah Lockwood sat upon a parapet by the old Everling Tree, gazing out across the city.

Something terrible was about to happen. She felt it in the homely air—too *tight*. She saw it in the marble towers, which spiralled from the cramped little shops at all the wrong angles. The timid winds carried the sound of a thousand voices to her ears, as well as the clapping of moving feet, and distant, chiming music.

Gods, but everything was *wrong*. The people moved with a frenetic haste, sweeping the glistening cobblestones, furnishing the spaceports with flowers of bright colours. It was the picture one might see before the arrival of someone very, very important . . .

"They're coming, aren't they?" Elenah said.

Gilgan stood behind her, crookedly leaning on his walking stick. Elenah glanced at him sidelong as a gust of wind rolled over the bridge and flung her raven hair across her face.

"Get down from there," Gilgan said, tossing away the white flower he'd been holding, which immediately began to shed its petals. "You're going to hurt yourself."

Elenah stood up, her toes hanging over the edge of the bridge. The wind's lively hands tried to snatch her, yet her feet seemed bound to the parapet's marble aura. She felt invincible, protected by the sky and the morning stars above. If she only stepped forward . . .

"Elenah!" Gilgan said, more intensely.

Elenah sighed and faced him, her back to the great drop. One might have thought that after sixteen years on this rock, she might actually be able to walk a few hundred feet beyond the palace. But her father's *hounds* just didn't ever seem to let go.

"Come down now," Gilgan muttered.

"Come get me," Elenah invited.

Gilgan smiled. "If only my balance was half as good as yours." He pointedly wiggled his black cane. "I can hardly stand on flat ground without falling over." Finally, he drew a deep breath and said, "Well, if you *do* fall over, I hope you know that *I* won't be sweeping you off the cobbles."

"I honestly don't think I would mind by then."

Gilgan shook his head despairingly. "You can't keep this up forever, Elenah. I know you're just doing it to spite your father, but you have to realise that you're not just some street urchin."

"I'm not that important, honestly."

"You're important to *me*. Now, would you please come down?"

Elenah took a moment to simply observe Gilgan's wrinkled face. He was getting old, and his sense of fashion was deteriorating as surely as his own body was. Today he wore a black duster, which was grim compared to the rest of the city.

Gilgan offered her his hand, and Elenah took it as she stepped back onto the bridge. "Ugh, look at your dress," Gilgan said, patting her down. "It's all crumpled. You know, you should at least make an effort to be clean. They'll be here soon."

Elenah grumbled. "Why are they even coming?" she asked, following the arch of the bridge. Gilgan joined her, clapping along with his cane. The bridge, like much of the city, was wrought of marble, and flanked by flowers of a multitude of colours. Flowers were symbolic here on Etheron; these ones had been planted and blessed by the current floran, Iris Tan, and were supposed to be some kind of wisher of good luck. "We're doing perfectly fine here."

"Not for long," Gilgan said. Then he added, "Something's happening." Elenah looked at him. Gilgan was never one to speculate, and he knew a lot more than other people thought. After all, Gilgan had ventured from one side of the galaxy to the other, and who knew what he'd seen? "There's been an . . . *imbalance* in the galaxy."

"Okay, well, what's that supposed to mean?"

"It means we're not necessarily safe here anymore."

"You do realise we won't be any safer with *them*, right?" Elenah noted the anxious expression that devoured Gilgan's face. His jaw tightened, and the sweat in his wrinkles looked more pronounced. "I don't trust the Council," she told him in all sincerity.

"Oh, I know," he said unevenly. "You've only told me a hundred times."

"You don't trust them either," she said.

"I have to; it's my job." He smiled. "Besides, the Forty-Ninth Council has done more things for this world than you can even count. It's in our best interest not to . . . *piss* them off, excuse my language."

Elenah wasn't sure why there weren't more people trying to make a stand against the Council; she knew in her deepest heart that it was not the benevolent hand it claimed to be. The galaxy moved in patterns, and what came before would come again. Why couldn't anybody see that? The leaders of the Council were master puppeteers, manipulating the influential percentage of the Inner Realm, orchestrating tyranny.

"I wish I could do something," she said as they passed a young, lanky man handing out leaflets. Elenah could just make out the headline: THE GREAT DECEPTION OF THE FORTY-THIRD CYCLE. She'd already read it, though she wished more people would heed its words. "This is all a game, can't you see, Gilgan? The Council is playing us."

"You shouldn't read that stuff," Gilgan muttered under his breath. "It's not good for you. Believe me, this is not the first time I've seen a force like the Council come to power. It certainly won't be the last. They're promising to protect us, and I say that's good enough for now. It's what the people need. *Reassurance.* The only thing those papers are going to do is inspire some sort of resistance, and all that's going to achieve is violence where violence has no place."

"Do you *actually* think the Council's going to come peacefully?"

Gilgan's silence, as it often did, betrayed his dumb façade. He knew more than he was letting on. Gilgan had seen this all before, in another time and another place. But Elenah had long given up hope that Gilgan might try to fix it. For some reason, he seemed reluctant to do anything these days. Unless, of course, it was demanded by her father. *But Father's probably the only person in this city even more reluctant than Gilgan,* she decided.

"I suppose they're going to take Teveran too," Elenah said.

"Your brother will be fine," Gilgan said with barely a flicker of hesitation. It was difficult to believe. Teveran was the High Prince of Etheron by birthright, which meant he was important to the Council. But as far as Elenah was concerned, the Council just wanted to get their hands on someone with a piece of this family's magical ancestry, someone they could use to defend their new order. Like playing with puppets.

Elenah sighed. "Isn't there anything we can do? He obviously doesn't want to—"

"You don't know that. Besides, I don't think he has much of a choice."

"Well, maybe he *should.*"

"Like I said, we'd be better off not making enemies of the Council." He put a hand on her back and smiled reassuringly, though it didn't do much to help. Gilgan pulled her to a stop by a garden of multicoloured flowers and dug into his huge duster. "Here." He pulled out a couple of silver square chits. "Go buy that book you've been waiting for. Put your mind at ease."

Elenah waved them away. "What's the point?"

"What's the *point?*" Gilgan asked incredulously.

"We're all going to be dead soon anyway."

"Just stop," Gilgan hissed, shoving the cold, silver chits

into her hand. "Nobody's going to die. The Council wouldn't risk that." There was something cryptic embedded within those last words that Elenah couldn't quite decipher. She merely lingered on Gilgan's silver-eyed gaze until he turned around and started hobbling off.

"Where are you going?" Elenah asked.

"I work here," Gilgan said, a little less jovial than he'd been seconds before. "I should probably start helping out. Oh, and Elenah?" He stopped and angled his head. "Please, for the love of all things holy, try to stay out of *trouble*. I presume their ships will be arriving soon." Then he went off with his stick drumming the ground.

Elenah watched him go, wondering if he suspected she might turn to trouble in such times as these. She gazed into the sky; there was barely a cloud. There weren't many places like this left in the galaxy. Untouched and untainted by the dark forces gathering. Soon it would be ripped up by the Council's fleet. *Protection*, they called it. Elenah didn't believe them.

She muttered angrily to herself as she stuffed the chits into her pocket, then spun and carved a path to the city streets. The planets were in turmoil, even Elenah knew that and she was just a sixteen-year-old girl with barely any stakes in the galaxy. Soon it was going to come here, to her father's Free Worlds. The peace he'd built would all come undone. And what then? What would happen to these glistening marble towers, and the hills and lakes and the magnificent city walls?

And what about the people?

Elenah slipped inconspicuously into a narrow alleyway and pressed her back up against the stone wall, bathed in the cool shadow beneath the eaves. The truth was, she hadn't come out here just to speak with Gilgan. There were other people in this city, people like herself who saw through the Council's lies and who were willing to fight back.

This was where they conspired.

She puffed out a shaky breath, then quickly followed the alleyway until she reached a dishevelled door wedged between a pot of dead flowers and leaking rubbish bags. She knocked once, twice, then stepped back and waited. A cold wind rippled through the alley, shifting pebbles and papers and a soggy leaflet with THE END OF THE FREE WORLDS TREATY? branded upon it. A moment later, the door swung inward and Elenah hurried inside.

"—been in contact with an informant off-world," came a voice across the repurposed storage room. It still smelt like potions and ointments of every sort, although seventeen years had tarnished the smell with rot, decay, and the bitterness of death. Shelves were toppled, the wood splintered and eroded. Chairs occupied the space where once there might have been benches; and a grim, low-key group of people loitered in the place of customers.

"Where have you been?" Oswald whispered, leaning against the dusty wall with folded arms. Oswald was probably the only person here she actually trusted, and that was saying something, because Oswald was currently a wanted man in several star systems. He wore a dusty top hat, which concealed his greasy brown hair, but did not hide his beard— which was, as always, far too well-groomed for the face of a criminal.

"I thought the meeting started at tenth chime," Elenah said, standing beside him.

Oswald sighed, but Elenah felt she deserved it; this was

not the first time she'd turned up late. Oswald ignored her tardiness. He asked instead, "Where's Korvis?"

"Korvis?" Elenah looked around. "No idea."

"Somebody had better watch that guy."

Elenah was just glad she didn't have to listen to him for once.

"I have no doubts," continued the bald ex-pirate, Morgan, "that the bastards will be using the clock tower as their operating base. I suspect it will only be temporary." They all knew what that meant. The Council wasn't coming here just to visit. Once their ground troops occupied the city, they'd move into the palace. It made a knot in Elenah's gut and she realised her father's ignorance angered her now more than ever. It was going to cost them all dearly if he continued to do nothing. It would probably end up with them all dead.

As she looked around at the gathered, she realised his inaction had already taken its toll. There were hardly a dozen of them left, for they'd fled to the north and west, seeking greater rebellions. Perhaps they'd even banded together to strike Tarthalus on their own.

"This may be the last time we speak before the Council's arrival," Morgan continued, now pacing up and down what was once an aisle flanked by potions. He swallowed, and a silence came that was interrupted only by the creaking of wood, and the dying, wheezing breaths of the old man in the corner—a *magician*. "I do hope it will not be the last time."

Morgan eyed Elenah over his grizzly beard. Perhaps, like herself, Morgan wished there was something she could do— after all, she *was* the king's daughter—but Elenah was as helpless as the rest of them. Despite her position, she did not have influence. Her role in this galaxy was merely a princess, a showpiece for her father, and not much else.

She wanted to explore, but she couldn't step one foot beyond the city walls. She wanted to learn magic with Gilgan—like Teveran did—but magic was outlawed here under the Treaty of the Free Worlds and Elenah wasn't "important" enough. So this was where the fates had led her: to a meeting of dissidents in a dingy storage room.

Precisely where she was not allowed.

"To all of you," Morgan said, "be vigilant, be steadfast, be resolute. We must not bow down. The Council aims to do one thing and one thing only: tear this civilisation apart." He nodded to a man standing nearby, and motioned for the old magician in the corner.

Elenah watched them with a nervous curiosity.

"Listen, Elenah." Oswald grabbed her arm and pulled her into the corner of the store, so that they couldn't be overheard. His breath stank like beer and smoke, which repelled her back into the half-light. "You'd better go back to the palace and keep a low profile for a while."

"What?"

"Just do it," Oswald said, his voice becoming lower and lower as he glanced left and right, incapable of appearing any more suspicious.

"I'm not giving up on this, Oswald."

"I know," Oswald quickly said. "It's just . . . It's a *feeling*." But he was as unconvincing as Gilgan. Elenah glanced from Oswald to Morgan, then to the magician.

"They don't want me in the palace," Elenah said.

"Whatever. Then just go away from *here*. Got it?"

Elenah bit her lip, but eventually resolved to nod. Maybe

he was right. Things were about to get real bad, and she had enough to worry about without getting caught conspiring against the government. Soon the Council would arrive and everything was going to change. They were going to take her brother, strip power from her father. And what did this mean for her? At least she knew she could count on these people if she ever needed their help.

"Bloody hell," Oswald said, pulling her from her reverie. "Go." Elenah nodded, hurried from the shadows, and flung open the door leading back into the city.

"Heed my words, citizens of Etheron!" a loud voice bellowed from amidst the swelling crowd. Elenah focused on it as she rounded into the bustling marketplace and slowed, trying not to be sucked into their frantic, mindless activity. Merchants scurried about, spilling trinkets and small handmade toys. She eventually emerged from the throng to see a tall woman standing on the large statuesque foot of Soris, Goddess of the Starsong. The woman was gesticulating wildly before the gathered crowd, a stark contrast to the beautiful god.

"War threatens the galaxy, war like we've never seen!" She had a glazed look on her face, her eyes wide, glittering in the morning sunlight. Her voice was shrill and powerful, and in the wind her pale dress was flung about majestically. "Countless cities are falling beneath a wicked shadow of terror. Warmongers, false prophets and magicians threaten our world!"

Elenah frowned, glancing about the crowds and feeling anger at their gleeful expressions. Did they really believe this woman's indoctrinating tunes?

"For two thousand years we've had chaos," the woman bellowed, "but the Council will liberate us! They will restore this galaxy to its former glory!"

Gods, they can't be serious, Elenah thought, moving along and leaving the voice behind her. She couldn't escape it all, though. Voices followed her. A woman muttered, "Have you heard? The chancellor of Oracle has abandoned the Treaty—"

"They say there's going to be a ban on old religious texts," came another.

Elenah descended a set of stone steps, crossed a road that smelt sweetly of flowers, tried to organise her thoughts—but the entire city was buried in deep discussion.

"I heard the Royal Family is cursed," said a man with round spectacles as Elenah brushed past him trying to look nonchalant. She wasn't sure if any of these people recognised her; it wasn't like her father paraded her around like he often did with Teveran.

"It's the king," said another in a hushed voice. "He's afraid of the Council, that's why this is happening . . . If he weren't so married to that Treaty, none of us would be in this mess."

By now, Elenah was hardly paying attention. She split through another crowd, rounded a corner—and then someone grabbed her arm and hoisted her behind a statue.

She gasped, leapt out of his arms and swung instinctively at his face. The man grabbed her wrist reflexively and looked into her eyes.

Korvis, she thought bitterly.

He was dressed differently today, in a neat white coat that contrasted his dark hair, and a single white glove that concealed a blistered burn he'd obtained about three weeks back. Though he was only two years her senior, Korvis looked much more a man even than her older brother, who had one year on Korvis. A strange thing, age and numbers.

"Come with me," he said, ushering her behind a small shop.

"What are you doing?" Elenah asked. "And why weren't you at the meeting?"

"Those guys don't have a clue what they're doing," Korvis said as they arrived at a garden covered in shade. The flowers here were dead, all wilting and colourless. There were grey, ashen leaves on the ground, and there was something in the air that made Elenah feel uneasy. Korvis eyed her with a vicious look and said, "I don't trust them and neither should you."

"At least they're trying," Elenah said. "Somebody needs to." She grunted, trying to placate her frustration. "Look, there is at least one thing I agree with my father on, and that's keeping this a *Free* World. I don't want my home to fall into their hands."

"You don't get it," Korvis said.

"What don't I *get?*" Elenah beckoned him.

"Those people you hang out with, they're *criminals.*"

Elenah simply eyed him, until she couldn't even bear to do that. She spun away, now watching the city folk crossing the roads back and forth, back and forth, as if they weren't even aware of what was about to happen. Once the ships of the Forty-Ninth Council came down from the sky, they'd all fall under the rule of the man who called himself the Architect, and they'd have all liberty stripped from them. She wouldn't allow that. She just *wouldn't.*

"Come with me, Elenah."

"What are you talking about?"

Korvis crept up behind her, rocks crunching underneath his feet. She could suddenly smell his pungent perfume, or whatever he used. "We can leave this place while there's still a chance. We can go where magic's allowed. We can learn it *together*."

"You're unbelievable," Elenah groaned. "I can't leave. This is my home. The moment my father finds out I've fled he'll have half the galaxy trying to hunt me down." She turned around to face him, then glanced at the dead flowers. They stirred feebly in the depressing breeze. It meant only one thing. "You've been practising magic here."

"I—"

"You can't *do* that, Korvis."

"Well maybe if your father wasn't such a *fool!*" His face twisted in a show of rage, and Elenah felt the air revolve as Korvis tapped unconsciously into his magical potential. That happened sometimes when you didn't have a proper teacher. Gilgan kept telling her, though it was often in bitterness towards her father. Elenah stood there firmly, her brow quivering. Korvis softened immediately. "Sorry, I shouldn't have—"

"I don't even care," Elenah said. "I should probably be looking for my brother." She spun around and tried to escape him. Korvis took her hand and she shook it off.

"Wait!" he said.

Elenah ignored him. "By the way, Oswald was looking for you. You might want to go and speak to him before you lose the few allies you have left."

"What's your problem?" Korvis asked. "I thought you *wanted* to leave." There was genuine disbelief in his voice now, causing Elenah to flush. "Besides, I don't think *you* have any right to admonish me like this. Haven't you been training with Gilgan?"

"You know I'm not allowed," Elenah said.

"Don't lie to me. I'm not an idiot."

She rounded on him heavily. "Don't call me a liar, Korvis!"

He sighed. "Fine. You know what? You're right. Maybe I *will* just leave. Etheron may be a Free World, but it won't be free much longer."

Elenah nodded. "You should do that. You'd be doing us all a favour—" She was brought up short by a deep rumbling in her chest. The ground shifted underneath her feet, a warm wind surged through the alleyway. She looked up into the blue sky. It began to ripple, and blur . . .

And then the sound of explosions rocked the entire city as silver Ragnaroks emerged from hyperspace. Elenah's breath caught. *Already?* The starfighters burst into existence, a dozen of them, throwing off wisps of cloud and space matter. She glanced at Korvis, who was frozen stiff, as though somebody had cast a spell on him. *But it's barely past morning . . .*

"Not good," Korvis gasped, striding through the alleyway to the crowded city streets. Elenah followed him, her heart racing in her chest. When she emerged in the blazing light, reality finally settled in, and everybody looked up as the Forty-Ninth Council arrived.

CHAPTER TWO

WAR GAMES

The galactic significance of the High Prince stemmed from the war hero, Ramadus Lamonte, who, after defeating the magician, Oradin of Cryptis, founded the famous Thirty-First Council and generated stability for thirteen years before his equally-famous fall.

Teveran watched the ships descend upon the city. Each time a new one appeared, there was a blast like thunder and the glass in his bedroom window rattled.

"They're early," he said. "Gods, they were supposed to come later."

"How much later, exactly?" his father, Bayle, inquired.

"Just later," Teveran muttered. He faced the window and fastened his sleeve's ivory cuff. His reflection stared back at him. Gods, but he didn't look much like the High Prince of Etheron. His ash-brown hair messily grazed his neck, his gleaming hazel eyes looked as though they belonged to a child—not a *man*.

But you are the high prince, he told himself. *You've got the blood of all the high princes before you.* His father often reminded him of the fact, said they would call him Grand Highlord one day, although Teveran wasn't sure if the title was anything to be proud of.

"It's time for you to become the man this galaxy needs," his father said, standing by the antiquated desk behind him. Teveran watched him stroll into the window's gaze, hands clasped—they trembled slightly. His father had just one eye; only white swirls and a thin red scar remained of the other. The lively sunlight revealed his wiry frame; it sank into his hollowed-out jaws and refined them. "You'll follow in the footsteps of your uncle . . . and all those before you. They'll gladly honour you among their ranks, I'm sure."

Teveran thought about this. He was not intimately familiar with his uncle, Ignus Thrakk, who was now serving as Grand Highlord among the Council's prime fleet. But the man's icy blue eyes were imprinted upon Teveran's vision: the burden of family legacy.

"What if I'm not good enough?" he whispered. "I've hardly got any training. I can *hardly* use magic. And gods, out there is a whole new world. Nothing like this." Everything was about to change. Merely its name, the *Forty-Ninth Council,* bore a reverence far greater than any council before it. Some said *this* was going to be the one that brought peace and order to the galaxy. This time they would finally break this two-thousand-year epoch of chaos and start a brand new age . . .

His father smiled. "And what would you know of the worlds beyond?"

"Gilgan told me," Teveran said carefully.

"They're nothing more than stories." He gripped Teveran's shoulder tight, causing him to flinch. Teveran tried to conceal his discomfort, staring straight ahead. Growing up, he'd always been quite tall, but his father still towered over him.

"I wish Elenah could come with me."

"It's unfortunate." Such a simple lie. His father didn't really care about Elenah and, if he did, he didn't show it. Teveran knew how much Elenah wanted to see the stars, to follow in Gilgan's footsteps, play with magic, explore, and go tell her own stories . . . The fact that she was denied so much angered him, although perhaps it meant he ought to take this far more seriously. Make the most of it. Live this adventure for the both of them.

"This is *your* duty, Teveran. Not hers."

"I know," he acquiesced. They'd raised him for this very moment. To go and join the Council's highest ranks, and lead their greatest fleets, like all the high princes before him. He should've felt so privileged, so grateful for this opportunity . . . but instead it frightened him.

It was Elenah, and what she'd told him: *Be careful, Teveran. Remember what Gilgan told us. There's a terrible danger in too much power. And I don't think I've ever heard of anybody with more power than the architects of the Forty-Ninth Council . . .*

He couldn't help but think she knew something that nobody else did. She saw something in the Council that was invisible to so many others, and it was starting to take hold of him too. Gods, but he hadn't slept a full night in weeks, constantly plagued by dreams of warfare, fighting on the front lines . . . Was that where they were going to take him?

"There's a rebellion," Teveran said, trying to think of something else—*anything* else. "The Galactic Liberation Movement . . . fighting in the west . . . What about them?"

"There are many groups that would call themselves

rebellions," his father said, "and they are not for you to be concerned about. They are nothing more than terrorists and they will be dealt with accordingly, when the time is right."

"But you've heard the stories, Father. You've *seen* it." He tried not to shout, but there were people out there trying to destroy the Council. His father *knew* this. He always spoke of it: Cities blown to pieces, mass burnings of troopers . . . He constantly hammered those truths into the minds of the populace, and now he was sending Teveran out there!

Yes, but it wasn't meant to be like this, Teveran thought, anxiety twisting his gut. *The rebels weren't here until a few weeks ago.* That was the word on the news. The rebels had previously fought on the skirts of the Council's sphere of influence.

But now . . .

And that's why the Council's really here. They haven't come here just to offer us their protection, or to take me. They're recruiting. Because there's war coming.

And that frightened him above all else.

"Father . . ." he started.

"It's okay, Teveran. It's not the role of the High Prince to fight on the front lines." Yet ostensibly reading the unconvinced expression on Teveran's face, he moved closer and tried to placate him with a gentle hand on his shoulder. "I would never do anything that would put you in danger, Teveran. You know that."

"You wouldn't really have a choice, though, would you?"

His father stared blankly, then retreated. "I would certainly do my best to." Then he stepped away and glanced out the window, towards the ships gathering on the horizon. "Look at them all," he mused. "I think it's best not to delay things further."

In that moment, his father looked like he didn't know what to do, what to say, faced with a son he might never see again. Teveran couldn't help but notice his sallow skin, accentuated by the rays of golden light. "I don't suppose they've changed their mind," Teveran said, trying to release the building tension.

His father offered a pale, bony hand. "I don't think so," he said with a smile.

Teveran took his hand, which was cold.

"You're the High Prince. Don't forget that. They'll take care of you."

"Okay," Teveran said warily.

"Remember what Gilgan taught you. Everything you need"—he caught Teveran's wrist and pressed it firmly against Teveran's chest—"is in *here*." As he said it, Teveran felt a spike in his magical potential. It was like an icy current somewhere even deeper than his soul itself.

Teveran nodded vacantly.

His father smiled, then released Teveran's hand and balled his own into a fist. He coughed violently, causing Teveran to cringe, then drew a deep, hoarse breath as he hurried away.

"Are you going to be okay?" Teveran asked.

"Yes," his father quickly said. "Yes, don't worry about me. Go." He stopped at the threshold of the doorway, leaning up against the frame. "Go and save this galaxy, Teveran." Then he walked out, leaving Teveran all alone with his sorry reflection.

ELENAH EMERGED ON THE MAIN THOROUGHFARE, and released a ragged breath. She'd managed to shake off Korvis, but now the Council was descending upon them, and they were worse.

She gasped as a huge troop transport landed swiftly before her, blowing up dirt on the cobbles. "A Manticore," she muttered. A knot of white-clad troopers marched down the landing ramp and onto the city road. Black highlights trimmed their striking armour plates. A narrow visor wrapped around the mid-section of each helmet, which arced up sharply at the ends, giving them an angry appearance that was probably befitting of such men.

Their lieutenant strolled ahead of them, twirling on the spot. "Set up patrols in the Corfalle District," he said. "We've got sectors four, seven, and nine." He began gesticulating about. "There are vantage points on—" Elenah stepped out of earshot as she arrived at the palace. Its emerald spires graced the sky, its many spears thrust up into the heavens. One could've called it beautiful, even majestic . . . Though it only reminded Elenah of what she was.

The air rumbled as another Ragnarok split the sky, throwing off beams of silver. Gods, but she'd be lying if there wasn't something wondrous about it. All her life she'd been sequestered inside the palace, hidden away from the real world and its spectacles. Sure, she'd had plenty of books—many of which were written by Gilgan himself—but the truth was, she wanted to *see* things, not just read their names scribbled on mouldy pages. She wanted to smell the alien air, taste their wonderful cuisines . . . Just imagine what lay beyond here, in worlds where great beasts roamed the skies and heroes walked the streets! Part of her, the smallest part, but also perhaps the truest, wondered if she *should* have run off with Korvis.

Too late for that, she told herself. So she sucked in a deep breath, raised her chin, squared her shoulders—like Gilgan had taught her—and took off.

Teveran was standing in the palace courtyard, beside a stone statue of Endius, the God of Knowledge. A long crack stained the side of the statue's leg. Crystals glistened across the book it raised towards the skyline.

"Are you ready?" Elenah asked.

Teveran spun towards her, startled. He cursed beneath his breath and scrubbed strands of hair out of his face. "Yeah," he recovered, but it was hardly convincing. He gazed past her, to the officers all moving about the streets, and the ships still descending between the towers. "What about you?" he asked. "You'll be okay here, won't you?"

"Well . . ." She thought of the Council, and what they were, and what they stood for, and wasn't really sure if she *would* be okay here. "That depends on whether or not I'm right."

"That's not very comforting," Teveran said with a boyish smile. He hardly looked his nineteen years. A glimmer of sunlight touched the emerald sphere he wore from a gold chain around his neck. It marked him as the High Prince. Elenah wondered what made the High Prince so special, and how such a title could make smart emen take foolish actions. Teveran stepped towards her, sunlight tangled in his perfect hair. "You won't cry, will you?"

Elenah shook her head, but she was suddenly reminded of the times they'd played out in the gardens, with Gilgan, and Old Rose, when their worries were non-existent. "No," she said firmly. "Just watch out for yourself. Where are they taking you exactly?"

"One of those shuttles should take me to their flagship."

"I hope they know which one," she commented, for there must have been scores of them all hovering and floating about. "I hope they know what they're doing."

"So do I," Teveran said, almost to himself. Then he asked, "Is something wrong?"

"No, it's just . . . I can't help thinking of Mother," Elenah whispered, heaviness in the backs of her eyes. "She never came back. Old Loris never came back. And Murell . . ."

"That was different, Elenah."

"I know. I'm sorry. It's just . . ." She fiddled with the three white buttons beneath her blouse's elegant collar. "Oh, just be careful, Teveran."

Teveran stepped forward and wrapped his arms around her.

She clutched him tighter. "Don't let them change you."

"Do you remember that game we used to play in Old Cob's shop?"

Elenah chuckled, although it came out nasally and harsh. "He used to make the best cakes." Teveran quietly laughed. She could feel his heart beating, and was afraid it might be the last time she ever did. "I miss Old Cob," Elenah said, salty tears on her lips. But they were not entirely tears of sadness; they were tears of anger and frustration, despair that somehow it all came to this.

"Excuse me, sir."

They stepped out of their embrace to see an important-looking man scrutinising them. He wore the uniform that Elenah recognised as belonging to a field officer. He observed

Teveran's emerald globe and said, "You'll need to come with me now."

Teveran nodded and stepped forward. "Bye, Elenah."

Elenah couldn't speak. She eyed the officer, fighting the urge to attack him. She'd never stood face-to-face with one of them before, but now that she was, she couldn't trust herself not to do something stupid. This was her enemy, the enemy of Etheron, one of the men who had come to take her home away. She held his eyes until the officer turned and left, with Teveran in his wake.

And Elenah just stood there, surrounded by silence and emptiness. Suddenly, the palace courtyard, and all of Etheron, felt too small.

Gilgan stood in the shade of a white-bole tree.

The sun beat down in scintillating rays. All around him, children played and laughed, and the mobile troopers of the Forty-Ninth Council steadily began to occupy the city. *Protection*, they called it. Gilgan knew that they meant the *location*, not the *people*.

He watched Teveran from afar. Gods, but he reminded him so much of the king himself. All but for one thing: the raging magical potential in his blood, his ability to harness, manipulate, and engage in this wicked dance with magic. Teveran had such brilliant promise, and it was a shame he might never complete his training. Though, it was a miracle Gilgan had been allowed to teach him in the first place. The king didn't fancy these "magicians" and it was only through Gilgan's stubborn insistence that Teveran learned how to spellcast safely.

After all, it was the powerful untrained who were most in danger.

As Teveran departed amidst the frantic crowds, Gilgan glanced at Elenah, and met her glistening eyes. She was smart, and she knew that the Council was not all that it appeared to be, but she would be okay. Besides, Gilgan didn't have the heart to tell her how bad the galaxy really was—how bad it would *become*. He certainly couldn't tell her that Teveran wasn't likely coming back, not any time soon, and that it was a feeling cloudy like a shroud of unending darkness.

Gilgan stepped away from the tree and climbed forward with his walking stick. It clapped the windswept cobbles in rhythmic tempo, in time with his tired heart. Why did it feel like there was something out there, something stale, moving about the crowds? It was a familiar disturbance, a spike of magic in a world where magic had been outlawed for seventeen years.

It's nothing, he told himself, watching Teveran's form disappear within the rabble.

Gilgan stopped beside a flowerbed, then glanced at Elenah and found she'd already moved. *I'm getting slow*, he realised. Then he gazed about and saw several shuttles already lifting off the ground, and troopers and officers headed for the clock tower and its surrounding areas.

This was all just a show of power. War games. The Council coming to offer their protection, fabricating lies about the scattered rebellion . . . Those rebels, fighting in the crime-ridden pockets of the galaxy, were not a threat to these Free Worlds. It was the Council that was a threat, and Gilgan knew this all too well. He pulled from his pocket the letter he'd been sent via imp; it tremored in his shaking hands, but the words were clear:

My old friend,

Fex is alive and he's serving the Forty-Ninth Council now. We are currently moving out of the Western Realm and our paths may very well cross—his and mine, of course. However, I must warn you: Keep the boy safe, and the girl as well, for I fear there is something far worse approaching.

- Jethre

Gilgan tore it up and fed it to the wind, then walked nonchalantly from his position. There was nothing he could do about it now, certainly not from this end. There was nothing more he could say to convince Master Lockwood that they should reconsider this "allegiance." All he could do was find Elenah and protect her, though he knew that he could not do so forever, and that she would soon find out the truth of this war . . . perhaps sooner than he would like.

CHAPTER THREE

HIGHLORD KLOAK

The year was 43c19 by the designation of the Eternal Cog, a number which would become significant in more ways than one.

Elenah listened to the ticking of her desk clock. It filled the emptiness of her bedroom. *Tick . . . Tick . . . Tick . . .* She lay on her bed, staring at the stark, white ceiling. Shadows from the buildings outside played across it. She watched them, and she listened. Outside her window, a long way below, white-clad troopers and uniformed field officers strolled about. Though, their presence hardly seemed to deter anybody, for the city was louder than ever.

Elenah, meanwhile, had a decision to make.

Everything was falling apart, that was a fact. She was beginning to realise Oswald and the resistance group she'd once believed in was hardly capable of putting a dent in the Council's force. Korvis was probably long gone by now, though where he'd gone was anybody's guess. Gilgan, like always, was so reluctant to admit anything was wrong. For some reason he was lying not only to himself, but to Elenah and maybe even to her father.

And Teveran . . .

She tried not to imagine him trapped within the Council's ranks, all alone, with those tyrants. Though, wasn't it better there than here? At least out there he wasn't being left to suffer, out there he had a *choice*. Elenah was trapped on this once Free World beneath the hammer of the Council, alongside millions of others who would never see their death-blow coming.

She sat up, the bed squealing underneath her. *There's so much I'll never get to see,* she thought, glancing absently towards the book sitting upon her bedside table, *The Unwandered Worlds* by Cartheius Draghelm, which she must have read at least a dozen times. She thought of Gilgan again. A long time ago, he'd promised he would take them to the worlds among the stars, show them the galaxy beyond Etheron . . .

Maybe if she found him, maybe if she could *convince* him, they could still run away from here. She drew a deep breath and glanced towards the window. Sunlight poured through the golden frame. She could barely see the glass for it was so often polished by the servants. *They* probably cared about her the most in this damned place. The sun had risen over the city, casting an opulent glow across the marble spires. She wondered if Oswald and the others were still out there somewhere, planning something dangerous. She wondered if they even cared about her.

Dammit, she thought, leaping from her bed to the polished floorboards. *There's still a way. I just have to find Gilgan and convince him of it.* And then with that, she fled the confines of her bedroom out into the palace proper.

She slewed into a corridor with emerald carpeted floor, then took a sharp left turn. She knew these halls as well as the stars outside her window. She knew the fastest way to get anywhere; after all, she had spent her whole life trapped inside it.

She emerged on the balcony overlooking the main hall, then descended the stairs two at a time. The main hall was dome-shaped, with marble columns pressed against the walls. The ceiling hung thirty feet overhead. A chandelier of jagged curves and edges twinkled from the dome's pinnacle. Through round windows embedded in the walls, golden sunlight spilled inside. This was a modern kind of architecture, designed by leaders in the Clockwork Architectural Society, although it felt too severe, like a temple, not a *home*. One of the servants, an older lady called Rose, hurried towards her as she swept the mahogany floors.

"Rose," Elenah said politely.

"Chasing someone?" Rose asked.

Elenah hesitated, then timidly nodded. "Do you know where Gilgan is?"

"Is everything okay?"

Elenah looked up and around. Other servants hurried about. They'd been working like this ever since news of the Council's visit emerged. Though, the palace—if Elenah were any judge of things—could not possibly be made any cleaner. But still they worked, on and on, sweeping the smallest grains of dirt. Like Gilgan said, it was probably in their best interest to present themselves in the brightest light. After all, the Forty-Ninth Council had all the power in the Inner Realm now, and it would do this family well to be in their good favours.

"I just need to find Gilgan," Elenah said.

"I haven't seen him all day."

Elenah huffed. That would present some problems. "What about my father?"

Rose shook her head, and her features adopted the sombre look they often did when she thought about Elenah's father. "I believe he's . . . occupied."

"Of course he is," Elenah muttered. Not that she really fancied a meeting with her father at a time like this. He'd been ignoring this for far too long.

"What's wrong, Elenah?" Rose asked determinedly.

"It's just . . ." She bit her lip. "I just want to see Gilgan."

"Is it about Teveran? You know there's nothing we can—"

"It's not him," Elenah said, feeling rather stupid standing there in the middle of the hall. But what could she say? That she wanted to leave right now? That she truly believed this city, and in fact this entire world, was all but lost to them? After all this time, why would anybody listen to her? They'd all mired themselves in a denial too deep. She turned to leave. "I'll find him my—"

"He's here!" one of the servants yelled across the hall. Elenah tensed. Rose cursed and brushed past her to where the other servant was waving about. "Get into your positions. Put away those brooms. Gods, Jakob, would you straighten that collar!"

They all began to rush about frantically.

Suddenly, the huge palace doors were thrust open and a single man walked in. He had a burnt face and flaming red hair. He was unaccompanied, which was strange as, judging by the way he dressed, he was a *highlord*, from among the Council's highest military ranks. Elenah felt herself shrink, but she forced herself to eye him down unwaveringly. As he stepped inside the main hall, he withdrew a silver watch from his pocket and held it up, swaying side-to-side before his eyes. Elenah could hear it ticking. *Tick . . . Tick . . . Tick . . .*

"My lord," said a servant, bowing in front of him.

"I'm here for Master Lockwood," the highlord said.

"Yes," the servant said, rising hurriedly to his feet. He stepped aside, then gestured forward, to where a dozen other servants stood with bowed heads—including Rose, several feet in front of her. "Right this way, my lord," stammered the servant.

"No," Elenah whispered, so quietly she could barely hear herself. "Rose," she gasped. The old woman finally lifted her head and the highlord disappeared up the emerald stairs. Elenah strode towards her. "Rose, why are we just *letting* this happen?"

"Be *quiet*, dear," Rose hissed.

"But—"

Rose cut her off with a sharp raised hand and piercing emerald eyes. "The Council is here to protect us, Elenah. It will do us no good to make enemies of them now."

But that's not true! She wanted to scream it out, but instead she simply glanced towards the top of the stairs, where several nervous servants stood, awaiting the highlord's return. "We shouldn't have to bow to him," she said, biting back anger. "He has no authority here."

"I'm afraid he does," Rose said.

"This is *our* home, not his."

Rose simply sighed, and Elenah decided she wasn't going to get any kind of intelligent response, so she asked instead, "Who is he, then? An emissary from Tarthalus?"

"Not quite," Rose said. "That's Highlord Kloak."

Elenah couldn't help but think of his burnt face. *He's a*

soldier, she thought. *Or he was. I wonder why he's here. I wonder if Teveran will end up like him . . .* The highlords were a circle of military advisors ranked just below the Grand Highlord. Some people believed that *they* were the ones who were really commanding the Council's fleets.

But if that were the case, then this was worse than she'd thought.

"What does he want with my father?" Elenah asked.

"I suppose they'll want to discuss the conflict," Rose said, but she sounded unconvinced by it. She turned around and offered an apologetic smile. "Will you try to stay out of trouble, Elenah, just for a few days? Just until the situation settles down. Please?"

Elenah sighed. "Okay, Rose."

Satisfied, Rose strode away with a broom clasped at her side, and Elenah couldn't help but think something terrible was about to happen. She thought of Highlord Kloak and his burnt face, the Forty-Ninth Council occupying the city for the rebels were "gathering a strike force." It wasn't true. There *was* no rebellion, or at least not one that was a threat to the Council. She considered returning to Oswald, but what good would that do? They couldn't help her now. So, instead, she grit her teeth and scoured the palace for Gilgan.

Gilgan found the insurgents in a dilapidated storage room, which reeked of stale magic. The door came off its hinges without hassle, and admitted him into their hideout. To tell the truth, he'd expected more, some sort of magical barrier or a protective charm at the least.

But it didn't surprise him; he couldn't say the same for the others.

Sweaty old men leapt up from their chairs. Several of them receded into the shadows. And the sooty-looking man who stood in the centre had already dug his hand into his coat, fetching for some kind of weapon. None of this bothered Gilgan.

"Don't waste your bullets on me," he said as the door fell shut behind him, failing to catch the latch and instead swaying back and forth. He ignored most of the men and instead strode up to their leader, who was a bald criminal with a purple runic tattoo across his left shoulder. Gilgan recognised it as the rune *ta*, which was quite useless on its own.

The man looked amused as he glanced around at his companions, who were now stepping back into the light, shaking off nervous laughs. "And who might you be, old man?"

"I'm a man who's concerned," Gilgan said softly.

"You're not welcome here," said the resistance leader.

"That's fine; I don't intend on staying." Gilgan took one step away from the man so that he didn't have to smell his rancid breath. The sooner he could leave this place, the better. It reminded him of his days before coming to Etheron, reminded him of the war, and rapped at his magical potential, which had lain unharnessed for almost two decades. "I just so happened to have heard of your little operation, and I think you should end it immediately."

The man simply glared at him, then burst out laughing, turning his back on him and striding towards a couple of his cronies who were also now giggling fitfully. It drew

Gilgan's attention to an old man sitting in the corner; he *reeked* of magic. His eyes were downcast, and his expression was one that Gilgan wondered if they'd done something to him.

"I mean it," he persisted. He pressed his walking stick down hard and stepped forward towards the tattooed man. "This is a terrible mistake. You won't be doing anybody a favour by provoking war with the Council." What he didn't mention was his disgust that they'd even attempted to draw Elenah into their affairs. It *sickened* him.

Though, he also wished she'd been smarter than joining a group like this. He thought he'd raised her better, but clearly nothing could thwart the stubbornness of youth, especially in such times. Gilgan had seen his fair share of resistance in the galaxy—it turned out there were already movements in the north and west—but a resistance here on Etheron, in a Free World, a resistance that utilised magicians and magical sympathisers . . .

"Oswald, come here," the leader said tiredly, waving to the sweaty-haired doorman dressed in a coat and top hat. "Kindly deal with our visitor."

The man called Oswald stepped forward and slammed an electric baton into Gilgan's gut which, from his experience being stunned with electric batons, was only three-quarters charged.

Still, it knocked him to his knees.

"Well?" the leader suggested. "Don't just leave him there!"

Oswald picked Gilgan up and lugged him back out into the alleyway. As he threw him into the dirt, he hissed, "How'd you find us?"

"It really wasn't very hard," Gilgan gasped, stunned. "This

being the only spot of *magic* in a city that has *outlawed* it for *seventeen years*. You could get in serious trouble for this."

Oswald grit his teeth, thought about saying something, then turned to leave.

"Wait," Gilgan said. He propped himself up on one elbow as feeling gradually returned to his body. "Just think about this before you go and do something reckless: The Council is stronger than you, and smarter. If *I* could find you here, then think of what *they* can do."

Oswald seemed to consider it.

"But I don't suppose you care about getting yourself killed—or *others*."

"Who are you?" Oswald asked, still standing before the half-closed door.

"I'm with Elenah. And I know she's been here. Just—"

"I've sent her back to the palace."

Gilgan suppressed his instinctive sigh of relief, for he still didn't fully trust this man. Once you got to his age, with the things he'd seen and lived through, trust was hard earned. "Oswald, is it? What are you doing here that requires a blasted *magician?*"

Oswald simply stared at him. "I have to go," he said, and then he went back inside, leaving Gilgan alone in the cold alleyway, wondering which god had placed this curse upon him.

Chapter Four

INTO THE FIRE

It's called the Magicus Eye, generally agreed to have been coined by the Asmorean astronomer, Sidra Zaihre, for its position within the "Magicus" constellation of space. If this is true, it is also one of the earliest suggestions of innovative life beyond our galaxy.

We're not going to the flagship, Teveran thought as he began to sweat.

He looked up and around, scanning the shuttle's silver walls. They called these ships Manticores, and from what he'd heard they were strong. Yet everything rattled, and groaned, and flakes of metal sprayed into his eyes. *I shouldn't be here. They put me in the wrong one.*

He looked down, remembering the rifle in his grasp. It felt unnatural. He couldn't help but think there'd been a mistake. He'd told them who he was, but he wasn't sure if they'd heard. No, they'd definitely heard him. But had they listened?

"This is *ridiculous*," spat the guy sitting opposite him. His dark skin, narrow eyes and stocky build suggested he was of Azich heritage. The white lights behind him illuminated beads of sweat speckled across his forehead. "Why don't *we* get armour like that?"

"Unfortunately, the rebels recently bombed one of our supply depots," said the commander, who stood against the rear wall in full trooper armour. "There isn't much left, and the workers are falling behind schedule. We couldn't salvage enough in time." He sounded distinctly human, yet machine-like. On his shoulder-plate was the black arced insignia of the Forty-Ninth Council, emblazoned by the cabin lights. It made Teveran's heart race, seeing it like this. Not a drawing. Not some flowery description. The *real thing.*

He averted his eyes from the commander, focusing on the other recruits. There were only a dozen of them, sitting in two rows facing each other, with perhaps four feet between them.

"How can you even see in that?" asked another man.

"It's made of twinsteel," the commander said gruffly; he sounded old—not as old as Gilgan, but old enough to have fought in at least one war before this one. He didn't explain what twinsteel was; Teveran guessed they were just supposed to know.

He turned over his rifle, forcing himself to put his mind at ease, examining the warm metal as it tossed back his reflection. *Is this the face of a hero?*

He gripped the rifle tighter in a fruitless attempt to steady himself. He was almost tempted to ask why the commander had armed them all with rifles—but he knew. They'd put him in the wrong transport shuttle, with a bunch of soldiers who were being pitched into battle. He'd told them this wasn't right, but it was as if they'd been put under some kind of spell.

He studied the rifle, making himself familiar with it. A small cylindrical canister slotted neatly into the rifle's main compartment. *Starfire cell*, he noted. They were the heart of all modern machinery. He fiddled with it, although couldn't quite grasp how it worked. The rifle had a scope, though there was a crack in it. Beneath the barrel was a place to clasp his hand, as well as an ammunition cartridge. *That's where the bullets go*, he thought, glad to find some familiar ground between the weapon and himself. He rolled it in his hands, searching for other secrets.

In all his time within the palace, Teveran had only been given very basic weapon instruction. Gilgan had been a magician, not a soldier, and his father had never seen combat. Teveran just hoped that, when people were shooting at him, he'd remember to shoot back.

"I can tell you're getting anxious," the commander said to all of them. "Thinking about what's to come, about where you're all headed. I'd encourage you all to take a deep breath before we get there. Keep in mind, we've done this a thousand times before. You can be in no safer hands than mine, and I'll make sure to carry you all the way."

Teveran felt a spike of dread. For a second, he could almost see the commander's cobalt eyes gleaming through his visor. He looked away, to the polished silver floor. His stomach heaved; he tried to force down bile. "Where *are* we headed, might I ask?"

The commander eyed him uncomfortably before saying, "Corion. It's a small world on the Starforged Spiral, edge of the Greater Realm. Any historians among us will know Corion's where the Entari warrior Irik'Tai Abitaar made his last stand against the Pulse."

Abitaar's Last Stand, Teveran thought, simply out of habit. *It happened in the thirty-first cycle. Here . . . In this very place . . . A thousand years ago . . .* He distracted himself by thinking of that famous painting. The lone Entari warrior outlasting the endless hordes, posing on a mountain of bodies. But it wasn't enough to make him forget what was happening.

We're not going to the flagship. As if something had changed, he became acutely aware of the rumbling engines. Starfire broiled within them, an energy source forged over thousands of years by the old mages. Gilgan had told him about them.

They were gone now.

He became aware of other ships, too. It was difficult to tell, but there must have been hundreds of them. They made a thundering sound as they ripped through space. This was something very peculiar, and even somewhat exciting, as Gilgan had told him this was the only galaxy in the entire universe where you could *hear* the sounds of space.

"You know what?" said a guy with a scar-crossed brow. "I'm kinda itching to find out how hard this rifle can rumble." He grinned wickedly, the pierced ring around his lip flashing. "How many bullets does it fire each second, do you think? A hundred?"

"Whatever, just don't shoot yourself in the head," said the woman beside him. "Or *us*," she added. There was some nervous laughter at that, but not much.

The ship began to shake. Teveran glanced at the commander, who quickly said, "No need to panic. We're entering Corion's atmosphere." How could he look so calm? Though, how could Teveran tell *what* he was feeling beneath all that ivory metal?

His heart kicked as the guy beside him tapped his arm.

Teveran looked. The young man stared back at him. He had cropped blond hair, ears like roses, eyes that reminded him of the skies above Etheron.

"Are you ready?" the blue-eyed kid asked, a weak smile on his pinched face. Dammit, but he probably should have been in school. *Are you ready* . . . It was the same thing Elenah had asked him, Elenah who had warned him about the Council, who he might never see again . . .

"Yes," Teveran said. But he wasn't. His gut was flipping as the ship rocked back and forth. He wasn't sure who he was lying to more: the boy or himself.

The kid peered down at his own gun, rubbed it with his small hands. "It won't be too bad," he said, a nervous tremor in his voice. "I think those rebels should be scared of *us*. They're running out of men, you know? And, the gods permit it, soon they'll be gone." He gave a little laugh, muttered something, and left Teveran unconvinced.

The gods could screw themselves tonight.

The commander glanced at him through the helmet. He knew that Teveran was the High Prince. But did he care? It was too late, and he felt that truth with more terrible dread.

How did this even happen?

The others watched him, weighed him, weighed each other. Who would die? Who would live? Blasts, they were just young. *Boys. Girls.* Not warriors. Teveran eyed a woman who might have been his own age, her brown hair in a braided tail. She looked almost happy, like she'd been waiting for this moment her whole life!

Teveran flexed his fingers and listened to his heartbeat. Blood hammered in his ears, drumming a staccato rhythm. He felt a cold shiver rattle through his body, so he tensed and gripped his rifle tighter—as if that would warm him. He tried to meet the commander's eyes, but the man was looking straight ahead, focused only on the door.

"We need armour," Teveran muttered, feeling a needle of heat streak through him. Head down, he didn't dare meet the eyes of the commander. "How the hell do we survive this?"

"Just follow my lead," the commander said. As Teveran mouthed a curse, something exploded outside. It was only distant, barely registering as a rumble beyond the Manticore's impenetrable walls. There shouldn't have been explosions. "Just do as I say and I will get you off this planet alive. All of you. But I *won't* have your insubordination."

Another rumble—closer this time.

A nervous air began to boil.

"Easy now," the commander warned. "*Easy*, you guys." His tense voice certainly didn't help ease anyone—particularly not Teveran. The shuttle began to slow. "From this point forward, you call me Commander Vallon. And, trust me, I want to get off this world just as much as you." He put a finger to his earpiece and listened for a couple of heartbeats. Teveran looked up and watched him, eager to hear what was going on. He didn't like being uninformed.

Soon, Vallon dropped his finger and rolled his shoulders. "It appears the rebels have locked up the airspace." Something cracked overhead, and a small brown backpack landed in Teveran's lap. "It will be difficult enough to bypass their blockade, let alone land." He nodded towards their packs. "So those are parachutes. Put them on and don't ask any stupid questions."

Teveran's stomach knotted. He almost said, *But these ships are supposed to be indestructible*, then thought that might count as a "stupid question."

Vallon strapped on his pack. Teveran just eyed his own, a heavy weight in his lap, crushing his blood vessels. He tried to open his mouth and tell Vallon again that he was the High Prince of Etheron, that they had made some mistake and his real escort was probably wondering where he was, but all that came out was a croak. It wouldn't matter, anyway. What were they going to do? Turn back the ship and drop him off?

No. He was going to have to think *positive*. There was no getting out of this situation. Sure, it was terrible, and death was breathing down his neck, but tradition didn't matter here. Being the High Prince didn't matter. All that mattered was winning the battle—whatever the battle was.

Once he got through this . . . *then* he'd start asking questions.

Besides, was Teveran not also a *magician?*

"Our objective," Vallon continued, safe beneath that armoured suit, "is to push north towards the rebel base. We're going in with the first wave. It's going to be messy. Just stay focused and stay behind me. It'll all be over rather quick, I'd say."

Teveran found himself nodding. He was afraid, so afraid, but he had no intention of dying. He owed it to Elenah to make it back home. The Council was going to turn him into a leader, into a hero, like his uncle and all the high princes before him. This was just one mishap, and once it was over they would take him to the flagship and he'd never have to do it again.

I can do this.

He buckled on the parachute.

"We're going to die," a young voice said. It belonged to a boy who looked fifteen, blond hair streaked with brown, sitting right beneath Vallon's gaze. "You've plucked us straight from home and you're sending us to the front lines. We've got no armour . . . We're a distraction, Commander. We're a *distraction.*"

For a while, Vallon said nothing. Teveran looked at him eagerly, heart pounding. A woman muttered, "Here I was thinking they didn't recruit *children.*" Teveran squeezed his eyes shut, wishing he could slow down time. Someone else said, "We're the saviours, aren't we? We're golden gears in the Council's great machine . . ."

"He's right," Vallon said. "You're our best hope now. And if you can prove yourselves, you'll be recognised all over the galaxy. Together we will *win* this battle. Not one man—or woman—left behind." He raised his eyes across them, fires in his irises. "For the Magicus Eye!" he yelled.

The response began as murmurs and grunts from sweaty lips. Then, the Azich man in front of Teveran raised his head and shouted, "For the Magicus Eye!" Others chimed in, one after another, like a chorus in a vibrant choir. Teveran gripped his rifle. He could feel the air loosen, could feel them slowing down . . .

And then they were hit.

Teveran lurched forward, the seat's leather straps straining against his skin. Klaxons blared, ringing in his ears. The pale darkness lit up with red lights. The Manticore careened to the side and they were spinning. And falling—*fast.*

Vallon stumbled forward, skidding across the floor. He landed on all fours. Then, within a single flash of red light, he rose to his feet, dragged out his rifle, and slammed his fist against the flashing panel beside the door. The whole shuttle seemed to quake.

And suddenly, the world roared to life.

The landing ramp unfolded, thrust out into the wailing winds. Teveran pulled himself tight against the seat, but then all at once their straps unbuckled and bodies crumpled out. Teveran floundered across the floor on hands and knees. The night sky appeared through the foreboding exit. He scooped up his rifle and looked up.

Shards of wind slashed his eyes.

"Pull the cord," Vallon roared, "before you hit the trees!" Teveran watched him, skin going taut. Vallon waved out into the darkness. It filled the cabin now. Teveran couldn't see the ground; he could only see the red lights splitting the pitch night, stars spinning *round* and *round* and *round*. Black smoke billowed around the ship. Fire roared. And gunfire crackled. And metal plates snapped and hurtled away. Gods, but they'd been *hit*!

"Now get the hell out of here!"

A missile slammed the shuttle, casting it to a crooked angle. The Azich man teetered forward and leapt over the edge, perhaps determined to lay the first kill. A pale-skinned boy joined him, tears leaking from his eyes. Another one jumped. And another.

And then something hit them from the other side, deflecting off the shields.

"Jump!" Vallon barked. "*Jump now!*"

Teveran scrambled with the ugly mess of bodies, mustering some sorry excuse for courage. The winds drew him outside, but he gripped one of the straps still hanging from a seat. *I can do this,* he thought. *I can do this,* he chanted inside his head.

"Go!" Vallon yelled, tossing them into the mouth of battle. Teveran edged himself forward. He grit his teeth with the rifle clasped against his chest, whispered a prayer that probably didn't matter, and leapt off the Manticore.

He fell.

Plummeted.

The night unfolded, shredded by his inexorable descent. He flailed through the air. He tried to scream but the wind stole the breath from his lungs. Down below, he could make out the mangled treetops of some sort of forest. Gunfire roared down there, loud and furious.

Pull the cord before the trees. Pull the cord before the—

He tumbled head over heels, watching the sky recede above him. Others were plunging all around: shouting, screaming, begging for dear life.

Overhead, the Manticore exploded and shards of metal and fire rained down. A Ragnarok rammed its side and combusted instantaneously.

Bloody hell! He rolled onto his front and spread his arms to either side, searching for balance. He thought of himself like an old starfighter falling out of the sky. In Gilgan's stories, they always managed to pull up at the last moment. Maybe he could do the same. Though, his skin warped and dragged and, by the end of this, he'd probably be a skeleton.

The trees and the moon hardly registered in his frantic mind; it was only the dim red star that triggered a memory. *Corion. Yes. We're on Corion.*

I'm on Corion.

Gunfire.

It came from beneath the crazy treetops of the dark forest. White flashes of light scattered beneath the overcrop. The air cracked, bullets screaming through the air. Soldiers were hit, bullets shredding bare flesh. Most of them had no armour. *We're a distraction*, the young boy had said.

What does that mean? Teveran wondered.

Bodies jerked back and tumbled through the sky. The cracks of yanking cords filled the airspace. White parachutes flared open. Men and women crashed into one another, their bodies twisting spasmodically as the parachutes broke their descents.

Bullets punctured anything they could, flinging bodies like ragdolls. Teveran fumbled for the cord. He was going to land in the thick of it. If these terrible odds won out, he would die within seconds. But Teveran didn't fancy death.

So he yanked the cord.

It took a few seconds. First, he felt the ripple in the air above him, then the gentle pull. Then the tug. Then the jerk that made his back crack. The parachute opened with a sound like a slap and his body lurched upwards.

Something crashed into him, and *shouted*.

And it sent him hurtling towards the treetops, towards certain death in the blind fury of the rebellion's remaining soldiers.

The other man wrapped his arms around him as the winds sang and the gunfire roared. Bodies splintered through the sky like the debris of a falling star.

"Get off me!" Teveran shouted, fighting against the man. A knee stabbed him in the gut and Teveran dropped his rifle. It flew from his grasp, spiralling away.

"Stop that!" the man screamed. "I'm trying to save your

life!" Teveran blinked, facing him, but all he could see was his gleaming armoured suit. "It's me! It's *Vallon!*"

Vallon hugged him as they fell. He yanked his own cord. His parachute shrieked open. Teveran wrapped himself tight, clenched his innards so they didn't fall out of his ass—

And then the parachute unfolded and thrust them both upwards. One minute they were hurtling through the sky, the next they were devoured by sharp twigs and branches.

It lasted an eternity.

Then, he slammed cold dirt ground.

"Get up!" was the first voice he heard. Teveran looked around, disoriented. There were hands on him, and then he was on his feet. Commander Vallon was shouting, cursing, sending bullets flying in every direction. "Get up, soldier!"

Teveran did.

Vallon tossed him a rifle, which he barely caught, and then waved him on through the battlefield. They weren't the first to arrive. Hundreds of bodies beat them, already strewn across the forest floor. *Gods, that could be me.* Trees had been torn down by explosives. *Oh gods, what* does *that!* Flames licked the darkness. Grenades had burrowed craters in the ground. Overhead was the faint rumbling of gunfire and ships. And everywhere around him was the constant screaming and shouting of men and women fighting, and the cracks of magical spells.

Teveran followed Commander Vallon, weaving in and out between tall, stark trees. Lives blinked out around him. Lights bombarded his eyes and he could barely see six feet ahead. He wondered what crazy turn of events could have thrown him into this position. They were supposed to take him to the flagship, not to Corion, not to the *battlefield!*

"Stop!" he gasped, heaving for air. "Commander, stop!" But the gods were merciless tonight. Tears burned his eyes. Bullets singed the air, hot like dragonsfire.

Then: an explosion.

He shielded his eyes and speared through it. A dead body tugged at his ankle. A discord of shouts erupted up ahead. Vallon reached out to him through the black smoke and fire.

Teveran just focused on the commander.

"Run!" Vallon roared, and it all happened in slow motion. Teveran tripped, skidded across *dirt*, then *wood*, and then he scampered past Vallon and a door closed behind him.

It was almost silent.

"Get up, kid," Vallon said, trying to haul him to his feet, but Teveran didn't even have the strength to be lifted. He just lay there, the rifle plastered against his chest. He could feel the magical pulses humming through the air, frantic and hopeless.

"I think," Teveran gasped, "we should go back!"

"Get off your ass *right now!*"

Vallon yanked him to his feet, and dragged him farther into the darkness. Teveran wondered whether he'd been blinded, or if a darkness so absolute was actually possible. "Down there," Vallon said, shoving him down a shallow set of steps. "Go!" Teveran hit the bottom, heard the hollow clap of a wooden door shutting.

And then gunfire exploded overhead, accompanied by Vallon's frightening roar.

Chapter Five

THE CLOCK TOWER

When the Forty-Ninth Council came to power in the year 42c78, the galaxy changed. There was order like there had never been, bolstered by the promise of eternal peace. It was, by many accounts, the greatest era since the years before the Battle of Haratheon.

Elenah jerked awake. She lay in her bed, staring at the ceiling. Silver beams streamed through the window, twisting and turning, cast from the stars.

She scrambled out of the sheets and into the cold. All she could hear was her stilted, ragged breathing. And there was something else, like the echoes of a thunderclap, fading into infinity.

"Teveran," she breathed. His name whistled through the room, going through one ear and out the other, back and forth, like a prize between two opposing entities.

She clutched her chest; her heart fluttered against her palm. *Something's happened.* She felt it like a dark force propelling her out of bed, into action . . . but what could she possibly do now? The damage had been done. They shouldn't have let Teveran go. They shouldn't have invited that highlord inside their home. They'd been digging, and digging, searching for a way out of this mess, and they'd unintentionally dug their own grave.

Subduing her anger, she scrambled out of bed and stepped onto the cold floor. Her bare feet absorbed the icy chill. Her reflection resolved in the mirror: a young woman of a meek sixteen, cloaked in a nondescript nightgown that draped the polished floorboards.

I have to do something, she thought. *I have to try.*

Cautiously, she crossed the dark room until she stood before her desk. Bathed in silver starlight was an old map she'd torn from *Charting the Eye, Illustrated Edition,* and she wondered if she'd be able to follow it if she did decide to leave this all behind. Her thoughts wandered back to Korvis, although she was not sure why. Gods, but what if she *had* decided to go with him? What if she still had a chance to? Would that make her a coward? Would she only be leaving Gilgan and her father to melt inside the Council's fiery grip?

Focus! she scolded.

She gently closed her eyes. It *frustrated* her. Her father was sick, and perhaps the sickness had played its toll on his ability to think clearly. But *Gilgan* . . . Gilgan *knew* what was happening. So why wasn't he doing anything to fix it?

I'm on my own now—

Crack! It rang outside her window. A bulb of red light swelled in the distance. She frowned, peering closer to the glass and resting one trembling hand against it.

I have no doubts, said a voice inside her head, *that the bastards will be using the clock tower as their operating base.* Suddenly, the room became much colder. Her shaky breaths fogged up the window. *Be vigilant. Be steadfast. Be resolute.*

" 'We must not bow down,' " Elenah finished with a whisper.

Her window lit up with *fire*.

She screamed, jerking away from it, but the fire was distant. It spiralled into the sky, illuminating the city and the black shapes that began to pour onto the roads. She could almost hear their screams. And, among them, she saw the unmistakeable white forms of the troopers.

"Oh my god." She covered her mouth. The clock tower! She could feel the flames from here, burning up the ice-cold night. *Gods, what have they done?*

Another loud blast cut through the night, like fireworks. The explosions were coming from within its walls, bathing it in a furious coil of flames. Elenah flinched as a fireball flew into the sky, crackling and fizzling and emitting beams of blinding light. She glanced towards the street and the troopers racing about. A field officer, judging by his uniform, sprinted towards the tower.

Elenah clutched her nightgown so tight her knuckles turned white. The stamping of feet, the bellowing of explosions, and thousands of terrified voices filled the night. And among them, she heard Oswald, although it was distant, and ghostly: *You'd better go back to the palace and keep a low profile for a while.* And Elenah realised that he had been *warning* her.

But it was too late.

Her chest began to ache, her breath coming hard and hoarse. *I can't wait here any longer. I have to leave.* She shut her window and stepped away. Another fiery flash lit her bedroom silently.

She could barely watch. Flashing lights crossed her vision,

drowning out the pale aura of the stars. It was all worse than she'd anticipated. Suddenly, she heard cracks of gunfire, and screaming, and shouting. What was happening? Who was shooting?

Elenah swallowed hard to avoid being sick. She spun away from the window and strode towards the door. She wrapped her fingers around the cold, bronze handle—but then her strength availed her and she slid feebly to the floorboards. *Oh god, what's happening?* Pain shot through her head. She felt like she were suffocating in the middle of all this chaos.

The Council is our only hope now, her father always said. *They're here to protect us.*

From what? she asked herself. It was all a lie, couldn't they see that? It was a lie to justify their mass recruitment, to finally cement their reign across the galaxy!

She looked from the window, to the bed . . .

And then some kind of creature *burst* into existence inches from her wall, tumbling wildly across the room and crashing into her wardrobe. Elenah screamed as it threw the doors off their hinges. She backed away from it furiously.

The creature couldn't have been more than two feet tall. It had shiny smooth skin pulled violently across its spindly bones, no visible mouth, but a snake's nose and two pale eyes that were far too big for its narrow inhuman face. When the creature finally composed itself, Elenah noticed in its hand a letter, which it tossed at her carelessly.

Then it was gone, puffed out of existence.

Elenah simply stared at the space the creature once occupied, her mouth agape. *Was that an imp?* she asked herself. Yes, Gilgan had told her of such things. Messenger imps that could leap through time and space. But they could only be harnessed by magicians . . .

She hauled herself to her feet, panting, observing the wreckage of her wardrobe and realising someone must have heard that. However, she found she didn't care in the least. Hesitantly, she picked up the folded letter and read it:

> *You have to run.*
> *Morgan's men have unleashed a beast inside the clock tower, and now they're looking for you. They want you as a hostage to intimidate your father into action. Whatever you do, don't come find me because I can't help you. Go to the spaceport if you can make it there.*
>
> *- Oswald*

She read the words again without taking in much meaning; they flashed beneath the crimson lights outside. *Oswald's a magician?* But even that fact paled in comparison to what the letter meant. Those people never cared about her. They'd been using her. Gods, she didn't know what she'd stumbled into here, but it was not what she thought it was.

She had to leave, but where would she go? She didn't even know how to fly a ship! Well, whatever happened, she had to go *far*. It seemed everyone she trusted was lying to themselves, and every second they spent denying this raging war, Teveran slipped farther and farther away, and the Forty-Ninth Council dismantled their grand society piece by piece . . .

She looked to the broken wardrobe, and to the small brown knapsack crumpled underneath it. The bag had been her mother's, once. Her clothes were arranged in rows within her cupboard: dresses and blouses and undergarments. She'd need food, but there was food aplenty in the kitchens. She'd need money, too, but there were loose silver chits of all shapes in her drawers.

Gods, how did it come to *this?*

It was time to leave.

GILGAN PRETENDED HE COULDN'T HEAR THE CHAOS raging outside. He channelled out the cracks of explosions going off in the night, tuned out the voices and the stampeding and the shouts of the troopers trying to contain the situation.

It was better like that, because he couldn't do a thing. He'd warned them but how could he have expected them to listen? None of them had been there amidst the horrors of the Daemon Wars. These people hadn't been there fighting on the front lines, facing death day after day . . .

Gilgan had come here to escape his past, but now it was happening again.

He navigated the winding halls of the palace, limping on his blasted, incompetent leg. "No," he said to Rose, walking abreast. "I don't know what's happening, and I don't know who's doing it." It was a lie, but the truth was, this was all much worse than he'd thought. There were magicians here. He could feel their dangerous arts pulsing through the palace walls.

"*Gilgan,*" Rose hissed, striding along beside him. "You're being ignorant."

"No, I'm not," he assured her.

"Jethre's letter—"

Pain lanced his forehead, and he had to stop a moment to compose himself. The words that had been written in that letter . . . The man who had written them . . .

Gilgan cursed, then set off hobbling through the halls.

"*Gilgan!*" Rose snapped.

"Not now," he said, trying to remain calm. He rounded a corner, teetered on his crooked leg, then came upon a corridor that was empty save for Ed brushing portraits along the wall. "Evening, Ed," Gilgan muttered with a nod.

"Are you okay?" Ed asked.

"I'm fine," Gilgan said. He glanced at the portraits as he passed. There were countless commissions of a rather healthy-looking Bayle, posing gallantly. Dozens of other kings and high princes from long before his time. When his eyes brushed the icy painted stare of Ignus Thrakk, the king's brother, he chilled. Thrakk was serving as Grand Highlord now; Teveran was on his way to meet him. In one of the portraits, baby Elenah and Teveran were painted in long strokes beside their father. They'd hardly changed. They only knew more.

A lot more.

"What are you hiding?" Rose asked as they left behind Ed.

Gilgan sighed. "I'm not hiding anything. This has all gone too far."

Rose rounded on him, planting her fists angrily upon her hips. Gilgan almost ran into her, barely stopping himself in time. Rose pursed her lips. "Blasts, Gilgan. I *know* you're lying to me . . . but you don't have to. This burden is not yours to carry alone."

Gilgan eyed her awhile. He saw *hurt* in her bright emerald eyes. He grumbled, then stumbled around her and threw open the door into Bayle's grandiose sitting room. "I'm sorry," he said as she strode in behind him. "It's just . . . I just feel so helpless." He'd failed Teveran, let him go off to be with the Forty-Ninth Council. And there was nothing he could do for Elenah, who so desperately wanted to be *something*. Maybe there was a part of him that wanted to believe the Council was here to do good, maybe he'd been played the fool, maybe he really *was* just so terrified to find himself in the middle of another galactic war . . .

The sitting room was an opulent chamber, with round walls and a simple ceiling. A glass chandelier hung overhead. The walls were carved of the finest wood from the forests on the other side of the planet. There were black leather seats and other showy furnishings set about the room, and doors perched in lamp-lit hollows. Gilgan could hear Bayle's voice behind the door to the right; he made slowly for that direction.

"You don't have to go in there," Rose said.

Gilgan stopped a few paces from the double-leaf door. It reminded him of a hundred other doors, the kinds of doors that rich, foolish men hid behind as they schemed.

"Gilgan," Rose softly said. "I hate what this is doing to you."

"Unfortunately . . . this is what I am now. Just a servant." The last words he spoke as barely more than a whisper. *Just a servant*, he reminded himself. *I'm just a servant.*

He creaked open the door.

"—inefficient," Bayle finished. Four heads looked up as Gilgan walked inside. Gilgan recognised Lord Orvall among them—an important man from Tarthalus. A spectacled woman dressed in deep blue sat beside him, with the pale-skin blond-haired look from someplace closer to the core—Kasnah, perhaps. A haggard-looking man sat across from her; he looked better placed in a fighting ring than a political circle.

"Master Lockwood," Gilgan said.

The king perked up, a scrutinising look on his face. The man was unwell, slowly deteriorating beneath an illness that had no cure. But he was still the leader of these Free Worlds, and he needed to start *fixing* things. "Yes, Gilgan?" Bayle answered cautiously.

Gilgan leaned on his cane, the cracks of explosions ringing in his ears. It must have been his imagination, for these four were oblivious to it. Or, they just didn't *care*. Make the troopers deal with it. Let them tighten their grip around this wonderful world. Gilgan wanted to berate the king, demand that he opened his eyes, but he was a different man now—no longer the hero from his stories.

"I . . ." He stuttered. "Could I entertain you with refreshments?"

For a while, none of them responded. Gilgan felt so foolish standing there before them. Finally, Bayle said, "No. I anticipate we will be finishing shortly."

Gilgan nodded, and retreated.

He found Rose sitting on one of the leather chairs.

"Why are you being like this?" Rose asked.

"This is my job. And it's your job too, if you'd forgotten."

"No. Why do you let him *do* this to you?"

Gilgan sighed. "Because this is not about me anymore," he said grumpily. "Bayle is the only reason I'm here. I owe him so much for everything he's done for me. You wouldn't understand. You don't know how bad things were, how far in the dark I'd fallen . . ."

Rose puffed her cheeks as she rose from the chair and trailed him back into the hallway. "This is not the Gilgan I remember. You're stronger than this. I can see it in your eyes. You don't like it. You're playing the role of somebody else, somebody weak." She paused, just briefly, but it was enough for Gilgan's thoughts to wander.

Gigantic beasts marching through the battlefields . . .

Demon eyes blazing in the bleeding skies . . .

"Is it about Jethre?" Rose asked.

"No," Gilgan said, gritting his teeth. "No. It's not about him."

"The stones—"

"*Certainly not!*" Gilgan snapped. A tense silence washed over them, tightening around Gilgan's chest as he hobbled into the dining room and sat down at the glass table. "It's Elenah. Gods, I want to help her. But . . ." But he was lucky to be here. He needed this. So he did what he was told, regardless of how much it pained him. Besides, Elenah needed to be *protected*, not encouraged, just like it said in Jethre's note. And Gilgan trusted Jethre more than anyone.

A bowl of fruit lay in the middle of the table, directly beneath another glowing chandelier. Along the walls were paintings of beautiful landscapes and faraway worlds.

His hands were shaking.

Rose didn't sit, but she was much stronger than him. "What's wrong?" she asked kindly. "What are you scared of? And don't say *nothing*."

He muttered a curse and tried to settle down. He was thinking of the chaos outside, of the Forty-Ninth Council and those who opposed them. He was thinking of Elenah, and Teveran, and how he'd let them both down . . .

"It's coming," Gilgan said vacantly, tears at the backs of his eyes. "The war. It's coming here. The Council's building some kind of advanced military base on our home. There's going to be a fight and we're right in the middle of it." He couldn't meet her eyes.

"A base? Is that what they're talking about?"

"Hmm. But that's not what frightens me, Rose. It's the *war*. It's been simmering almost forty years now." He curled his hand into a fist to try to stop it from shaking. "But this war . . . It's larger than any of us ever thought. It's not just the rebellion in the west. There are more sides all competing for power and it's getting out of hand." He had to stop a moment, to catch his breath and suppress his panic. "And it's Teveran . . . fighting it alongside . . ." Memories he'd fought so hard to repress came clawing back into his mind. "And Elenah . . . I'm worried about her."

"She's a smart girl."

"She's also *young*." He gave a mirthless laugh. "And all she's ever wanted was to leave this damned place and see the *real* galaxy. Not this, this . . . fabrication!"

"Gilgan—"

"But I don't blame her," Gilgan continued. "You know, it's mostly my fault." He lowered his head in shame. "I glorified it."

A gunshot. *Closer.*

It rang out in the night, causing Gilgan to jump. Rose almost leapt onto the table. *Gods.* Gilgan scratched his hairless chin, slid his hands into a steeple. *I tried my best, I promise.* The gunshot still echoed when the shouting began. He closed his eyes but he could see them: the troopers fighting the rebels, children screaming. *Dammit, but it's just going to get worse.*

"Gilgan," Rose breathed.

"Yes, Rose?"

"What will we do about the Council?"

Gilgan frowned. It was all falling apart. He wasn't sure why Jethre had sent him that message, but he didn't need it. He knew what the Council was playing at, and the terrible truth was, the Council was all they had now to keep the Free Worlds together. "I just hope they know where our allegiances lie," he said.

CHAPTER SIX

IN THE FORESTS OF CORION

*The mobile troopers wore an impressive make of armour,
ostensibly an improvement on the successful stormline
build. Designed for efficiency both in cost and combat, I
wouldn't be surprised if it becomes the benchmark for all
future soldiers.*

The world stopped shaking.

Teveran awakened to find himself sitting against
the cold wall in a room so dark he couldn't even see
his own hand. His heartbeat thudded unevenly in each ear.
His breath rasped, tremoring with each shiver. *Where am I?
How long have I been here?*

He wondered if the battle was over. He wondered if
Commander Vallon was still alive, or if the rebels had mowed
him down. Would they come for *him* next?

No use waiting around.

He felt his way to the stairs, then climbed them on hands
and knees. *Why is everything aching?* There must have been
bruises all over him. Sweat drizzled down his forehead,
burning his eyes. Streams of blood trickled along his arms
and smacked the splintered floor. He tasted it on his lips.

Come on, Teveran. Pull yourself together! He heaved against the door, and the door squealed open.

Three troopers sat inside the room beyond, their rifles lying on the ground beside them. Bronze bullet casings littered the floor, reflecting the light of the single swaying lamp. Pockmarks were scattered across the walls, like some kind of painting. Nobody wore their helmet, but Teveran wouldn't forget the cobalt eyes of Commander Vallon so soon.

Teveran climbed ruggedly to his feet and crumpled against the wall opposite the commander. His legs buckled and he crashed to his backside. "I'm alive," he muttered, meeting Vallon's gaze. "I'm alive . . ." It didn't sound true.

Vallon wore the face of a dead man; the battle had erased any fury there'd once been. In its place were tears carving trails through the dirt. Bewildered, Teveran crept forward. "Are you all right?" he asked in a shaky voice.

Vallon wiped his tears and jumped up, hooking his rifle in one hand. He had brown shoulder-length hair, longer than Teveran's, and a square beard all ruffled from wearing his helmet. The other two troopers gave him their attention. "You're him, aren't you," Vallon said glumly. "You're the High Prince. Teveran Lockwood."

"I . . ."

Vallon waved. "I'm sorry. They did tell me we'd have you on board. I don't . . . I don't know how this happened. Gods have me, but I'll get you out, get you to the flagship and to your uncle." Teveran could barely move. "Just stay close," Vallon said. Then he pointed at the other troopers, calling them Krosse and Snake; Teveran wasn't sure if those were names or call signs. Grim, heavyset faces stared back at him, unblinking, unwavering, like statues.

"It isn't every day you get to be in the presence of royalty," Krosse said, the light rolling over his dark Azich skin. As he stood up, he fetched a red ribbon from his pocket and pinned back his greasy black hair. Silver flecks peppered his beard, suggesting he'd weathered more years than Teveran automatically guessed. A deep wound punctured his gut—the bullet must have gone right through his armour. Teveran cringed, wondering how he wasn't either dead or screaming. He must have been hit with something terribly nasty.

The other trooper, Snake, had snowy blond hair and held two rifles. He slung the first across his shoulder, then checked the starfire cell on the second, before bearing it in his arms. Hanging from his waist was what looked like a . . . flute.

Teveran guessed it wasn't just a flute.

"Put on your helmets," Vallon instructed them, though he didn't don his own. Instead, he proffered it to Teveran. "Here."

"Me?" Teveran asked.

"Your life is worth more than mine right now."

Teveran frowned, but he took the helmet anyway—it resembled a facemask in its unfitted state—and pressed it against his face. The helmet clicked, then made a machine-like hiss as it wrapped around his head. Darkness enveloped him, then the visor beeped online. Light returned all at once. The helmet seemed to disappear, and everything else resolved into view.

A second later, the heads-up display came alive with various numbers and readings, most of which made little sense to him. But what he did make out were the names attached to each trooper, popping up as he looked at them. *Krosse. Snake. Vallon.*

"Cool," he muttered, peering about the room.

"Krosse," Vallon said. "Are you still less than half-dead?"

"I'm fine, Commander."

Vallon frowned at the Azich man's bleeding gut. *Fatal,* Teveran's HUD said. "We're getting that fixed. There's a village nearby."

"I'll be fine," Krosse said, determined.

"No wonder, you'll be *dead.*"

Krosse muttered a curse as he slammed on his helmet; it wrapped around his head. Vallon muttered, "You're not invincible. I don't care what the others say."

Teveran eyed the wound. There were certain spells that could heal something like that, though it was a delicate stream, one that Teveran had never quite mastered. He wondered if these three were also magicians, if they could spellcast like himself. Gilgan had taught him how to *feel* the magic, how to grasp it . . . But the magic here was cold, sour, and mostly all dead. It twisted his gut in all sorts of impossible knots.

Dark magic could do that.

He turned his gaze and met the emerald eyes of Snake.

"Have my gun," Snake said, proffering his slick black rifle. There was blood smeared across the metal; it dripped onto the ground. Teveran nodded a silent thanks and reluctantly took it, getting blood all over his clothes. "I assume you know how to use it?"

"Yeah." *Are you kidding? No you don't.*

"Please put on that helmet, Snake," Commander Vallon said in a tired, fatherly tone, striding between them. Snake slapped on his helmet; the white metal flashed and the visor lit up with a vague red glow. "The rebel base is nine clicks north. I assume it will be well fortified, so we'll hit the village first,"—he pointed to Krosse—"and patch *you* up. From there, we go direct. Cut a straight line through this hell-hole. Kill anything that moves." Teveran caught his eye, and felt his gut wrench. Vallon turned towards the door, and said again, "Stay close, Teveran."

"Are we the last ones?" Teveran asked, though he dreaded to hear the answer.

Vallon looked away, and simply waved them forward. Krosse and Snake followed. They slapped Teveran's shoulder wordlessly as they scurried past him.

Okay, Teveran thought, taking a deep breath. He needed to trust these men, trust that they'd get him through this crazy plight alive. It wasn't like he could run. Corion was a planet somewhere far away from home, and there was no way back—just *forward.* He blew a ragged breath through his new helmet, and tried to remember what Vallon had told the rest of them on the shuttle. *Our objective is to push north towards the rebel base . . .*

The rebellion.

"We need to get going," Vallon said in the doorway.

Teveran snapped out of his reverie, followed him outside . . .

. . . and a vicious slap of death whacked him across the face. It surged through both his nose and mouth at once, a vile stench that made his eyes water. It was worse than that time he'd found the dead cat in the attic. Worse than Old Teri's spilled sewage. It caught his throat, and he gagged reflexively. "*What the hell is that?*" he cried. "Tell me that isn't—" He opened his mouth again but someone might as well have fed him bile.

"You don't fancy the smell of melted corpses?" Krosse asked.

"Should I?" Teveran replied.

Krosse laughed in response, but it quickly turned into a guttural fit of coughs. Teveran cringed, reminded of his father.

"Keep up," Vallon said.

Sticks and shrubbery cracked underfoot. He couldn't make out much more than the flames flickering upon machinery, and embers scattered across the dirt, glittering sporadically.

The night had not lifted.

Gilgan's stories welled up inside his head: *For thirty nights we waited for the sun, yet all we ever saw was that bleeding red star: glowing, watching, mocking.*

Teveran glanced upwards, but only saw the treetops.

"I swear to the gods," Krosse said, "I'm *fine.*" The readings on Teveran's HUD said otherwise. *Rate of blood loss: Deadly. Seek immediate medical attention.*

"Isn't there a magician here?" Teveran asked.

Vallon laughed weakly. "Not after a battle like this. Too much ill-inspired spellcasting. Too much fury, and pain . . ." His face soured. "It's all gone stale, dead . . . not so unlike the planet itself. Besides, poor man's magic can't heal a wound like that. You'd need a master magician. Those are gone. The Dead Winter killed them off."

Teveran chilled at that, but nobody argued; they simply followed Vallon between the imposing trees, picking through shrubbery and winding round bodies.

Vallon glanced at Krosse over his plated shoulder and said, "You could almost fit a *tank* inside that— Ugh, and you're leaking all over the place."

"You're exaggerating," Krosse murmured, trying to mop up the blood with his hands. He vaulted a fallen branch, then fell into a series of long strides.

There was urgency in their movements now. Teveran never had much reason to run, but he was coming close to it. *Slow down*, he thought. At least the haste warmed him, which was a reprieve for there was barely a fleck of heat in this pitch forest.

It was like walking through a nightmare.

Bodies posed, arms reaching towards the sky. Gaping holes punctured faces and chests. White armour glowed in the moonlight, reflecting the fickle light of flames. Bullets protruded like teeth from the metal, glinting. Bodies hung from the treetops. Broken Ragnaroks had flung chunks of rusted machinery everywhere. Arms and legs were pinned beneath toppled tanks. Skin still bubbled from the flames of grenades, emitting a sour stench . . .

"Where are we going?" Teveran gasped.

"There's a village ahead," Vallon said as he clambered over a rotten log. "And there's a colony of Taurans there. I'm sure you've heard of them."

"Taurans . . . Aren't they potion masters?" Teveran recalled.

"Yes, and it's the closest thing we have to magic tonight."

Teveran was about to ask if the Taurans might also treat them all to some *tol'riva* tea, which he believed was made from the *riva* leaves here, when something splattered down beside him, crushing his little toe. "Ouch!" he croaked, hopping out of the way. The troopers turned their rifles towards the disturbance. A severed arm lay on the ground. Teveran twisted his face and raised his rifle shakily toward the canopy. Blood dripped down and, in the amber light of embers and flame, he could see the silhouette of a skeletal body dangling above.

"You all right?" Snake asked, kicking the arm gently.

"It almost broke my toe," Teveran muttered.

"We can fix a broken toe," Vallon said. "But if we don't get moving, you will have a list of other wounds that aren't so repairable. Come on. Keep up."

As they ventured farther from the landing zone, the bodies thinned out, the craters in the ground flattened, and the vehicles seemed to have been abandoned—not destroyed. Despite Gilgan's lessons and his many illustrated books, Teveran still failed to recognise most of it. Were these weapons of the Council or the rebellion? Did they belong on the land or in the air? His mind buzzed with questions, but every time he opened his mouth he tasted dead people, and it tasted worse than when Gilgan had given him that rotten citric fruit from Jiara.

Krosse shot him a sidelong glance. "Do you know Ignus Thrakk Lockwood?"

"I . . ." He caught Krosse's glance and shook it off. "He's my uncle."

"Thought he was. Your uncle's made a big mark on the galaxy."

"So I've heard," Teveran said, trying to keep his voice steady. "I never really met him in person, though. He left before I was born."

"He's serving as Grand Highlord now," Krosse said.

"I assume he already knows that," Snake said. Krosse muttered something about Snake's mother marrying a half-breed Vukosan, but Teveran wasn't paying attention.

He wondered if he would ever be like his uncle, a man who was practically worshipped by his fleet, leading them into some of the greatest battles in recent history . . . He wondered if that was even what he wanted anymore. Elenah had never quite trusted the Council. She wasn't convinced the galaxy would ever regain its stability. She said that powerful men were dangerous, and the Council had some of the *most* powerful.

Was he about to become the very thing she feared more than anything?

He tried not to think about it. Instead, he focused on the tremoring ground and the distant sound of magic, a hum and a whir and a vaguely-familiar tune. Everything shook, as though the world hadn't yet realised the battle was over. Tree branches rustled, and fire whistled, and black clouds of unharnessed starfire hissed.

The world looked so dead . . . yet it felt so *alive*.

Something caught his eye in the bushes. Snake raised his rifle and said, "I saw it too." Teveran watched the settling leaves of a bush that sprouted red buds in every direction, sweating as he searched for the shape again. It had been too quick for his HUD to register.

Another black figure darted through the shrubbery.

"Snake? What is it?" Commander Vallon whispered.

"It's exactly what you're thinking," Snake said resignedly. "Iridel." The way he said it, you would've thought "iridel" was a new breed of cat. Teveran glanced at him, heart hammering, but he couldn't speak fast enough. Vallon sped into motion, traversing the forest floor.

"What's . . . *iridel?*" Teveran asked, struggling to keep up.

"Sneaky little things," Snake said. "Normally, they don't

care much for man-flesh, but tonight I'd say they're especially hungry."

"Why's that?"

"The battle must have driven off or killed most of the living wildlife. Also,"–he tripped on a vine and then took a moment to compose himself–"they don't eat dead things."

"Brilliant," Teveran grumbled.

Vallon pulled to a sudden stop behind some bushes, and the others slowed, giving Teveran a moment of respite. He could hear their thoughts whirring round and round, crashing against one another like waves. They all exchanged silent looks. A twitch of the eye, a curve of the lip. Finally, Vallon turned to Teveran and said, "That must be Werrek."

Teveran saw it through a gap in the skeletal trees, and it almost reminded him of home. Though it was small, and the largest thing was a wooden house with three floors wedged between three trees, there was something *homely* about it. Smaller huts lay scattered about the base of the house, their square windows lit by yellow firelight. They were each barely large enough to fit a family of three or maybe four. There was a lake by the courtyard, becoming black with soot, with shards of metal bobbing on the surface.

A silence swelled between them that highlighted Krosse's hoarse, clunky breaths, vaguely inhuman beneath his mask. "You think there'll be anything there?"

Vallon sniffed, counting the figures moving within the village, observing their every twitch, constructing some kind of plan. "They're *Taurans*, Krosse. They'll have supplies," Vallon said. "Ointments of some sort, magic potions . . ."

"You know," Krosse started, "I'm really not in that much pain." Teveran glanced at him, awed by the man's strength.

But Krosse was moving ever slower, his pace uneven, grabbing his gut as thick red blood oozed across his fingers.

Vallon grunted, not sounding very amused. "If you're expecting your mother to come hurtling through those treetops to kiss it better, you're more crazy than I thought." He spat a glob of spittle onto the forest floor, and shook his head despairingly.

"What are you going to do?" Teveran asked, annoyed at the fear in his voice. Gods, why was he so scared? Hadn't he always wanted this? Wasn't he *meant* for this?

"Just stay close," Vallon told him. "Stay behind us."

Teveran chewed his lip and clutched the shaking metal of his rifle. It threw off a gentle thrum and a scorching heat. He looked at Krosse, then Snake, searching for some sort of comfort, but there was little comfort to be found when all he saw was the metal of their masks.

A moment later, they were off again. Vallon led them out of the trees and into the glade. He emerged from the shrubbery. Behind him came Snake and then Krosse, and finally Teveran. *Focus*, he thought. *Stay behind them.*

A blue-skinned Tauran, maybe seven-feet tall in a brown chequered coat, looked up from his crops. His blue eyes bulged, his mouth opened in the shape of a scream.

Vallon *shot* him.

The body hit the ground with a damp *thud.*

Teveran froze. *What?* He stood there stupidly. But the others pushed forward—forward into the inhabited village of Taurans. *Stay close,* Vallon had told him. *Stay behind us.* Snake and Krosse raised their rifles, like wings trailing their commander. They emerged from the darkness and showered the place in bullets. *No, no, no, no, no . . .*

And then: screams. A tall male gasped an unfamiliar kind of name as a hundred-some bullets opened him up. A cloaked female fell to her knees and clasped her hands, as if in prayer, and she pleaded for her life as Snake filled her mouth with bullets.

Pale blue skin ripped messily off the bone. Milky green fluttered like streamers caked in blood. The elderly died first, and then the children, too petrified to move their legs. Mothers died rushing for the young. Fathers protecting their wives.

There must have been three dozen dead, *slaughtered*, in a matter of seconds.

But not Vallon, nor Snake, nor Krosse, stopped there.

They might as well have been shredding pages of Gilgan's books. Docile creatures from Gilgan's tales blown to pieces before his eyes.

No! he gasped. *What are you doing?*

The troopers pressed forward, converging upon the door to the central house. Vallon glanced back with a livid expression. His blue eyes seemed to *glow* with rage. "Teveran!" he screamed, as if to wake every person in this village.

Teveran couldn't move.

Do something! his mind pleaded.

"Get over here!" Vallon yelled.

He forced himself into motion. It made him sick, but he had to keep moving. If for anyone, then for Elenah and Gilgan, and for all of Etheron, and for the worlds at the farthest reaches of the galaxy, worlds that would fall apart if not for the Council.

Commander Vallon shoved open the wooden door in a shower of splinters, threw it off its hinges and sent it slamming into a Tauran man on the other side. Snake burst through beside him, and all Teveran heard was the roar of gunfire.

Then, he saw only Krosse.

The Azich man grabbed Teveran's shoulder and stared into his eyes through the visor. "Listen," he said. "You're gonna be fine." It was a wonder he could even stand with that mess in his gut. "I know how you feel. I know what's going through your head. But what this is, what you have to do . . . It's building *legacy*, and *order*. The Council will restore order to this galaxy. *We* will restore order, and bring back the age of *heroes*!"

Teveran fought back tears with all the strength he had left. He flinched at every crack of gunfire. His blood curdled beneath the screams of the innocent people dying inside. These Taurans, they were people too . . . weren't they?

"Follow me," Krosse said, turning on his heel, rifle blazing, blood streaming down his armour and his hands. Teveran tripped on the threshold of the door, splashed and slid on a pool of shimmering blood, but it didn't matter anymore. By the time he arrived, it was all over.

The three troopers strolled throughout the room, weaving around the dead Taurans splayed across the ground, picking things up and tossing them around, as if searching for something. The room, stark though it was, looked a great deal more colourful with all the blood on the ground. Despite his disgust, Teveran couldn't take his eyes off the bodies. They didn't look like they could last two seconds in battle, all sinewy limbs and jutting joints.

"This isn't right," Teveran whispered, and was glad no one heard him.

"Clear the second floor!" Vallon roared, and the troopers followed him up the stairs. For a moment, it seemed they'd forgotten all about Teveran, left in his own sullen silence. He almost jumped out of his shoes when a glass bottle crashed to the floor and shattered, spewing bubbly concoctions across the wooden boards. The wind through the door was icy cold. Firelight flickered in lanterns upon the walls.

Teveran struggled to breathe as he navigated across the bodies and crumpled to his knees against a toppled chair. "This isn't right." Frightened he might be violently sick, he deactivated his helmet and jerked it off his head. It slammed against the floor.

A dead female lay in the corner of his eye, her white hair unkempt across her thin blue shoulders. *Gilgan . . . they're killing Taurans!* he wanted to plead. But Gilgan wasn't there to comfort him. He was all alone now, with *murderers*.

When he closed his eyes, he saw Vallon sitting against that wooden wall, crying. He struggled to make sense of it. *We could've just asked . . . We could've bloody asked!*

"*Lavok . . .*" choked a Tauran.

Teveran forced his eyes open, and saw that the dead female was not in fact dead. Blood glittered in her ashen hair. She looked at him, and if these Taurans aged like humans, she couldn't have been thirty.

"Oh, *Lavok . . .*" she said again, and Teveran wasn't sure if that was a name or a place or maybe even some sort of word that meant *you bastards* or something worse.

Teveran shook his head; it was all he could do. "I'm so sorry about this."

She closed her eyes, her lips forming words that would never be heard. Teveran looked away, unable to watch her die. His rifle clattered to the ground beside his helmet. *What's happening? I shouldn't even be here!* He squeaked when gunfire exploded overhead, rattling the wooden rafters. He pulled himself tight. *Gods, I need to escape.*

But there was no way out. His father had told him, *It is the duty of the High Prince to fight for our world, to fight for our freedom, and for the freedom of the galaxy.* And he saw his father's burning hazel eyes in the eyes of the dead. *Make us proud, like all the high princes before you.*

"Elenah . . ." he muttered, a single tear rolling down his cheek. "Help me."

CHAPTER SEVEN

ESCAPE FROM ETHERON

Nine streams of magic form the basis of all modern magicianry: a circle construction composed of the restoration triangle, the incantation triangle, and the conjuration pillar, kept in constant balance by the equilibrium.

Elenah ran.

Night engulfed the city of Esther. Flame-lit towers pierced the heavens, and emerald spires twisted like the shells of fantastical beasts. The city had been so beautiful once, but now the roads were swarming with its terrified populace, and troopers with guns. There were frightening flames scattered across the sky as the clock tower burned.

It was like nothing she'd ever seen.

"Elenah, *stop!*"

She turned around to see Gilgan in the shadows, his wrinkled hand grasping the top of his cane. Gilgan, who had ventured across the galaxy, who had fought in so many wars, who had saved so many lives . . . They were on an empty road sprinkled with debris, about twenty paces apart. The fog of night rolled across the ground, curling around her ankles like death's hands.

"Gilgan," she breathed. With one hand she anxiously fingered the three buttons of her white blouse, and with the other she clutched the strap of her shouldered knapsack. Her pleated grey skirt billowed in the hot breeze, short enough not to constrict her movements, long enough not to earn her father's ire—not that it really mattered anymore, for she had no intention of turning back after tonight. Beneath it, she wore ivory stockings which were a gift for her fifteenth birthday. In her knapsack was a change of clothes, a woollen sweater, and a handful of chits, for she didn't really know where she might end up.

"You shouldn't be out here," Gilgan said as he crept forward across the ruined road. His silver eyes seemed more vibrant beneath the flames, but his voice carried none of the mirth it often did, none of the joy, none of the calm. "Let's talk about this. Just you and me."

Elenah frowned. A storm of feelings and thoughts all tumbled through her head. Bad things were happening. War was brewing. She'd meddled with the wrong sort of people and now they wanted her for bait. The Council was occupying the city. There were rebels fighting in the west and the gods knew where else. Teveran was gone. And it was becoming more and more clear that none of them were safe here, like the Council wanted them to believe.

There was more to this. So much more.

"I'm not going back," she whispered, heart aching.

He swallowed. "Let's talk about this."

"No, there isn't time," she said, and she shook her head

as tears began to form behind her eyes. "We have to leave here. *Now*."

Gilgan grumbled, approaching her through the darkness. Somewhere, a gunshot went off and echoed wildly through the empty roads. It cleared her thoughts, and made her realise that the clock tower attack would only give the Council an opportunity to demonstrate their protection. It would let them slowly close their grip around the city and the people—and then the entire planet. How could she have been so foolish?

"Gilgan," Elenah persisted, stepping forward. "We can't stay here, and you know that. The Council's already taking possession of the city, stealing the trust from our people. And you know that Teveran is out there now . . . They've *got* him." She clasped his free hand and looked up into his glittering silver eyes. "We can go together, like you always said."

Gilgan shook his head. "Please don't do this to me. Don't make me choose. You *know* I can't take you anywhere, not now, not with everything as it is." He worked the muscles in his jaw and his eyes darkened. "Believe me. You do not want to be out there now. And certainly not *alone*," he added with warning eyes.

"But I do! And what other choice—"

"Look at yourself!" He waved at her, and it hurt like he'd cast a fiery spell at her. "Dressed like that. You're only going to get yourself killed. And that,"—his voice tremored, his eyelids quivered—"that is something I just can't live with. You shouldn't have messed with those dissidents, Elenah. What were you thinking?"

"I don't know what you're talking about," she lied.

"It's okay," he said, softening his voice. "I don't blame you. But this is something else entirely. Leaving Etheron, leaving the safety of the Free Worlds . . . You don't really *know* what's out there. How could you? Gods, Elenah . . . It's not the wonderful paradise you think it is. The galaxy is dangerous. The *real* galaxy. Not mine."

Elenah looked at him despairingly. She didn't understand what he was so afraid of. She didn't understand why he was being so *infuriating*. Gilgan had seen the galaxy, he'd lived among the stars, seen things that should have set his nerves in steel . . .

"You're still so young," he said.

"What does that have to do with anything?"

"You have your whole life ahead of you."

"You don't understand. I'm not safe here anymore . . . And if you cared about me, Gilgan, then maybe you would try to help. But if you're so scared, then I'll go myself."

"Don't you trust me?" Gilgan asked.

Elenah averted her eyes, focusing on the swelling fog. Why was everything suddenly so grim? She brushed a curl of raven hair from her forehead and tucked it behind her ear. "You never were going to show us the stars, were you." She stopped, but Gilgan gave no response. "And once the Council gets rid of my father, they'll bring Etheron under their control. They'll make this my prison. They . . ."

"Etheron already belongs to the Council," Gilgan said.

Elenah's heart shot up into her throat.

"Maybe you've forgotten, but your brother's the High Prince. He has no choice but to join their fleet, and to help them help us scrape through this goddamn war."

"What are you hiding from?" Elenah asked.

"It's not that. We can't fight the Council. We need them."

"*You* need them."

"Yes," Gilgan said, exasperated. "Yes, I do."

Elenah wanted to cry, standing there like a complete fool. "But Gilgan . . ." Something was going to happen, and she had no intention of being here when it did. She didn't even know what to believe anymore.

"It's safer here," Gilgan said. "We have their protection."

"They don't care about us!"

Gilgan staggered forward, and Elenah thought she could hear his bones cracking and complaining. She stepped towards him before he could fall over and hurt himself. "If you go out there, you are putting yourself in grave danger. You're not *trained*."

"Well, whose fault is that?"

"Your father did not permit it."

"My father's a fool!"

"Don't say that," Gilgan snapped, then softened his tone. "Oh, it's dangerous out there. Much too dangerous. Stay here. Stay with me, and when it's all over I'll take you. By the gods, I *promise* it. I'll take you wherever you want to go. But this is Teveran's *duty*."

"No," Elenah whispered. "That's what you *always* say!" A tear rolled out of her eye; she brushed it. "Stop lying to me, Gilgan. I'm not a child anymore."

Gilgan's face fell flat, his wrinkles deepened. Tears blurred Elenah's vision. She felt them, like cold rivers running down her cheeks. "Come here." Gilgan stepped forward and threw his arms around her, and Elenah melted into his warmth.

"I'm going to go now," she said.

It seemed an eternity before Gilgan answered, "You

remind me a lot of my younger self. More so than you think. And . . . I don't suppose I can stop you, not really. Maybe I ought to face the truth: This world is coming undone. Maybe you *are* better off away from it all."

Elenah squeezed her eyes shut. All her life she'd been shelved away, disregarded like she was just some dusty old gadget. As if she didn't have her own feelings, and hopes, and ambitions. Why couldn't she be the High Princess of Etheron, like she was *meant* to be? Why couldn't she be just like Teveran and write her own stories among the stars?

"Let me go," she said, and Gilgan did. She stepped away and looked into his eyes. She'd stared into those very eyes as a child, when Gilgan had propped her on his lap and told her stories. He had explored the vast galaxy beyond anyone's imagination. He had been in battles and wars and revolutions. He had walked beside great heroes. And what was she but a weak little girl? "So are you going to help me?" she asked.

Gilgan sighed. "I can't. Not this time."

Elenah nodded and let him go. "I understand. You're . . . You're old."

"Old, am I?" Gilgan asked. "Now, that's not fair."

"No, it's true," Elenah said. She walked away from him, stepping through the debris and the scorched grass that reached up between the cobbles. "You can't take me." She gestured flippantly to his cane. "Gilgan, you can't even walk."

When she looked back at him, a huge frown dominated Gilgan's face. He hobbled towards her, black cane digging into the ground. "Sometimes all we can do is make the best of the cards we're given," he said. Firelight streamed across his face, accentuating all those wrinkles, and scars, and his mutated leg. "Be careful out there, Elenah. The war changed me, and it will change you too. I pray that it is for the better."

Elenah nodded. "Please be safe," she told him. Gilgan just watched her, tears glittering in his eyes. She'd never seen him cry before. She couldn't even look at him.

"I will try my best," Gilgan said.

Elenah lingered, sketching his face in the heart of her mind. Then she turned, replacing her sadness with burning determination, and hurried off down the road.

FROM THIS POINT FORWARD, everything had to go right.

Elenah kept her head down as she ran. She needed to get off-world as swift as possible, because she seemed to be the only person here who saw through the Council's mask.

The roads were shrouded in darkness, the lights of fire and lamp obscured by smoke. If there was still a clock tower, she supposed it might be chiming close to midnight. Everywhere she looked, there were troopers and field officers. Children scurried about, pulling along their mothers and fathers and pointing nervously. Wedged between the marble towers were small shops and houses, with painted wooden walls sparkling under the flames.

She realised she was holding her breath. This was as big a gamble as ever she'd taken. To run away from everything—from safety, and her father, and Gilgan—into a galaxy rife with total warfare. Merely the thought dug a gaping pit in her stomach. But they'd lied to her, deceived her all her life. The Council was the enemy, and now they were here.

Gilgan's words were trapped inside her head, bouncing

around and rattling against the walls of her mind: *You do not want to be out there now. And certainly not alone . . .*

Her eyes darted around, searching for someone she knew, someone familiar. She *wasn't* going alone. Doors opened and closed, feet clicked cobbles, bright lights sprayed from arched and tessellated windows. A small shuttle bus flew past carrying wounded.

Then she saw him, hovering in the shadows. Oswald's long brown duster was caked in ash and blood. His top hat was crooked, his hair dishevelled, his bushy beard frayed and drenched in spittle. "Oswald?" she gasped, running towards him.

"Oh, it's you," Oswald croaked as armed troopers with rifles sprinted across the road and headed for the clock tower.

"What happened?" Elenah looked at him in bewilderment. He was wearing all matters of charms and bracelets, flung out as if he'd put them all on in a hurry. He was losing blood fast, but Elenah couldn't find his wound. "Who did this to you?"

Oswald shrugged her off. "Did you get my message? They're after you."

"You don't look so good," Elenah commented.

"I'm fine!" he persisted. "Why are you here? You won't be safe with me . . ." He seemed to be running out of breath. "I'm not taking you, Elenah . . . I'm not—"

A silver light slammed the wall beside Oswald's head, throwing debris in their faces. Elenah jerked back, staggering on her feet, and tried to pinpoint where it had come from.

"Move!" Oswald shoved her out of the way, onto the cracked cobbles. An icy surge split the night and there was a distant cry of pain. Elenah rose just in time to glimpse a body splayed across the icy ground ahead, like winter had suddenly come and gone.

"Oswald?" Elenah tremored.

He grabbed her by the arm, tight enough to cut off her blood flow, and then pulled her into another long stretch of road. Elenah shook herself from his grip and risked another glance over her shoulder. A dark figure spun around the bend, right on their heels.

"What's going on?" Elenah gasped. "How many are there really?"

"More than I thought," Oswald grunted. He grabbed her by the elbow and whisked her onto another road. "Look, you've gotta get to the spaceport. I can probably arrange—"

"Let me come with you," Elenah said.

"No, it isn't *safe!*" His very last syllable became a grunt and then a shout as he spun around unsteadily and launched an icy spear through the air. The effort sent him stumbling backwards, crashing onto his hands and knees, but he propelled himself back up and spun into an alley without wasting a second.

Elenah followed him down, shadows and lights flashing over them. "Why didn't you tell me you were a *magician?*" she demanded. "That would've been helpful, you know."

"I'm not a magician. I'm a *trickster.*" He grunted as he brought her to a brief stop in an alcove. "And you need a pilot, don't you."

"Clearly," Elenah said. "Do you think I'd still be here if that weren't the case?"

"Oh, all right," he spat. "I wasn't planning on taking anybody with me, but I don't suppose I can just leave you here." He pointed at lights in the distance; his finger trembled with exhaustion. "That's the spaceport. Can you run?"

"Can I run?" Elenah asked, incredulous. "*I* can. What about *you?*"

"I'll try," Oswald said, then he turned, duster billowing out behind him, and she followed him out from within the shadows and onto the road towards the spaceport.

IT LAY JUST BEYOND THE CITY: a debris-strewn field that stretched towards the horizon. The towers upon the field were spear-like and silver-white, although they were bathed in darkness. One of them had *collapsed*. On circular platforms lay ships: a red delivery shuttle, several that must have been leased to the visiting nobles, and a luxury Pegasus emblazoned with violet and white.

Oswald's was an old AT-13 shuttle, shunted off on its own. It looked suspiciously like the kinds of spacecraft smugglers used to move piracy. Though, it was no surprise considering his past. "Hurry up," Oswald said. "Get inside." He gestured pointedly at the door and it *jolted* in its frame. Then he dragged it open, brusquely commenting, "Protective charm."

They stumbled inside. Oswald slammed the door shut, causing several hanging trinkets to clatter against each other. They were everywhere, those trinkets. Mystical things that made Elenah wonder if Oswald wasn't trying to ward off some sort of demon. Gilgan had spoken in brief of this kind of magic, mostly that it was very unreliable. Oswald clearly didn't mind. He crossed the main lounge and plunked himself down on one of the couches.

"Luran blood," he panted, pointing. Elenah tried to follow

his finger's trajectory, peering about the lounge, heart racing. It was only a cramped little thing, and smelt like a disposal yard for sewage. The trinkets cast a multicoloured glow upon the air, clinking against one another in song. "Over *there*," he persisted. "*There*, Elenah!"

She found it stashed in a small wooden crate. Within the vial was a bright blue liquid which felt cold to the touch. "Got it," she said as she raced back to him.

Oswald downed it quickly.

"Do you live here?" Elenah asked, noting the pillow and sheet draped across one of the couches, and the empty cereal bowl on the table.

Oswald nodded, gasping as he finished the potion. Then he closed his eyes and seemed to fall into a trance. The trinkets rattled, as though an invisible wind were rushing through them. Elenah felt beads of cold air sliding over her skin and she shivered.

Finally, Oswald jumped up and ran into the cockpit.

"Let's go," he said. Elenah watched him with bemusement as he entered the cockpit. A huge viewscreen spanned the curved bow of the ship, revealing darkness outside.

"Why were they attacking you?" Elenah asked.

"Who can say?" Oswald said without much conviction, busying himself by pulling switches in the cockpit. "Sit down while I get this started."

Elenah let her knapsack slide from her shoulders and lowered herself onto one of the painfully-hard gravity couches. There were two of them, curving round a disc-shaped table. "Sure you're okay?" she timidly asked. "You were half-dead just before."

"Do you want to get off this rock or not?" Oswald asked.

Elenah frowned. "Where can we go?"

"I think I know a place," Oswald said. "But that's as far as I'm taking you."

"Well, I wouldn't want to ask too much of you," Elenah said drily. She sat back on the couch and drew a sharp breath. This could all go so terribly wrong; a nagging voice in the back of her head told her so. But she couldn't return now. With Teveran out there, resistance fighters hunting her down, and the Council's grip around her father tightening, she *couldn't* go back.

Oswald pulled a switch and everything began to rumble.

Am I doing the right thing? She imagined Gilgan and her father, and the others inside the palace. The troopers. The rebels. The good people of Etheron who were slowly falling under the Council's control . . . And she who was deserting them.

The ship came alive with flashing lights and sounds. The various trinkets around the place started jingling about.

Where will I go? she wondered.

"Let me introduce you," Oswald said. "Ship's called the *Voyager*. It's an AT-Shuttle—well, one of the older models, but it gets the job done. Bought it cheap off some merchants back on Cleave. Oh, and try not to play with anything. Keep your hands to yourself. I bet you half of this stuff doesn't work, but I don't feel like playing the odds."

"Oh, good," Elenah said, glancing about. The lounge had two tinted windows, running along the walls; Elenah peered through them, palms growing sweaty. The engines revved up, aft propulsion cannons roaring to life. Fizzling flashes of starfire swept across the dark platform, crackling about. The *Voyager* tilted backwards and Elenah was surprised not to be flung to the back. It must have been using some sort of artificial gravity.

"Now," Oswald said, "let's hope this thing doesn't fall straight back down."

That made Elenah's stomach turn.

She glanced towards the viewscreen, but saw only black sky and wisps of smoke. Firelight poured into the shuttle, making her squint. Her heartbeat quickened. The *Voyager* grew louder, choking, starfire gushing around it. A cabin light blinked out.

"Does this always happen?" Elenah asked.

"Usually," Oswald said, voice strained. He accelerated. The *Voyager* screamed. The force threw Elenah's body against her seat. Her blood pulsed excitedly. The clouds blurred and the sky became a tunnel. Winds thrashed the ship, rocking it.

And then they emerged.

In *space*.

Strange black specks burst to life around her, floating within the beams of beautiful starlight. *Fabledust*, she thought, reaching out to touch it. *Gods, it's beautiful.*

She slid off the couch and dragged herself towards the cockpit. The unfamiliar pull of artificial gravity made it a balancing act until she righted herself against the wall and looked inside. Before her, Oswald visibly exhaled.

Beyond him, stars stretched into infinity. The beauty sucked her breath away, like no painting she'd ever seen, like no passage of feeble words could describe. *We're out. I did it.*

She twirled and scampered to the portside window, pressing herself against it. The moon, Angel III, lay below her, barely a speck. She followed the curve of the window until her home, Etheron, sauntered into view. *It's so small.* There before her lay everything she'd ever known. Her entire world, compressed into the size of a grape.

A morbid thought: *Gilgan's down there.*

And her father. And Rose. And thousands of others. What would happen to them once the Council crushed the meek resistance and began taking the city as their own?

Oswald walked in. He was still covered in blood, but he hardly seemed to be in any pain. "I'll admit, I haven't flown this ship in years." He laughed a little to himself, then breathed out a long, shaky breath. "I'll get you something to drink. How about some tea?"

A metallic bang drowned her answer.

"Is there anybody else living here?" Elenah asked warily.

"Uh, don't worry about that."

"What's behind that door?"

Just as she said it, the door fell open and a spindly figure stumbled out. Elenah yelped, backing away. Oswald cursed as he shoved her back and put himself between her and the *thing*. "Eukaloo!" he barked. "Get back inside that room, you sneaky Troff."

"A *Troff?*" Elenah gasped. The realisation threw her back inside Gilgan's books, to a faraway world where Troffren roamed the streets alongside humans. Eukaloo was a rather tiny fellow, with arms barely thicker than sticks, and a narrow face jutting from the end of a long neck. He wore a grey cloak which looked handmade, but by no means inexpensive. Beneath the cowl he had scaled, reptilian skin, and bright yellow eyes.

"*Dubah shubah,*" it croaked.

"Back!" Oswald yelled.

"You can understand it?" Elenah asked.

"*Barely*, but I wouldn't call it a blessing. Come on then," he said to the Troff, "back inside, and try not to make a mess in there."

Eukaloo grunted, skulking back inside his dark room at the back of the ship, the door shutting behind him. Oswald turned back to Elenah, cursing under his breath. "Tea?"

"Tea's fine," Elenah said.

"Good. Sit down and get comfortable. I'll drop you off at Highshore. While it's not very far, this ship doesn't have a very strong hyperdrive accelerator. Besides, I wouldn't risk exposing a trash-keep like this to that much force."

"The Troff," Elenah said as Oswald began walking away to the kitchens. "Are you keeping him a *prisoner* here? How did you come upon him in the first place?"

"It's complicated," Oswald said, and then he was gone. Elenah glanced at the door, behind which stood that lanky Troff, and she wondered what it was doing here. But her last thought was looking at the stars, hoping she'd made the right choice.

CHAPTER EIGHT

FOREST ASSAULT

The gods are dead, but there are places in the galaxy where I have felt their presence. Within the sunburnt cities of Skarros, upon the mountains of Azia, inside the forests of Corion . . . And I've always wondered: Is there a pattern or am I finally going mad?

Teveran watched Vallon work on Krosse's injury, sticking things into his gut and mopping up the blood with rags. It was messy business. If Gilgan were here, then Teveran was sure he'd be able to do a much better job of it with some kind of magic.

But there were no magicians here.

Krosse no longer wore his helmet; it lay on the floor, splattered with blood. Snake sat at the other end of the room, one rifle slung across his shoulder, the other in his arms, his helmet still covering his face.

"Hold still," Vallon said, forcing a metal rod through Krosse's broken armour plates and into the wound. Teveran only glimpsed a sliver of the needle before it disappeared inside him. His dark skin sizzled. Milky steam rolled off. Teveran cringed at the burnt-flesh smell.

Veins throbbed in Krosse's face as he bared his pale teeth. His bulky hands locked into fists, thumping the ground. "Aw, hell!" he roared. "I told you I didn't want you to— *Ugh!*" He screamed, but Vallon was no longer listening. He squeezed a trigger on the metal rod, invoking more wrangling wails from Krosse. Teveran wondered what the hell that thing was. He looked from the wound to Krosse, then to Vallon, and realised he couldn't sit there any longer. He launched himself off the floor and hurriedly walked away. Krosse's screams followed him out the door and into the dark forest. Snake came hurtling out after him.

"Don't stray too far," he said.

Teveran ignored him, traversing the field of dead bodies. He hadn't bothered to put his helmet back on; he found he no longer cared much for it. Snake, however, had not touched it. He was the picture of a perfect soldier, one from the storybooks, the ultimate weapon.

"It's okay," Snake said, grabbing his shoulder and holding him in place. "Let me tell you, Teveran, twenty-five years I've been fighting and even *I'm* not used to it yet." He brushed past him, gazing off into the distance. It didn't make Teveran feel that much better, knowing there were twenty-five more years of this hell. He sniffed the scent of rot and tried not to be sick.

"I want to be alone right now," Teveran said. He wanted to forget where he was, but he could still hear the ringing gunfire, and the screams, and the fruitless pleas. *Lavok,* the female had rasped. *Oh, Lavok . . .*

Snake removed his helmet and hooked it to his belt. Wavy blond hair flowed onto his shoulders. He turned, emerald eyes glistening. "Walk with me," he said in a voice that was far more human. Teveran hesitated, but decided he'd rather not be left standing in the middle of nowhere. There were, after all, creatures called iridel stalking about.

He followed Snake to the skirts of the village, where the trees seemed to grow forever, so close to one another you could only see shards of silver moonlight. They stood abreast, staring into the endless distance. Teveran wondered how far you could walk without reaching the edge. His heart knocked at his throat as he gaped at the towering trees.

"I'm sorry you had to go through this. I know it's probably not what you were expecting. But your uncle is a good man. He's a strong leader. In fact, he might be the best we've had in years. And if you're anything like him, well . . ."

He could have been talking to himself for as much Teveran cared. He glanced at him sideward. "What is this, Snake?"

"What do you mean?"

Teveran locked his jaw and clenched his fists. "What the hell are you *doing?*" He rounded on him. "Gods! Those Taurans did *nothing* to deserve that."

"Hey," Snake said. "No need to get angry."

"I think I have every right. You're murderers, that's what you are. You can't just *kill* people. Especially when they're not even shooting at you!" Anger burned through him now. He tried to figure out what was going through Snake's head. *Maybe those Taurans were aiding the rebels.* But it tasted wrong. *They had to save Krosse.* But even that was no justification.

Snake's emerald eyes darkened. "It helps not to think too much."

"But those Taurans were clearly *unarmed.*"

"And what if they weren't?" Snake retorted.

"They're Taurans!" Teveran snapped. "They wouldn't

hurt you if you'd set fire to this whole damned forest! Hell, even I know that and what the hell do I know? You could have asked nicely. We need to be making allies. I'm sure they would've helped."

"You need to settle down, High Prince."

"Don't call me that." He spun away from him and tried to put a few paces between them. "I'm not even meant to be here. Gods, how did this happen?" His mind clicked over a hundred scenarios, each one more frightening than the last. In a smaller voice he asked, "Did someone . . . *do* this? But who would want me dead? I haven't *done* anything."

"I think it was just an innocent mistake," Snake said. "I'm sure they'll work things out. Let's get through this first." After a while in silence, he added, "Whatever happens, I've got your back." Teveran eyed him, but suddenly wished he could turn invisible and run away.

He drew a deep breath. "Is that a flute you're carrying?"

"This?" Snake whipped it out. "Yes, it was my sister's. Wouldn't want to play it here, though." He carefully secured it back inside his belt. "I'm not very good. I only know one song: *The Sailor Son of Selas*. My sister used to play it all the time."

"What happened to her?" Teveran asked.

"She was killed by a cruel, cruel woman."

"I'm sorry."

"It was a long time ago." But the way he said it made Teveran think his wounds had not yet healed. Teveran couldn't even imagine what it would be like to lose Elenah . . .

A sudden voice rang out behind them: "Let's keep moving."

Teveran and Snake turned to see Krosse blundering out of the house, clasping his smoking gut with one hand, swinging a rifle in the other. His helmet concealed where there might have been tears. "Goddamn needles," he grumbled. Vallon emerged behind him, hauling two brown bags across his back. Both men were covered in blood, but neither of them seemed to mind.

"I didn't think the Azichs could cry so much," Snake jibed.

"I'm only half Azich," Krosse grumbled.

As Snake said something about Azich dragon riders, Teveran found his eyes wandering. In Gilgan's stories, Corion was a vast place with a dark beauty that daylight never touched. There'd been hundreds of species here, thousands of peaceful creatures that lived among the trees. Was it still beautiful? It surely took his breath away, but he couldn't say it was beautiful. Not like this. This was a graveyard. Everywhere he looked, he could see those Taurans.

Breathe, he told himself. *Breathe.*

Something shifted behind the trees.

"Did you see that?" he gasped.

Snake fastened his helmet and raised his rifle. Something else shifted there, in someplace unseen. Teveran's gut sank into the dirt and leaves. Vallon must have seen the terror in his eyes, because he turned and saw it too. "Is it the iridel?" Teveran asked.

Lights. Movement.

Crack!

A sizzling bullet punched a hole through Vallon's head, splitting his brain and throwing shards of skull across the ground.

Nobody moved. It took them all a while to realise what

had happened. Vallon stood for several heartbeats more, wavering on the spot. Then, he fell, gaping hole in his head.

"Oh *crap!*" Krosse roared.

"It's a sniper!" Snake bellowed.

Teveran's mind reeled.

"*Get down!*"

A shower of bullets folded across them. Krosse heaped up Vallon's bags and sprinted for the shelter of the trees. Snake pulled Teveran out of his frozen stupor, grabbing his shirt, throwing him forward, and shouting, "Run, Teveran!"

Teveran wasted no time at all, taking off after Krosse. Snake lingered back, returning fire through the trees, his flute drumming against his thigh. When Teveran glanced his way, the trees had shunted him from sight. He looked straight ahead, and he was hot on Krosse's trail.

Bullets thinned the trees around him, flicking off chips of wood and bark. People shouted and cursed. The white flashes of gunfire burned his eyes. Krosse turned sharply, then threw himself down a hill. Teveran barrelled down after him. Bark, dirt, and grass choked him.

A rock slit his palm.

A twig cut his brow.

At the bottom, he splashed in water.

He came out coughing and spluttering, scrambling for the bank, but Krosse emerged in front of him, tossing the bags away and throwing Teveran backwards. "Follow the river!" was all he screamed, before unshouldering his rifle and sending bullets flying into the darkness.

Teveran realised he wasn't holding his rifle anymore. He opened his mouth, but no words came out. Bullets spat in his direction, kissing the water. Fish scuttled about, darting back and forth. Red fish, the colour bleeding from their scales like ink, and white fish like skeletons. Six-legged insects the size of his palm clung to Krosse's back, wings fluttering, dripping water. The Azich man ducked behind the shallow hill, black water rolling down his armoured suit. Starfire coiled around his rifle like lightning. It launched his bullets through the air at a frightening speed.

"Go!" Krosse bellowed.

Teveran hastily splashed to the other side of the river, floundered over the muddy bank, grabbed strands of dead grass and hauled himself up. Somehow, he found his feet. A bullet struck his ankle and he screamed, falling headlong into the dirt. His nails dug into the mires. He glanced over his shoulder. A bullet whacked the ground beside his hand, flicking dirt into his eyes and mouth. He flipped onto his back.

Through the haze he could see the brown coats of the enemy, painted crimson gears flashing upon their shoulders like devil eyes. They were converging on Krosse's position, and Teveran knew they were going to kill him. There was no way out. No way—

"Blast it," he snarled. "Pull yourself together!" Teveran lurched to his feet, half-blinded by dirt. Hot, furious pain howled in his ankle, throwing him back down. He grinded his teeth, suppressed a scream. Lights bombarded his eyes. *My helmet*, he thought. *I left it in the house!* The trees twisted and grew a thousand feet taller. He could hear them singing, and laughing. He could feel the frantic pulses of magic swimming through the air, swirling around his exhausted, hopeless form. *I need to keep moving.* He reached down and grabbed his ankle. The ground crumbled beneath him, dirt tumbling into the black river. He raised his eyes. Gunfire popped in the distance. He turned, and rose, and began to hop.

He didn't know where he was going, or if he would just end up hopping right into the rebel base where they would surely kill him. He just knew he couldn't stop, not with this agonising ankle, not with his heart in his throat.

Gunfire thundered behind him. Was Snake still alive? Krosse?

Gods, they were all going to die . . .

Every time he blinked, he saw Vallon's face burrowed out by a single sniper's bullet. Dead in a heartbeat. It felt like cheating. It was so unfair. So quick. So *sudden*.

Teveran's ankle snared a vine and he came crashing back down, sliding through the mud and dirt. He almost screamed, but every fibre of his body was numb. He propelled himself back up, spluttering on the back of his hand. *Just keep running*, he told himself, dragging his swelling ankle through the dirt. *Run, Teveran. Don't stop.*

Maybe he could escape.

The gunfire softened as he drew farther and farther away, rumbles of bullet rain replaced by cracks of twigs and leaves, desperate shouts by chirping birds. His breathing came hard, and his brain begged him to stop, to just take a damn breath. Confined behind the walls of the palace, Teveran never had much reason to run.

He tripped again. His head struck a jutting stone, and pain lanced through his face, rattling his skull and overwhelming him with nausea.

In an effort not to scream or vomit, he bit down until he tasted blood. He glanced back the way he'd come, but the darkness had somehow grown deeper.

There was a sudden, chilling silence, save for the crackling sounds of the forest, and blood in his ears. A patchwork of silver moonlight illuminated leaves and rocks strewn about. He tried to get back up and keep running, but the world was spinning.

As he lay there in the leaves, he focused and tried to cast a restorative spell. Nothing happened. He couldn't concentrate! He reached for the magical spheres surging across the battlefield but could not make them listen. Hopelessly, he bent out his arm and tried to cast a beam of light, but all he managed was the faintest coil, which faded.

Leaves rolled and swirled around him. There was birdsong overhead, rustling bushes all around. He couldn't remember where he was, or how he'd come to be there, but he closed his eyes and pretended he was back in the city, back home.

He could see it now. The lush green fields. The brilliant marble spires of the palace. Red and blue flowers along the verge, simple green trees that weren't impossibly tall, lakes and rivers that reflected the cloudless sky's beauty and not fire. He would've cried, had his tears not dried up before they touched his eyes. He tried to lick his lips, but they were parched and cracked. *How did I get here?* he wondered. *Why is it so . . . quiet?*

Something exploded, waking Teveran from his daze. His eyes shot open, his body flared with sensation. The cold wind against his skin, the pain in his wrist and in his ankle . . .

Off in the distance, fire surged through the sky.

Teveran yanked himself to his feet and tried to amass a better look. *What the hell?* He was already too scared to panic. He turned every way he could, hoping nothing was coming to kill him—iridel or worse. *What's happening?* He tried to recall the mission. He racked his brain trying to remember. He couldn't. He just watched the inferno.

The sudden sound of gunfire rattled him. His heart danced around. He stumbled maladroitly to the nearest tree and crumpled against it. To one side lay the fire and explosions. To the other, the incalculable blasts of bullets. He folded to his knees, closed his eyes—

And then: "Let them burn! Alert the extraction team!" Another trooper emerged from the bushes. Half his suit was smeared in blood. He stuffed the radio back inside his pocket and ran to Teveran. "You all right, soldier?" He offered a hand. "Where's the rest of your squad?"

Teveran passed out before he could answer.

Chapter Nine

CHOICES

Is it the inherent use of magic that causes widespread phenomena such as the Rending Winds, or does it require a perfect set of circumstances; an equation of sorts? This question once led me to ponder if magic also possessed the ability to conquer death.

It was raining again. Beyond the windows that encircled the king's sitting room, storm clouds swirled and thrashed in the skies. Thunder bellowed so loudly that the lights threatened to douse them in darkness. A result of the sudden imbalance of magic in the Free Worlds.

Gilgan watched King Bayle Lockwood, standing in the middle of the room with a glass of wine clasped in his hand. The echoes of his last words still roared through Gilgan's ears: *Where is my daughter?* Gilgan felt sick, cold, as if all the life had drained from his body. He had failed him, *betrayed* him . . . betrayed the man who had done so much for him.

"I don't know, sir," he mumbled.

Fire swelled in Bayle's one good eye; once hazel, it was now the colour of burnt wood. The muscles in his jaw grinded and popped, like the turning of gears. He tightened his grip around the glass, then threw it upon the table. It shattered. Red wine sprayed the carpet like blood. "Look at me when I'm speaking to you!" he snapped. "Look at me, Gilgan!"

Gilgan tried, but he could barely stand the shame. He was the one who'd left her there that night when all hell was breaking loose. He'd watched her walk away.

Bayle's emerald robes fluttered as he stepped forward, the golden gilt reflecting light from the chandelier swaying overhead. Thunder shook the foundations of the palace, and though he barely moved, he seemed to grow as tall as the domed ceiling. "Well? *Where did she go?*" He made an effort to enunciate each word through gritted, crooked teeth.

"I don't know," Gilgan said dumbly. He felt so pathetic, so helpless. A torrent of guilt clutched his frail bones. It poured through his blood.

"You must," Bayle pleaded.

"She could be anywhere in the whole galaxy by now."

Bayle pinched his forehead, slick with sweat and laced with furrows. "Gods, we're in trouble." He looked out the window, plastered with fog, battered by an unstoppable sheet of rain. "It's like the Dead Winter. The Treaty was supposed to prevent something like that from happening again. But now there are magicians among us, and look at what they've done . . ."

Gilgan knew all too well the consequences of using magic, especially in disastrous quantities—*especially* when no magical spell had been cast here in seventeen years. Gilgan had come here to escape all that, he'd come here so he wasn't tempted, or drawn back into that way of life . . .

"I shouldn't yell," Bayle apologised. "It's just . . . I always knew this would happen, and I should've acted sooner. Why didn't I?" He was talking to himself now, pacing, rubbing his hollow jaw. He skirted the mess he'd made on the carpet and walked to a tapestry of an ice-capped mountain surrounded by black birds. "All these years I was *blind*. Blind to the Council's games, and to my own responsibilities—not as the king of these people, but as the father to my children." When he turned around, pain flickered in his eyes. He pulled out a white kerchief and coughed into it. Gilgan flinched. It *hurt* to see him like this. Eaten alive by this terrible sickness . . .

"Look at what I've become," Bayle said, waving the bloody kerchief. Black blood. You saw its kind in darker worlds, places overrun by cursed vermin. "This is why Misra left. My own children couldn't care less about whether I live or die." Gods, he felt bad for the man. Bayle had taken him in when he had nowhere else to go. He'd taken him in despite the crooked leg, despite the nightmares and delusions, despite what he was and where he'd come from.

But what could he say?

"I'm not asking for your pity," Bayle said with a solemn shake of the head. He crossed the room and threw himself into the couch. He clasped his hands and stared at the bloody stains of wine. "But I can't keep doing this. It's tearing me apart."

He wasn't talking about the children anymore. Bayle, as the founder of the Free Worlds Treaty, carried such a burden that Gilgan was surprised he hadn't folded sooner. All that had kept him going was the promise of building a better world for his children, and their children . . . But now that they were gone, perhaps drawn into the Council's fight, he had nothing left. Magic was used here last night, Gilgan could feel it, and it had upset the stability of the planet. He wasn't sure how long this storm would last, but it wasn't subsiding anytime soon.

"There's nothing you could've done," Gilgan said. "Whatever you chose, it couldn't have saved Teveran." And that was the closest truth Gilgan could find. Teveran was the High Prince. Six hundred years of tradition bound him to the Council's cause, and they really couldn't afford to make enemies of *this* Council. Elenah was right when she'd said they were taking over Etheron, and he hadn't lied when he'd told her it was already too late. The walls were closing. This would soon become their prison. The Council was going to build some kind of base here, and use it in their efforts to bring the galaxy under their complete, merciless control.

"But what if there was?" Bayle asked. "What if we fled?"

"They would find you." A fork of lightning flashed outside the window, throwing in silver light that was almost precisely the shade of Gilgan's eyes. "I know how hard this was for you. But this doesn't mean the end."

"Isn't there anything we can do?" Bayle asked.

Gilgan eyed him warily. "In what regard?"

A single tear glimmered in Bayle's eye. "I don't want this place to become my grave. These people are depending on me. I should never have agreed to it in the first place."

"You never could've known what they were going to do."

Bayle averted his eyes ashamedly. "No. But I *should* have. What we're up against is something far worse than I ever imagined. What the Council wants, and what they stand for . . ."

"Nobody could have predicted it," Gilgan said. "Not after all this time."

"*You* did." Bayle's eyes widened now. "You knew, Gilgan.

You've known it all along. It's where you came from, isn't it?" He seemed utterly desperate now.

"Do not speak as though I ever dealt with the Forty-Ninth Council," Gilgan snarled, painful memories tugging at his temple. "I am *not* one of them."

Bayle grumbled. "Highlord Kloak will return in four days to begin the instalment of the base." He looked up at him. "I won't rest that burden on you. But . . . But Elenah will listen to you. Maybe you can bring her back. Maybe you can save them both—for me."

"I . . ." Gilgan's breath caught in his throat. "I don't know what to say." He forced a weak chortle, and leaned on his black cane. "Master Lockwood, I can hardly walk."

"They *need* you."

"They need *you!*" Gilgan said, eying him intently. He shook his head, drew a deep breath, and let it out slowly. "You're their father, goddammit!"

Bayle looked at him hopelessly. Within his one good eye, Gilgan could see the two children of Etheron, pleading for his help. But Gilgan couldn't save them. His days of travelling the galaxy were gone now. It would be simple foolishness to go back out there.

"This is *your* responsibility."

"Dammit, Gilgan!" Bayle roared, slamming his fist into the couch. He twisted his face and his eyes turned to fire. "Would you not help a dying man?"

"Don't give me that *crap!*" He stepped forward, driving his cane into the wine-soaked carpet. It almost slipped and sent him doubling over. "You know I can't go back out there, Bayle. Not with everything that happened. I did some terrible things. There are people who will—"

"My children are going to die," Bayle simply said. "I wish there was a cure to this disease. I would cross the stars for them if I could . . . But I can't, Bayle, and they're all I have left."

Gilgan's forehead burned with sweat. It reminded him of the battlefield. It was *his* fault Elenah was gone. He should have stopped her. He *could* have. He'd fought armies, and some of the most powerful magicians ever to manifest in the galaxy. Then why . . . Why hadn't he tried? *I'm going to be sick,* he thought, spinning around and hobbling back across the chamber. *I can't do this, Bayle. I won't go back. I won't be the person I was!*

"Gilgan!" Bayle snapped. "You can't run away forever!"

Gilgan tossed the door open and bolted through the halls. This mutation would be the death of him. His parents had abandoned him, he'd been called *impure* by the only family he ever had, left alone to wander the galaxy, just trying to stay alive . . .

The corridors of the palace curved and split in every direction. He stumbled around every bend. His leg was aching like it had never ached in years. There was a time long ago, in the heat of battle, when he didn't need his cane, when it was like he'd never been born with this mutation at all . . . But those times were far gone now. These days he could barely walk from one side of a room to the other without falling over and making a fool of himself.

He threw open the door to his study and his cane slipped on the polished floorboards. He grunted as he barrelled forward, landed on his crippled leg to keep his balance, then shouted as he hurled his cane halfway across the room. It slammed his desk with a crack. *What have I done?* He floundered over to his bed, but collapsed to his knees before he reached it.

You can't run away forever . . .

So are you going to help me? He saw Elenah's face in the darkness, a bright light behind all this rage. He was weak. He was afraid.

And she was far too strong for her own good.

"Rysenthor's flame," he groaned, dragging himself up against the side of the bed. "Damn." His crooked leg folded, pain lancing up his thigh. The study was cramped. It held nothing more than his creaky old bed, the dusty antiquated desk, three dirty bookshelves, and papers strewn across the ruddy floor. A lamp hung from the ceiling, emitting hazy yellow light. There were maps plastered across the walls, and a stained writ from the long-dead chancellor of Thrall. Gilgan didn't come in here often anymore; it was a place of too many bad memories. "I don't know what to do." He grabbed his cane and pulled himself upright. "I—"

The door swung open.

"Please leave," Gilgan said, breathless.

Rose stepped into the room, the door swinging shut behind her. Gilgan smelt her sweet perfume, like a knife. He struggled away from her, leaning on his cane. He stumbled over to his desk, then locked his jaw to stop himself from screaming at her. "Gilgan," she said, her velvet voice untouched by age. "I saw you running across the hall. Are you okay?"

"This is all his fault," Gilgan muttered, anger rising into his voice.

"Whose fault?" Rose timidly asked.

"Their father's, of course! I told him to let me train her. I told him that Elenah was strong, that she'd be in terrible danger if I didn't teach her how to control her powers . . ."

Rose stepped quietly across the room.

Her hand found his shoulder.

"Elenah is more capable than you think," Rose told him.

He shook his head. "No, Rose. It doesn't work like that." He tried to calm himself with a sharp intake of breath. He failed. "I warned him. But maybe it's my fault for telling them all those stories." He knelt before one of the lowest desk drawers and broke the lock binding with a simple, silent spell. The drawers squealed, spraying dust against his burning face.

Within: a cold emerald stone, glowing vibrantly, which spanned the length of his palm. Despite its pleasant shade, there was magic inside this stone so dark it made him wish he didn't have it. He could feel it pulsing through him, tapping excitedly against his own magical store.

"Gilgan?" Rose murmured. "What are you doing with that?"

Gilgan grabbed the stone and slowly turned around. It seemed to leech the fickle light. "We're chasing the wrong shadow, Rose. It's not the Council. It's *him*." Wicked chills grabbed his spine. Death's hands clutched his throat. "He's got Teveran."

"Jethre?" she gasped incredulously.

"No. Not him. *Fex*."

"But—" She'd hardly rasped the single utterance when it faded in the room's dusty chokehold. "Gilgan . . . But it's been so long. He must be dead!"

"I told you about Jethre's letter. I didn't tell you what it said, but Jethre's seen him—or, at least, he's felt his presence. I have too, even from here. Fex is still out there somewhere."

"Gilgan, don't . . ."

"Go find Dockson," was all he said in response. "Tell him to prep my old starfighter. *Revenant.* It's a modified Starsinger. He'll know which one."

"Gilgan?"

"Please, Rose."

"Don't do this."

"I should've done it years ago."

She worried the hem of her beautiful flowery dress, twisted the silver ring around her finger, then retreated in acquiescence.

Gilgan tucked the stone inside his pocket. He didn't like this, not one bit, but he had to be strong, just like he'd always been. For Elenah, and for Teveran. He was Etheron's last hope now, the only promise of bringing its son and daughter home.

And what a weak, weak promise he was.

Chapter Ten

MOKUURA

Starfire (more accurately called Element SG-18) is the beating heart of innovation and, importantly, civilisation. It was discovered in the year 10c15 by an old friend of mine, Jorv Landis, sparking the Mechanical Revolution two years later.

Elenah lay on the hard gravity couch, eating a packet of Oswald's sweet-tasting gorsa beans. They had a thin shell, which crunched, admitting a leathery layer of chocolate, and finally a kind of filling that Oswald called gorsa-spawn, which was warm and unbelievably addictive. She'd found several of the packets scouting the kitchen—which was not at all strange, considering this ship *did* double as Oswald's home.

"How many other languages can you speak?" Elenah asked as she reached into the packet to withdraw another bean. "That *was* Troffese before, wasn't it?"

"My great grandfather was a traveller," Oswald said, sitting on his own couch and shuffling through a deck of azherok cards. "I guess I just picked up those languages from him."

"That's not possible," Elenah said.

"Well, as I said, I'm not very good at it. For one thing, I can only *speak* one language and that's this one, Foundation. Pass a bean, would you?"

She tossed him one. "There aren't many left, are there? Troffese must be one of the only ancient languages still spoken across the galaxy."

"You know a lot, Elenah."

She blushed. "I read a lot."

"Knowledge can be a dangerous thing, especially with times as they are. Once we reach Highshore, you'll want to keep quiet for a bit."

"And where am I supposed to go from there?"

"You can go wherever you want. Hell, you could stay, but you won't be staying with me. The gods know if I'll even be there very long myself. That's generally how it works."

Elenah popped another bean between her teeth and closed her eyes, trying to tune out the tension around her and focus on the sweetness. The aft thrusters emitted a constant hum throughout the ship as they rolled in full force, sending them precariously towards Highshore. She'd gotten used to the musty scent, but it was still there, lingering in the background. She hadn't bothered to ask about Oswald's charms, but she did wonder how they worked. Perhaps that was a question for another time; as her mind emptied, she found a more pressing concern.

"Oswald?"

"What?"

"Do you think I can find my brother?" Sudden memories of him resolved in her mind. Running through the palace halls, playing childish tricks on Gilgan. She cast them away by chewing on another bean.

"The galaxy is a large place."

"So I've heard," she said, almost resignedly. "But I can't help but feel he's in trouble, and I'm scared the Council's going to make him do something terrible." She kept staring at the ceiling, but she could hear Oswald thinking, shuffling those cards. Would he help her? Or would he truly abandon her once they reached Highshore? Whatever happened, she had the entire galaxy at her fingertips. She could go anywhere she wanted, *do* anything she wanted . . .

Suddenly, the ship *jolted*. A high-pitched whine shrieked from behind the wall panels, and Oswald threw himself off the couch. He cursed at the ship as he trudged to the bow.

"What's that?" Elenah asked, sitting up straight.

"Gods of mercy," Oswald grunted as he slumped down in the pilot's seat. He whacked a button that silenced the keening, though he looked suddenly quite defeated. Elenah chucked the packet of beans onto the table and stood up, trying not to feel so wobbly. "I thought this might happen. This ship is more dead than I thought."

Elenah walked up behind him. "What's happening?"

"It's the damned starfire cells."

"Meaning?"

"Nothing." He shook his head. "I messed up. It's my fault. I should've checked them before we lifted off. They're old and, uh, almost empty."

"Well, what can we do?" Elenah asked.

"We'll need to land somewhere close."

"What about the . . . GSC? The Galactic Support Centre?"

Oswald groaned. "Oh, don't get me started on them. If you ask me, they don't even exist. The number of times—" He trailed off. "I shouldn't have brought you with me."

"What is it now?" Elenah demanded.

He slapped a switch that threw up a sketchy-looking hologram of a planet that could pass as a moon. "Every heard of Mokuura?"

"Once or twice," Elenah said, recalling Gilgan's stories.

Oswald grabbed his sweaty locks of hair, pulled down on his neatly-groomed beard—nervous habits that had become quite pronounced since they'd left Etheron. "We might have to make a brief stopover," he muttered. "Sit back down and I'll bring us in."

Elenah followed this tentatively. Mokuura was certainly not one of the places she'd had in mind when she thought of all the planets she wanted to visit. And the look on Oswald's face didn't help her confidence very much. "Are they looking for you there?" she asked.

"It's been five years. I hope they've forgotten me."

They arrived at Mokuura several hours later.

Elenah leapt out of the *Voyager*, her shoes slapping the glossy stone of the overflowing spaceport. Lights flashed across every surface, amber and blue and occasionally vibrant greens, but the city was not *colourful*. The sky was black, and there were no stars nor a sun. Shivering in the chill air, Elenah pulled her grey sweater across her blouse and exercised her cold hands.

"There's a lot more people here than I remember," Oswald said, ushering Eukaloo from the shuttle. Elenah watched the Troff, whose thin face swivelled upon his long, grey neck as he took in these new surroundings. His large, yellow eyes darted about. The light slithered across his greenish-grey skin, slipping in the cracks between his reptilian scales.

"You're bringing *him?*" Elenah asked.

"Not because I like him. Because I don't trust these people not to kidnap him," Oswald said as he led them briskly away from the ship, and through an archway that became a broad tunnel.

"I thought it was locked with a protective—"

"If you'd looked around, you'd find that Mokuura is *not* a Free World. There are magicians here and all breeds of other dodgy sorts. Just keep your eyes on the road and don't stare." Elenah wondered what made Eukaloo so special, and what Oswald needed of him, but her thoughts were soon whisked away as she glanced up and around and examined the city.

Windows overlooked a dark metropolis to either side of them. Ships hovered steadily through lanes in the sky. Buildings rose up awkwardly, jutting unevenly into the great dark. Elenah realised it was the first extra-terrestrial world she'd ever stepped foot on. It was also nothing like she'd imagined. Cold, dead, depressing.

"It's certainly become a lot grimmer," Oswald said, tipping his top hat so it shaded his face. He brushed a curl of brown hair out of his eyes. "But that's not saying much."

"Why is it so bad?" Elenah asked.

"Who knows? One day, I'm sure this place won't even exist."

They skirted to the side as a short creature passed them through the tunnel. *Is that another Troff?* Elenah wondered, glancing at its yellow bulb-like eyes and grey reptilian skin. Walking several strides behind him was a taller nonhuman with broad pink arms ringed with tattoos, and a snout that stuck pointedly from the centre of his face.

They emerged from the tunnel and into some sort of shanty town, with buildings that looked fit for slaves: slanted corrugated roofs, sphere-shaped lamps hanging from the eaves, trashcans spewing papers and scrap metal. Elenah clutched the straps of her knapsack tightly, afraid that somebody might steal it—not that it contained anything of value.

"Best you don't talk to these folk," Oswald told her, leaning close. "They'll do anything to swindle, bribe or murder you." Elenah followed his eyes towards an old lady sitting in front of a burrowed-out building, proffering a grey tankard that rattled with chits. Beneath the soot and scraggly hair, Elenah could've sworn that was a human.

She averted her eyes and quickened her pace to keep up with him. "What are they?"

"Beggars," he said. "Quite unfortunate. Nobody wants to live in a place like this. And if anybody says otherwise, don't believe them." Elenah screwed up her face as a bad smell wafted past. "Most of these people, they're either hiding from something . . . or they're just trapped here."

"I hope nobody steals your ship," Elenah said, wishing they'd walk a little faster. The beggars were everywhere, sitting along the skirts of winding roads, smoking, playing dice and cards, scrounging through the trashcans. They reminded her of rats, flitting about, and she wondered why nobody tried to help them. "Will they hurt us?"

"Not if you keep your distance," Oswald said. "Come here." He turned a corner and led them out of the town. Buildings here rose two or three times higher, but they remained dark and crooked. Other people lurked among the shadows. They scurried about with backpacks or grey sacks, riffled through fried vehicles and toppled structures. Scavengers. The only thing that hadn't changed was the acrid, sweaty smell clinging to the air.

"Now, this might be difficult," Oswald said awkwardly, hauling Eukaloo to a stop and rounding on them outside a shop lit with amber lamplight. The sign was written in glowing alien strokes. A bald-headed creature stood behind the counter with greasy yellow skin. He had one customer: a guy whose face was concealed by a high brown collar, whose eyes were metal spheres that rolled about, blinking red and white. "It might end up taking longer than I would like it to. If you want to take a wander, just don't go too far."

Elenah nodded, and Oswald also did—just a little less surely. Then he stepped away with Eukaloo and vanished amidst the crowds. Elenah couldn't help but notice how well they seemed to blend in. She shouldn't have been surprised; after all, Oswald *was* a criminal.

Is that what you were warning me of? she wondered, thinking of Gilgan. *Am I putting too much trust in him?* She turned away from Oswald and Eukaloo, and gazed about.

The ground level presented itself as a disposal yard for the rest of the city. Flakes of black dust fell from the sky. Metal and rubbish skittered across the ground. Snaking wires threw sparks where people walked.

Higher, crooked buildings with broken windows and stripped stone slabs stood like black statues against the pitch sky. Beyond them, huge walkways cut through the haze—bridges of some sort, impossibly suspended. Shuttles and cruisers hovered in their midst.

She came upon a courtyard that opened up the lower dwellings. Scavengers hurried from place to place. Residents smoked cigars. A big fellow—a Grall, blind crime lords from Gilgan's best stories—stood by a set of descending steps, bulbous grey flesh hanging off like sticky paste. A tall skeletal creature stood beside it, at guard, with a sweeping white cape. She'd read how the unsettling Skaar often served as bodyguards to the Grall.

In the centre of the courtyard rose four giant monoliths, scattered with no ostensible order. Hundreds of glowing amber symbols were carved into the stone. Elenah stepped closer to one. Parts of the monolith had eroded into nothing.

She reached out to touch it.

"They called it *Krakensvouf*," came a voice from the shadows.

She spun around to see a slender figure emerge. The first thing Elenah noticed was her feline face, and her yellow cat-like eyes, though she was perfectly humanoid and quite pretty. Her wavy pink hair hung down past her shoulders, slipping out from beneath a long grey cowl.

"Sorry?" Elenah said, recovering from her shock.

"Krakensvouf," the woman said simply. Her voice lilted as she spoke. She couldn't have been much older than Elenah. In the light, rough patches of brown in her hair became clearer, and Elenah guessed she'd coloured it herself. "A curse." She nodded towards the strange shapes and carvings etched into the monoliths. "Those are runes. They're meant to keep the beast at bay. But I think it's just a waste of time."

Elenah chilled. *A curse? A beast?*

The woman smiled warmly, flicking something off Elenah's shoulder. "I'm Hannah." She brushed past her and gently touched one of the runes; it beamed, and some sort of black steam rolled off the stone, writhing around her slender fingers. "You're a magician, aren't you."

Elenah looked at her strangely. "What makes you think that?"

"You have a *shade*."

"A what?" She was starting to regret ever leaving Oswald. What had he said about there being all breeds of dodgy sorts here?

"Only magicians can carry them," Hannah said, but Elenah was already trying to get away from her. "It's the *Sandred*, the king of dragons. Who gifted it to you?"

"What are you talking about?" Elenah asked, watching her warily.

Hannah seemed to consider her next words carefully. She was still running her lithe hands across the monolith. "I've been looking for the one who wields the Sandred's power. I've been looking for *you*." Lowering her voice, she asked, "What's your name?"

Elenah didn't have a clue what she was talking about.

"I'm not going to hurt you," Hannah said.

"I'm Elenah," she said. "But . . . I'm not staying here."

Hannah studied her for a moment, then stepped away from the monolith, clasping her pale green hands against her torso. Elenah also took a step back. Whatever magic they'd used to summon this protective seal, she could *feel* it, like a sheet of water against her chest.

"Elenah, I have to talk to you," Hannah said, gliding closer. There were residents of the city skulking about, like spectres moving through the shadows. "How about a drink? There's a bar down here; it isn't far."

Elenah bit her lip, not quite sure what to make of her.

"I need your help," Hannah said urgently.

"Okay," Elenah conceded. "Make it quick."

OSWALD LAUGHED. "I thought you were *dead!*"

The shopkeeper, a lanky blue Tauran called Hilka, didn't look impressed. She cocked her narrow face at him. "I thought you said you were never coming back."

"Trust me, it wasn't my intention."

"Ha. I thought you might want to apologise to my daughter."

"Your *what?* Gods, Hilka, I never—"

"Tell that to her face, you scum."

Oswald stepped away from her stall, bumping into Eukaloo. The Troff chirped, scuttling out of the way and into the path of grumbling pedestrians. The marketplace in Arkait Square was packed tonight, more so than he ever remembered. "Look,"—he raised his hands in defence and tried on a smile—"I just want to buy a couple new starfire cells for my ship."

"*Brikt mokta,*" said Eukaloo.

It roughly translated to: "*Scum woman.*"

"Who's this?" Hilka asked, flippantly addressing Eukaloo.

"No one of any consequence," Oswald said. That was true enough, though Hilka didn't look convinced. She folded her arms. Somebody riffled through the wooden crates at the back of the shop—Hilka must have gotten herself a new assistant.

"What have you done now?" Hilka snarled.

Oswald sighed, plucking off his top hat and clenching his

locks of hair. He stepped forward and plopped the hat onto the edge of the storefront. He lowered his voice and said, "Look, I've got a lot going on right now. I'm . . . I'm going back to Highshore."

"Highshore? Of all places? I thought you had a death sentence there."

The reminder made Oswald suddenly cold. "Yeah . . ."

"It's Liethral, isn't it?" Hilka said.

He nodded. "I'm going home, Hilka. I'm going to set things right and . . . and I might even ask her to marry me." He wasn't even sure if Liethral would remember him, or if she would even care, but he'd realised something on Etheron: Time was running out to fix things.

Hilka drew back, furrowing her thin brows. "Oswald, I'm sorry to say, but you're just not a marrying man. You can hardly take care of yourself."

"I can take care of myself just fine."

"Then when will you cut off that *thing* you call a beard?"

Oswald scrubbed it self-consciously. "Look, I didn't come here for your advice, Hilka. Will you sell me some starfire cells or not?"

"*Pfft.* After what you did?"

Oswald cursed and scooped up his hat, throwing it on his head. He spun around angrily and gestured Eukaloo back along the marketplace thoroughfare. "You're a devil, Hilka!" he yelled so everyone could hear. "After everything I did for you!"

"You broke my daughter's heart and disappeared! *Twice!*"

"That wasn't me!" He fell into stride with Eukaloo, muttering, "That was *not* me. Oh boy, can you believe her?" Eukaloo responded with a guttural phrase that translated to something like *"Never trust a Tauran."* Oswald laughed and said, "I think I can agree with you on that." As they ventured along, they passed a number of species. Oswald inclined his head downwards. He didn't want to be seen by the wrong pairs of eyes. "What about *you*, little fella?" He shot the Troff an eager, sidelong glance. "When are you going to tell me how to use that *talisman* you found? Here's your chance. There must be a thousand ships outbound here. Tell me what I need to know, and I'll let you go free."

Eukaloo chirped dismissively.

"Have it your way," Oswald said, pulling him along.

ELENAH AND HANNAH WALKED through a squealing metal door into a dingy tavern. Tables dotted the ruddy floor. Lamps dangled from the ceiling. Slats in each wall carried lights from outside to within. A pleasant smell wafted to her nose, much more inviting than the sour smoke outside.

She followed Hannah to the bar, where a scantily-clad barmaid was effortlessly drying stacks of glasses and humming to herself.

"Two glasses of stormjuice, thank you," Hannah said, throwing several silver chits onto the bench. Then she led Elenah to a round table a few paces away. Out of the corner of her eye, Elenah glimpsed a tall, lanky Tauran with milk-white skin appear behind the bar. Elenah had to stop herself from gaping; the Taurans featured prominently in Gilgan's stories.

"Stormjuice is a light drink," Hannah said. "Nothing too fancy."

"Yeah," Elenah said, not fully paying attention. She couldn't help but gawk at everything. It overwhelmed her: The smells of ale and fried meats, the clattering of plates, and the chirping of alien voices. Only now did she truly realise what had happened. This was no longer Etheron. She was in a completely different world. She was one of the travellers in Gilgan's stories, where she'd always wanted to be. Among all the voices, she understood a few:

"Did you hear? The Uzrean are planning a migration to the Greater Realm."

"This ale tastes like a *Grall* crapped in it."

". . . and they shut the turbo lifts to the upper city!"

"Mother said it's dangerous out. Better luck finding—"

"I'm from Feluria," Hannah said suddenly. Elenah blinked, returning to the present. "I'm probably the last Felirean in the galaxy now, but there was a prophecy . . ."

"A prophecy?" Elenah asked. Then she caught herself. "You're from Feluria?" That name sparked something in the back of her mind. The Purge of Feluria . . . The Kerrean warlords . . .

"They think I'm dead."

"That's why you're in disguise."

Hannah nodded.

Elenah shook her head. "I don't think I can help you, whatever you need . . ."

Hannah reached across the table and grabbed her wrist, staring pleadingly into her eyes. Hannah's were yellow, like the eyes of a cat. *The last Felirean in the galaxy . . .*

"Here are your drinks," said the milk-white Tauran, plodding the glasses in front of them and forcing Hannah to recoil her hand. The Tauran smiled, bowed amiably, then retreated. Elenah eyed the swirling liquid within; it was strangely energetic.

"I need you to come with me," Hannah said. "You're the one they spoke of—"

Explosion.

Distant.

The tavern shuddered. The lamps all shattered. Dirt and metal trickled from the ceiling. The tables slid, glasses and pans toppling. The door roared open and slammed on the ground. Elenah's heart leapt. Hannah's yellow eyes bulged from her face, the black pupils expanding. She pulled the grey cloak's cowl across her face. Elenah tried to mouth *What was that?* but she couldn't breathe and she couldn't speak.

And then: a high pitched keening.

It grew, and grew, and grew . . .

First came the screams, and then the shouts, and then people started spilling into the tavern from outside, followed by amber lights flickering on and off. Hannah scrambled to her feet. Fifty different alien voices exploded, but they were quickly drowned out by the keening, the sound of scraping metal . . .

A metal bridge the size of two buildings screamed through the ceiling and crushed the front half of the tavern. Elenah yelped and floundered backwards, falling off her chair as a wave of dirt folded across the room. Tables and chairs went flying. Pipes burst, releasing unharnessed starfire. People rolled across the ground. Elenah rammed her head into something, and all she saw were stars, spinning, spinning, and then a sudden splash of black.

CHAPTER ELEVEN

THE COUNCIL'S WRATH

The greatest achievement, perhaps, of the Forty-Ninth Council was their innovative Legacy-Class of ships. Dare I say it, this was a turning point in total galactic subjugation.

"My lord?" Fleet Officer Bredin squeaked as he scurried onto the main deck of the *Subjugator*.

Grand Highlord Thrakk stood by the huge glass viewscreen, gazing down upon a stark, crimson planet, which glowed so brightly Bredin assumed it must have been mostly gas. He stepped closer, suddenly conscious that the Grand Highlord might not have heard him. It was chaos upon the bridge; the Grand Highlord was leading a mining operation in the debris field over Rust. People hurried back and forth, crossing the slippery floor wildly.

"I have a message for you," Bredin said.

"Report," Thrakk said. Bredin chilled, heat burning right through him. Gods, he'd only just arrived three weeks back and he was already reporting to the most important man in the fleet.

It was a tale of the times.

Bredin crept closer, trying not to slip. Thrakk was the only still figure in the bridge. Red light bathed his statuary figure, casting him as a silhouette before the blinding glass. Bredin's glasses were spammed by the immense light and for a second he wondered what might happen if that was not Thrakk, and instead he was delivering the message to the wrong person . . .

"Report, Officer," Thrakk repeated, growing annoyed.

"The High Prince's extraction was . . . um . . ." Bredin tried to stop his voice from shaking. "There was a problem," he gushed. Then he waited. But the Grand Highlord did not respond. *Did he even hear me?* Bredin wondered. "The boy was drafted into the wrong troop transport," Bredin continued, "under the watch of Commander Vallon. And, well, the commander and his men didn't make it. But the boy is safe and he's recovering on . . ." *Crap, where was he again?*

"I don't care for excuses," Thrakk said. "If the boy does not arrive in due time, there *will* be consequences." His voice cracked and Bredin saw the Grand Highlord's shoulder slouch. But it might have just been a trick of the light. "Do I make myself clear?"

"Yes, my lord."

"Anything else?" Thrakk asked expectantly.

"One more thing," Bredin offered. "Highlord Pandion wished me to inform you that his battalion has launched the first strike on Mokuura's capital city."

"Good. Tell him I will be there shortly to offer my support."

Bredin nodded.

"Thank you, Officer."

Bredin was already on his way out.

ELENAH OPENED HER EYES, glanced around, and realised she was on her back. Blood rumbled in her ears. Shadows flickered across the walls. Disoriented, she scrambled up and levelled herself on the crumpled ground, hefting her knapsack.

"What— Where—"

Amber and sapphire lights spun and flashed through the glittering atmosphere. Elenah stepped over bodies and clambered over the fallen bridge, which was a huge metal structure spilling cables and black, gaseous starfire from its gut. Arms and legs jutted out from underneath it, fried or turned to mush. People were writhing and squirming, screaming out names.

"Oswald!" Elenah gasped, scrambling through the darkness. She could hardly find a breath amidst the smoke and debris. She heard sparks and hissing, the howl of starfire bursting out of pipes along the rafters. She needed to get out of there.

She emerged outside.

A massive Pegasus cruiser cut through the sky, twisting and falling in a coat of violet flashes. Billowing smoke and bright blue flames trailed it. Below, mouths were gaped in horrified screams, but all she could hear were the explosions. The Pegasus smashed through bridges and walkways carelessly, tearing the city in two. As if in slow motion, the ship drilled the side of a skyscraper and disappeared in a cloud of broiling flames.

Elenah searched for Oswald, for *Hannah*—anyone!— spinning left and right. She could barely see anything. Tears scorched her eyes, but she couldn't afford the distraction. She hastily blinked them away and followed the other survivors in a furious flounder along the road. People lay dead all over the place. Others wailed in all sorts of languages.

She didn't know what to do.

It's the Council, she thought. *Gods, they're here . . .*

A large troop transport emerged from the haze, a mighty beast straight out of Gilgan's books, throwing off silver lights. Three of them. Four. Five.

And troopers leapt out of them.

Elenah's heart lurched. Her feet were rooted to the spot. Her skin burned in the humid, malodorous air. People scampered around her, brushing past, trying to flee. They couldn't. *Is this what will become of Etheron?* she wondered.

The first blasts of gunfire rang louder than any scream, louder than the explosions and the ships plummeting from the sky. She began to feel dizzy, began to feel as though there was something burning inside her, something that she could almost—

A hand on her own snapped her reverie.

Hannah's feline face cut through the darkness. Her bubbly pink hair had floated out of the cowl, which now lay across her shoulders. There was a long gash in her cloak. "Follow me!" Elenah barely had time to think, but decided she had no choice.

Together, they hacked through the frantic crowds. Hannah's hand was sweaty and clammy and Elenah could barely hold on. She fought to keep up.

There was a crack. And then another. And the sky lit up with an effervescent explosion. A missile dug a hole through one of the buildings, throwing off streams of white, red and blue. The second missile, gone astray, blew up the back of the floundering crowd and severed limbs sprayed through the air. Elenah wanted to close her eyes and block her ears, but it was fruitless.

She screamed, thrown back by another blast. She landed on the ground, dirt and debris collapsing around her. She struggled to her feet as another missile ripped through a building and glass sprayed outwards. She couldn't see the starfighters swooping back and forth, but she could hear their thunderous roars, rattling her ribs, distorting her vision.

Glass fell from the sky. Shards slashed her skin back and forth. She heard the high-pitched cry of another missile, felt the whir of a Ragnarok arcing through the air just above her head. She tripped on a dead body. Her hand splashed in a puddle of blood. Bone and cartilage spewed over her. She tasted it, smelled it, and furiously fought her muscles to get off the ground and run. *Can't breathe.* She gasped. *I'm going to die . . .*

"Get up!" Hannah snatched her hand and hauled her to her feet. For a moment that felt like eternity, Elenah could do nothing but stagger, peering through the smoke in all directions. Black smoke. Fire. Limbs. Hannah yanked her along. Elenah saw the young Felirean's pink hair, mottled with brown, the only colours save for the crimson of blood, frantically flapping ahead.

Her delirious mind began thinking of the four monoliths and how they were probably blown to pieces. And she thought of Krakensvouf . . .

Someone else called out her name from a place unseen. A man. She strained her eyes, then a body slammed her side and sent her somersaulting. She thumped the ground, rolled, then threw the dead man off. She climbed to one knee and sought out Hannah—*again*. Those who could were running as fast as their legs allowed. Others simply lay on the ground, searching for their various body parts, clawing at their blinded eyes and ruptured ears.

Why are they attacking?

"Elenah!"

Where are you?

"Elenah!" Oswald's face emerged through a crack in the crowd.

"Hannah!" she screamed, jerking a finger in Oswald's direction. "This way!"

They ran to him.

"Go inside!" Oswald gasped, waving at a nearby door hanging ajar. He was kneeling on the side of the road. His beard was frayed and sooty. Blood gushed down his arm, though he'd tied a makeshift rag around it. His hat was gone, and sweaty locks of hair melted around his shoulders.

They all scrambled inside the little house. The door slammed shut behind them, spraying acrid dust. Hannah collapsed to her hands and knees, gasping for breath. Oswald stumbled. Elenah skirted to a wall and almost passed out.

"Gods," Hannah gasped. "This is my fault . . ."

"Who's that?" Oswald asked, though there was barely anything left of his voice.

"They're coming for *me*," Hannah complained.

Elenah stared, panting. "What are you talking about?"

"*Kokta rhuki!*" interrupted Eukaloo. He stood beside someone who looked vaguely human in the room beyond. It was dark inside, with no light but the fiery rays that streamed through the shuttered windows. Further on, the ceiling slanted and everything became much smaller. The room's only furnishing was an old couch with a pillow on one armrest. An orange radio stood on a bench in the corner, but the wires were frayed and it was covered inch-deep in dust.

The human, hunched as she was, stood only a couple inches taller than Eukaloo. She was an old crone with a shrivelled nose over shrivelled skin, grey wispy hair and a coat that seemed to be made of paper. Dirt stuck to her skin, pasted by sweat soaked deep inside her wrinkles. The crone clasped her hands against her chest, licking her lips through toothless gums. She opened her eyes as wide as sleep-encrusted eyes could open.

"*Takru. Batta!*" Eukaloo screamed.

Oswald strode from the group, blood snaking down his arm and onto the floor. The magical charms he wore jangled with every step he took. Thundering past them, he closed his fist around the old woman's shoulder and hacked out, "We need to access this passage."

"They're . . . coming." Her muddy accent suggested she was not speaking native Foundation. Her wrinkled cheeks quivered with every syllable. She reeked of terror, but Elenah couldn't blame her. This was nothing like the stories Gilgan had told her. Her legs were trembling, her heart thumping against her ribs. She glanced at Hannah, who was slow to her feet with tears in her murky eyes. She was the last Felirean, and she looked genuinely rattled.

Oswald shook the crone. "The passage! *Now!*"

Her small, fragile eyes opened in fright, eying them each in turn. Then she finally nodded and plodded through the house, bare feet slapping the splintered wood. Elenah had always considered herself quite short, but even she had to duck her head as they ventured inwards. The crone threw her hands into the couch, as if she could push it on her own.

Oswald reached her side, slamming his good shoulder into the couch and straining. Blood squirted out of his other arm. Elenah hissed through gritted teeth and dragged herself across the room. She flattened her palms against it. Eukaloo came hobbling along on spindly reptilian legs. Hannah grabbed the end. And all four of them pushed for their lives.

The couch grinded against the floorboards, flicking up chips of wood and dust that might have been in darkness for centuries. Elenah coughed and spluttered as dust caught in her throat. She heaved, and strained, and the couch steadily moved. And then they slammed it against the back wall . . . revealing a trap door underneath.

The crone knelt and worked the latch. She cracked it open, lifted it, and looked up at them. "Dark inside," she croaked, grabbing a lantern that emitted a playful white light. "Take this." She proffered it at them. "*Take it!*"

Oswald snatched it, then skirted towards the pit. "Bring the Troff," he said. Eukaloo tensed, his yellow eyes radiating their own lights in the darkness.

Elenah glanced at the old woman. "Shouldn't we take her with us?"

"No, we can't," Oswald said.

"We can't leave her here," Elenah protested.

"Look at her!" Oswald roared, and for the first time Elenah saw fury in his eyes, in his tightened jaw and pulled-back skin. "We have enough to worry about. Down there she'll only be left to rot." He glanced at Hannah. "What about you? Can you walk? Can you *run?*"

Hannah thought for a moment, then nodded firmly.

"Then do it," Oswald said.

Elenah looked at Eukaloo, at the crone. Two complete strangers, united in their doom, victims of the Council's wrath. *I'm letting her die,* she thought. *I'm so sorry.*

Oswald entered the pit, the white light following him down. About a second later, his boots crunched the ground at the bottom.

Hannah went next at a gentle gesture from Elenah. Beside her, Eukaloo croaked and looked at her. She still could not fathom why Oswald was keeping him around. "Go on," she tremored, throwing her hand into the Troff's back and ushering him towards the pit. The old crone watched her fearfully. For a moment, she adopted the form of Old Rose, emerald eyes so full of life, a smile on her wizened face . . .

This is what we've let into our home, she thought.

She squeezed her eyes shut, tears cutting through the dirt on her face, and climbed into the pit after Eukaloo. When the trapdoor closed above them, another door opened. And the last thing Elenah heard was gunfire, and the old woman's brief but horrifying scream.

Chapter Twelve

SUBJUGATOR

The Forty-Ninth Council acted not out of haste or desperation, but out of careful, coordinated political and military manoeuvres inspired and refined by forty-eight galactic councils before them. You could say they were overqualified for the job.

Teveran opened his eyes and thought, *I'm alive.*

Then he blinked, white lights coming into focus.

But where am I? He felt weightless, cold. It was deathly quiet. *This isn't the flagship.* He sat up and rubbed his eyes.

As the lights began to clear, he managed to process these new surroundings. It was a medical bay, although it seemed the only things separating its patients were thin, tarp-like walls erected like makeshift cubicles. The bed was soft but not expensive. A tall metal pole stood beside it, suspending a sack of clear fluids that was linked by a tube to his body, like he was some sort of robot. He stripped it off and swung his legs out of the coverlets.

"Careful, High Prince."

A lanky doctor stood within the entryway, datapad pressed

against his chest. He wore a white suit. His greasy black hair reflected the lights overhead.

Teveran frowned. "Excuse me?"

"Be careful," he said, more intensely, then lowered the datapad and strolled into his partition. Behind him, Teveran noticed another bed set further back, where an injured woman lay. Several nasty burns striated her face, like strips of bacon, and black and purple bruises peppered her skin. "You don't want to do any further damage to yourself."

"How do you know who I am?"

The doctor smiled warmly. "You're not the first child of Etheron that has washed up in my hands." He drew a small pendant out of his pocket and waved it at him. "Although, this little trinket might have given it away." Attached to the end of a long, golden chain was an emerald globe that appeared to glow. Teveran tore it back in cold, callused hands.

"You suffered a mild concussion," the doctor said. "Dehydration. Exhaustion. And, by the gods, you were shot in the foot. But you'll live."

"What about the others?" Teveran muttered, licking his cracked lips. "Krosse . . . Snake . . ." He couldn't remember much, but those two names were printed on the back of a hazy memory. He looked up at the doctor, into those calm, blue eyes. "Did they make it out?"

"It's hard to say," said the doctor, frowning at his datapad.

Teveran tried to remember what had happened. He'd been put in the wrong shuttle, they'd given him a rifle but no armour—the rebels had bombed a supply depot. He remembered the Azich man and the thin blonde woman. They'd all been forced to leap out of the flying Manticore, which the rebels had blown up so easily.

He'd been fighting on Corion. Their commander—*what was his name?*—had taken a bullet through the head, in a village. A small village. He racked his brain trying to remember why they'd been in a village when the objective was to reach a rebel base . . .

"Did we win?" Teveran asked.

"In a war like this," the doctor said, "a war of attrition, there *is* no winner."

Teveran dropped his gaze to the emerald globe in his palm. It was, perhaps, the only familiar thing around him. Gods, but this had all gone so *badly*. Even if the mission *had* been successful, he couldn't remember doing anything to help. He'd only run. Had he even fired off a single round? He could scarcely remember holding the rifle at all. "So . . ." Teveran began. "What—"

The Taurans.

They'd slaughtered the Taurans. He felt a wash of dread as it all broke through the murky waters of his mind. The way the blue and white flesh ripped off bone. The way they'd screamed. How they'd stood no chance at all. The heroes of the Council, they . . .

"People are dead because of what happened to you, High Prince." The doctor snared him with dire, bloodshot eyes. "On behalf of them, I'm sorry you had to go through what you did. We'll take you to the Grand Highlord. He'll make you welcome."

"What?" He was trembling. "No, you have to help me."

"You'll be relocated to the *Subjugator* once I conduct a few more tests."

Teveran swallowed. He'd known something wasn't right the moment that shuttle had lifted off the ground. Even *before* then! How did this happen? It was as if somebody had orchestrated it . . .

No, he told himself. *Why would anybody do that?*

He lowered his head and scratched his messy hair, staring at the white sheets. He needed some fresh air. His mind was still going in circles trying to process everything that had happened. How long had it been? Days? Weeks? Where had they taken him?

He should've been grateful that they weren't going to send him back out there. But, instead, he felt a pit of fear open up inside his stomach. It was the uncertainty. He hated it.

As the doctor sat down to do his tests, Teveran began to second-think this whole experience. So, they were finally going to take him to the flagship, but he wasn't sure if he liked that idea so much anymore. The name *"Subjugator"* certainly didn't help.

He became rather tense.

I need to get out of here.

Teveran splashed his face with icy water, then stared at his reflection in the mirror. White lights glittered across his skin. Where once he'd worn the emerald globe was nothing but sweaty skin. Putting that on again felt like a death sentence, so he'd tucked it into his deepest pocket. The clothes they'd given him were thin and uncomfortable: a low-necked white shirt, and loose pants that were two sizes too big.

Breathe, Teveran, he told himself. He'd decided most of these people didn't know he was the High Prince. Hell, they'd sent him all the way to Corion and back without batting an eye towards the fact! He just needed to find a way out before the Grand Highlord—his *uncle*—got a hold of him, because there'd be no coming back from there.

Drying his face with a towel, he strode out of the bathroom and into a wide hall bustling with voices. Doctors hurried back and forth, men and women in white coats splotched with blood and grime. Did any of them know who he was? What were the odds of his father having transmitted pictures of his face across the galaxy? He checked the corridor left and right. Puffing a long, uneasy breath, he hurried right and quickly stumbled upon the exit.

The glass doors opened up onto a field of doctors and patients, makeshift beds sprawled across trimmed grass and dirt. The sun hung in the distance, sitting upon the shimmering ocean. There were no other stars in the sky. He shielded his eyes and saw an array of ships scattered upon the grassland, mostly small shuttles. Still, the force was intimidating.

We're on some sort of island, he deduced, walking about. Despite the breeze that wafted off the ocean waves, he could only smell the sickness and death in the air, sour as the winds of Corion. Doctors and nurses rolled beds along on rusted, squealing wheels. Bodies lay discarded to the side, draped over with white cloths. A woman rushed by him in a sheet marred with blood.

It was not the kind of place he wanted to be in.

Several feet ahead, a long-haired doctor had his head burrowed among a pile of ledgers. Teveran ducked away towards him. "Hey," he said. "Can you spare me a moment?"

The doctor turned around, looking him up and down through crooked spectacles. He wore a button-up shirt, and had unruly stubble plastered across his hollowed-out jaw. "Sure," said the doctor, then frowned. "Is there a problem?"

"Where are we?"

The doctor grunted, wheeling on his heel and walking to a nearby bench. "Hmm. How long have you been here? And are you well? Are you . . . right in the head, I mean?"

"Yes," Teveran said, bemused as he chased after him. "I . . ."

"This is Medical Station 441. I'm not sure that I'm cleared to disclose the precise location to patients." The doctor withdrew a water bottle from beside the bench and proffered it to him. Teveran took it. The doctor sniffed, then blew his nose in a crumpled kerchief. "Are you thinking of running? Think you can sneak out before they realise you're missing?"

Teveran froze.

"You're not the first one. My advice: Don't try it." The doctor showed warning eyes and, before Teveran could argue, he slapped him on the shoulder and turned back around. "Don't go making enemies of the Council." The intensity in his gaze made Teveran regret ever speaking to him in the first place. "Anyway,"—he suddenly sounded jovial—"I should be going. You should, too. Next outbound shipment leaves in an hour."

Teveran watched him saunter off, frustrated. He didn't care what anybody told him, he needed to get off this planet, or whatever the hell it was. Maybe he could take one of those shuttles—but which way was home? Hell, who was he kidding? He couldn't fly.

If only Elenah was here; she always knew her way around a control board.

But she's not here, Teveran. You're on your own.

So he strode through the camp, trying to ignore the dead bodies. Another ship hung in the sky, an enormous Banshee deployment machine, slowly descending like an insect's bulging head. Gods, that thing was huge! It emitted a thundering howl, which shook the waves and even made the grass quiver. Doctors gathered beneath it, hurrying back and forth.

"Teveran!"

He spun to see a familiar face sitting on a plastic chair, one rifle strapped across his back, another leaning up against his leg. "Snake?" Yes, it was him. He was alive! But was he an ally? Teveran's heart bounced back and forth. "Snake, I—"

"Are you hurt?" Snake asked, waving him over.

"No," he uttered, following his gesture. "But . . ." A terrible realisation dawned on him. *He knows I'm the High Prince!* And that meant a ticket to the Grand Highlord himself!

Snake's emerald eyes were even brighter beneath the sunlight. They reminded him of Rose, and that gave him a strange sort of comfort. Snake still wore his trooper armour, scratched and dented yet unbroken; his helmet lay beside him. "Here," he said, tossing over a muesli bar caked in white chocolate. "To keep your energy up."

Teveran almost dropped it through his trembling fingers. "Thanks." He tried to steady his nerves as he crept closer. A burning question rose to his lips: "Is Krosse . . . ?"

"No. Krosse didn't make it," Snake said. "But that's all right. It wasn't your fault." He waved him closer until Teveran could smell his stench. "I'm so relieved to see you here. There's a private shuttle outbound in a couple of minutes. Best to catch it."

Teveran wished he could make himself say no. He could

see it again: Snake's thundering rifle and the terrified, screaming Taurans. He opened his mouth, his lips cracking. He glimpsed the small, wooden flute Snake carried by his waist. It belonged to his sister. "Snake, I have to—"

"I'll get you out of here," Snake said. "Straight to the flagship. This time, with no stops in between. I hope I'll be able to convince you I'm not so bad. Maybe we can get along."

A wave of dread crashed through Teveran, but he could do nothing but stand there gaping. His soul cracked a little. *Oh, great,* he thought. *Now what?* He doubted Snake would take anything else for an answer. But . . . he had to get back home, get away from this madness!

"What's wrong?" Snake asked.

"Nothing," Teveran quickly said, chastising himself. "Nothing's wrong. Nothing at all."

Snake groaned as he stood up, grabbing the rifle that lay against his chair, and his helmet, which he clipped to his belt. "The shuttle's leaving soon."

Teveran just nodded, and instantly hated himself.

THEY STEPPED INTO THE HANGAR of the *Subjugator* side-by-side, and Teveran was surprised at how cluttered it was. Every plot of shimmering metal floor was covered by ships and machinery. Some were as small as the shuttle he'd taken there, others could've fit a battalion of troopers.

He followed Snake down the landing ramp, the trooper's white armour reflecting a cascade of blinking lights. Other mobile troopers patrolled the hangar, clad in full armour, rifles clasped across their chests. Several deck officers walked among them. They wore an austere type of uniform, with high collars and striking black lining.

"Keep up," Snake said through the machinelike distortion of his helmet. "Don't be intimidated. These guys aren't that frightening beneath the masks."

Despite what he said, Teveran felt their scrutinising stares as he followed Snake through the hangar. His legs were trembling, his knees threatening to buckle underneath him. He drew focused breaths, one after the other, and just tried not to be sick.

Footsteps echoed along the floor. Men and women. Troopers, officers, and grey-clad mechanics. They walked among the ships, hurrying back and forth.

Isn't this where I always wanted to be? Teveran asked himself. *Isn't this where I was meant to be?* He glanced up and around, processing everything. Some sort of robotic machine—like a flying spherical toolbox—spun through the air, beeping. Teveran watched it, mouth agape. He'd never seen anything like that on Etheron.

They walked through a door and entered a narrow corridor. As they ascended a shallow set of lurid white stairs, a young officer passed without batting an eye towards him. It felt strange. *They don't know who I am.* It felt almost . . .

Liberating.

They stepped inside a lift. The doors closed behind them, and a pit of anxiety opened up inside his gut. He wiped his sweaty palms on his pants. Gods, they were too big! He felt so out-of-place, like a child who'd wandered into his father's workplace.

"Hey," Snake said, breaking the silence. "I'm sorry about what happened on Corion."

Teveran kept staring ahead. Snake could apologise, sure, but no apology could ever make him forget those events. He could still see the troopers shredding those Taurans apart. He could hear their screams, and their pleas. It would give him nightmares, no doubt for the rest of his life, and no apology in the galaxy could change that. But it was *an* apology, and it was better than nothing. "Okay, Snake," he said. "I get it. You had your orders."

"It's my battle instinct," Snake said, as though he were ashamed of it. "They've drilled it into me so badly, turned us all into these . . . *war machines*. I can't look at a Tauran—or anyone, for that matter—and not feel like they're going to kill me."

Teveran nodded. "I'm sorry for getting angry."

"No, you had every right—like you said."

He glanced at the trooper, trying to find comfort in his presence, then glanced down at his shoes. He wondered who had worn these clothes before him, and if they were still alive.

"So, what's next?" Teveran asked. "For you, I mean. Now that . . ."

Now that everyone is dead, he almost said.

"I made a promise," Snake said.

"A promise?"

"I promised to keep the squad alive if Cartus wasn't there to do it. Hell, I'm barely a speck in their grand army, but I know my way around. I'll set things right."

Cartus, Teveran thought. *Cartus Vallon,* their dead commander. A horrific image flashed before his eyes, of a sniper's bullet hurtling through Vallon's face. "I'm sorry."

"The gods spared him," Snake said.

He was glad when the doors parted on the highest level,

and they stepped out into a chamber almost twice as large as the hangar. Teveran gasped, blinking, but everything only seemed to expand. Every surface but the floor was a window into the endless expanse of space. White beams ran along the edges and corners, but through the spotless glass he could see everything so clearly. His heart thudded. Snake tapped his arm to hurry him along.

There were no other troopers inside the chamber, just busy officers, beeping computers, and a quiet hubbub of voices. Silver and black webbed holographic displays were raised throughout, spinning upon round platforms. To his left, a young blonde woman stood in quiet conversation with another man. To his right, a man with a burnt face watched everything unfold, clutching a pocket watch by its thin, silver chain.

"I was wondering when you'd arrive." His uncle stood several paces ahead, hands clasped in front, his shoulders level and his chin inclined.

Snake stopped and waved Teveran forward. Teveran swallowed as he stepped closer. His uncle wore a tight-fitting white shirt, immaculately designed, beneath a long half-cape, black as the deepest galactic depths.

He's the Grand Highlord. His father's training had taught him what this title meant. He held the highest rank in the fleet. He answered to no one but the very heart of the Forty-Ninth Council itself: the *Architect.* He dismissed Snake, who Teveran was not delighted to see go, and then stepped forward. His onyx cape billowed behind him.

Teveran swallowed, clenching his sweaty hands. He sucked in the slow-moving air, tried to steady his leaping nerves. This was not some nightmare; it was real, it was happening.

There's nothing you can do, he told himself. *Just don't look like an idiot.*

"High Prince," his uncle said, then motioned for Teveran to follow him through the chamber. They walked abreast, so slow that Teveran had to drag his feet to match his uncle's pace. "I was told you'd be here soon. You look just like your father."

Teveran shot him a wary sidelong glance. His uncle had been taken by the Council seven years before Teveran was even born. But he had those eyes . . . Vibrant blue, like the ocean—his mother's eyes—and the posture, and the voice, and the nature of a very powerful man. Teveran had seen him in the paintings all over the palace walls.

Ignus Thrakk Lockwood.

"I do hope it wasn't *your* idea taking a detour through the forests of Corion," Thrakk said with a hint of jest. "The battlefield's no place for the High Prince, of course." Teveran wasn't sure whether to be relieved or scared. Finally, they arrived at one of the grand windows, which filled Teveran's vision. Beyond the glass, he could see nothing but the endless stars, lights, and countless other ships of the Council. Banshees, Ragnaroks, Harpies. He couldn't trust himself to stay on this side of it. Gods, it was beautiful.

"It wasn't my intention, trust me," Teveran said.

Thrakk nodded, satisfied. "I will have to investigate, then, surely, but you're lucky you weren't *killed*." He softened his tone. "These are, indeed, terrible times."

Teveran scratched his chin with jittering fingers. He remembered what the doctor had told him shortly after waking up. *People are dead because of what happened to you,*

High Prince. Teveran tried to work moisture into his mouth, but he wasn't sure if he was allowed to speak.

People are dead because of me . . .

"Teveran," Thrakk began.

"Yes?" He tried to steady his voice.

"Just relax. Take a deep breath." His blue eyes shimmered beneath the lights of the stars glowing beyond the window. But he said nothing more, just patted his shoulder and walked away from the glass. Teveran followed.

"I wouldn't know where to start."

"Then let me show you." They strolled to another wall of glass, separating them from an impossible field of stars. Teveran tried to count the ships. He wondered how they could afford all this while there were a thousand worlds out there that could barely afford enough food. He supposed it was the accumulation of wealth and power from all the failed Council's before them.

"See that?" Thrakk nodded towards a grim-faced planet in the distance. It was small, and charred. "That's Mokuura. Once, it had one of the most beautiful cities in the galaxy." He turned with charcoal eyes. "The rebels have a base there now."

Teveran felt a sick stirring in his stomach, but he nodded all the same.

"A strike force has already been dispatched," Thrakk went on, then pointed to a cluster of stars and floating debris. "But the battle is far from over. We have intercepted an enemy transmission. Rebel reinforcements are inbound." He paused a moment. "Surely you know of the rebellion. They're calling themselves the Galactic Liberation Movement. Your father despised them." Teveran nodded again. Someone might have thought he had a problem with his head. *Traitors. Terrorists. Conspirators.*

"I've heard of them," Teveran said.

"Then you know they must be stopped." Thrakk rolled his shoulders, and Teveran heard them crack. "Their downfall has already begun."

"How long do we have?"

"Until the fires of the first strike die down."

Teveran didn't know what that meant, but it sounded like they'd already *started.* Thrakk raised a fist to his mouth and coughed into it. The sound was not pleasant, yet unsettlingly familiar. *So soon?* Teveran thought, playing it over in his mind, wondering if any of this was possible. Maybe this was all a dream, and he was still dying on Corion.

No, he told himself. *Don't be stupid.* Besides, lying wouldn't get him anywhere. It was clear these people needed him, clear that they *wanted* him. And they were the heroes of his childhood. And Teveran had promised his family that he would make them *proud.*

He eyed the black atmosphere of Mokuura, and wondered if it had been like Etheron once. Then he licked his lips. "What am I supposed to do?"

"You will accompany me here, on the bridge," Thrakk said.

"Seriously? I just *got* here." He stepped away from him, ignoring the blinding stars beyond the window. "I know what I am, but . . . I don't have much training."

Thrakk rounded on him and Teveran choked on his words. *Gods, he's intimidating.*

"You're the High Prince, Teveran," Thrakk said. "Start acting like it."

Teveran wilted and remained silent. "Yes, Uncle." Thrakk watched him, like an apex predator might regard his prey. Then, he coughed into his fist and prowled to one of the holograms. Teveran could hear his father in those coughs. He observed the Grand Highlord's ghostly skin, and wondered if he was also unwell.

Thrakk cleared his throat, and the officers surrounding him perked up their heads. Barely raising his voice, he said, "Man the battle stations," and the bridge came alive.

CHAPTER THIRTEEN

LOOSE ENDS

It's a secret society of magicians, operating between the cracks of galactic politics and inadvertently deciding the fates of civilisations a thousand worlds away.

E4 Station slowly turned, revolving through the atmosphere of Tannis II. It grew larger as Gilgan approached; if the hackers there were watching him, his Starsinger would appear like a yellow stain in the distance, slowly becoming larger.

The station had changed since the last time he'd paid them a visit. A huge planet-like hologram was projected in the centre. Above and below it were half-spheres made of silver metal that reflected the nearby moon. A long metallic pillar—the shell of a turbo-lift—ran about three hundred feet from the bottom of the hologram. Halfway down, it was ringed by a halo-like walkway. At the far bottom extended four disc-like docking platforms. Blue lights glittered all over the station, some of them flashing erratically, others like stars in their purity.

Silver lasers scanned his ship as he docked, sending cold shivers down his spine. There were auto-turrets erected along the walls, and he stared them down, wondering if the station's inhabitants could see him, if they would remember him.

He shut down his starfighter and leapt out. Gods, it was cold in here. Docking Bay 3, a place of many fond memories, hadn't changed at all; if anything, it was even colder. The ships were still docked all over the place, and it was quite devoid of life.

Whistling an old radio song, he wandered from the docking bay and down a corridor that led into the painfully-cramped turbolift, which scanned him with a grid of diaphanous blue lasers as it carried him up. The lift, as it had done all those years ago when he last rode inside it, was made of twinsteel and therefore let him peer out into the starscape. The azure haze of Tannis II licked up against the walls. In the distance was its mother planet Tannis, which was a far less exciting thing to look at; it was grey and looked vaguely metallic.

When the turbolift finally reached its destination, Gilgan hobbled out and entered the main communications bay.

"Morning," he casually announced. Everybody looked at him. A couple of them cursed and reached for their weapons. Gilgan smiled and stepped forward, leaning on his cane; it clicked along the sparkling metal floor. "It *is* morning, isn't it?"

Nobody moved. Gilgan pinched his brow rather tiredly, then walked from the door along the walkway. It skirted a replica of the spherical hologram outside, only it was much, much smaller. Several doors hung along the walls, extending to chambers and kitchens and other trivial "necessities." On the edge that overlooked the hologram were computers and switches, beeping frenetically, and a railing that went all around.

The station had hardly changed. There were only a lot more people; from the top of his head, he guessed there were maybe two hundred of them all up.

"Gilgan?" the lone familiar face gasped. Threpe wore a dirty white shirt emblazoned with a picture of a comical unicorn. He stumbled towards him, his white hair frayed like he'd been struck by lightning. Aleria's ghost, he hadn't changed at all.

"What have you done to the place?" Gilgan chirped.

"Brightened it up a little. Is it not to your liking?"

"You might want to check the security. It let *me* in."

"That's because *Astral* recognises you," Threpe said. "You were lucky. With how many bastards that machine stops, there'd be a field of broken ships here were it not for the pull of Tannis II." He paused, simply taking in the sight that was Gilgan and his walking cane, clothed in charcoal trousers and a long black duster. "Gods." The way he said it, you'd think he was staring at a ghost. "I almost forgot you ever existed, old man."

"I doubt that, Threpe, what with the posters of me all over your bedroom wall."

Threpe smiled. "What is it you need?"

"I need your help."

"What's happened?" Threpe quickly said. "Is it . . . ?"

"No," Gilgan retorted.

Threpe frowned—he frowned an awful lot; it seemed not even two decades could change that. "Well," he said, softer now. "You'd better come in, then."

Threpe led him through the station, beneath the wary eyes

of all these new officers. He had to assure more than one of them that Gilgan was *not* a spy.

Their sheer numbers still surprised Gilgan—delighted him, too. It had been Threpe's dream to have a contingent of hackers all running his secret galactic-wide network. Threpe had promised him that one day he would reveal it to the galaxy and have it replace the current network—which was, quite honestly, utter rubbish. The last time Gilgan had come to the station, there'd only been thirteen of them, and the place was less than half the size. He glanced at the huge hologram in the centre, speckled by dots of all manners of colour.

"You haven't yet made intergalactic contact?"

"No, not yet," Threpe said. "I've put that aside for now. What we're operating currently is . . . Ah, I can already see you're falling asleep."

"I promise it's my age," Gilgan quipped.

Threpe laughed, then finally turned around and slapped his arm around Gilgan's shoulder. "I can't believe you're back. Gods, we even had a bet and I swear to Fergda I betted on this day!"

"I'm sure you did." But his mind was falling to other things, to the tension in the air, the dead note in the magical symphony. Where were the others? Where was Caston, and Grish? Elkair? He didn't need to ask. He already knew the answer.

"Alas," Threpe said as they left the main chamber, "what is it you need?" They entered another room, smaller and familiar. When the door shut behind them, it chopped off the last vestige of sound, and all that remained was the beeping of computers.

"You're still living in this hole?" Gilgan asked, glancing over the portholes in the walls, the overflowing trashcan in the corner, the buzzing computers and flashing screens.

"Now I *can*," Threpe said, pointing. "You know . . . Now that I don't have to worry about finding you and Avery all curled up in my bed."

Gilgan blushed; he didn't know he still could. "That . . . That was *once*, Threpe. And, might I add, hardly what you thought it was."

"Oh, sure. I *found* you once. The gods know what I missed."

Gilgan finally glimpsed the bed tucked away in the corner, with its crumpled sheets and sunken pillow. *Has it already been twenty years?* he asked himself, finding that he couldn't quite believe it. The last time he'd been here, Teveran must have been in the womb. Last time, he'd never stepped foot on Etheron, which he'd eventually call his first real home.

"Gilgan?"

He looked at Threpe, who seemed not to have aged a day. It must have been close to a mirror reflection, Gilgan with his greying hair and angular cheeks, and the eyes that had been weathered down from too many violent storms.

Threpe sat down at his chair. "What happened?" When Gilgan stared blankly, Threpe said, "You know what I'm talking about. What happened to the *Starforged?*"

"I don't want to talk about it."

"What about Jethre?"

The name lanced his chest.

"Jethre's not coming back. None of them are. And, before you ask, no: I'm not either." He hobbled across the room to the second seat by the flashing screens. This seat must have been new; it felt different, firmer, colder. "I haven't seen any of them for *twenty-three* years—and I don't plan to break that run. It's quite relaxing, you know, doing nothing all day." He didn't mention Jethre's note, his cryptic communique; it made him sick thinking about it.

"Hmm. But you brought that damned stone," Threpe noted.

Gilgan's heartbeat quickened. He could feel it pulsing in his pocket, as always, packed with dark magic. Threpe had never been a very powerful magician, but he was finely attuned to the frequency of magic. "I couldn't leave it there," Gilgan said. "Not on Etheron." He hesitated. "It's all falling apart, and the gods know who's out there—twenty years later."

Fex, he thought. *Fex is out there.*

Threpe scratched his chin. "Well, I know one thing: You're not here to sightsee. You're going to fight them, aren't you?"

"The day I fight again will be a dark day indeed." But he could feel those dark days chasing him—or maybe *he* was chasing *them*. He could feel the remnants of the Starforged out there in the vast galaxy, like broken machines coming back to life.

Threpe didn't look convinced about anything. "Then why are you here?"

"For now," Gilgan said, "I just want you to hack the Council's channels."

"Oh. Is that all? I thought we'd be doing something a little more . . . *exciting*. Gods, how my brilliant skills have atrophied these past twenty years."

"I want you to find their flagship."

"And what do you plan to do with that information?"

Gilgan frowned, the stone throbbing by his thigh. "I have

to set things right," was all he said, and it must have been enough, because Threpe finally turned to the computers, pulled on a headset, and minded his own business.

Gilgan reclined in his seat and breathed a sigh of relief. A moment to reset was all he needed, just to steady his nerves, before venturing too far out. The stories he told to the children of Etheron—stories were all they were. Far out in space was a dangerous place.

For him, it was worse. What he was, what he'd *done* . . . He closed his eyes and listened to the melody of magic surging all around. A force of creation, it kept things in movement, kept the world's spinning, kept life thriving and evolving. He let its aura calm him down.

But then it struck him again: the memory of the Starforged, of four magicians who'd made a promise of blood and will, who'd travelled the galaxy trying to put things right.

Hell, but he wasn't feeling too good.

"It's Fex," he admitted, sweat in his brows. The name had a sour taste. "I don't know how, but somehow he knows about the stones, and I'm afraid he's coming for them . . ."

Threpe perked up, dividing his attention. He looked unwell, but Gilgan didn't blame him. In his last days, Fex had gone mad. He'd started playing with dark magic, started tracing dangerous roads . . . And he'd found something terrible: the ghost of the *Dark Lord.*

"He's going to bring him back," Gilgan said.

"After all this time? He must be crazy!"

Gilgan nodded. "I can *feel* him." Gods, it felt like a lifetime since he'd last seen Fex. "I may yet see him again," Gilgan said, although this would be no happy reunion.

Threpe looked unsettled by that. "Ah, well . . ." he said,

feigning composure. "There it is. A Leviathan. Not many of those left. The . . . *Subjugator*." He spun on his chair and threw the headset back upon the control panel. "*Astral*, open the star map." A white and blue hologram shot from the holopad attached to the wall, throwing up a planet in the centre of the room.

"Mokuura," Gilgan observed.

"Won't be the first time I've sent somebody there."

"Wait . . ." He leaned in. "What's *that?*" He pointed to an array of disorganised white blips, barely touching the edge of the hologram. They looked like ships. He peered closer to it, but though the map showed such splendid detail, he could barely make them out.

"Gods," Threpe said suddenly, swivelling his chair.

"What is it?" Gilgan asked.

"It's . . . It's the liberation."

Gilgan's heart leapt up into his throat. "The liberation?"

"The rebels—"

"I know what they are," Gilgan snapped. "But . . . Are you sure?"

Threpe nodded. He opened his mouth, but Gilgan had heard everything he needed. He leapt off the chair, sending it shooting towards the edge of the room, and strode off for the door. Then, he stopped, as the door rushed upwards. "Wait, Threpe."

Threpe stood up from his chair. Gilgan withdrew the emerald stone from his pocket. He could barely look at it; the thing was heinous. Instead, he turned around and proffered it to Threpe.

"Take it," Gilgan said in a rattled voice. "Please. It isn't safe with me."

"Gilgan . . . If they come for me, there's nothing I can do."

"They will never find you here." He walked back across the room and pressed it into Threpe's wrinkled palm. "I'm going into the heart. And if I face Fex, I'm not sure if I'll be strong enough to defeat him . . . not this time."

Threpe took the stone and his eyes drew in its emerald glow. It reminded him, for the briefest moment, of Rose back inside the palace. "I'll keep it safe," Threpe whispered.

"Thank you," Gilgan said. Then he turned on his heel and rushed back through the door. And he couldn't help but feel he'd seen Threpe for the very last time.

CHAPTER FOURTEEN

THE WASTELAND BEYOND

The Four Stages of Starfire:

1. *Purest; appearance of a black crystal*
2. *Unharnessed; appearance of black gas*
3. *Harnessed; appearance of white sparks*
4. *Residual; appearance of ash*

Everybody out!" Oswald said as he kicked down the metal grate at the end of the tunnel. It *shattered*, flecks of metal spraying through the darkness. He leapt out, bringing with him the light, and was quickly followed by Eukaloo, then Hannah . . .

Elenah stepped out last, heart hammering. Dirt cracked underneath her feet. Unlike the world within the city, the darkness here was pitch black; there was no colour save for the dim lights of faraway ships in the sky. "Where are we?" she asked, breathless, clasping the straps of her knapsack; one of them was coming loose.

"I couldn't say," Oswald said, raising his lantern. It emitted a pale white light, powered by a single coil of harnessed starfire, which leapt about within the glass. The only thing prolonging its life was the metal sphere affixed in the centre of the lantern: a *permanence orb*. "Just stay close to me." With that, he led them onwards at a brisk pace.

They passed tufts of brown grass, weeds, and twisted, chipped bones. All dead. All left behind long ago. The quartet stalked through the darkness, barely an arm span's length from one another. Elenah's heartbeat drummed in her ears. She could count each one. *Thud. Thud. Thud.* She wondered what lay out here beyond the city within this stale, stale darkness. She kept seeing things shift in the black. It kept her on-edge, kept her looking about, brushing shoulders with Hannah. The Felirean smelt sickly of smoke.

All those stories Gilgan had told her started coming to life. Of enormous insectoid creatures with hanging jowls, brown fur and a dozen hungry pincers. Of ghosts and apparitions that fed on fresh souls. Of the terrifying Krakensvouf . . .

"I know what you are," Oswald said, his voice carrying across the wastes. He didn't shift his forward-facing glance, but Elenah knew he was talking to Hannah. "I know what happened to Feluria. But I still don't know what the hell you're doing here. I thought your kind were gone, murdered by the Kerrean in some kind of mass genocide . . ."

"Not all of us," Hannah said, her voice weak.

"Clearly," Oswald said. "Are there others besides yourself?"

Hannah took a moment to respond. "I ask myself that question every day." Elenah watched the young woman's cloaked back. She looked several years older down here in the dark. Her pink hair was frayed and dirty, ruffled and woven with blood. Her skin resembled flaking marble, paper left out in the rain. Yet it wasn't human skin. She was different. A *Felirean* . . .

Maybe the last one in the galaxy.

Elenah wrapped her arms around herself, watching her breath evaporate into mist. *There was a prophecy*, Hannah had said. *You're the one they spoke of . . .*

"Can you hear that?" Oswald whispered.

Elenah shook herself from her reverie. "Hear what?"

Suddenly, there was a *burst* of lightning starfire. It hissed among the darkness, startling everyone. Hannah jumped. Oswald cursed as Elenah grabbed his coat.

"Calm down!" Oswald spat. "Calm down, calm down . . ."

A clash of metal on metal echoed though there was nothing for the sound to reflect off. A bright white light went on with a clap. Elenah shielded her eyes. The light beamed off a panel affixed to a pole ten feet off the ground, angled towards the sky.

Another one illuminated, painting stark white light across the dirt fields. There were three of them. Four. Five. Six . . . They clapped on in sequence. Elenah turned her head this way and that, each clang and crash making her heart jump.

It all carried on for several seconds more.

And then, as if nothing had ever happened, it stopped.

Oswald lowered his obsolete lantern and gently placed it on the ground. The fields were entirely illuminated, revealing nothing but a flat stretch of endless wastes.

"I'm guessing it's too late to turn back," Oswald muttered. Elenah stepped ahead of him. The ground beneath her feet cracked with every step, as if she were treading on bones.

Eukaloo grumbled and pointed at something.

Oswald bent down and tested the dirt. Hannah strolled several paces away, whispering to herself. Elenah stroked her hair as it settled across her shoulders. Her fingers trembled.

Gods, but why did it feel like there was something . . . *familiar* about this place. She looked at the panels of light, at the great expanse, and smelt the wet, humid air. It was like she'd stepped into the sketches of Gilgan's books. She wet her lips.

"I . . . I think I know where we are."

The others looked at her, even Eukaloo; she felt their eyes digging into her back. She reached into the deepest confines of her mind, into places where memories had buried themselves. She extended her arm and caught flakes of starfire sediment on her hand. "This is a Foundry."

For a while, there was stunned silence, as if none of them had ever heard of a Foundry before. Elenah turned around and faced them, wiping the solidified starfire onto her skirt. In her excitement, she felt a smile begin to wrap its way around her face. She forgot about Mokuura, about Teveran . . .

She *knew* about this.

"Gilgan told me about them," she said. "Great Foundries all across the galaxy. And the old magicians inside, creating the starfire we use to fly ships, and charge lights, and power technology and . . ." She paused to catch her breath.

Oswald exchanged a look with Hannah.

Elenah stared. "The Foundries." She looked at them all. Oswald's brows creased, Eukaloo blinked and kicked up a thread of dirt, and Hannah hardly twitched. A sudden streak of hot frustration ran through her; it made her want to bound up and yell at them. "How else do you think your piece of junk ship can fly?"

"Hmm," Oswald said, stroking his messy hair. "I've heard of them, but . . . No, we buy the starfire off merchants now. It's cheaper that way. They *mine* it."

"No." Elenah shook her head. "You're wrong. *That's* not how it works." She had to stop herself from crying. "Gilgan told me. Gilgan . . ." She spun away from them before they could see her cry, striding into the shadows. *Oh, I'm so sorry. I never should have left!*

"Elenah," Hannah called after her.

"No, this is stupid!" Elenah said, trying to suck back in her tears, to stop them from flowing down her cheeks. She walked to the metal pole of one of the giant light panels, and sat down on the cracked ground, hugging her folded knees.

"Hey, come on now," Oswald said, joining her. "We can't stay here all day, Elenah. We have to keep moving. Come on. I'm sorry."

But Elenah didn't move. She just sat there beneath the buzzing lights, and she thought of Gilgan, and Teveran, and her father. And she wished she'd never left. She'd been stubborn. There was nothing for her here, nothing but darkness and death.

Oswald knelt beside her, gently touching her back. "We can't afford to stop. The Council will be searching this area very soon." But Elenah couldn't look at him. She couldn't raise her face and look at any of them, not like this, not looking like a complete fool!

"The Council . . ." Elenah said, trying not to sound like she'd been crying. It was all she managed to get out before images of Teveran flooded her mind, the sound of his voice in her ear. "The Council took him away. They're ruining everything. And . . ." She dropped her head into her knees and cried. "Oh, and I shouldn't have come out here."

It all sounded so foolish. What was the point of leaving? Would it have been so bad to die alongside Gilgan? At least she wouldn't have been alone! Gilgan had warned her. Gilgan had told her not to leave. But she'd turned her back on him and left him there.

Please don't go, he'd said. *For me.*

"You were never told, were you?" Oswald said. "This stuff wasn't in the books. And so I suppose that's why you're here, looking for adventure in all the wrong places. I'm sorry. I really am. I should've stopped you. Blasts, I knew this was all a bad idea."

"They're not the galaxy's heroes like they say they are," Elenah said. "They're not out there keeping peace and order and defending us from the rebellion in the west."

"I've heard the stories," Oswald said. "I've heard their lies."

Elenah felt more angry than she'd ever felt before. Knowing that it was true, that she hadn't been crazy, that even Gilgan was terrified of this gathering storm . . . And the fact they now had Teveran. These *criminals.* A part of her even began to realise the choice she had to make.

She stood and kicked up dirt. "I'm so stupid!" Tears streamed down her cheeks. She missed home, she missed Gilgan and Teveran, and her father, and by the gods even *Korvis!* She'd made a terrible mistake coming out here, and now she was going to pay the price.

"You're not stupid," Oswald said. "Listen." He followed her as she stalked across the wastes. "You're not going back. *That* would be a terrible idea. You're coming with me. I'll get you to Highshore. And then . . . I don't know, we'll think of something. But running away won't do you any good. Maybe we've got a crack. Maybe we can topple this thing." Elenah looked at him, though he was distorted behind her tears.

"*Boruuka!*" Eukaloo shrieked.

"Oh, hell," Oswald grumbled. "Don't move."

Elenah started. Though she could hardly see, she followed Oswald's gaze, followed his half-raised arm, his pointed finger . . .

And her eyes landed on the huge black bird perched on top of one of the nearby lights. The creature made a high-pitched keening and fluttered up into the darkness, its wail following it all the way into the sky and through the beams of light.

Silence. Nothing remained but a single black feather, posing between Hannah's slender fingertips. They all gaped, as if the feather could transform into an eleven-headed monstrosity at will. It was as long as Elenah's elbow to the tips of her fingers. She gasped.

"What was *that?*" Elenah choked.

"Birds," Oswald said, climbing to his feet.

"Birds aren't that big," Hannah tremored as she threw away the feather.

"Well, this may not be a Foundry," Oswald said, "but I think it was a mine once. And the starfire . . . It has a habit of . . . *changing* things."

"Mutation," Elenah whispered, and Oswald nodded. He brushed sweaty locks of hair out of his eyes and, striding forward, said, "Let's not wait around."

THEY VENTURED THROUGH THE GLOOMY WASTES, trudging over pieces of smoking metal. Craters pockmarked the ground. Black, unharnessed starfire curled and writhed through the air, seemingly drawn to the panels of light.

Elenah felt a rattle in her chest. Was it excitement or fear? Hannah's heavy footfalls shook the ground beside her. Putting the birds aside, the city was still under siege from the Forty-Ninth Council, and they were running out of time. Escape would not be easy.

Eventually, the metal shards became chunks, and then discernible *ship* parts. Some of them still bore flakes of paint: reds and yellows and whites. And before Elenah could think they might be stumbling upon the mystical Foundry, Eukaloo pointed excitedly towards what was unmistakeably some graveyard of ships.

Churned-up ground and derelict wreckages littered the wastes for miles. Starfighters were shattered like glass, plastic and metal flung everywhere. Starfire floated out of the engines in its unharnessed gaseous form. Two light panels lay on the ground, the poles crunched and twisted awkwardly, inviting a heavier darkness.

"We're going to have to salvage something here," Oswald said, hastily walking ahead. He and Eukaloo began picking through parts, eager to find something useful. "I need a new ship anyway."

"What do you think happened?" Elenah whispered.

"Looks like there was a battle," Oswald said.

Elenah wondered if this had been another assault launched by the Council, or if they were stalking through relics a thousand years old. Nearby, Hannah turned over a long rod of fried metal, then chucked it back down and moved on. Elenah followed her. "Hannah," she said.

"What is it?"

"Is the Council after you?"

A troubled look fell across Hannah's face. "I don't know."

"In the shack . . . You said—"

"They might be," Hannah said, exasperated. Then she huffed and kicked a loose pebble. "If they are, then my odds of getting out of this alive are very slim." She glanced at her, and there was a hint of something dark behind her yellow, cat-like eyes.

Elenah grabbed Hannah's arm. Gods, she was thin, almost like a stick. Her yellow eyes twinkled; she sniffed the hot and stinky air. "You saw my shade. The Sandred?"

Hannah nodded reluctantly.

"It was Gilgan's," Elenah whispered as she released Hannah's arm. There was no recognition in Hannah's eyes— why would there be? "Gilgan had the Sandred before me . . ." The realisation had just come to her in a rush. Gilgan did mention it once.

"Well, that makes sense," Hannah said.

"He . . . gifted it to me." That was generally how it worked. Shades were a kind of guardian force gifted through generations of magicians, all through the ages. "But why?" she asked—pleaded. "Why would he give it to me? He still has a battle to fight there. He . . ."

He knows there's no escape, she realised.

"But why can't I see it?" she asked.

A loud crash sounded as Oswald hauled open the door of a tri-winged starfighter. He made a long, thoughtful hum. "Yes," he announced. "I think we're onto something here." Hannah ducked out of Elenah's reach and walked briskly towards the ship.

"*Jinra yokulo*," Eukaloo chirped, drumming his spindly fingers against the rusted hull.

"You're right," Oswald grumbled. "It's missing a shield core."

"What about this one?" Hannah asked, pointing to another ship. "It still looks whole." She knelt down and ran her hand along the glowing bronze hull, then yelped and jerked quickly away. "It's *hot*."

"Looks old, too," Elenah said.

"It's even smaller than the *Voyager*," Oswald said, slapping the hull. Eukaloo's gangly form hobbled along beside him, scratching his pointed chin. He was right. The shuttle was maybe half the size of his own ship. But still, Oswald gave it due consideration. Eukaloo pointed at golden writing that must have been the class. MAGICUS.

Oswald weighed the cobalt brand. "Gods . . . Magicus?" He scrubbed dust off the hull, and muttered the name that was painted across it: "*The Divinity*." Eukaloo dragged open the door, unleashing a waft of gaseous starfire that caused them all to back away. "It's *really* old," Oswald said, stroking his beard. "Never seen a model like this before. Tri-thrusters . . ." He laughed. "These wings have no shielding." He tapped one and frowned. "It *looks* like an AT but— What are these?" He knelt down and ran his hand across an array of ventilation slats.

"It would suggest we're standing in the ruins of an ancient war," Elenah said.

"Magicus-Class ships have not been in production for *millennia*," Oswald said.

Elenah started as Eukaloo sauntered inside, covering his reptilian mouth with his cloak. Oswald ignored him, frowning at the slats and the MAGICUS brand, mesmerised.

"I can hear something nearby," Hannah said. Elenah perked up, but she could only hear the shrieking starfire, and Eukaloo making a mess inside that shuttle. Oswald stepped away from it, looked up into the sky, and swallowed hard.

Then she heard it, too. A high-pitched wail that split the silence, driving through the buzzing of the lights. They all looked at once.

A screech, like the crack of lightning.

Hannah screamed as the creature emerged from the darkness and descended upon her. She threw herself sidelong, but one of its wings slashed her shoulder and *slammed* her to the ground in a messy coil. The bird wailed, splitting through the group and returning skyward, leaving a whirlwind of dirt, sticks and rocks in its wake.

"Hannah!" Elenah cried instinctively.

"Don't move too quickly!" Oswald barked. Another inhuman scream replaced his voice, and this time Elenah saw the bird before it struck: a huge figure piercing the air, breaking the beams of white light. It had no eyeballs; the only feature on its face was a long, pointed beak. Its wingspan could undoubtedly wrap two people, maybe three.

Oswald roared and thrust out his arm. Flames unfolded rapidly across his forearm, snaked across his hand, then a bolt of fire exploded from his palm. It barrelled frantically through the air, before striking the mutated bird and sending it up in a cloud of ash. Flames sprayed across the ground, glittering and eating up the dead strands of grass.

Elenah dived to the dirt, shredding her hands and

forearms. Oswald cursed. Hannah fumbled up a rusted pipe and stepped into an awkward fighting stance.

"Get inside the ship!" Oswald roared, slamming the bronze hull. "Eukaloo! Get the *Divinity* in the air!" A bird swooped Oswald, coming down like a hammer. He backed into the hull and the bird narrowly missed him. One more hurtled through them—obsidian-like beak agape—bringing with it a sound like thunder. Hannah lunged forward and cracked its back with the metal pipe. The bird squawked, crashing down in a fountain of dirt. She converged on it, raised her pipe, but the bird drilled upwards and hid in the twisting shadows.

Elenah did not think Hannah was capable of such force.

Another bird came soaring downwards. Elenah heard the wail of yet another. She glanced up and wished she hadn't. More birds than she could count now laced the sky, soaring through lights and shadows, disappearing and reappearing closer, and closer, and closer . . .

Oswald slammed a fist against the *Divinity's* bronze hull. "Get it moving, Eukaloo! Get the bloody thing moving!"

And then: lights.

The *Divinity* roared to life, choking, silver starfire crackling out from underneath it. Oswald threw open the door before Eukaloo could reach it, almost flinging the small Troff off his feet. "Ha!" Oswald cried. "Not bad for a Troff. Get inside!"

Eukaloo saluted and said, *"Kokral oska!"*

Black birds slammed the hull, printing dents in the rusted metal. They screamed and broke their beaks, blindly ramming the thing. Elenah scrambled to her feet and shouldered her knapsack. She called across to Oswald, "Why are they attacking us?"

"Must be that they're trying to ward us off," he panted. Then his face tightened as another bird rushed past, black wings slapping. He pursued it several wobbly strides, and lashed out as though he were trying to get rid of something stuck to his hand.

Elenah felt the *ripple* in the air; the shockwave almost knocked her off her feet. The bird froze mid-air, as though caught in an invisible web, then Oswald hurled it downwards, breaking its bones in the dirt. Elenah glanced up at him, heart hammering. Magic surged through his charms, and slipped off him like the plumes of a gas giant.

Then, it stopped abruptly.

"Dammit," Oswald hissed, holding the dun shards of his bracelet.

"What happened?" Elenah asked.

"Get inside the ship, Elenah."

She simply looked at him.

A *scream.* Elenah twisted to see two huge talons grab the back of Hannah's cloak and snatch her up into the air. She slipped from its grasp and they both pummelled maladroitly into the dirt. Elenah bolted for her. "Get up!" she said, grabbing Hannah's sweaty hand.

They floundered for the shuttle.

It hung three feet off the ground, spewing spider-webbed waves of starfire across the dirt. The birds chased the sound, attacking and leaving their shapes in the metal.

Hannah screamed, and Elenah's arm went painfully taut. She turned and tried to wrench her free. A mutated bird clutched the back of Hannah's cloak with its huge, obsidian-like talons. Its wings beat furiously, shedding feathers everywhere. "It's got me!" Hannah cried. It jerked her off the ground. Elenah grasped Hannah's wrist. The bird squawked and tried to drag her up and away. "Let go!" Hannah yelled, flailing mid-air.

"No!" Oswald shouted. "*Don't let go!*"

Elenah glanced at him; he sprinted towards them. "Go back!" she cried. Suddenly, the bird retreated, tearing a huge gash out of Hannah's cloak. She crumpled into Elenah's arms. The bird careened off through the air. "Let's go, Hannah."

Oswald stopped, his boots scuffing up dirt and rock. "Come on!"

A single bird dived through the air and grabbed Oswald's back. He cursed. The bird screamed as it carried him off into the endless darkness.

"Oswald!" Elenah cried. She bit down on her lip and blood pooled across her teeth. Without thinking, she grabbed Hannah's hand and hauled her towards the ascending shuttle.

She released Hannah at the last moment and they both scrambled on-board. Eukaloo armed the controls, spluttering words that no one could understand.

Elenah climbed off the floor, untangled herself from Hannah. "Go!" she screamed, but Eukaloo retorted with a roiling blabber. Birds slammed the hull. They chirped, screamed, and squawked. The whole world shook, like an egg about to hatch. The *Divinity* choked as it struggled to gain altitude. "Eukaloo!" Elenah roared.

Eukaloo recoiled with pointless jabber.

"Do something, you idiot!"

"I've got it," Hannah said. She grabbed the Troff's cloak

and flung him off the chair, into the wall. The shuttle lurched to the side. Elenah rolled across the floor.

"*Bitka!*" Eukaloo screamed.

Hannah threw herself before the controls, so hard she almost rolled right off. Something crashed on top of the roof. Hannah slammed forward the accelerator and sent the ship screaming skyward. Elenah and Eukaloo were thrown backwards.

Stars broke through the viewscreen.

Everything stilled. Endless dark lay before them once again. For a long moment, no one spoke and no one moved. Fickle fabledust sparkled through the air, rolling and tumbling. The particles blinked and collided, disappeared and reappeared. Fascinating. Enchanting.

Eukaloo bounced back up. He gathered his cloak around his gaunt reptilian frame and thundered to the viewscreen. "*Guthra,*" he said. "*Bitka! Chookra ock!*" Eukaloo had almost made it to the co-pilot's seat when Hannah stood and shoved him away.

"Are you trying to get us killed?" she spluttered.

Eukaloo slipped almost comically and then flopped down like a sinuous bundle of vines. A silver sphere rolled out of his cloak, throwing off lights at impossible angles. Elenah watched it tumble across the floor, then trapped it beneath her palm.

"What's this?" she demanded, picking it up. The sphere was the colour of Gilgan's eyes. It had some heft, though it fit neatly within her outstretched fingers. It was not a perfect construct; it looked almost *carved*, or *moulded* into form. A strange kind of chill emanated from within, a thin layer of cold air hanging half an inch off the metal. "What is it, Eukaloo!"

Eukaloo backed away from her, but said nothing. Gods, could he even understand what she was saying? But he'd understood Oswald, hadn't he? In his silence, she searched through Gilgan's stories, but he'd never spoken of anything like this.

"This is what Oswald was after," Elenah realised. "But why?" She met Eukaloo's golden eyes, and for a moment she saw something in them that looked strangely like . . . *relief*.

Elenah stuffed it into her knapsack, then rose unsteadily to her feet. "Hannah," she said, suddenly realising how tired she was. "Get us out of here."

Chapter Fifteen

CONVERGENCE

Just as magic binds the worlds of the galaxy, there is a link between magicians, not necessarily tempered by age or potential, that enables the transmission of telepathic messages across time and space. We call this phenomenon clarency; though, it is often impossible to control.

Gilgan soared through the tunnels of space, his bronze Starsinger rumbling with starfire.

The charred world of Mokuura lay ahead, barely a pinprick in the distance. A wave of fear rolled over him and his hands grew sweaty around the yoke.

"Oh, pull yourself together!" he told himself. "Think about the children. Gods, they don't deserve this!" But the stones . . . and the great, foreboding dark . . .

The remnants of the Starforged . . .

No! You're their only hope now!

And there, shining like silver stars: the fleet of the Forty-Ninth Council.

Gilgan reduced the fighter's starfire propulsion and sent it floating steadily towards the blackened world. It was a sad sight. He'd never seen it prosper, for that was long before even his time, but he'd known many who'd shed its wondrous tales. He wasn't sure how it had become so dour, though it was likely a combination of two things: the dark shade Krakensvouf, and the starfire mine—one of the largest in the galaxy—right there outside the city.

Out of habit, he began to count the massive silver shapes arranged in the void. There was a single Leviathan—one of the Council's bold-faced beasts—though there couldn't have been many more of those in their arsenal. Ragnaroks drifted among them, alongside Banshees, and Harpies . . .

"Blast it," he muttered. "They brought their whole damned force." He lay his eyes upon the Leviathan. It hung there ominously. Teveran was in there, Gilgan had no doubt in all the galaxy. But he could feel something else, something familiar: a tremor in the void, the cold air of space fluctuating around him.

There was something out there—or some*one*—who was very, *very* powerful. A feeling he'd felt before, like strings pulling taut, curdled inside his chest. His days with the Starforged came hurtling back. Memories he'd tried so hard to suppress . . . The war had torn them all apart.

"Fex," he breathed.

He heard the second fleet before he saw it. A thundering through space that rattled his Starsinger from end to end. He glanced to port and saw another fleet emerge from the shadows, approaching the Council's force.

There they were: the rebels—or what was left of them.

Gilgan coursed starfire through the engines. His bones began to shake and rumble, and then he shoved the steering yoke forward and streaked towards Mokuura.

ELENAH LEAPT TO HER FEET, scurrying towards the cockpit. The *Divinity* was beeping, and its proximity radar threw numbers and readings everywhere.

Two massive fleets were converging on their position.

Hannah hadn't moved from the controls, though her green skin was turning pale, and there was blood racing to the small of her back. Eukaloo stood hunched against the wall, muttering anxiously. Elenah wished she could understand what he was saying. Maybe it had something to do with the sphere, now tucked away in Elenah's knapsack.

"Hannah," Elenah croaked. "Can you do something?"

"I'm trying," Hannah gushed. "It's just . . . This ship is so *old!*" Elenah swallowed bile. Every time she blinked, she saw death. Oswald being carried away by that mutated bird, Gilgan and her father doomed beneath the Council's shadow . . .

Hannah had thrown them off somewhere beneath Mokuura. She couldn't see the other ships, but the planet swirled above them now. She wondered if it had been like Etheron once.

Gods, what have I done? She buried her face in her hands and turned her back on the viewscreen. Once, she would have given anything to be out here, to follow in Gilgan's footsteps and explore the worlds beyond her home. But now she wished she'd never messed with those insurgents, never gotten into that damn ship with Oswald . . . She wished she'd never traded the safety of Etheron for this terrible nightmare.

But Etheron *wasn't* safe.

Nowhere was.

She thought of Teveran. She could feel him through the mystical tunnels of magic, lost, frightened. She could almost hear his thoughts, and they were as confused as her own. *I'm so sorry.* But it was too late for apologies. Perhaps it was too late to do anything at all.

Something exploded outside. It racked the ship. She grunted, stumbled across the floor. Klaxons screamed, but they sounded half-dead, like a dozen whining babies. The klaxons looped over and over, a red light flashing half a second too fast, too slow, too fast . . .

Cold dread filled Elenah.

"Dammit!" Hannah moaned. "They've come to finish us off." She bunched up her hands, then punched the controls and leapt to her feet. "It's useless. I can't get it working."

"You've gotten us this far," Elenah said, trying to sound encouraging.

"No I didn't. I pretty much did nothing!"

Outside, impossible thunder sounded as ships exploded.

Eukaloo strode forward, yellow eyes blazing. *"Rok tik eht!"* But he could have been telling them where to find more of Oswald's gorsa beans. Elenah closed her eyes . . . and saw Teveran's face. *No. I can't die here,* she told herself, striding across the cabin. *I can't–*

"Rok tik eht!" Eukaloo repeated.

"No one can even understand what you're saying!" Hannah said. Elenah looked at Eukaloo despairingly, thinking of the silver sphere, wondering what it was and why Oswald had been so fond of it . . . And she realised she needed to keep Eukaloo alive and on her side.

"There's no use fighting," she said, though there was heat

in her voice. "We have to work together if we're going to get out of this. We have to work—"

Something hit the ship, throwing them downwards away from Mokuura. Elenah screamed, slamming the wall and sliding to the ground. Darkness and silence consumed them. Metal pipes and contraptions groaned and choked. Starfire hissed from the engines.

There was a pop, and then *weightlessness*.

And Elenah was floating.

"Hannah?" she gasped. All she could see were the stars twinkling beyond the viewscreen. Shockwaves of explosions rattled her bones. *The artificial gravity's been disabled.* She tried to move, but she was suspended in complete darkness. Her stomach turned. Breath choked her. Starfighters thundered by in silver blurs, swooping over and under, headed for the battle.

Then, everything powered up again.

"Backup generators activated."

Elenah fell fast, slamming the ground. When her vision reoriented itself, she watched Hannah struggle to her feet, gasping, blood leaking from her mouth. Eukaloo wandered to the huge viewscreen, his yellow eyes alight, determined.

The *Divinity* hung crookedly. Elenah dragged herself to her feet and peered out the viewscreen. Fighters speared past them like silver darts crossing space.

One of them barrelled *towards* them.

Elenah climbed up beside Eukaloo, hauling herself across the back of the pilot's seat. Her eyes drooped. Consciousness burdened her. The stars whirred before her.

A Starsinger approached. Hadn't they been out-of-production for almost two decades? Still, that ship was nowhere near as old as this. It was such a small thing, almost trivial in the grand scheme of everything. Yet, for some reason, the Starsinger *became* everything.

Wait . . . Where had she seen it before?

Memories of home, of her childhood, of the times Gilgan used to show her his ship and tell her stories. Memories of Teveran, and the realisation that the Council had taken him away from her. Acceptance that she was probably the only one left who could save him.

Save *Etheron*.

And through the dusty viewscreen: Gilgan's face.

"Gilgan . . ." she breathed. "*Gilgan!*"

"THERE!" TEVERAN POINTED AT THE RED BLIPS falling beneath Mokuura. Another fleet officer joined them around the hologram and shouted a string of numbers. Teveran licked his lips; they were cracked and his throat was parched. "They're escaping!" he cried.

Grand Highlord Thrakk towered beside him. Maybe Teveran ought not to interfere, but he couldn't keep quiet when there were enemy ships escaping the world. He felt . . . some sort of *urge* to stop them. It frightened him.

"There are life forms aboard," one of the other officers said, a middle-aged man with a reddish moustache and short-cropped hair.

"Destroy them," Thrakk said—but his voice was hoarse. The officer grabbed the coordinates of the fleeing ships, then turned and ran to the men at the computers. Teveran watched him go. The Leviathan's cannons propelled missiles and bullets through space, causing everything to shake. The engines were thrumming loudly, and metal grinded metal as the giant weapons shifted and changed positions.

Teveran played such a small role in this fight, but he was still so scared, so apprehensive. Bullets rattled against the hull of the *Subjugator*, slamming the windows that encased the bridge, then bouncing back off into space. He'd never seen anything so *powerful*.

Thousands of starfighters split through space outside. Seven Banshees hovered among them; he could hear their monstrous wails, the sound of impending doom. Debris littered the starscape, unharnessed starfire spewed from punctured engines.

Hundreds of voices were thrown back and forth, officers relaying messages and commands, Thrakk pacing around and shouting orders, calling for status and damage reports. Desperation streamed down his face, gushing off in burning rays.

Teveran's eyes were drawn back to the holographic display, at those ships beneath Mokuura. He wondered where they'd come from, what had led them to this doomed cause. *They're terrorists*, he reminded himself. *The Galactic Liberation Movement is a terrorist organisation. The rebels are enemies of peace.*

Sweat cracked his forehead.

Gods, and I've killed them.

"Teveran." Thrakk stood beside him again.

Teveran spoke instinctively. "There are more," he stammered, pointing to a handful of ships emerging from the planet's dense atmosphere.

"Shall we fire?" someone asked.

"No." Thrakk stabbed a long, callused finger through

the holographic display and prodded at the flickering red image of a massive ship—a cruiser?—approaching alongside Mokuura. "Target their flagship," he said. "Blow it out of the stars."

A HUGE TRACKING MISSILE ripped through Gilgan's starfighter.

The engines exploded, fire billowing in the vacuum of space. It threw him against the dashboard. Elenah screamed— sweet Elenah Lockwood—but he couldn't hear her. Oh, how much he would do just to hear the voices of the two children of Etheron one more time.

Blood trickled down his face, dripping from a wound in his forehead. He gasped for breath, but it tasted like ice. The back half of his Starsinger was gone, spinning away from him. Forty years ago he had first sat in the cockpit of this thing. He had travelled the galaxy with it, had gone places men only dreamed of going.

And now . . .

No.

He diverted all the remaining starfire to the engines, jerked the steering yoke and sent the Starsinger in a downwards strife. *I'll come back for you, Elenah.* Stars striated around him. Everything rattled, and spasmodically shook, and if this didn't work then death would certainly take him. Mokuura spanned out below. He fell towards it, throwing all the power he could into the thrusters. Starfire screamed, gurgled, ripped holes in the overflowing engines.

Down, down, down he went . . .

And then he smacked something. *Another ship.* They spun away from each other. Gilgan's bloody grip slipped from the controller. Three ships spiralled towards him, three silver darts that belonged to the Council. Across his viewscreen appeared a message:

WARNING: YOUR SHIP IS BEING DISABLED

ELENAH SCREAMED, watching Gilgan tumble out of focus.

Another blast slammed the *Divinity*. She slumped against the controls, splattered with blood and debris and flickering fabledust. "No," she whimpered, locking her hands into fists. "Not now." She raised her tear-stained eyes towards the viewscreen.

Silver Ragnaroks crossed the starscape.

I have to get us out of here.

Eukaloo grabbed her knapsack and tried to heave her off the control board.

"Get off me!" Elenah shouted, throwing him to the ground. Eukaloo squawked, climbing back to his feet persistently.

"*Shields at 39%*," came the voice of the ship's computer.

Elenah faced the controls, recounting the maps and illustrations from Gilgan's books. Diagrams, numbers and measurements flashed before her eyes, seemingly thrown into existence by the countless pale explosions. She blinked, and saw Gilgan's face in the Starsinger's cockpit, tumbling away into the endless abyss. Tears rolled down her cheeks.

He'd gifted her his shade . . . the legendary Sandred, king of dragons . . . but why? It didn't matter anymore. The transition was complete, and all she could do was thank him.

But now she could *not* let him down.

She drew a deep breath, and felt it again: the pull of magic, the manifestation of what she was, but what she'd never been trained for. It gave her focus, gave her strength even without her summoning its power. She exhaled. *I'm the only one who can save us now.*

Her fingers darted across the controls. *Okay. It's not like Oswald's.* She'd known that since she saw it back on Mokuura. This was some sort of primitive shuttle, maybe thousands of years old. Her eyes flicked back and forth over the screens, over the panels, over the frantic field of stars outside, and then suddenly things began to unravel themselves. *Tri-thrusters,* she thought, running numbers and schematics through her head. *Grade Three shields. Class One . . .*

"Hyperdrive," she gasped. She'd read about this, how it let a ship harness the galaxy's magical currents to create a magnificent charge of energy and jump thousands of light-years through space, all in a single heartbeat.

The viewscreen lit up with the schematics of the ship in a three-dimensional wire outline. Elenah's heart thudded. Her fingers moved by instinct, as though she'd done this a hundred times before, and a rusty voice dictated her commands.

"Starfire supply rerouted."

Something smacked the starboard side.

"Shield core damaged."

Beeping and lights darted across the viewscreen.

"Hey!" Hannah croakily cried. "Watch it!"

Eukaloo threw himself into Elenah. She gasped, the breath knocked from her lungs as she slammed the ground. The shuttle spiralled out of control. Eukaloo hijacked the main console.

"No!" Elenah cried, but searing pain ensnared her.

"Stop him!" cried Hannah, wobbling forward.

Elenah could hardly draw breath. She tasted blood on her tongue. She'd bitten it. Blood rolled across her lips. "*Eukaloo . . .*"

"*Hyperdrive ready.*"

Eukaloo pulled a toggle and armed several more switches. Elenah's strength availed her. She fell back down, and resolved to watch the Troff take control of their lives. Then, as if totally exhausted, he collapsed to one knee. Elenah took her chance.

"Get away from that!" she yelled, leaping at him.

Eukaloo spun with blazing eyes and brandished a gleaming opal charm. "*Caska rithkai!*" he screamed, and the air cracked with lightning as Elenah went flailing across the cabin, slamming the rear wall. Pain seared right through her. She saw blinding lights and distorted figures, a cloaked creature veiled in darkness, with two gleaming blood-red eyes . . .

Eukaloo's rippling form climbed back to its feet and turned towards the viewscreen, slamming the charm onto the control board beside him. It flashed, and glowed, emitting a furious surge of magical energy. Elenah clambered up, steam rising from her body. She climbed forward. Closer. Closer. With all the pain sizzling through her skin, she wondered if Eukaloo's spell had somehow fused her body to the metallic floor of the shuttle.

She was a hand span from Eukaloo's throat when the Troff pulled a lever and everything *jolted*. Elenah felt the *Divinity's* systems draw an incalculable amount of magic. Flashes of light crackled across her vision. A thousand voices all rang inside her ears. Everything vibrated, whirring louder and louder. Outside the viewscreen, time began to quicken and distort, and the stars and ships elongated, blurred, striated, covering the whole of space in white . . .

And then Eukaloo sent them through a blast of light.

CHAPTER SIXTEEN

OPEN YOUR EYES

*He was the greatest magician who ever lived, so powerful
that to call him anything short of a modern god would be
an insult.*

Teveran woke to the sound of his own scream.

He threw off the rough covers and sat on the edge of the bed. Gods, he was still shaking. The chaos from the night before still circled through his mind. Red blips and explosions flickered across his eyelids. Thunder crashed in his ears, like waves of bass that rumbled through space. *I killed people . . .*

A chill rippled through his body, from his feet to his knees to his gut and to his throat. The room was small, with only a bed and a table. A pale light on the wall flickered on and off intermittently, and beams of starlight streamed through a porthole beside it. He stared into space as he tried to settle his breathing. *What was I thinking? What have I done?*

He wasn't a murderer. He tried to tell himself the rebels were terrorists, that they were a threat to this galactic order—but was it even true? Wasn't it the *Council* that launched this attack? It wrenched his gut, made him want to run away and hide from it all. He just wanted to see Elenah again. And he needed Gilgan: his stories, his comfort.

"It doesn't get any easier," came a voice from the shadows.

Teveran started, his heart leaping. "Who's there?"

A tall figure sat on the floor in the corner, just beside the door. His emerald eyes glittered as harsh white light rolled over him. He cradled a rifle across his knees.

Teveran frowned at him. "Snake?" He recoiled, pulling the sheets back across his bruised, lanky chest. "What the hell are you doing here? How long have you been watching me? How— How did you . . ." He sighed and rubbed his forehead.

Snake just stared from within the darkness and rolled his shoulders. He no longer wore his trooper armour, but an ivory suit that would have put him in rank with those who operated the bridge. Fleet officers, they were called. "The nightmares. Even I still have them."

"You do?" Teveran asked quietly.

Snake offered the softest smile of comfort, then flicked soot off his rifle's starfire cell. "All you can do is learn how to manage them."

Teveran stared vacantly at him. "Why are you here?"

"They want me to keep an eye on you. Your uncle's concerned."

Teveran cursed. He felt numb. He wanted to tell someone that he couldn't keep doing this, but he felt so alone now. Look at Snake with his scars and bruises. He was a warrior. *And what am I?* Teveran asked himself. Just a boy, just thrown in the middle of a galactic war. He was no hero, no saviour, like the men from Gilgan's stories. All he wanted was to get the hell out of there. Maybe if he wedged that porthole open he could jump out.

"Get dressed, Teveran."

"For what?"

"Just put on that uniform." He pointed to a set of clothes hanging from the wall. Teveran hesitated, then threw off the sheets and hurriedly shrugged on the coat and pants—they still couldn't get the damned size right. The belt didn't have enough pips to keep them up. Silently, he stalked to the edge of the room and stepped into his shoes. This wasn't a real uniform. It looked *nothing* like what the other officers wore. It was like wearing a fake costume.

"You still have a long way to go," Snake said. "But things *will* get better. For now, your uncle's organised you a mentor. Says it'll help you out for the time being."

"A mentor? What about you? Why can't *you* help me?"

Snake chortled. "Oh, I wouldn't be very good."

Teveran wasn't so sure he liked the idea of a mentor. Did his uncle think he couldn't handle himself, that he needed someone to hold his hand? It made him angry—angry because it was true, and he was ashamed of it. Everything was just so wrong.

"Though," Snake added, "if there's anything you want to talk about, I'll do my best to be of some help. I *have* had my fair share of experiences here."

Teveran shook his head and strode on past him. "That's fine, Snake. *I'm* fine. I should get going. Uh . . . Thanks, I guess."

"Off you go, then. He'll be waiting for you in the second level cafeteria—the better one, if you ask me. Take the turbolift before Block C. First corridor—"

But Teveran was already through the door.

THERE WAS A BANG, the sound of a door slamming shut.

Gilgan awakened.

Metal cuffs gnawed on his wrists, chains rattled across the floor. The world became scuffling, breathing, pressure on his head, on his arms and on his shoulders. Someone yanked the bag off his head and six armoured troopers levelled rifles on his chest.

They threw him to his knees.

This went poorly, he thought, grimacing at the pain.

He dragged his gaze up to the pale lamp hanging from the ceiling. It rattled side-to-side, spraying lights across every ridge, scratch, and dent. There'd been battles inside this room. It was a prison cell, and Gilgan had seen enough of them for one lifetime.

Troopers crowded the cell, surrounding him. Their gazes were penetrating beneath those thick black visors. He could smell their sweat, hear their trembling bones. Magic enhanced one's senses, and let him know their fear. Their orders would have been to keep him alive, which meant that Gilgan didn't have to comply with anything they told him.

They broke their lines and a man strode through. He wore the garb of a field officer: open, high-backed collar, a coat, and a thin black tie. He appeared to be unarmed.

He knelt in front of Gilgan. The light betrayed his age. The man couldn't have been much older than Teveran, with brown hair hanging between his eyes. He had a crooked nose, freckles, and eyes that belonged to a lonely soul. It was a fortunate truth that this long struggle had probably killed most of the veteran soldiers, leaving these ones in charge.

"Gods," Gilgan muttered. "Look at yourself."

The field officer scratched his naked chin. His breath

smelt of stale fruit. A shallow cut ringed his lip, as if he'd bitten it recently. He simply observed Gilgan's face. All was silent save for the whine of creaking metal, of starfire rushing through rusted pipes. The ship, whatever it was, had to have been quite large—maybe a Leviathan, maybe their flagship.

Gilgan ran his eyes across the troopers, each of them standing frozen around the chamber. "You flatter me," he said dully, returning his eyes to the officer. "Truly."

"You have something we need," the officer said.

"You're wasting your time."

The officer frowned, light swimming through his hollowed-out jaws. Gilgan felt the air whir and shake. He felt the cold steel biting his wrists. He channelled deep down and silenced the sensation. He drilled his gaze into the young man's eyes.

"Who do you report to? *Fex?*"

He didn't wait for the officer's response. Fex's power ran hot through the Leviathan's metal walls. It frightened him, for Fex had never been so strong. Once, they'd been like brothers, long before the Daemon Wars, before Fex betrayed them, before he succumbed to the temptation of dark magic . . . and now the Forty-Ninth Council!

"Where is he?" Gilgan asked.

The officer bit his lip. Gilgan saw fear within the young man's eyes. The officer slowly stood, then swiftly motioned with his hand and all the troopers left. Now on his own, he paced back and forth, footsteps ringing across the metal. "Fex couldn't be here, unfortunately."

"That's unlike him."

"Huh." The officer stopped pacing, his eyes pressed against one of the burnished silver walls. "But he did have a question, *Gilgan*, and I am going to repeat it to you using the very same words: What have you done with those stones?"

THE CAFETERIA WAS A LONG WAY from where he'd been the night before. Unlike the sleeping quarters, but not unlike the bridge, it was chaos. Officers scurried about with various intentions. He'd learned how to tell them apart. Mechanics in cheap grey livery, ensigns in silver-grey, fleet officers in pure white. There were no weapons save for the pistols half-concealed behind their backs, but that did nothing to help settle his nerves.

A chill breeze blew through the hall, causing his hairs to stand on end. Warm aromas of various meats and a sour sauce wafted through the air. Teveran's stomach growled like a monster. He looked around self-consciously, hoping nobody heard it.

Okay, Teveran, he thought, trying to relax. *This isn't so bad. Look, it's just like on Etheron. They're not aliens; they're humans, just like me . . .*

"You must be Teveran." The old man stood when Teveran approached the table, offering a firm gloved hand. He smiled and bowed his head. "Lost your way, did you?"

Teveran felt like he was standing beside a god. He made an effort to pat down all the ridges in his shirt, to appear at least half-presentable. This man was dressed with splendid care to detail, the insignia plastered across his breast. He looked so composed.

"Sorry," Teveran said.

"Oh, don't worry. It's a pleasure to finally meet you. I'll

be the one they call your mentor." Teveran shook his hand. "Take a seat." Teveran followed his gesture down.

He must have been Gilgan's age. His gloveless hand was pale and wrinkled. His grey brows were fluffy, drooping over the tops of his eyes and snaking across his balding forehead. He wore the immaculate uniform of a highlord, meaning he was important.

"Most people around here call me Fex," he said. "I have heard many good things about you." His voice was calm, each word carefully enunciated. He plucked a blue grape from the bowl of fruit between them. "Thrakk informed me of the details of last night's battle." Teveran would've been better off without the reminder. Fex popped the grape into his mouth. "There is something about you High Princes . . . Brilliant architects of the future."

"I—"

Fex waved him to silence. "Have some fruit."

"I'm not hungry."

"Sure you are."

Teveran grunted and picked out one of those blue grapes.

Fex lay his right hand across the table, absently pulling his black glove up tighter. "Thrakk has great belief in you. He wants you to lead this fleet one day."

Teveran nodded, yet his heart was someplace else. *Keep it together*, he thought. But he wished none of this had ever happened. He just wanted to go back home, back to Etheron, to be with Elenah and Gilgan. But how? No one was going to take him, not even Snake who was probably his best chance. Fex smiled, his face cracking with wrinkles.

"He's my uncle," Teveran said stupidly.

"Yes. He did say so. Etheron has always been very much

an ally of the Galactic Council. Almost since the beginning. Do you know why?"

"Not really," Teveran said.

"Neither do I," Fex admitted with a weak smile. "I doubt your uncle knows."

Teveran almost smirked, but was hit by a sudden image of Elenah, which ripped it off his face. He saw her standing on Etheron, with Gilgan, and his father . . . Tears threatened him. Weren't they depending on him? Didn't he promise to make them all proud?

He told himself to be strong, for *them.*

"My uncle . . . He's sick," Teveran said.

Fex's eyes narrowed, as if weighing his thoughts, but then he finally nodded. A grim nod, only the subtlest tilt of the head. "Yes."

"My father was, too. Will that happen to me? Will I end up just like them?" He'd seen what the sickness had done to his father. It had cost him almost everything. He'd watched his father become irritable, watched him grow frustrated by his own incompetence. What was worse, there seemed to be no cure. It was a death sentence, as sure as a bullet to the head.

"You're not like them," Fex simply said. When he spoke, his eyes grew smaller, skin folding over skin. He was a thin man—thin but not sickly—and his skin hung loose in too many places. "You've come far. Tell me: What's waiting for you back there?"

Teveran averted his eyes, suppressing the memories of home.

"These thoughts will make you stronger," Fex assured him. "Give you purpose."

"I . . . have a sister," Teveran softly said, focusing on not tearing up.

"A sister," Fex said carefully. "Interesting. I suppose she is also a magician?"

"A magician . . ." Teveran wondered how much else they'd told him. "No." He shook his head, trying to find meaning behind Fex's inscrutable stare. "She wasn't trained like I was."

"A shame. You have confidence in your abilities?"

Teveran shrugged. "Not really. I mean, just a little."

"I imagine we'd ought to change that, don't you?"

It sounded tempting. There were so many aspects of magic that Gilgan had never taught him, so many spells that he'd said were too dangerous—spells that could also make him into one of the heroes he had read about in so many of Gilgan's books.

"Maybe," was all he said.

"Your uncle has asked me to." Fex reached across the table with both hands, and brought them in together. "See, the galaxy is in chaos. For two thousand years we've not had but a fickle semblance of order, fleeting as a young man's love affair. Perhaps you would know." A glint in his eyes. "This won't be easy; it isn't meant to be. That, I know for a fact. It will test you, just as it will test all of us. But we are in this fight together. You and I . . . and your uncle, and . . ." He looked troubled. "And in the end," he recovered, "we will build something *grand*."

But those Taurans. He couldn't forget that. He couldn't just pretend it hadn't happened. He'd *seen* it, watched the troopers gun down those innocent Taurans in the dark forests of Corion. How was that the recipe for building something grand?

Gods, I'm not ready for this. But he knew he should have been, and he knew he was letting them all down by being so timid. Gilgan always told him this day would come. They all had. That he would be fighting for all of Etheron, and for all the galaxy.

It just wasn't meant to be like *this.*

"Fex," Teveran said. "I killed people last night." He wished he didn't have to listen to the tremor in his voice, revealing his apprehensions to the whole galaxy.

Fex said nothing, merely rested his gloved hand over Teveran's, fingers wrapping around his wrist. He gazed into his eyes sternly and, within them, Teveran saw his own frightened face. "That's okay," Fex said, his voice barely more than a whisper. "You will come to understand it."

Teveran nodded, swallowing.

Fex stood up. "Are you ready?"

"Ready for what?" Teveran asked warily.

"There's something I'd like to show you." Then he waved Teveran off his seat and led him through the bustling cafeteria. Teveran followed nervously; his legs felt like they were moving through sludge. As he looked around, he realised they drew many glances. People were watching them and trading whispers, probably wondering what this *kid* was doing with one of Thrakk's trusted highlords.

"How have you found your accommodations so far?" Fex asked as the cafeteria faded away, replaced by a short corridor lit by lamps in the ceiling.

"They're fine," Teveran said.

"The *Subjugator* is a powerful vessel. I think your uncle would be willing to argue it has the best shields in the galaxy, and the most advanced weaponry for lightyears."

"Would you believe him?"

"I've yet to see it engage a formidable foe." He led him through a door into a turbolift, which emptied them into another short corridor on the fifth floor. Fex strode briskly out. Teveran hurried to match the old man's pace. This ship was a maze; he didn't want to get lost.

"I'd say the *rebels* are pretty formidable," Teveran offered.

"They're hardly the most dangerous enemy in the galaxy. Have you *seen* them?"

Teveran realised that, no, he hadn't. His mind wandered in circles as they entered a cramped meeting room with a round table and high-backed seats. Along the walls were doorways leading elsewhere throughout the ship. Teveran could hear a gentle buzz of voices, although he couldn't make much sense of them. The meeting room branched out into a series of narrow corridors, and then to a door that led out into darkness.

As it slid shut behind them, white lights flickered to life. There must have been a hundred of them, tiny bulbs blinking on every wall.

Teveran stepped ahead of Fex, peering about the chamber. "What is this?" Along the walls were metallic pillars, twisted as if of some ancient design, spiralling up towards the stout domed ceiling. Glowing white spheres were attached to each pillar. They pulsed and hummed. Teveran felt the familiar *twinge* of magic at work.

Fex walked forward, his feet clapping against the floor. Teveran followed him a short distance to the small black orb in the centre, sitting directly below another identical one on the ceiling.

His every heartbeat, every breath, and every tingling nerve

resounded through his head. Was he really there, or was it just a dream? He wondered if he was still on the bridge, ordering those ships to be destroyed. It would give him nightmares forever, that would.

"Where are we, Fex?"

"Watch." Fex stepped forward and clicked his fingers casually before the orb. The lights went out. The mysterious humming grew louder. Teveran felt warm pulses against his skin. He could barely make out Fex within the strangling darkness.

Then the room became a hologram.

Strobes of black and silver streaked across his face, blinding him. He gasped. It was everywhere. Stars, worlds, ships, lines, things he couldn't even name . . .

He was standing in the centre of the galaxy.

And the centre of the galaxy was cluttered. The galactic core, brighter than his eyes could comprehend, hung in the middle of everything. Beside it: the Dawn Star, and the mystical Gods Haven. He eyed it, barely able to comprehend it.

"Forty-three cycles of the Eternal Cog and nineteen clicks to the right," Fex said, stepping away from the galactic core and scrunching his fingers into a fist, "and it has brought us here, to this very moment. Me. And you. Pioneers of a new galactic order."

Teveran frowned, unsure of what to say, what to *think*.

Fex began to pace through the chamber, and Teveran followed him. Planets passed through his face, bright lights that should've burned but felt like cold whispers of wind. "Countless hours I have pondered the patterns of the stars. Scoured the depths of space." He turned suddenly and snapped Teveran in a viper's gaze. "Do you know how many there are?"

Teveran's breath caught. "Sorry?"

"Have you counted the planets?"

Teveran simply shook his head.

"Ninety-four," Fex whispered, stretching out his hand and *feeling* the stars that swam between his fingers. "Well, that's all that remains. Only ninety-four, and I have visited them all."

So has Gilgan, Teveran thought, but still the size of everything was underwhelming. He'd always grown up believing the galaxy was so much grander, that space was the great unexplored region of everything. And to see it all now . . .

Fex scratched his angular jaw contemplatively, then stopped pacing. Teveran stared at his back, merely a silhouette webbed by a thousand white lines. "They want me to train you," Fex said. "Help you to realise what you are, and what you must become."

"Yeah," Teveran said. "They think I'm weak—and they're probably right."

"That's not true," Fex said as he ran his hands through a cluster of planets nearby the Dawn Star. "You just need some time to settle into this new way of life, and to realise your importance in this galaxy, so that you will have the courage to *save* it."

Teveran shook his head. All he could do was think about those poor Taurans on Corion, and the troopers gunning them down. He could still hear their screams, their pleas . . .

"This galaxy needs a hero," Fex said.

"Might need to search a little longer." Teveran squeezed

his eyes shut and spun away from the swirling planets, the vibrant stars. "You've got the wrong person. I can't do this stuff. The Council . . . The rebellion . . . I'm not like them, Fex. I realised that on Corion."

Suddenly, Fex's hand found his shoulder. "Never are there merely two sides to a war." It was barely more than a whisper. "It's time to open your eyes."

"Maybe I don't want to." He knew it was the wrong thing to say.

Fex turned, amber lights dwelling among his wrinkles, and Teveran turned with him. "You will." The old man stopped, and the galaxy swirled and reshaped itself as if by his own command. Planets and stars striated, then reappeared much larger.

And Teveran saw Etheron.

It burst into flames. Embers and black smoke seemed to fill the entire chamber. Etheron was gone, reduced to a crisp. The galaxy twisted, and turned, and slowly crumbled into nothing.

Teveran felt his emotions being pulled on, steered, reshaped to follow the spiralling course of the deteriorating galaxy.

There were two spiral arms extending from the galactic core: the northern Godsworn Spiral, and the southern Starforged Spiral. They burned now, disintegrating wickedly.

Fex stepped through the chaos of exploding worlds, through flames that engulfed billions of people every time another massive star turned black and exploded.

Fex quickened his pace, bones grinding as he returned to the centre of the galaxy. "This is what awaits us if we do not try to change it. For two thousand years the galaxy has been decaying. But we can restore the majesty we forgot. We can build it anew." His voice grew coarse now, folds of skin growing taut. "This is barely the beginning. There is so much more ahead."

Teveran tried to catch his breath. A warm trickle raced down his cheek, and he quickly scrubbed it away. When he spoke, it was barely a whisper. "I don't . . . I don't understand." Gods, he sounded like an idiot. "Why are you showing me this?"

"Something terrible stirs. You have to understand what we have at stake." By its own will, the light in the chamber returned. Fex flipped out a calm, gloved hand, and a *flame* came alight above his palm. "Let's begin proceedings. After all, we came here to make you ready to face this war head-on, did we not? So, we must define what you can do. What have you already learned?"

"Um . . ." He bit his lip, taking a wide step away from Fex. The flame swirled over the old man's palm, throwing out embers across the room. Teveran could feel magic pulsing around him, the very essence of creation itself. It was said the galaxy was formed in the debris of a magical explosion, and that it still burned furiously with its lingering power. Well, this was proof like he'd never seen before. He could feel it now, as furious as if it was swirling within himself.

Fex drew a long, steady breath. His hand momentarily convulsed, and the ball of fire grew larger, more vibrant. For a second, Teveran wondered if Fex was going to attack him with it. He didn't know many defensive spells; Gilgan had never really prepared him for combat.

"I . . . I'm not *going* to be sent to the battlefield, though,"

Teveran uttered. "I'm the High Prince, not a soldier. Surely . . . Surely my uncle told you that."

"You still need to be trained," Fex said sternly. "I feel your connection to the source; it is very strong. You will be a danger even to yourself if you do not learn to control it."

Teveran frowned. "But I'm not going to touch it. I'm not—"

"*Listen* to me, Teveran!" He expelled the bolt of fire and strode across the chamber. "This has nothing to do with the Council. The Council fights their own battle now."

"What are you talking about?" He stepped backwards.

"What I'm offering you," Fex whispered, "is an *alternative*."

An alternative . . . ?

"Does my uncle know about this?"

Fex shook his head. "You would be better keeping it between you and me. But I promise I will hold him to my word and I will make you stronger, make you ready to face what's coming. Just . . . The Council will not last much longer. We have to ensure we do not fall when they do."

"If they're going to fall," Teveran started, "shouldn't you *tell* someone?"

"They won't listen to me. But we're getting derailed." He cast another firebolt and it danced upon his palm. "Come on then, Teveran. Show me what you can do!"

Teveran locked his jaw. He curled his hand into a fist, drew a deep breath, then lashed out with everything he had. The dry air twisted several paces before Fex, then cracked like a whip and Fex slid back on the scuffs of his feet. Teveran gasped, struggling to remain standing.

"Good," Fex said, watching him keenly. "A focused conjuration . . . Excellent."

Teveran cursed. "Are you sure about this?"

"As sure as ever." He seemed joyful, which made Teveran want to run away even faster. He did not like this at all. Suddenly, Fex's commlink beeped and he simultaneously extinguished the ball of fire and fetched the small comm device from his belt.

"Report," Fex said. Teveran couldn't hear the other speaker's voice, although it must not have been a very good report, for Fex's face showed nothing but anger—or frustration, or maybe it was some other emotion. Gods, the man was hard to read.

"Leave him," Fex eventually responded, though his voice was sweltering. "I'll speak to him myself, in due time. Just don't let him out. I want your men keeping a close watch on him at all times. Do not underestimate him. He's *dangerous*." Fex listened for half a second longer, then stowed away the commlink and cursed angrily.

"What was that?" Teveran asked.

"Get out of here," he said, voice shaking with feigned calm. "Go and get some rest. I suppose you'll need it. We'll continue this later."

Teveran nodded, and gladly obliged.

CHAPTER SEVENTEEN

HOMEWORLD

Eyes of violet . . . Skin that hums with emotion . . . Hearts attuned to the frequencies of magic . . . The Kerrean are dangerous . . . They are coming . . .

The *Divinity* burst out of a hole in space, tumbling. The shuttle rolled. Pipes and contraptions in the walls screamed. Elenah braced herself as the force threw her backwards, skittering across the metal floor. The stars beyond the viewscreen became white smudges, smeared across the charcoal canvas of space. Eukaloo roared something out, but who could understand him? He'd done this.

He'd killed them.

Fire scorched the *Divinity's* hull from bow to aft, causing everything to rattle, and giving the electronics countless problems.

Elenah glanced upwards, but she could no longer see the stars through the viewscreen, just the huge green whorls of a massive space object. And she saw Eukaloo lunge for Oswald's magical charm as it loosed from his grip and shattered on the floor.

Elenah felt the magic *vanish.*

Then the shuttle lurched forward as it speared through the planet's atmosphere, flinging Elenah backwards maladroitly. She screamed, tucking herself in close. Several inches away, Hannah squeezed her eyes shut. Elenah prayed the death was painless . . .

SHE OPENED HER EYES IN AN UNFAMILIAR PLACE. Charred and fractured metal littered the blackened grassland around her. Embers flickered upon the wreckage, causing her eyes to water. Groaning, she dragged herself out of the wreckage, pulling metal shards off her jumper.

The burnt ground gave way to grass, which she grasped within her bleeding hands to haul herself up. She squinted, blinding sunlight peeking over the distant horizon. What she made out were rolling hills dotted by pink and white trees. Among them stood domed huts held together by bands of metal. Large lakes interminably broke up the verdant fields. And, though it couldn't have been midday, red fires danced upon wooden posts.

I don't know this place, she realised. But why should she? She'd lived sixteen years on Etheron. The only other planet she'd ever stepped foot on was Mokuura, where . . .

Wait. Where was Hannah?

She scrambled to her feet, but her legs buckled under this unfamiliar gravity. The grass spiralled up and snared her ankles, pulling her right back down. *Dammit,* she thought as she landed. *Please don't be dead.* She wasn't sure why, but a part of her needed Hannah alive, to learn about her shade, and understand what this was all about—

There in the corner of her eye she saw the fleeing form of the Troff. "*Eukaloo*," she hissed, but he didn't turn back. He ran through the clear air, beneath blue skies, towards . . .

A dozen gangly shapes were sketched in the distance, barely discernible in the glare. They had large yellow eyes and long cloaks of varying colours. As their forms resolved into view, other senses returned to her: the smell of vegetation, and life, and beautiful prosperity; a soothing breeze across her body, ruffling her tangled hair. Overhead, a flock of flaming red birds streamed by. Her vision began to clear, and she realised those distant shapes were other Troffren, small and lanky. *He's taken us back to his homeworld,* she realised.

"*Korook ta biklo!*" Eukaloo shrieked, glancing over his shoulder and almost tripping over himself. The leading Troff stopped ten strides from the edge of the village, her colourful cloak trailing behind her. It jangled with dozens of dangling charms, not unlike the ones Oswald had worn, the ones that were probably all gone now, destroyed in the Council's rage. The Troff held a tall twisting staff, which glowed with the light of a yellow gem embedded within the top.

Eukaloo reached out towards her. "*Korook ta–*"

The other Troff slapped him across the face. A crack of yellow light flashed between them, coiling around her hand, and Eukaloo flew ten feet away and onto his back.

"*Inska litarta!*" she bellowed, her cowl spraying off her head. Wispy white hair spilled out, touching the tips of her eyes. Several tall Troffren towered behind her, carrying handmade spears. "*Buk buk Eukaloo!*" the female snapped.

Eukaloo whimpered, struggling to his feet.

"Elenah . . ." came a weak voice from behind her. Elenah

glanced around to see Hannah crawl out of the wreckage. She looked as though she'd risen from hell, a nasty black gash painted down the side of her face—as if *roasted*. "Where are we?" she murmured.

The elder Troff was watching them. She said something to her spearmen and they carried Eukaloo away. Finally, the elder kicked back her heel and marched towards them with several spindly Troffren in a surrounding knot. Why did she have need of guards? Elenah wished she had the strength to shout, to tell them what had happened, that Eukaloo had done this to them . . . but she could barely organise her thoughts.

"Elenah?" Hannah muttered.

"He's taken us back to his homeworld," Elenah said, pulling herself and Hannah off the ground, then patting herself down. She could still see the wisps of cloud and ripped-up atmosphere in the sky where they must have entered, stirring weakly. "Can you walk?"

Hannah nodded, though she looked delirious. Her pink hair looked somehow *duller* in the sun; her natural brown was more pronounced.

"Don't move," said the elder, her voice coursing through the air like streams of magic. Elenah froze, heart in her throat, wondering if she'd heard correctly.

"He . . ." Elenah started. "He tried to kill us . . ."

"It's okay now," the elder said. "I can help you." Elenah just stared. The elder spoke in a haggard yet warm voice that enveloped her like a woollen blanket. Alongside her contingent of guards, she eased her way towards them. "You have come a long way." A smile crept across her thin lips. It was only a small gesture, but it looked almost friendly. As she rolled her shoulders, the charms stitched across her cloak rattled. "But," she added, "*how* far?"

She took Elenah's hand, which was trembling.

"Etheron," Elenah said. "We—" A sudden surge of power swelled through her body. It started in her hand, where the elder had touched her, then slithered up her arm, to her chest . . .

Her pain and lethargy faded; she felt . . . reborn. Hannah exchanged a similar look of disbelief, as she too appeared refuelled. Hannah's bleeding had clotted, and her eyes had regained focus.

"What did you do to us?" Elenah asked, backing away.

The elder barely took her eyes off Elenah as she gently bowed her head and took a careful step back. "I have healed your wounds. May it be a gift for bringing my Eukaloo back."

"We didn't bring him back. He tried to—"

"Please," the elder interjected. "Please accept my gratitude. Please come inside. On Telaron, it is the greatest offense to refuse respite for the galaxy's *travellers*." She spoke the last word as if it were some sort of title, or worthy of being one. Elenah bit her lip, but gods was she hungry, and so eager to sit down and consider her options. "You have been through so much," the elder said. "Come. You must still be exhausted." She gestured towards the village. "We have plenty of food. And beds, might you need them. Let us trade stories, Travellers."

THE ELDER CALLED HERSELF AMOHRIA: a name that she'd said was almost holy.

The other Troffren all dressed similarly, in colours and

patterns more playful than even the flowers on Etheron. They wore skirts held up by strings of colourful beads, and cloaks encrusted with crystals, draped with fascinating trinkets.

Elenah glanced about, absorbing these new surroundings. The huts were large enough for families, crafted of white wood that reminded her of the colour of the buildings back home. Trees with bright pink leaves broke them up, nestled by winding sand roads. Signposts stood at every intersection, painted beautiful colours. It looked calm, maybe *too* calm, and she couldn't help but feel anxious to be there, surrounded by so many Troffren.

The spindly, reptilian-like creatures scuttled about the hills, laughing, playing and joking. Elenah couldn't understand their language, Troffese. It appeared only Amohria could speak Foundation, and she spoke it with an elegant grace as she told them how Eukaloo had run away from the tribe five years earlier. She promised them a place to rest and recover their wits. Though, Elenah had no intention of staying very long. Something had changed during her plight on Mokuura. It had changed when Hannah told her about her shade, when Oswald was snatched up by the birds, when she saw Gilgan's form plunging into the depths of space . . .

Is he really gone? she asked herself. He couldn't be dead . . . could he? It didn't seem possible. Gilgan *couldn't* die! Gods, the things she would do to see him again, to hear his voice, to hear him say things would be all right. If only she could return to the old days, when she would sit on his lap and close her eyes and listen to his stories.

Life had been so simple then—the life she'd run away from.

"Tonight is very special," Amohria said. The wind rushed

through the trees, carrying pink and white leaves across the hills. "Tonight is the passage of Iridenia ot Batrumn."

"Who?" Elenah asked.

"Daughter of the moon and sea. Once, she was our guide between the islands. Perhaps she brought you here, of all the places in the galaxy."

She led them onwards, her spearmen close by. Other Troffren watched them, distrust and wariness all swirling within their beady yellow eyes. Elenah couldn't blame them; after all, had she not left, she might as well have been *with* the Forty-Ninth Council.

A worried-looking Troff scurried up to Amohria as they arrived at a flat of grassland between the huts. Amohria leaned in, and her expression began to marry that of the Troff's. She spoke hastily to him, before slapping his shoulder and watching him scamper off. She then waved Elenah and Hannah forward again. "Here we are."

The square was dotted by more of those pretty pink trees. Leaves lay across the ground, tossed about by the wind. There were two Troffren standing by a well on the corner. They were laughing and eating some sort of foamy white broth. Several were playing an unfamiliar game with different coloured beads, another seemed to be painting on a rock. Elenah watched them keenly. Despite her apprehensions, this place was like no other she'd ever been to. It was as though the troubles of the galaxy didn't *exist* here.

But how long could it last?

"*Chok rokto buht,*" Amohria said, twirling her staff and sitting cross-legged in the grass. The two guarding Troffren chirped something in response, then fetched them each a bowl of broth. "Please, sit." Amohria gestured towards fresh patches of grass.

Elenah hesitated.

"We are not going to kill you," Amohria said kindly. Elenah felt a tug on her skirt, then looked down to see Hannah, sitting cross-legged, gesturing to the grass.

"I appreciate this," Elenah said, sitting down beside Hannah, "but it really isn't necessary. We don't plan on staying." She placed her knapsack between her legs, clutching it close. From somewhere deep within, she felt the burning hum of Eukaloo's silver sphere.

"And how do you plan to go back?" Amohria asked, apparently humoured.

Elenah pursed her lips.

"Why are you so nervous?" Amohria asked her.

Elenah caught herself drumming her fingers against the knapsack, and clenched them into a fist. "I'm not," she quickly said, giving an apologetic smile. "I'm fine. Really."

Amohria narrowed her eyes disapprovingly.

"I said I'm fine," Elenah said.

Amohria raised a brow at her.

"Short on time is all."

"Do you have someplace to be?" Amohria asked as the Troffren returned with bowls of broth. Elenah took hers reluctantly; she wasn't going to complain. She glanced at Hannah, who took hers and didn't wait before sipping it. Elenah looked back at Amohria to consider her question. *Where would I go?* Did she even have any chance of smuggling Teveran out of the Council's ranks, let alone *finding* him?

"If you have nowhere to go," Amohria said, "then please eat."

Elenah lifted the bowl to her lips. Its heat touched her tongue like a viper's bite, but it was not unpleasant for more than a couple of seconds. In fact, it reminded her of potato and creamed mushrooms. The smell was familiar to the kitchens back home.

Amohria seemed pleased. "I am sorry for Eukaloo. He has made it a habit of getting into trouble. This time, perhaps a little bit too much." She made a sound like a laugh, though it was closer to the sound of a shell breaking. "I always tell him: 'In the real galaxy, every wrong turn, even the smallest mistake, has terrible consequences.' But"—she shrugged nonchalantly—"Eukaloo *still* does not listen to me. He is too much like his mother."

"Where is his mother now?" Hannah asked.

"A terrible thing has happened to her," Amohria said. "Taken by the Shadow Reaver." She shook her head sadly, as though remembering it. "It often comes to those who delve too deep into the unexplored galactic depths. I was afraid the same fate might befall Eukaloo. Though, I suppose only time will tell. Currently, all he needs is a *slap*."

Elenah smiled, her face in her broth, but Amohria's eyes had not left Hannah. "You know," she said. "When I first saw you, I thought I'd been drinking too much *ieelk!*" Her yellow eyes brightened upon Hannah. "You are very, *very* important."

Hannah averted her eyes as she said, "I'm not so special."

"Oh, but you are," Amohria said. Elenah focused on Hannah's catlike eyes; they were the same colour as Amohria's, only far dimmer. "There must not be a hundred left of your kind. I wish I could help you, young one. It saddens me that I cannot."

Hannah looked away. "Sometimes I do better without the reminder."

"You should not run," Amohria said.

"I wish I didn't have to."

"I think it's sad that you think you *do*."

Hannah looked up. "What do you mean?"

Amohria simply smiled and flicked her eyes skyward as another flock of crimson birds darted by. Elenah turned to Hannah, thinking about her prophecy . . .

"Something terrible is about to happen," Amohria said absently. "I am weaker than I once was, but I feel it even now. Right *here*." She lay a gentle hand against her heart. "A shadow falls across the galaxy, a shadow darker than any that has come before it. This war is just a vessel, a tool . . . like a *knife*. There are dark forces out there that are using it to fuel their cause, to construct their armies, to achieve terrible, terrible deeds. For you two . . . it would be best to *leave*."

"Leave?" Elenah asked, almost spilling her broth.

"Yes. There is a way."

"Where would we go?"

"Away," she simply said.

"Can you see the future?" Hannah asked. "Are you a seer?"

"No," Amohria said. "It is just a feeling."

"And what about you?" Elenah asked. "Are *you* just going to leave, then?"

"No. I will stay and fight—fight for my people."

Elenah was close to offering her own help, but decided it was a burden she wasn't capable of bearing. Already, she'd been given one burden too many: Gilgan's shade, and the prospect that he was equipping her with the power to save Teveran and her homeworld.

"There's nothing you can do, child," Amohria said as though she'd read her thoughts. "If you choose the same path as I, then you will beg for death, I assure you."

Elenah swallowed.

"This war is not about the Council," Amohria reminded them. "Soon they will be gone, yes . . . but there is more to it. Soon, it will take a much darker turn, and from there . . ." She simply let the word hang, and Elenah conjured a thousand different endings for it.

Amohria smiled. "But please, rest easy. You will need it. And you must eat. You may stay here with us tonight, stay for the festival, but if you wish to fight, then I must ask you to leave this place. It will not be safe here for very much longer. Not for you."

"Our ship . . . It's broken," Elenah whispered.

"I will do my best to fix that," Amohria said.

Elenah wasn't sure if that was possible, but she couldn't be bothered arguing with her. Instead, she put aside her empty bowl and stood up, relaxing her skirt, hauling up her knapsack. "Come on, Hannah," she said, intending to seek some peace and quiet.

Hannah sat there for a moment longer, as if she hadn't heard.

"Are you coming with me?" Elenah asked.

"Oh," Hannah said, as though shaken from a trance. "Yes. Of course." Then she, too, collected herself and walked away from Amohria. Elenah eyed the Troff elder, wondering if she really intended to help them. Then she turned on her heel and wandered off.

CHAPTER EIGHTEEN

THE GATHERING STORM

By the year 39c52, they were calling him the Dark Lord.
Though, what truly frightens me, even to this day, is that
after our single encounter I could almost call him a friend.

Gilgan sat alone in his prison cell.

He closed his eyes, for he didn't need them. Instead, he listened to the flow of magic. He felt the icy breeze against his skin, and the pale white light flickering across the walls, burning the backs of his eyes. The air was tight, and stale, and it reeked of impending disaster.

I can feel it.

A gentle throb from the centre of the galaxy. Indecipherable imagery, impenetrable terror. He'd felt it before, a long time ago.

A *storm is coming.* If only he knew what exactly. He'd weathered many storms travelling the galaxy. Ever since he'd been banished from Tarthalus, banished from all of human society because of these mutations, he'd weathered every kind of storm.

But this one was different. It rumbled through the ship. An inferno unfolding like a flower from a seed. This . . .

This was something far, far worse.

Gilgan's eyes snapped open and reality refocused itself. The four metal walls, rusted and blackened by char. Metal and dirt skittering across the floor. There'd been troopers in here earlier, and that young field officer without a name.

What have you done with those stones? he had asked.

Not his own words; they belonged to Fex.

The worst part of it was that Fex knew about the stones at all. There were nine altogether, scattered across the galaxy in the hands of those he trusted most. They each held a portion of the Dark Lord's wicked, ancient power. But, if he wasn't careful, Fex was going to find them.

Fex was going to finish what he failed to do before.

Gilgan shut his eyes again and simply listened. The whispers of dead men bounced about: officers and troopers all around the ship. They'd taken him to their flagship, one of their last Leviathans . . . And somewhere, he knew that Fex was aboard it too.

"What are you up to, old friend?" Gilgan asked the zestful darkness. The only response was the squealing and rattling of the lamp from the ceiling.

He felt a sudden flash of anger. *If you dare lay one hand on Teveran, I will kill you.* It hadn't even occurred to him that Fex might know about Teveran, that he might try to use his unkindled power to fulfil his own dastardly plans—or to tear out answers from Gilgan. Of course, Teveran didn't know about the stones . . . But that wouldn't stop Fex.

He curled his hand into a fist. It was up to him now. Seventeen years it had been since last he ventured through the depths of the galaxy, but now he was back and he had no plans of running away. Not until he knew for certain that

Teveran and Elenah were safe. He might not survive—he'd accepted this fact long ago—but his survival was not what mattered; that was why he'd gifted his shade, the Sandred, to Elenah. What mattered now was ensuring the *children* stayed alive, and ensuring the stones did not fall into Fex's hands.

If he could do all that, then death didn't matter.

"He's insane," Teveran said. Gods, but speaking with Fex, and seeing the galaxy map, just pulled his soul in all sorts of directions. What the hell did Fex want? Did he want him to become Grand Highlord, like his uncle? Or . . . did he want something else?

What I'm offering you is an alternative, Fex had told him. But Teveran didn't like the sound of it. Whose side was Fex on, really? And who the hell knew about it?

Snake riffled mechanically through barrels of weapons, checking the starfire cells and replacing those that were faulty. "All I want to know," he said, "is why the hell you're with *Fex* now. That guy's trouble. From what I've heard . . . He can kill a man just by *thinking* about it." He unclipped one of the starfire cells and tossed it into a discard bucket, then replaced it with one that had a little splash of red paint on it.

"He's a magician," Teveran said. "And he's powerful."

"You should be very careful around that man. I don't trust him."

"Well, my *uncle* does. That's what I'm worried about. He's got Fex in his inner circle. But . . . Gods, he's telling me all these things . . ."

The Council fights their own battle now.

Teveran's gaze became unfocused. *What is his game? What*

is he going to do? What does he want with me? That last part, the most *important* part, had been bothering him ever since he'd left the star chamber. There must have been a thousand better magicians out there!

"I don't suppose I can go back home," Teveran tried.

"No," Snake said. "You couldn't go back even if you had a choice. Etheron's under their control now. Besides, you've been given this opportunity, so try not to waste it. Do you know how many people would kill to be standing where you are now?"

"Isn't there a better way?" he asked, remembering the screams of those Taurans, the sting of the forest cold, and the rumble of bullet-fire and explosions. Whatever he decided, it would make him a murderer, and that was something he didn't want to be.

"Sometimes the best way is not an option."

"I don't care. This all feels so wrong."

Fex's voice resounded in his head. *Never are there merely two sides to a war . . .* It almost aligned with something his father had said, a lifetime ago: *There are many groups that would call themselves rebellions . . .* But what did it mean? Gods, he didn't want to be a part of it!

"It doesn't make any sense," he growled. "None of it makes any bloody sense." He looked at Snake despairingly. "I don't think Fex is on our side. Does my uncle know? Does he know what Fex is talking about? Maybe we should report him or something."

Snake puffed a breath through his nose. "No. Your uncle will *not* like that. Don't start doubting his integrity, or his decision-making. Especially not you." He resigned to his quiet work, slapping a new cell into the gut of the rifle. "I might have a word with him, if time permits, but your uncle has enough to think about." He tossed the cell into a barrel, then pulled out another. He lay it on his lap and rapped at the side.

"Well, I don't doubt that Fex was very competent once upon a time," Teveran said. "But he is crazy now. I mean . . . I've heard of it happening, you know? The Daemon Wars, it changed people. Soldiers came back home like reprogrammed machines. Some of them worse, like . . . I don't know, like their circuits had been *fried*. Maybe that happened to Fex."

Snake stopped working, as though lost in deep thought.

"What is it?" Teveran asked.

"Nothing."

"Were you . . . there?"

"It was a long time ago," Snake recovered, forcing himself back to work.

"I'm sorry. I should've known . . ."

"You couldn't have," Snake grumbled, then looked back up. Teveran thought he could see explosions going off in Snake's emerald eyes. "Teveran, this fleet will need you."

"That's what I'm afraid of." *But I promised them, didn't I?* He'd been thinking it over and over. All he'd ever wanted was to make them proud, and be the man they needed him to be. Honour his family's legacy. Had it been so hard for everybody else?

But there was another variable. If Elenah knew the Council's real agenda, if Gilgan had any idea of the things Fex was going on about . . . If they knew how powerful Fex was . . . If they knew what he was trying to *teach* him . . .

If his uncle could see that Fex was a threat.

"Don't be afraid," Snake told him. "Listen to your uncle. He's been in this far longer than either of us. I'm sure he'll know what's best for you."

"My uncle's half-dead."

"It makes him no less of a man. He's all that's keeping this fleet together."

Teveran sighed and leaned up against the doorframe. He wasn't ready for this. It scared him. Fex, and the power he was promising, and the sickness in his blood. Would it take him too?

Loud footsteps came thumping down the hall, startling Teveran. He turned to meet the eyes of a young ensign in his silver-grey outfit. "I'm sorry to interrupt," the boy said. He couldn't have been sixteen. He nodded diffidently to Snake. "Officer."

"What is it?" Snake asked.

"It's a message for the High Prince." He clasped his own hands, which tremored, and softly said, "The Grand Highlord wants to see you now."

Teveran grunted. "Okay, I'll be there." Though, he wasn't looking forward to it. The ensign nodded hurriedly, then scurried back off up the hall. Teveran turned back to Snake. "Thanks for helping out. I appreciate it."

Snake nodded and gave a small salute. "Off you go."

HIGHLORD KLOAK RAN THE NUMBERS THROUGH HIS HEAD as he crossed the bridge towards Thrakk. He'd been given a major role in all this, and he wasn't going to screw it up. In a matter of days, Etheron as the galaxy always knew it would fall.

As a Free World, it was an easy target. What made it even

more alluring was its location among the stars, so close to the core, so close to the *source.*

But he needed more men if he was going to take it cleanly, men that only the Grand Highlord would be able to afford him. His own specialised force. He knew they could spare the numbers for it; it was just a matter of convincing Thrakk.

"Highlord Kloak," Thrakk said, turning towards him. "Is there a problem?"

"I'd like to request my own guard," Kloak said, wasting no time. He knew the Grand Highlord had already requested the High Prince's presence up here, so Kloak was running on a short time slot. "We *will* face resistance down there, as I'm certain you're aware."

Thrakk seemed to consider this. "How many do you propose?"

"A dozen will do," Kloak said, hardening his voice. He could turn any number into a force that felt like a thousand. Though it sometimes seemed a lifetime ago that he was carving boys into warriors at the old warcamps of Alakhar, his skills had not languished over the years. "However, Grand Highlord, if I may request someone in particular . . ."

"Go ahead," Thrakk said, but only half-listening.

Kloak hated it when Thrakk's mind wandered like this. Sometimes he couldn't even tell if the man was conscious or not. He was difficult to read, that was for certain. "There's a man in Corona Squad. Lieutenant Renarik. I have been made aware on several occasions that he has demonstrated immense talent on the battlefield. Consider it a promotion for his service."

Thrakk's cobalt eyes focused on something behind Kloak as he said, "Very well. But I cannot spare you twelve men.

You will be accompanied by a guard of six, alongside the ninety-four of the Eighty-First Battalion."

"There are others," Kloak said, glancing briefly to where Thrakk was looking. The boy, Teveran, had entered and was looking around. "Other soldiers I'd like to request."

"You have my authorisation to select a guard of six," Thrakk said, slowly moving away from Kloak. "Take them to fulfil whichever means you see fit. Excuse me."

"Thank you, Grand Highlord," Kloak said, then departed for the lifts.

TEVERAN STRUGGLED TO CONTAIN HIS AWE as he looked around. Gods, but it still took his breath away. The galaxy he'd heard so much about spanned forever in every direction, an endless creation beyond impenetrable glass.

As always, the bridge was bustling with people. Officers worked tirelessly, observing and making notes around holographic displays, sitting at data pads on the walls, or running about, relaying messages between different operating sections. The highlord with the burnt face—Kloak?—passed him as he entered, taking the lift back down. He had a sneaky look on his face, as though he was planning something against the Grand Highlord's will.

Teveran peered through a gap in the chaos, where Thrakk stood, looking much sicker than usual. Cracks had started to appear in his sallow skin. But he tried his best to hide it, standing straight-backed, hands clasped behind him. "Sir?" Teveran said, walking up to meet him.

Thrakk regarded him. Teveran had always been quite tall, but Thrakk was nearly a full head taller. He now brandished dishevelled grey stubble, and deep bags had unfolded beneath his eyelids. "I've been meaning to ask about your sister," he said, simply.

"I . . ." He didn't know what to say.

"In all honesty, I didn't know you had one."

"How did you find out?"

"Fex told me."

Teveran went taut. *Fex.*

Thrakk waved him onwards, and Teveran followed. They crossed the bridge slowly, between dozens of immaculate fleet officers. Some of them glanced over curiously, although most hardly seemed to notice anything amuck. "I am intrigued as to why your *father* never told me. Though, I shouldn't be surprised; he was always a man of many secrets. Perhaps that is why he became so . . . disliked by his own people."

"That's not true," Teveran said.

"Oh?"

"His . . . His people respect him."

"They *did.* At least, that's what *I've* heard."

Teveran frowned, watching Thrakk as he walked several paces further. Eventually, he stopped and turned around before the strobing lights of an unfamiliar planetary hologram. "Recently, news has reached us that your sister is gone."

"*What?* What do you mean she's gone?"

Thrakk coughed, then rubbed his ragged face contemplatively and licked his cracked lips. "Your father has issued a missing persons report. He's alerted every planet in the realm."

How? Had Gilgan taken her? No, Gilgan would never do something so defiant of his father's word. And there had been no galactic maps just *sitting* around the palace; Elenah wouldn't know where to begin. It was as good as suicide!

"Please leave her out of this," he said.

Thrakk nodded. "Of course."

It was unconvincing but, then again, what would Thrakk want with Elenah? The Council didn't need her. Gods, but whatever happened to *him*, and whatever cruel things they made him do, he didn't want Elenah anywhere near it. He didn't want her by danger's nasty door, where any stray bullet might just . . .

And then he saw him: the phantom figure, standing with folded arms beside a hologram in the distance. Though Fex's eyes looked vacant, unfocused, Teveran knew they were watching him.

I have to do something, Teveran thought. Yet suddenly he felt completely bewitched, as though Fex had placed some sort of spell on him. Teveran believed what Snake had said, that Fex could kill a person just by looking at them . . .

"Is everything okay?" Thrakk asked him.

Teveran looked back at him hastily. "Yes."

Thrakk nodded, as if that were the only acceptable answer. "We're going to be landing soon," he said, clasping his wrinkled hands and turning his head to gaze out one of the windows. "There will be a conference held on Kasnah. I want you to be present."

Kasnah, Teveran thought as he joined his uncle gazing through the glass. That was where it all happened: the great Battle of Haratheon, the last day of peace. There was something . . . ominous about the prospect of returning there. Especially now of all times.

As he stood beside Thrakk, he could hear the old man's

strained breaths, hear the sickness clawing at his chest. *He's all that's keeping this fleet together,* Snake had told him.

"This conference," Teveran said. "What is it about?"

"I see no reason to disclose that information at this time," Thrakk said, and if Teveran wasn't mistaken, he even sent a glance sidelong to the phantom figure of Fex. Teveran suddenly felt very uncomfortable, and was glad when his uncle finally dismissed him.

Before leaving, Teveran met Fex's watching eyes. Something unseen ran between them, before Fex drew a visible breath and strode off through the bridge with another highlord. Unnerved, but glad to be somewhere else, Teveran walked off in the opposite direction.

Chapter Nineteen

SHADES AND SPHERES

The detachment of the shade, Krakensvouf, was the strongest suggestion of sentience and free-thinking within these guardian forces.

Y"ou have to tell me what's going on," Elenah said, sitting on a rock by the edge of a lake, trying to make ripples on the water using nothing but sheer magical will.

Hannah stood behind her in the shade of a tree, the sleeves of her cloak pulled up, and her pink hair roughly matching the colour of the leaves, which rustled above them and drifted occasionally nearby.

"Firstly, you can see shades," Elenah said. "Secondly, you mentioned a prophecy—like this is some kind of *storybook*. What is it you're after?" She grunted upon the last syllable, annoyed at the water for being so stubbornly still, even despite the breeze.

Why was it so hard for her? When she saw Gilgan doing magic, he'd performed the most complex spells so effortlessly. Even Teveran could make things happen without paying much attention. Gilgan had told her she had a strong magical potential, so surely she could at least stir the waves! *He gifted me his shade, the Sandred . . . But does he expect me to use it?*

"I can't see them all the time," Hannah said. "The shades, I mean."

"Can you see it now?"

Hannah's watery reflection shook her head. "They only come out sometimes. You know, when you need it. Although . . . that doesn't explain why I could see it before."

"No, it doesn't," Elenah said, picking up a pebble and tossing it as far as she could. It landed halfway across the lake with an almost silent *plop*. She watched the ripples from the impact shake the water. Out of nowhere, a pink leaf fluttered down and landed lithely upon the surface, rocking back and forth like a boat.

Dusk was settling across the sky, but the stars were bright and illuminated the horizon. Hannah sat down beside her, brushing up against her side. They stared at the motionless lake, and the pink flower bobbing along.

"It's the Fifth Dimension," Hannah said, clasping her slender pale-green hands. "That's where they come from, the shades. That's why I can see them sometimes."

"I still don't understand," Elenah said. "Another *dimension?*"

"I can see into it, but I'm not sure why. Not many people can."

"Then how am I supposed to?" As far as she was concerned, she definitely couldn't see into this Fifth Dimension. "More importantly, how do I *use* it? Gilgan wouldn't have given it to me if he didn't think I could use it . . . would he? And how can I use it if I can't even see it?"

"You don't *use* them, Elenah. They're like . . . guardian

forces. They are bound to you. This one was bound to you when your friend, Gilgan, gifted it to you. I suppose he foresees trouble ahead, or the possibility of it. That's when it will come."

"And if it doesn't?"

"How much do you trust this man? Gilgan?"

Elenah bit her lip. Of course she trusted Gilgan . . . didn't she? As she thought about it, she realised she didn't trust him as much as she once had. Not *this* Gilgan. Maybe the old one, the one who had ventured across the galaxy. But Gilgan had changed. He was older. Wearier. Maybe he expected too much of her. "I . . ." she started. "I just don't like putting my faith in something that might or might not actually turn up when it needs to."

And if this shade wasn't really here at all? What if Hannah was just making this up? Gods, but she really didn't want things to get so desperate that she relied on an imaginary force . . .

Hannah stood up suddenly, and as Elenah looked up she realised it had gotten a whole lot darker. Behind her, in the heart of the village, she could even hear the first inklings of the festival. Jovial voices, stringed instruments being tuned, drums being banged.

"And what about the prophecy?"

"It doesn't matter—"

"Yes it *does!*" Elenah snapped, slamming her fist into the dirt. She recoiled, cursing as she rubbed her stinging hand. "Ugh, I'm sorry . . ." But when she looked back up, Hannah's form was receding in the distance. Elenah blew a deep breath and scrunched her hand into a fist.

Gods, but she didn't know what to do. She simply watched

the lake's surface, stirring as a strong breeze rushed past, distorting the silver and red reflections of the sky. *Are you still out there, Gilgan?* she thought, focusing her attention on the single pink leaf, floating in the middle of the lake. *Is this what you wanted me to do? Save Teveran? Save our home?*

There was a spell to make things move, *Lashio*, although it was incredibly difficult—almost impossible—to control. But she knew she could do it. She knew she would *have* to do it, eventually. Whether that was today, or tomorrow, or a month from now. If this was the task Gilgan had set for her, and if he'd trusted her enough to gift him his shade, then she needed to start practising. Relaxing her whole body, she imagined the spell inside her head. *Lashio . . . Lashio . . . Las hio . . .* She reached out towards the leaf and—

Nothing.

Dammit! Gods, she felt like crying. Even as the festival started firing up behind her, she wanted to run away and hide, and bawl out her eyes. Sure, the Troffren could act like nothing was wrong with the galaxy. They could play music, and dance, and laugh . . . but that wouldn't change the fact that there was war between the scattered rebel cells and the Forty-Ninth Council, that countless worlds were falling apart, and people were dying in masses . . .

How could they celebrate when everything was so *bad*?

She decided to busy herself by pulling out Eukaloo's silver sphere. She wished she could ask Oswald what made it so special, but now he was either dead or desperately out of reach. She slowly turned it in her hands, its tessellated patterns rolling against her palms. The metal sucked in bright lights, which swirled and roiled like flames, then bounced off in multicoloured streams. It *had* to be something. It had to *do* something.

"You are a very interesting girl."

Elenah gasped, spinning around and scrambling to her feet. She looked up from the shadows to see Amohria standing in the light. Her rainbow cloak billowed around her, thin reptilian hand encircling her twisted staff. This time she'd come without her spearmen, though Elenah couldn't tell why she needed them at all. Amohria could handle herself just fine.

"Where did you get that?" Amohria asked, carefully approaching.

"I . . ." Elenah choked on words.

Amohria shook her head. "I did not mean to surprise you. I am sorry." She poised herself a few feet in front of Elenah, clutching her staff in two hands.

"Eukaloo had this," Elenah said.

"Yes," Amohria breathed. "Hmm." A cold breeze rushed by, bringing silence. Elenah focused on the sphere, cradled before the hem of her pleated grey skirt. The clothes reminded her of home, and of her last day there. How different things might have been if she'd never run off, never left Gilgan behind, just did as she was told.

But would things be better or worse?

"Do you know what it is?" Elenah asked.

Amohria shrivelled up her face. "Perhaps."

"Tell me."

The elder Troff laid out her hand, and Elenah stepped forward, setting the sphere inside it. Amohria raised it to her eyes, turned it round and round, like a metallic moon in slow orbit. "Hmm." She gently placed it back inside Elenah's smaller, sweatier palm. "Yes. Indeed."

"Amohria?"

"It is a *Talisman*. A machine of the Asmoreans."

"A Talisman," Elenah repeated. "Asmoreans . . ." Her heart drummed along with the primitive music of the festival. "What is it? What does it do?"

"It's a map."

"A map?"

"Yes."

"Oh my god." It was all she managed. She looked at the thing—this unopened map—and wondered if it could lead her to Teveran. She felt like crying out, like grabbing Hannah right now and telling her what she'd found but . . . "Why did Eukaloo have it?"

"I would not be surprised if he stole it," Amohria said. "I see no other way. I have certainly not seen its kind in a very long time. You should be careful."

Elenah pondered that for a moment.

"You will not be able to open it," Amohria stated.

"Why not?" Elenah asked hurriedly.

"It requires a very ancient form of magic: the *Asmorean Script*."

"Of course . . . Do *you* know how to open it?"

"The Asmorean Script perished long before my time."

"But"—she proffered it to Amohria eagerly—"you know what it is. A *Talisman*."

"It is more complex than that. I have seen only one other in my lifetime, though I have never made one work." She drew a sharp intake of breath as if to say something else, then stopped, and a heavy silence fell between them. "You're looking for someone."

Elenah frowned, feeling that familiar jab to the gut, the tightening around her chest. When she thought of Teveran, and what he must be going through, it felt like the whole galaxy was caving in on itself. She realised that, if there was any way to help him, any way at all, she would risk her life trying. "My brother," she said. "The Council took him away."

"I understand."

"You do?"

Amohria nodded. "I have experienced the spectrum of your . . . *human emotions*. I do understand, Elenah. Very strongly." She smiled warmly. "That is why I know I cannot convince you to leave . . . but I suppose I *can* show you the way."

Elenah's heart leapt. She opened her mouth but no words came out. All she could do was look down, into the yellow bulbs of Amohria's eyes.

"I am not very powerful," the elder said, "but I know someone who can help you. An old man. Very old. He lives in a castle, alone, on a moon called Saecon IV."

"Does he know the Asmorean Script?"

Amohria chuckled. "Oh no. He is not *that* old. But he can tell you where your brother is. He might even be able to take you there. But . . . you will have to be careful."

"Thank you," Elenah whispered. She proffered the sphere, glowing with the surrounding lights. "What should I do with this? If Eukaloo did steal it, then I really don't want to meet whoever's looking for it."

"I will take it for you," Amohria said, offering her hand.

Elenah eyed her warily, then nodded and handed over

the sphere. Amohria quickly stowed it away in her cloak and took Elenah's hands in her own.

"Stay the night," Amohria said. "You will need the rest. As for your friend . . . She cares about you deeply, I think . . . You should talk to her."

"She barely knows me."

"She is very lonely. I see it in her eyes. But you can give her what she longs for: friendship, someone to care about. Perhaps she will come to be a powerful ally." Amohria smiled, but it was very feeble. It was probably difficult for her to find much to smile about in such times.

"Okay," Elenah said. "I'll go find her. Thank you, Amohria."

"When you wish to settle down, come find me and I'll make sure you have a place to sleep. You and your friend both. And if you'd like to wash up, I can arrange that too."

Elenah smiled graciously, and then watched the Troff walk off. Wasting no time, Elenah followed the winding sand roads into the village. Troffren dressed in garish colours danced and twirled to the feverish beating of drums. Others clapped, rocking from foot to foot, smiles lighting up their reptilian faces. She brushed by palm trees in cloaks of bright lights. The moon sat upon the ocean, waves of silver glimmering. A cool breeze washed through the island as Elenah peaked the hill. She wrapped her arms around herself, dark hair flapping.

"Hannah?" she called.

The Felirean wasn't there. Elenah huffed and strode onwards through the village. She diverged from the path and traversed glowing bushes and scrub, between palm trees and into darkness. There was nothing ahead but rocks and limestone cliffs. She spun on her heel and descended to what looked vaguely like a cemetery. Stray trees, back-lit against the starry sky, threw pink and white lights across the grass and branches. And there was a thin layer of mist, rolling between the gravestones: tall, pious things that looked pointedly reverent.

And there was Hannah, standing by one of the altars with her pink hair blowing across her shoulders. "I suppose you're leaving now," she said.

"No . . . not entirely."

"If you don't want me to come with you, then just say it."

"That's not it . . ." Elenah started, but found her voice faltering.

"I guess I was just trying to find meaning where there was none. There is no prophecy. It was a child's rhyme. I was being foolish." She turned around, and Elenah saw tears quivering in her eyes. "You keep going. Take the *Divinity* and save your brother."

"I didn't mean to get angry," Elenah said in a placating voice.

"Do you know what it's like? I'm the last of my species, Elenah. There's nobody else like me out there! And it's not just that . . . The Kerrean warlords who invaded my homeworld eleven years ago . . . They're hunting me. They've been hunting me for as long as I can remember. And I'm afraid they've also allied with members of the Council." She choked on her words. "What Amohria said is true: There are more forces than you can imagine all fighting to topple one another, all fighting to grasp control. This war is just growing, and I don't think I can keep up."

"Hannah . . ."

"Let me stay. Let me leave with the Troffren."

"You don't want to do that. Don't let them win."

"Have you *seen* this galaxy?"

What could she say? *No, Hannah. No, I haven't.* That would be the truth. After all, what did she know but what she'd read in Gilgan's stories? The Felirean's dim yellow eyes burned with hurt. Elenah stepped towards her, reaching for her arm, but Hannah jerked back.

"Stop," Hannah said.

"Let me help you."

"But what good will it do? This thing will never end."

Elenah closed her eyes, imagining the sweet scents and landscapes of Etheron, imagining the safety and peace she had left behind.

"You can find your brother, Elenah, but you can't stop this war. None of us can. Not this time." She was gripping the sleeves of Elenah's woollen jumper. "Look at me."

"It will end."

"How do you know?"

"Because I'm not alone," she said. "I have the last wish of the bravest man I've ever known, right here." She gestured to her heart. "We can fight this together, Hannah." She took her cold hands and peered into her moonlit eyes. "You don't have to run away. You can fight. We both can."

Tears glittered in Hannah's eyes.

"Do you trust me?" Elenah asked.

Hannah shifted, releasing Elenah's hands and wandering several paces through the graveyard. Why had she come here, to such a terrible, lonely place? Elenah watched her closely, clutching the grey wool of her jumper. "Hannah? Do you *trust* me?"

The sky lit up with a vibrant white light. A single star appeared overhead, slashed both vertically and horizontally by silver streams. A billion more stars came flourishing to life around it, enchantingly. Elenah offered her hand as Hannah turned around.

"I've made up *my* mind," Elenah said. "I'm going to fight the Council, and I'm not going to stop until every last one of them is dead. If that means going to Tarthalus, taking out the Architect on my own . . . then that's what I'm willing to do."

"Do you really think you stand a chance?" Hannah asked weakly.

Elenah bit her lip. "Not alone. But we can build something together. We can find others, people just like you and me, victims of the Council's death march. Maybe we *do* stand a chance, but only if we stand together. And we *can* topple this thing, like Oswald said."

Hannah hesitated. "Okay."

"Why don't you rest? Amohria has told me where we can find help. I'm going to need you to fly us there at the break of dawn. Can you do that?"

The Felirean stepped towards her. "I guess I can try."

Chapter Twenty

CONFRONTATION

*Of all the magical alliances I've studied, the Starforged
has me intrigued like no other. Four highly-skilled
magicians, one of which has descended from a very curious
bloodline . . . I still wonder if they're out there, and I
wonder if they'll ever come back.*

Gilgan watched the cell door creak open, letting in a
tall shadow, which fell across the chamber floor. He
tightened his jaw, peering up at the dark figure. The
door slammed shut, and the lamp on the ceiling shook back
and forth, back and forth . . .

Slowly, the figure became a man, and the pale light fleshed
him out: tall, with grey hair peeling off his forehead, bushy
grey brows furrowed, lips cracked and frozen in a perpetual
frown.

Fex dragged his black glove further up his wrist, then
curled his knuckles until they popped. It sent a loud crack
ringing through the chamber.

Gilgan just watched him. It had been so long since he
last saw the man, so long indeed that they'd both been
young men when he did. But seeing him now . . . It was like

nothing he could have prepared himself for. It inspired an anger inside him so deep it frightened him.

"What are you doing, Fex?" Gilgan rasped, bunching his fists under the restraints of two steel cuffs. They grinded against his skin, pinching him like needles, but he stilled the pain. "You've become the very thing you swore to destroy. What you're doing is going to hurt a lot of people—yourself included."

"I would disagree." Fex paced back and forth, his white uniform flapping at the cusps. He'd changed since their last encounter, more than two decades ago, back when they'd fought side-by-side as magicians of the Starforged. Fex had surrendered to the galaxy's dark magic. It had torn apart his mind. And now . . . Now he was with the damned Council!

Fex stood there facing the wall, hands behind his back. "You are a fool, Gilgan. Did you really think you could hide from me? Hide the magic in those stones?"

Gilgan grimaced. "I did it for your own good."

Fex shrugged, pacing beneath the fickle white light. Shadows laced his wrinkled skin like a black spider's web. Gilgan welcomed the silence, blood boiling. He wished he could stand, but they'd chained him to a pole affixed to the ground.

"Why are you with the Council now?" Gilgan asked. "What are you trying to achieve?"

"I'm going to find those stones, and bring order to the galaxy!"

"By destroying it? *That* is the only thing you're going to do."

"Oh, but you're mistaken," Fex said promptly. "I'm not with the Council. *They* will destroy the galaxy with their warmongering. It's been two thousand years, Gilgan. You cannot expect things to get any better from here. Not through any natural means."

"You're playing with dark arts."

"Dark . . . Light . . . They're simply shades of the same thing."

Gilgan cursed. Once, they'd been like brothers. He could hardly believe—he hardly *wanted* to believe—that Fex could become so reckless, that he would ever dream of enslaving the galaxy with chains of fear and raise his own army fuelled by dark magic. "You're making a big mistake. You've never been very strong, Fex—admit *that*, at least!"

The muscles in Fex's cheek tightened, and he lashed out, sending a blast of energy into Gilgan's chest. Gilgan jerked backwards across the metal floor. The chains restraining him tore apart. He slammed the back wall and crumpled down in a pile.

Fex strode towards him. "Tell me where you've hidden those stones."

Gilgan tried to draw breath, but he had none left in him. *Hell. It's been too long.* In Fex's eyes he could still see the man he'd once been: a friend in a galaxy that had all but given up on him. As Fex approached, hands balled into fists, a great evil warped off him, a dangerous madness that clung to his body and refused to let go. It was *consuming* him.

"No," Gilgan gasped. "You cannot control this power!"

Fex grabbed Gilgan by the scruff of the neck and dragged him up along the wall. Gilgan held his breath, baring his teeth. "Tell me where they are!"

Gilgan's mind became a splintering mess. In the final days of the Daemon Wars, he had barely managed to stop Fex from reawakening the Dark Lord. In his desperation, he'd bound the power of Fex's necromantic spell to nine debris-flung stones. The sudden imbalance of magic had caused the Dead Winter. *He* had caused the Dead Winter. But in the aftermath he had divided the stones amongst nine people across the galaxy.

Somehow, Fex had found out.

Whatever happened, Fex could *not* recover them.

Fex's breath was like fire against Gilgan's face. His grip around his throat tightened. With his other hand, he spread his fingers over Gilgan's forehead . . .

Gilgan's mind came alight with pain. His vision distorted, lights and shadows blending together and adopting terrifying forms. He squeezed his eyes shut as Fex's face took on a frightening expression. Gilgan howled in agony, the sound more terrifying and more painful than anything he had ever uttered before. But in his pain he conjured *magic.*

Gilgan broke the chains around his wrists and swept his arms furiously through the air. The whole room shook, dirt and metal spraying upwards. The lamp on the ceiling snapped off its hinges and slammed a wall, but the infused light kept it running. Fex crashed against the far wall, dropped to his knees, then drew himself upwards, cursing.

The spherical lamp rolled halfway between them.

Gilgan delved deep into his mind's eye and pictured a gleaming black blade—a soulblade—and then he *summoned* it into existence. His arm shook, the room thrummed, and a short black sword clapped into his grasp with a spasmodic jerk. Black lightning bolts surrounded it.

Across from him, Fex had done the same.

Gilgan leapt forward and swung at Fex with everything he had.

Their blades clashed, exploding in a shower of black sparks. The strike echoed through the chamber. Gilgan grit his teeth and pressed down harder. Sweat streamed down Fex's face. Blood dripped from his eye and traced his rough-hewn cheek.

"You're weak, Gilgan!" Fex roared.

"Look at yourself!" Gilgan spat. "Look at what you've become!"

Fex's muscles bulged, veins popping like obsidian. His fingers grew tense, his hand sweeping between them, fingertips straining . . . *straining.*

Gilgan grunted, slipping his hand before Fex's and casting a bolt of ice. A crack of light ripped through reality and an icy kiss, colder than the winds of Kasnah, slapped him across the face as ripples spread outwards. Frost sprayed across the walls.

The flash of light threw him backwards, but Gilgan didn't wait to regain his full vision. He pelted forward, half-blind, through the sizzling air, and blasted Fex through the door with a precision-based spell. They emerged inside a massive cylindrical chamber. Fex rammed a metal-barbed fence, one that overlooked an impossible drop. The fence rattled. Gilgan pursued him, short black blade fizzling, into the vast prison complex.

A wide walkway skirted the chamber, surrounding the drop. There must have been dozens of levels, hundreds and thousands of prison cells. Light streamed from the ceiling, and portholes in the walls revealed lamps and endless space.

Gilgan roared, bringing down his sword. Fex was ready.

They clashed.

Once.

Twice.

Sparks rained upon his face like falling stars. Fex twisted away, sending Gilgan's blade gnawing through the metal fence. He cursed, clutching the hilt with both hands and spinning back upon Fex. His sword carved a crackling wound through the fence and, had it been a man, he'd be dead a hundred times over.

"Admit that you have failed, Gilgan!"

Their weapons met again. Fex kneed him in the gut and Gilgan staggered backwards, gasping for air. His leg buckled and he folded to one knee. *Goddamn mutation!* It had burdened him all his life. His master, Ithrial, had always told him how powerful he might be had he not been born with such unfortunate handicaps. Two. Only two—and by the gods, one was simply the colour of his eyes—yet two felt as good as a hundred.

He spat blood. It dripped onto the metal, shimmering, throwing up his reflection.

"Admit that you are weak!"

Gods, Gilgan thought. *He's fast.*

"You were my friend," Fex said. "Don't make me kill you."

He's so much stronger than I am . . .

Fex took a clunky step backwards, sweat cracking through his wrinkles. His black blade spewed sparks into the air. Blistering cold winds roared from the endless drop beyond the metal fencing. It was twisted into diamonds. Gilgan could see places where it was weaker, where maybe there'd been a fight, where maybe it had been put back together.

He gasped, "It doesn't have to be like this."

"Your fear has blinded you," Fex said, then started laughing. It was a darker, grimmer, more sinister sound than Gilgan had remembered from the old days. "Surely you have felt it. The parasite that is tearing this galaxy apart. The darkness that will break us."

Gilgan flipped his sword upwards, but Fex effortlessly parried it.

He swept his sword across Fex's body, but Fex flicked it away like he were some child.

He swayed to the side, his palm driving into the cold stone wall. His eyes burned with sweat. If this was where it ended, so be it. Gilgan was ready to die. But if he could take Fex with him, then it might mean the difference in this war. He grasped the hilt tightly. It whirred with the magical powers of the galaxy. He swung it behind his back, and launched another blow at Fex.

Fex met the forward swing with his own. *Crack!* Gilgan's body shook. Black sparks like fabledust erupted from their blades. Gilgan twirled his sword, and unleashed another swing. Fex deftly nudged it away. He lashed out again, from another angle, but there were only so many angles and Fex deflected those too.

Finally, Gilgan pummelled forward, breaking Fex's defences and striking his chest with his palm. Then, he spellcast with all he had left. Magic surged through him, like a violent storm. It erupted in a wave of energy. But this time the magic did not obey him.

He froze.

Fex grinned, then grabbed Gilgan's chest and dragged him closer. "You've wasted away, old friend." And then he jerked forward, extending his gloved hand, and blasts of lightning exploded from his fingertips. Striking pain lanced through Gilgan's body as it hit him with its full force. It threw him backwards. His sword flew out of his hands, the blade exploding into minute shards. He hit the ground on his back, breath hissing from his lungs.

"*Ithrial!*" Fex demanded. "He's got one too. Where is he?"

Gilgan rolled over onto all fours, his body half-paralysed, slipping into total shock. He managed to shake his head, but it was as much as he could do. His head was spinning. He thought of Teveran, and Elenah, and how he'd let them both down.

"Gods, don't do this," Gilgan hissed, trying to haul himself back up. For the first time in so many years, he could feel it again: a raw, unrelenting anger dragging at his body. Fex towered over him. His arm shook and his blade vanished into minuscule shards.

Gilgan climbed to all fours, feeling the power slip away. "You're making a terrible mistake. You're playing with magic of the kind that you are simply *incapable* of controlling." He managed to climb back to one knee, peer up into Fex's charred, death-sworn eyes. "You can kill me. Hell, you can find the others and kill them too. But it won't change anything. And, trust me, you will sorely regret restoring power to the Dark Lord."

"Where is Ithrial?"

"We have to work together, Fex."

"Where is he? And where are the others?"

Gilgan felt the barrel of a pistol against his forehead, black metal throbbing with the energy of starfire. It summoned memories of the two children of Etheron. Of Teveran out on the green fields, so full of life and joy. Elenah, who had always dreamed of seeing the stars. He'd seen her out there, in the battle over Mokuura. "You're making a mistake," he gasped. "If you do this . . . You're going to cause so much pain . . . So much suffering . . ." A tear fell from his eye and rolled down his cheek. "Fex . . . This isn't you. It never has been."

"They're all going to die, Gilgan. All because of *you.*"

"Just hear me out," Gilgan gasped. He couldn't fight back, no matter how hard he tried. To cast a spell would be like chasing a thread of silk in the darkness. Its allure was elusive. His body felt broken. "Fex," he breathed, rising off the ground, the barrel of the pistol tingling his forehead. "Fex . . . If you return the Dark Lord to his full strength . . . He will destroy you. He's not from this age. He's not a mortal being! Just *listen* to me . . . as your friend!"

Gilgan grabbed the barrel of the pistol and tried to shake it off. He summoned every last ounce of strength, but soon the pistol was all that held him up, and Fex's hand around the grip.

"Please," he rasped, sagging to his knees. He felt the hot rim burn a mark above his eyes. "You have to stop this. Stop this madness."

Fex looked down upon him. The muscles in his cheek quivered, as though he were suppressing something terrible. "Do you have one with you?" he calmly asked.

Gilgan shook his head. "No."

Fex took a long moment to respond. His jaw tightened, his eyes darted across Gilgan's body, and eventually he resolved to silence. Gilgan knew, deep down, that Fex believed him. Not because they were once the closest of friends, but because the magic in those stones could be felt by even the weakest of magicians. Fury flashed across Fex's face, but he seemed to be fighting it. His finger tightened around the trigger, and Gilgan closed his eyes.

"Don't do it, Fex."

Fex roared, slapping the pistol across Gilgan's face and sending him sprawling onto the floor. In Gilgan's fading vision, he saw Fex withdraw a commlink and say, "Pandion, alert the others." His voice was sharp, tempered by anger. "I have a powerful enemy magician in my hold. I want him relocated to the Tower immediately." Without waiting for a response, he killed the connection and gazed upon Gilgan again. "Until next time, old friend."

Then, the shadows took him.

CHAPTER TWENTY-ONE

THE FROZEN WORLD

*There's something about the Architect, leader of the
Forty-Ninth Council. My attempts to have an audience
with him went unanswered, and there are even rumours
he reports to an unknown advisor now.*

Nine troopers escorted them from the *Subjugator*, two
ahead, one behind, and three on each flank. Not
that Teveran could really see them through the haze.
Gods, he thought, teeth chattering. They'd given him a
jumper, a coat, a jacket, and an ivory scarf, but the blizzard
still froze him to the core. He stared through a pair of ice-
encrusted goggles as snow pelted his face. Icicles slashed his
cheeks, and when he tried to draw up his scarf to take a
single breath, the wind just tugged it right off.

"Hell," he spat. "Are you sure this is safe?"

"Safe, sir?" Snake laughed, trudging along beside him.

"Yes," Teveran hissed through gritted teeth.

"Nowhere's safe. Here just overtly less."

When they finally reached the Kasnan complex, Teveran
hurried through the massive glass doors and released a
shuddering breath. It evaporated in a puff of white mist. He

shook off the snow that covered him and exercised his frozen muscles.

There were six representatives from the *Subjugator*. One of them was his uncle; he wore a long coat that hugged the backs of his legs, and goggles that protruded from his face, painted white by the blizzard—they concealed his sickness. Fex was there, too, although he looked wildly unhinged; he'd hardly said a word. The rest comprised of various fleet officers and highlords. The burnt-faced Kloak. One who Fex had called Pandion.

Teveran blew a long breath and yanked off his goggles, stuffing them into a pouch hanging from his belt. *Let's get this over with.*

Two guards, dressed head to toe in white, multilayered robes, with pale marmoreal skin and beady black eyes, met them within the entrance. *Kasnans*, Teveran thought. They were a holy species similar in biology to humans, that had evolved and populated the world in the hundreds of years following the Battle of Haratheon. They watched him stoically, clutching vertical spears that divided their faces, but made no move to interfere.

"Keep up, Teveran," Snake said, slapping his back.

A short while later, they emerged through mahogany doors into a large, almost *reverent* chamber. The walls rose sixty feet, ending at a glass ceiling that revealed the storm outside. The room must have been one hundred feet wide and one hundred feet deep. Giant marble statues of various historical figures formed an inner circle fifteen feet from the walls. In the dead centre stood a table that could undoubtedly fit forty or fifty people. Upon the table were microphones; behind them, high-backed seats. Two thirds of these seats were filled.

Thrakk pulled him along, and Teveran sat down between him and Fex. Soon they'd all taken their seats save for Snake and the other troopers, and the Kasnan guards, who stood by the statues. Teveran wished he could stand beside them, not here beneath these scrutinising eyes. What did they all see in him? Were they stifling laughter at this very moment?

"I'm glad you could finally join us," said a healthy but aged man who sat behind a plate reading MATHRADEL. Teveran looked at the woman beside him, stern-faced, with a plate that read ATHAEA. Strange to see a so-called *Perfect Human* here.

In fact, these people had seemingly come from all over the galaxy. Teveran half-expected to see his father, in those emerald robes, observing through that single hazel eye.

He was doubly glad not to.

"Let's begin proceedings," said a grim-faced man behind KINGDOM.

And they did.

They chirped on about building new trade routes between this world and that, spent thirty minutes trying to move a fleet from point A to point B, argued over whether or not they should employ a new security force around Tarthalus . . .

Fex hardly spoke; outside the circle of discussion, Teveran tried to read him—but failed. Gods, it rattled his nerves just looking at him. Snake had told him Fex could kill a man just by thinking about it. After what he'd seen in the star chamber, Teveran believed him.

What felt like three hours later, Teveran woke to the sound of Thrakk slamming the table and shouting, "We *need* your cooperation!"

"It just isn't efficient," said the man from KINGDOM. "Our resources are too far spread."

"We're falling apart!" Thrakk rasped, then fell into a nasty coughing fit that sprayed his white kerchief with bubbling black blood. He wiped his lips pointedly and scrunched the kerchief hastily back inside his wet coat. "Please, just *listen* to me."

He's all that's keeping this fleet together . . .

Teveran anxiously wrung his frostbitten hands. Did they even know what they were doing? Had they become so large, so powerful, that they couldn't keep it under control? It was just as Fex had told him: The Council was breaking under its own weight.

"We have bigger problems now," said a woman behind ORACLE. She couldn't have been thirty, with auburn hair that burned amidst the beams of firelight. "You may not be aware, but there is a growing force nearby: a paramilitary threat that we can no longer contain."

"Bloody defectors," somebody muttered.

"We'll shut them down," Thrakk grated. "Just like we always do. They're nothing more than miscreants. But *this* . . . This is urgent. Gods, but I only ask for fourteen thousand credits."

"I think that is a much larger number than you think," the woman of ORACLE said, almost mockingly. She had deep bags beneath her eyes, as if she'd hardly slept.

Thrakk's second, his most venerated, Highlord Kloak, leaned forward over his steepled fingers and said, "Your support on this matter is *vital.*" He spoke in a more civilised tone than the Grand Highlord. His fiery hair seemed to have sucked in the lights of explosions. "We are struggling every day to meet the quotas set by the Architect."

Teveran jerked upright. *The Architect. He's the one in charge, the one on Tarthalus . . .* The Architect was the cause of all this trouble, all this despair . . .

The woman from ORACLE said, "It is because we are distributing our resources in the wrong places. War *evolves*, Grand Highlord, and we must adapt to fit its changing mould."

Thrakk laughed; it was a sick, horrible sound. "Do you wish to see this Council collapse? What you are proposing will only promise us a brisk and hurried *defeat*."

"You already have your new base," an old Azich man behind GORSE said. His dark eyes narrowed, and wrinkles crossed his forehead. "Your project has already been funded, Grand Highlord. What more do you need?"

"That's not the point," Thrakk persisted. "Without your support . . ."

It all became background noise. Teveran was still thinking about the Architect, and wondered what it would take to kill such a powerful figure. It was said the Architect's rise to power was one of the swiftest and most peaceful in recent galactic history, but you certainly wouldn't think it, not now. He often wondered if the Architect was a magician. Did he have magical guardians? Was he even a human being . . . or something else?

"No," said the woman from ORACLE, jerking Teveran from his reverie. "Inquiry declined. I'm afraid we just don't have the money."

Thrakk shook his head grimly, and his shoulders sank. "You fools," he muttered, and played no further part in the ongoing discussion.

The next time Teveran woke up, night had almost fallen and he couldn't feel his legs. He raised his goggles onto his head and drummed his fingertips upon the table, trying not to fall asleep. *How many planets does the Council control now?* he wondered; it was all that kept him awake until Fex touched Teveran's hand and whispered, "Stop that."

Teveran sighed, righted his back, and acquiesced to listen.

"Tell me again why I needed to be here?"

Fex sighed as they walked through one of the halls within the Kasnan complex. The sanctuary covered more ground than he'd thought, and every single corridor adhered to a pious sort of architecture, all vaulted ceilings and marble decorations.

He shot Fex a wary sidelong glance. The man looked tired, like he'd stayed up all night filing reports and doing whatever Thrakk's most trusted men did. He also carried a limp, which was new, and Teveran thought maybe he'd taken a bad step in the snow.

"You did well," Fex said.

"I did *nothing*."

They entered another chamber, smaller than the others, with a flat ceiling and a wide window spanning the wall. A red couch sat alone to the right, there were tapestries of dead kings on the walls, a glass coffee table tossed to the side, and a deck of cards on top.

Teveran followed Fex timidly to the window, where they gazed out across the landscape of Kasnah. Now that the storm had subsided, he could see much more. Dozens of ships, docked on stone platforms, and lights in the distance that suggested the sites of other civilisations. But who would willingly live out here, Teveran could not decide. He folded his arms and said, "I'm starting to think I'm just not cut out for this. Maybe it'd be better if I went back."

"Oh? And where would you go?"

Teveran glanced at him. His anxiety worried the food he'd eaten for breakfast. He had to be careful not to provoke the man. Teveran didn't really fancy death, and who knew how dangerous Fex really was? He swallowed, worked moisture into his mouth, then settled his shoulders. "I'm not a soldier. I'm not a hero. I shouldn't even be here."

"Blast it, Teveran! That's not true and you know it."

Teveran quietened. He would be doing a disservice to Gilgan's training if he admitted he couldn't feel the magic pulsing around Fex. The man was powerful, that was certain. Teveran lowered his gaze, taking keen interest in the icicles plastered against the glass. *Fex is dangerous*, he recounted. But his uncle trusted him. Why? What had Fex done to earn the Grand Highlord's trust? *And what the hell does he want with me?*

Fex brushed jagged shards of ice from the window, causing his face to become so much clearer. Folds and wrinkles. Bright blue eyes. "Something terrible is about to happen. I know this for a fact. The galaxy is falling apart. You've seen this, Teveran. You've seen the Forty-Ninth Council and the ruin of those that have come before it." He eyed him sharply. "Everything you know. The Council . . . Insurgents . . . Ma gicians . . ." He grimly shook his head. "This is something far, far worse. And that is why you're here. The galaxy needs you."

Teveran just stood there. He felt himself weaken, and fold,

like a piece of metal under a boiling, boiling flame. "You said the Council won't last much longer," he uttered. "Well, how long do we have, then? How long until it falls apart?" Was he really considering this?

"It is a tedious process, dismantling an army like this," Fex said, almost tiredly. "But it has already begun. I know you've seen this too. They're beginning to fight themselves."

The frightening truth was: Teveran *had* seen this chaos. But he'd also heard it, not just from the mouth of Fex, but from Snake . . .

"And if I follow you," Teveran started, "then we're just going to abandon the Council and do what? What's your plan? Do you even have one that, you know, doesn't involve me walking around and killing people? I'm sorry, but that's just not who I am."

Fex eyed him darkly, but Teveran made an effort not to lose his cool. Fex might have been a very powerful magician . . . but so was Teveran. "Peace doesn't win wars."

"I'm not going to be your weapon."

"I don't need one," Fex said. "But the offer still stands. A chance to be a part of something larger than the sum of us both. A chance to escape the Council, and maybe even end this war. Though, you're stuck with me either way. I've promised your uncle that much."

"This is my alternative," Teveran said, almost to himself.

"Your alternative to what you saw on Corion."

Teveran's gut lurched. His heart rattled. He slowly looked over at Fex, who buried his hands in his massive white coat. "What did you say?" Teveran stammered.

"They're lying to you, Teveran. All of them. Your father . . . Your friends . . ."

"You don't know what I've seen."

Fex smiled. Gods, but he looked so old, like a man left too long in the ocean, resurfacing only to pass on his ancient tricks. The snowfall reflected in his cobalt eyes.

Those eyes . . .

Suddenly, he recalled their mission to Corion, and what Commander Vallon had said: *I don't know how this happened.* And Teveran felt himself go stiff.

It was as if somebody had orchestrated it . . .

"It . . . It was you, wasn't it. You sent me there." But how was that even possible? How could you pull off something so calculated, so terribly inconceivable?

Fex just stared through the icy glass.

"You tried to *kill* me," Teveran hissed.

"No," Fex said. "I tried to open your eyes to the *truth!*"

Teveran sidled away from him. "I'm . . . I'm going to be the Grand Highlord one day. I'm going to lead this fleet." But he was only regurgitating his father's own lies. He saw the officers all sitting around that table, clueless. Nobody knew what they were doing.

He saw the troopers blowing apart those Taurans.

He saw his uncle cough into his bloody kerchief.

"Soon there will be no fleet," Fex said.

Teveran's eyebrow twitched. *And by the gods, I believe you,* he almost said. He turned vacantly towards his reflection in the window, covered in melted snow and layers of clothing. He was beginning to sweat under all this. Fex paced several feet closer, staring speculatively out the frosty window. Teveran tried to figure out the man, but there was nothing in those eyes save for the reflection of snow. "You're going to destroy the Council from the inside."

Fex simply stood there, hands clasped, magic pulsating around him.

"You're crazy, you know that?"

"Not as much as you think."

Teveran didn't like this at all. Thrakk was supposed to be in charge here, not Fex. *Thrakk* was the Grand Highlord of this fleet. *He* was meant to be issuing all the commands . . .

Not *Fex*.

His mind flew back to that galactic star map, to the fury wreaking havoc upon worlds. He'd seen Etheron be charred, everyone dead. What had Fex seen? What did he know?

"It's okay to be afraid, Teveran. But I've known men just like yourself. Some of them I have failed, but within you is a very powerful magician. You can make a difference. You can make your family proud." They stood only a few paces apart now, the snow falling behind the glass.

Teveran looked at Fex, and almost saw *Gilgan*.

Gods, no, don't think like that. He couldn't afford to. Fex wasn't going to help him. He was talking madness! He was a threat to all of them . . . wasn't he?

No. Not to him. Not to *Teveran*. To him . . . he was an ally, an ally in a galaxy that had all but turned against him. Maybe there was a way out. Maybe he could save him . . .

"Who are you, really?" Teveran asked.

"What you have heard is most likely the truth."

"I haven't heard much that would make me trust you."

"Hmm. What I think is more curious is . . . who are *you?*"

"You know who I am."

"It's just that I couldn't help but notice how . . . *similar* your spellcasting technique was to that of a man I used to know." Teveran felt himself go cold. Fex stood merely a few feet away from him now. "You were taught by Gilgan, weren't you?"

Suddenly, everything seemed to freeze. It was as if the blistering winds had smashed through the glass, as if suddenly the ice had begun to set him in place.

"Gilgan?"

"He was my friend. Unfortunately, after the Daemon Wars, we all went our own ways. Thought it might be best if we all put our pasts behind us."

"He never spoke much about the war."

"I don't blame him. It was truly terrible."

Teveran was shaking. He could feel it again, the surge of spellbinding magic revolving around Fex. It was like nothing he'd ever felt before. He almost believed that Fex could achieve his goal of rebuilding the galaxy. "Gilgan raised me up more than my father. I mean, he taught me all I know. I . . . I miss him."

"It's okay to miss the ones you love."

"Do you think I'll ever see him again?"

"If the Council does not get him first."

Teveran nodded half-heartedly, then spun around and started towards the door. "I should be going. We still have a few days here, right? Maybe I should rest."

Fex stopped him. "Wait, Teveran."

Teveran froze, snowflakes sliding off his clothes. He turned a fragment of an inch and met the corner of Fex's eye. "What is it?"

"Take care."

Teveran remained standing there for a while, then puffed a shaky breath and threw open the door back into the long, winding halls. He needed to get away from Fex so he could delve back into his own thoughts. Was he actually considering his offer?

He knows Gilgan . . . But why hadn't Gilgan ever mentioned him? Teveran picked up his pace, searching for Snake. *He's lying. He can't possibly know Gilgan.*

But there was so much *truth* in everything he said . . .

After navigating the halls for several minutes, he began to wonder if he would ever find the exit. Standing in a narrow corridor flanked by marble statues of gods and various other historical figures, he started to regret leaving without Fex.

He was my friend . . .

My friend . . .

A door opened up behind him, and Teveran turned to see a young man walk out. The man let the door fall closed, looking up. Their eyes met, fire and ice.

"Korvis?" Teveran breathed. No, he must have been seeing things now. It couldn't be Korvis. Korvis was supposed to still be on Etheron . . .

"Teveran," Korvis breathed, and a wide smile lit up his face. It was him. Korvis walked down the corridor to meet him, dark hair somehow neater than the last time Teveran had seen it. He wore a white coat and gloves, an attire not unlike Teveran's own. "I was told you'd be here."

Teveran caught himself grinning, and tried to adopt a more passive expression. He'd only spoken to Korvis a handful of times before leaving, and had never really been fond of the man, but, truthfully, he was just grateful to see a familiar face.

He shook Korvis's hand as they met halfway down the hall. "How the hell did you get here?" he asked. "Nobody told *me*. Gods, I thought I was the only one they'd taken."

"How is everything?" Korvis asked.

"It's . . . fine." But then, staring at this familiar figure amidst all this craziness, he was struck by a sudden thought. "Do you know what happened to Elenah? Is she okay?"

Korvis's smile faded slightly; he looked slightly concerned.

"Dammit, tell me what you know!"

"I don't know anything," Korvis said, shaking his head.

"My uncle—sorry, Thrakk—told me she *left*."

"Gods, I don't know anything about that. Fex found me the day the Council came and that was the last I saw of her." He turned to face the statue by the wall, rubbing his chin. "I'm sorry."

"Wait, you've been with Fex too?" Teveran asked, bemused.

"Not entirely," Korvis said. Another door opened somewhere along the corridor, and a trio of Kasnans walked out, each of them dressed in holy robes. They didn't glance in the direction of Teveran and Korvis; they walked the other way, talking in low voices. "I've been training with someone else. Man called Damian."

Teveran choked. "*Training?*"

"It's not like Etheron here, man," Korvis said in an enchanted tone of voice, as though this were not a military campaign, but a holiday. "There are magicians among us."

"Here? In the fleet?" His heart was pounding. Who was Damian? The only magician he knew of was Fex . . . Surely there weren't more . . .

"Yes."

Gods, he hadn't even considered it before. Fex wasn't the only one. This was much larger than he'd ever thought. It was power like he'd never known. No longer was it just him and Fex. Now . . . He was beginning to feel something he hadn't felt before. Something invigorating.

"Korvis, how many are there?"

"I couldn't say. I suppose two, at least."

Teveran found himself smiling again, but he wasn't entirely sure why. The sight of Korvis reminded him of Etheron. Together, alongside however many magicians there were among this fleet, could they restore things back to normal? Could they actually end this war?

An order of magicians, like the ancient times . . .

"We should head back," Korvis said, starting back up the corridor in the direction the Kasnans had gone, "before all the shuttles are gone."

"Do you know the way?" Teveran asked.

"I hope so. Come on."

Chapter Twenty-Two

SAECON IV

In the immediate years following the Daemon Wars, magic underwent a state of paralysis. The Magical Inquisition fell. Magicians fled into the outer regions. It was the end of what was, perhaps, the greatest era of magic we've ever seen.

The morning brought a troubled wind to Telaron. It moved in a spiralling motion, whipping up leaves and catching them in slow, tedious orbits. Elenah stood in front of her hut, dragging on her grey jumper and staring at the *Divinity*, which was docked in the distance.

"I have repaired your ship," Amohria said, standing beside her. She'd come to wake her at the break of dawn, although Elenah hardly needed it. She didn't get much sleep, for her dreams were filled with pictures of Teveran and Gilgan, and the mission he had left her.

The galaxy was falling apart, and it needed a hero. She had to save her family, and her home, and she had to stop the Forty-Ninth Council.

"How did you do it?" Elenah asked.

Amohria smiled. "We Troffren . . . We have our ways."

Then, she wrapped her hands around the staff and started walking to the shuttle. Elenah followed her. Hannah was already there; she'd volunteered to help them correct the navigational computers. "It should be able to carry you to Saecon IV," Amohria said. "But you must remember to be careful. A terrible storm has raged over the moon for many hundreds of years."

"Thank you so much for your help," Elenah said.

"I hope you find what you're looking for."

A group of Troffren had gathered to wish them farewell. Their yellow eyes followed her as she emerged from behind a thicket of trees and strode towards the *Divinity*. Hannah was standing out the front, her arms folded, smiling weakly.

"One last thing," Amohria said. Elenah stopped where she was, then turned, glancing at the little Troff bouncing along behind them. It was Eukaloo, dressed in a sapphire cloak, with a band of colourful lights around his forehead.

Eukaloo bowed his head ashamedly. "*Bokne carta*," he muttered, proffering a single necklace made of glowing yellow beads.

"What's this?" Elenah whispered.

Eukaloo pointed exaggeratedly to his neck, and Elenah hung it around her own. The beads were strung up in the shape of a swirl; it fell to the top of her chest. She turned to Amohria. "What is it?" she asked again.

"It is the aura of *Orilight*," said Amohria. "It will keep you safe."

"Orilight . . ." She tested the name. "Thank you."

Amohria rested one hand on Eukaloo's shoulder. "Remember," she said, "the man resides in the castle, alone.

He will show you to your brother." Her eyes flashed, then she said, "But you *must* be careful."

Elenah looked from one Troff to the other. Eukaloo's eyes glinted, reminding her of the Talisman, the *map*. She'd returned it to Amohria.

"Thank you," Elenah said. "Really."

"Then you had better be going," Amohria said. Elenah drew a deep breath, her stomach tickled by nerves and excitement, and she let it out slowly. *I can do this.*

She spun around and strode towards the *Divinity*, the ancient shuttle from Mokuura's wastes. Hannah greeted her by the entrance. She, too, wore an Orilight necklace. "Ready?"

"Can you fly?" Elenah asked.

"I'll do my best," Hannah said, following her inside.

The grass, the trees and the lights of Telaron shrunk and faded as they ascended. Starfire hissed through the engines, propelling them into the sky.

Elenah looked to the stars.

I'm coming, Teveran, she thought. *Just hold on.*

THEY LANDED AMONG A STORM, rain hissing against the viewscreen, spitting down from swirling grey clouds. Hannah navigated the *Divinity* through the darkness, and set it down on a muddy bank. Water and mud sprayed out in all directions, jetted outward by the ship's thrusters. Tall trees were battered by the damaging winds. Sticks and shrubbery went flying. Animals fled.

"I'm sorry," Hannah said. "I'm not a very good pilot."

"It'll do." Shielding her eyes, Elenah stepped out of

the shuttle and took in these new surroundings. Thunder crashed in the skies over Saecon IV. There was a vague emerald glow in the air, emitted from the planet far above. And silver bulbs of light glittered about, showing the way. Elenah shivered, drenched by the rain, but she didn't mind it. The only thing that mattered was finding this man, the recluse that lived somewhere on this stormy moon.

"Are you sure this is the place?" Hannah asked.

"Yes." Elenah stepped several paces forward, sticks crackling all around. Amohria had warned her of this moon, and the warning was rightfully deserved. There *was* something different here, a presence in the storm, pulling on her emotions and causing her thoughts to whirl astray. She tried to ignore it. She *had* to, if she was going to find this man. "Come on, Hannah. We might not have much time."

Side-by-side, they sloshed through the mires, sticks and dirt flying through the air. Hannah had landed in some sort of jungle clearing—probably one of the only places they *could* land. Within the screams of thunder, Elenah could hear birds squawking, and animals darting through the bushes. She tried to peer beyond the trees, but could only see a livid, rolling mist, tainted with the ever-present emerald glow.

Elenah . . .

She shook her head. Her raven hair threw off steaming raindrops. It drizzled down her skin, and felt like some gentle form of fire.

The knights are gathering . . .

"It's this way," Elenah said forcefully, trying to distract herself. She turned on her heels and led Hannah out between the trees. Their Orilight-infused necklaces threw yellow lights across their path, illuminating bugs that crawled on ten legs, insects with great shells that hid in the bushes as if pretending to be rocks. The orbs of light, floating like dandelions, seemed to be *leading* them somewhere.

"Do you think he's still here?" Hannah asked.

"I hope so." But she couldn't help but think he wasn't. After all, who would live in such a terrible place? And even if he *was* still burrowed behind those castle walls, then what if he told her that Teveran was dead? What if this was all for nothing? Where would she go?

Stop thinking like that, she chastised herself.

Skeletal insects buzzed through the air. Keening whispers came from the bushes. Twigs and leaves cracked underfoot. Elenah's feet splashed in more puddles than she could count, puddles of water and mud that were far deeper than they telegraphed.

"You know, it's not so bad," Hannah said, her voice barely audible over the thunder. A crack of lightning sent a flock of birds shooting out of the treetops. Elenah brushed hair out of her face and squinted against the daggers of rain. "Saecon IV is an *anomaly,* you know?" Hannah said, lifting her voice above the crashes of thunder. "A glitch in the galaxy."

Her voice faded in the storm's hallowed screams, replaced by a deep voiceless whisper that seemed to make the plants shrivel in terror.

Why have you come here?

"Who are you?" Elenah muttered, ducking her head against the winds.

I am the voice of the thing that can help you save your brother.

"How do I know I can trust you?"

Do you trust yourself?

Elenah blinked hard. *It isn't real.* She looked at Hannah,

who seemed to be interested in a leaf she was carrying. *Nobody's talking to me. I'm just . . . I'm delirious.*

The castle emerged through a gap in the trees.

It rose up between uneven ground and emaciated trees, plastered against the darkening sky: an imposing sight. Glass and broken metal speckled the ground. Large, bulbous flies nestled in cracks in the black stone. This was an ancient structure; it must have been many thousands of years old.

As they drew closer to the heart, Elenah was struck by the vile stench of death. She quickly covered her mouth to stop herself from gagging. "This is bad," she muttered.

The castle walls were crumbling. The obsidian towers posed among the heart of the storm, surrounded by coils of vigorous lightning. Deep cracks split the battlements from top to bottom: memories of conflict and war, all frozen in time.

"Gods," Hannah gasped. "It's all dead."

They stepped onto a courtyard speckled with rotting bodies, mostly skeletons. The things posed in all sorts of demented positions, limbs and faces twisted in displays of horror. Elenah couldn't even tell if they were human. She was sure that many were not. Ahead, parts of the castle's face had been completely decimated, as if by explosives. The ground shimmered with bullet casings. Yet, there were no bullet holes in these bodies.

"They're all dead," she breathed, standing motionless. Limbs were detached, pasted to the ground with dried blood. She could smell them, hear their desperate cries.

She thought of Teveran.

She *had* to find this man.

"Elenah?" Hannah whispered. "I don't think anyone's here."

"You don't have to follow me if you don't want to," Elenah told her as she pinched her nose and made her way across the courtyard, weaving between the bodies. "Whoever did this . . . They're no longer here." Somehow, she knew this, though she wasn't quite sure how. It was just a feeling, like a single dead note in a symphony . . .

Elenah gazed around, searching for movements, for signs of life. *Anything.* There were battlements high up, with flagpoles that had long lost their flags. Stone watchtowers, with wooden ladders still propped up beside them, stood strategically at the corners. This place had been important enough to require a good defence, whatever it was.

Thunder crashed.

What if it's a trap? she wondered. Amohria wouldn't lie to them, would she? Hannah must have been thinking the same thing; she had a scorching look on her face. It said, "Maybe this isn't such a good idea." Elenah ignored it, glancing at the bodies, fighting the urge to be sick. These people had been massacred, not by bullets, but . . .

She frowned, following a bloody trail. As lightning cracked, she heard Hannah's soft, indecipherable voice. Elenah tuned it out, and focused on the way this man had been killed.

Someone had cut him in half.

Gods . . .

"Hey!"

Elenah snapped her head upwards, leaping away from the body. Upon the battlements stood a massive group of people, merely silhouettes against the flashing grey sky.

Elenah gasped, raising her hands as they pulled out rifles and descended upon them.

"Don't move!"

Elenah backed away, her foot skidding across a puddle. She tripped on something solid and splashed in the mud. It drenched her skirt. She groaned, rolling onto all fours. Hannah pulled her back to her feet. "Careful," she whispered.

There were more than a dozen people with rifles, converging upon the courtyard. Elenah's heart hammered. *I'm going to die.* Rifles found their aim. Human men, women . . . Some of them looked twenty and others could have been sixty. *Nonhumans,* too.

"Identify yourselves!" The man speaking hardly looked older than Teveran. He wore a jacket soaked through, a ragged red scarf around his neck, and he carried a long-barrelled pistol . . . within a shimmering *skeletal hand.* Elenah gasped, choking on her breath. The man raised the pistol just a tad, threateningly, and the rain splintered off the metal.

And then she recognised the crimson gear on his shoulder. *The rebellion . . .*

"Did you follow us?" the man asked, glancing from her to Hannah then back again. The strange exoskeleton grew from his fingertips and up his arm, disappearing beneath the sleeves of his coat. Elenah could do nothing but look at him, and wonder why they were here.

The others moved in to surround them.

The man beside the first looked older. He wore the very same jacket, with a matching crimson gear. It was perhaps Elenah's hindered eyesight, but it seemed as though his skin shifted to match the colours of the surrounding storm. He murmured to the skeleton-man, though what he said was inaudible over the howling winds.

"Did you do this?" Elenah croaked.

The man with the skeleton-hand shook his head. "They were dead when we arrived." His voice still carried the same weight. He didn't lower his weapon. "What are you doing here?"

"I . . ." She couldn't form any words. "What . . . What have you done?"

"We didn't do it. Answer my question."

"We're looking for someone," Hannah said firmly, stepping forward. She still had her hands in the air, rain slapping her pale green skin. Elenah tried to grab her arm, but she slipped away.

"You won't find them," said the leader.

Elenah felt the air tighten. She felt the terror of the dead, like a stain in the air. Who were they? Soldiers? Rebels? Troopers? Had this castle belonged to them, or had they come here to take it? Splashed on the backs of her eyelids was the man who had been bisected . . .

The rebels were coming closer now.

"You're with the rebellion?" Elenah asked.

"We're some of them," said the man, and he'd come close enough now that Elenah could make him out clearly. He was young, with dark eyes not too unlike her own. The rain had drenched his hair half-black. "What's that?" He pointed to the glowing gift from the Troffren.

Elenah grabbed it defensively.

"Put it on the ground."

"But—"

"*Drop it.*"

She worked it off her neck and tossed it into the mud. Beside her, Hannah parted with her own. The warm yellow glow flickered, lighting up puddles of blood, viscera, and severed fingers. Then, it burned out.

"It's not safe here," the young man said. "You'll want to come with us. We have a base, and we have numbers. This moon is not safe for any of us."

"But . . ." She had to find the old man. He lived here. He could help her find Teveran. If she failed, she might never get this chance again. "You have to help me," she said, striding forward in desperation. "I need to find—"

He grabbed her arm. "The one you're looking for is dead."

"*Dead?*" It wasn't possible. The fact leached away her emotions and left her feeling hollow. Tears dribbled from her eyes, although she wasn't sure if they were tears or just the rain. Everything seemed to move in slow motion, and all she could think of was Teveran, and Gilgan, and Oswald, and Eukaloo, and Amohria . . . and she felt her body go limp and soon all that held her up was the skeleton hand of this young, stoic soldier of the rebellion.

"He can't be dead . . ." Elenah gasped.

"He's either dead or gone. Long gone by now." Then he yelled over his shoulder, "Graham! Help me take these two to the ships. I think the captain will want to see them."

Chapter Twenty-Three

THE LESSER EVIL

The man, Armenis Ignatious, was by all definitions a madman. Though, respectable by all accounts. It was his crazy mind that gave birth to the game, Azherok, which I have been wont to play on occasion.

Bayle Lockwood, King of Etheron, stood before his palace doors. The deep mahogany wood, harvested from the forests on the other side of the world, glistened within the lights of lamps and chandeliers. He clasped his hands tightly behind his back in an effort to stop their trembling. It wasn't a frightened tremble, but a side-effect of his new medication.

By now, it was the only thing keeping him alive.

Two palace guards flanked the door, trying not to look at him. He could barely make them both out, for he only had one eye. Gods, but he'd never gotten used to losing it. If he'd not been burdened with this disease, the lack of an eye might have been what got him killed at the end of all things. He could never be sure what lay there in the emptiness.

Bayle drew a deep breath, his stomach twisting into a vicious knot. *Just breathe,* he told himself, yet even that was no simple task these days. His chest burned, for he spent each night in raging coughing fits. He'd employed a new doctor in the last couple of weeks, a young woman from Oracle who knew complex brews and magic charms. But Bayle saw in the sadness on her face that there was little she could do for him now. Not even magic could save him. Bayle's sickness had no logic, no cause . . . It was just *there*, and it was slowly eating him alive.

But you're still their king, Bayle, he told himself, *and these people are relying on you to fix this mess.* He nodded towards the guards, and they moved to open up the doors.

"Wait!" came a croaky voice from behind. Bayle grunted, turning his head to the side. The guards looked at him expectantly, and held the doors shut a moment longer. "Bayle," the woman said. She sounded tired, her voice awfully weary.

Rose, he thought. She'd stayed behind when he'd told them all to leave. It angered him; he didn't want her to get hurt once everything fell apart. And things would. Very, very soon.

"Let me come with you," Rose said.

"Stay inside the palace," Bayle told her, yet it hurt even to speak. A cough swelled inside his chest and he half-reached for his kerchief. *No,* he told himself. *Be strong.* His long-dead father had taught him how to rule a kingdom. Bayle had never been the High Prince, was never meant to join the ranks of the Galactic Council, but he still had a kingdom to protect.

And he was failing.

He righted his back and wiped the beads of sweat from his forehead. Rose emerged in his vision. She took his hand

and stood in front of him. Bayle couldn't bear the pain of looking at her. He would never forget the vibrant young woman she'd been, the one who had helped to raise him up when his own parents couldn't always be there.

"Bayle," Rose said. "Look at me."

Somehow, he found the strength to.

"Let us face them together," Rose said.

"I can't let you come with me. They're here for *me*. I'm the only one they'll reason with. But even still . . ." He grabbed her shoulders and forced himself to stare into her eyes. They were emerald, like the gilt on his robes. "I want you to stay inside the palace, and make sure everyone else is safe. Can you do that for me?"

A tear twinkled inside Rose's eye. For a while she simply stood there, her tight lips pursed. Then, she *smiled*. It was so subtle that Bayle might have just imagined it. "Your children would have been so proud," she said.

"I failed them," Bayle conceded, gently pushing Rose away and motioning for the guards to open up the palace doors. He righted his slouched posture, shoved back his shoulders, sniffed in the musty scent of the palace and his own sickly body. "But I will not fail this kingdom."

The palace guards swung the doors open.

Bayle stepped outside. The hungry fog raced past him, throwing his cape backwards and ruffling his greasy hair. The air smelt of petrichor and soot. Pale morning sunlight, colourless and grim, sprayed across him. Though, after being refined to these palace halls for so many years, even this sad, dreary light was almost refreshing.

A huge Banshee machine hung in the hazy atmosphere, throwing off glittering lights and silver Ragnaroks. It spun slowly, emitting a thunderous rumble that resounded all around him. The roars of swooping Ragnaroks untangled his gut, rattled his heart.

The roads were noticeably less crowded; he'd evacuated as many people as he could, and as many as were willing. They'd used every single ship in the spaceport. But his people had been replaced by more troopers, and more fleet officers, all parading about.

The city, and the world along with it, was almost all theirs.

A bright red shuttle descended from the sky, wisps of fog streaming off its wings. He felt a twinge of anxiety in the pit of his stomach, but decided he didn't have much left to lose.

He started down the stairs.

One step forward. Another. And another.

Gods, it hurt. His body ached, like he'd not exercised for years. This sickness was stripping away his muscle, carving away his bone. He'd never expected to feel so weak, so incompetent, at barely thirty-eight years old.

He reached the last stair as the crimson shuttle landed. Dust blew up off the cobbles and rolled through the air. A dozen troopers assembled at the shuttle, clearing a perimeter. Bayle picked up his pace. The shuttle's landing ramp flew down, slamming the cobbles with a crash. And then a tall man emerged from inside: a highlord who served beneath his older brother—now the leader of one of the Forty-Ninth Council's last remaining fleets.

Bayle slowed, then stopped, and waited for the highlord to meet him halfway between the palace and the crimson shuttle.

The highlord was accompanied by six of his own troopers, each of them bearing rifles and two crimson streaks on their left shoulders. He wore a neat ivory suit, with a flat collar, and the arched insignia plastered beneath it. His hair was the colour of fresh blood, and half his face was blistered and burnt, as if by hot irons.

"Master Lockwood," he said carefully, twisting his hands behind his back and raising his clean-shaven chin. The sun fell behind his stark figure, almost casting him in the form of a silhouette. Accompanied by his own personal guard, he looked intimidating.

Bayle tried to hide the sickness that betrayed his guise, grabbed his hands to stop them from frantically shaking. "Well met, Highlord Kloak."

Kloak was the overseer of the Council's secret project here, which was due to commence this very day. Bayle, however, had no intention of letting it. This was Etheron, a Free World, not a *battlefield*—and he would not let it become one.

Highlord Kloak glanced about, sunlight sliding through rivulets in his melted skin. Bayle wondered what he'd done to earn it. Had it been an accident, or a *punishment?* "It is a wonderful place," Kloak said, his voice warm like the flickering of fire.

"A shame it will become the base of something so terrible."

Kloak eyed him warily. Bayle pretended not to notice the way the highlord's right hand crept slowly behind his back, to where they often wore their pistols. "I do hope you're not thinking of breaking such a healthy alliance with the Forty-Ninth Council."

"Don't tell me you care about them," Bayle said. Kloak smiled. Bayle took one step towards him. Fog streamed around their ankles, as though they were standing in very deep water. "I know your kind, and I also happen to know that the Council is *vulnerable.*" He began to exercise his fingers. "A man like yourself would struggle to contain his excitement. A chance for glory. A chance to have a slice of power in this galaxy. Tell me I'm wrong."

"You're quite good, Master Lockwood."

"I know my brother, and he's just like you."

"Hmm. Well, we all know where your brother stands," Highlord Kloak said, his eyes glinting as though he knew something Bayle didn't. "But please, tell me: Where do *you* stand?"

"Where I've always stood," Bayle said. "With my people."

Kloak smiled, but there was no joy within his half-burnt face. The muscles in his jaw began to twitch. Slowly, he nodded, feigning calm. "Well then, Master Lockwood . . . I think it's simply fitting that you shall *die* with them."

Kloak whipped his pistol around his body and thrust it against Bayle's gut. Bayle grabbed the barrel and bent it downwards. The pistol went off, a bullet slamming the cobbles and throwing up chinks of rock. The chamber revolved frantically to the next bullet. Bayle brandished his own pistol and fired two shots into Kloak's stomach. The highlord jerked backwards, then bounced back and slapped him over the face with his gun.

Bayle skittered, the world shaking around him. His head pounded. He teetered on the spot, lifted his pistol once again—but found he was holding nothing.

Kloak roared, lunging forward on the momentum of his last hit, and cast a bolt of *fire* out of the air. It erupted halfway between them, swallowing Bayle in flames.

Screaming, Bayle crumpled to his hands and knees.

Behind the wall of blistering fire, Kloak dropped to one knee, grasping his bleeding gut. A livid expression flashed across his face as he dragged himself off the ground and waved his pistol about. "I want them all dead! Every last one of them! Etheron belongs to *me*, now!"

Bayle collapsed, feeling the flames gnash at his clothes, chew at his skin and bone. There must have been a hundred troopers gathering, bullet fire going off everywhere. "We could've done this peacefully!" Bayle cried. He snarled, tried to rise to his feet, doused in fire. Kloak's six troopers closed in on him, mere shadows against the blazing sun.

"Peace has failed you!" Kloak screamed.

"My children . . ." Bayle whimpered; a stray thought. Suddenly, a conversation he'd had with Gilgan came crawling back into his mind. *Let me train her,* Gilgan had begged, when Elenah was still just a child. *She's strong. In fact, I believe she might be just as powerful as Teveran. Untrained, she may become dangerous—to herself and to others.*

No, Bayle had told him. *You must train Teveran, and Teveran only.*

He could still see Gilgan's vacant eyes.

It was his biggest mistake of all.

Bayle managed to summon a sorry, mocking laugh. Blood and bile escaped his mouth, foaming over teeth and broken lips, streaming down his chin and splashing on the charred cobbles. "You fools," he gasped, wringing his bloody, burnt hands in front of him. "Soon you'll see what you've done. You'll see what this galaxy has become!"

"Gods, he's mad," Kloak spluttered. "Take the city," he said. "Do it as peacefully as you can. Take prisoners if you must." Then he pointed at Bayle. "On my command. *Fire!*"

Teveran tossed another square chit into the centre of the table, raising the pot by another fifteen credits. The chits were a dull silver in colour, lightweight and cheap to manufacture. As well as the squares, there were triangles, worth five credits each, and circles, worth only one. The pot sparkled with the shapes of all three varieties.

Across from him, Snake looked up from his hand of cards, his emerald eyes narrowed suspiciously. Counting the pot, perhaps. There wasn't much there, maybe seventy credits all up. He looked back down at his cards, then shrugged and lay them face down.

Teveran smirked. "I thought you were good at this."

"It's just my luck," Snake said dismissively, scooping up his glass of water and reclining in his seat. "I fear it's betrayed me today."

"You don't believe in luck," Teveran said.

"Oh, he does," Fleet Officer Bredin said, "when there are *cards* involved." Bredin was an even better azherok player than Snake. He had coppery hair and freckled cheeks, and wore round wire spectacles that he must have made himself.

The *Subjugator* was still stationed over Kasnah. As it would happen, each day the elected highlords and officers would shuttle down to the planet's surface for several hours of discussions and arguments. With all the luck Teveran had left, it turned out he wasn't required for the rest of the conference. This gave him time to think.

"Hell," Bredin said, laughing to himself. "I've only been here three weeks, mind you, but I think half the people I beat have blamed it on bad luck."

"Maybe you're just lucky," Snake suggested.

"*I* don't believe in luck," Bredin said with a smirk, sliding forward one of his own square chits. It caused a stir in the pot. He chortled as he looked at Snake. "By the way, everyone knows you don't fold when you're only playing for chits, especially not when you've barely played a card."

Snake smiled. "The way I'm going, I won't be able to afford lunch." Bredin nodded in agreement, then looked at Teveran expectantly. Teveran looked down at his cards.

In this quiet game of azherok, each player could hold four cards. Teveran had *Alden of the Night*, *Hapless Ori*, *Moonshrine*, and *Windsong Staff*. Not his luckiest hand. The goal was to build a sequence of five cards, with a total value of twenty-seven. Bredin said the number was holy to the ancient Asmoreans. But, to make things harder, your sequence required one card of each variety: *Hero*, *Weapon*, *Conflict*, *Location*, and *Magic*. It was like storytelling, and Teveran thought the game mechanics could make for some interesting stories.

"Play or trade," Bredin yawned.

Teveran scratched his chin contemplatively. Each turn you could *play* one card—thereby adding it to your final sequence— or *trade* one. He'd gotten quite used to trading; that was the general flow of the game. The only other winning condition was to accumulate the sequence called the Azherok, a word of the Asmoreans meaning something close to *Dominion*, though Snake said he'd only managed that once, and Bredin didn't believe him.

"Here," Teveran grumbled, proffering *Hapless Ori* to Bredin, then nodding towards the face-down card at the top of the main deck. "And I'll take that." Trading let you choose the face-*down* card at the top of the main deck, or the face-*up* card at the top of the discard pile. Teveran was feeling lucky; besides, that *Paper Flute* certainly wasn't going to help.

Bredin took *Hapless Ori*, chucked it at the top of the discard pile, then passed him the mystery card. Teveran swiped it from him eagerly and glanced at the image on the front.

His heart leapt.

It was *Fex*: stoic, calm, cryptic.

He almost dropped the card. He blinked and the image went away. *What the hell?* He stared at it for a while longer, but it was just the *Ghost of Ethril Dai*, most likely just some figure of ancient Asmorean mythology. His value was zero.

"Teveran," Snake chortled. "You need to work on your tell." But Teveran hardly heard him.

They're lying to you. Fex's voice . . . But why could he hear him now? He looked up and around, at the troopers and officers all bustling around the cafeteria. It was here that he'd met Fex all those days ago. Or had it been weeks? Months? All time had been compressed into the space of mere moments. *Soon there will be no fleet,* Fex had told him.

Snake had said the same thing.

Suddenly, he was back in the Kasnan chambers, listening to the men and women bicker about trading and weapons and new forces of security. He blinked to try to forget it all, but it kept knocking at the back of his head. One fact that he knew was all too true:

The Council was falling apart.

And in its place . . . A new order of magicians. Fex, Korvis, the man called Damian—who had been teaching some of the younger magicians—and who knew how many more? He was sweating, his heart palpitating. Puzzle pieces were falling into place.

Snake's commlink suddenly beeped across the table. He jerked it out of his pocket and raised it to his lips. "Lieutenant Hartwell speaking," he said rather sternly. There was a moment of silence; Teveran watched him eagerly, his heartbeat racing. Snake nodded—uselessly, at that—to the speaker on the other end of the network. "On my way."

"I suppose that concludes our game?" Bredin asked.

"Yeah," Snake grumbled. "Sorry about that."

"What happened?" Teveran asked, throwing down his cards and the remainder of his chits. Snake eyed him uncomfortably. *Elenah*, Teveran thought, but it was not her.

"There's been a resistance," Snake said.

Cold dread washed over him, and all he could do was sit there and look up at Snake, who had stood from his seat. *Gods, it's happening*, Teveran realised, though he wasn't sure how he knew. *They've attacked Etheron.* "What are you going to do?" he asked.

Snake grumbled to himself, stepping away from the table. "I have to take care of the situation," he said, almost tiredly.

"My father . . ." Teveran gasped.

Snake averted his eyes.

Teveran leapt up and slammed the table. "*Tell me.*"

"I'm sorry, Teveran. Please . . . Sit down."

"Bastards," Teveran gasped, but suddenly he had no strength left to stand.

Bredin pulled him back down into his seat. "I'll take care of him."

"I don't need taking care of!" Teveran snapped. He looked

pleadingly at Snake, but the trooper said nothing, just turned and strode away. He was not the only one; about three dozen other troopers were rising to their feet now. Bredin, a fleet officer, was among the handful that stayed behind. Teveran watched them all, heart racing.

A resistance? he thought. *But who? Surely not my father . . .* He grew colder the more he thought about it. He became aware of how quiet it had gotten.

"He did this," he whispered.

"Sorry?" Bredin asked.

Teveran leapt to his feet, almost toppling his seat. "It was Thrakk. He's not fit to lead this fleet. And now he's killed my father. I know it . . ." He trailed off into mere breath, suddenly feeling exhausted. Bredin was eying him like he'd gone mad.

But Teveran wasn't mad . . . and neither was Fex.

"I have to find him," Teveran said, striding away.

"Who? Thrakk?" Bredin hurriedly asked. "Wait—"

No, Teveran thought. *Not him. Not him . . .*

THE STAR CHAMBER WAS EMPTY but for the old man standing by the central orb. He was bathed in shadows and silence, with a concentrated look that bespoke of deep thought, as he absently picked at the fluff on his ivory highlord's uniform.

The galaxy surrounded him.

"Fex," Teveran said, breathless. He'd run the whole way, and only now did he realise he was lucky not to have gotten lost amid all the winding corridors. Was his memory that good? He slowly stepped into the chamber and the door slammed shut behind him. Beams of light crisscrossed in every direction. Planets and moons and mysterious twinkling bulbs were speckled across it. "Fex, he did it."

"Yes," Fex said. "I suspected as much."

Teveran barely heard it over the rasping of each breath. His feet rang loudly as he crossed the chamber. Fex, just another old man to the untrained eye, stood crookedly, as if something were weighing him down. The burden of this fleet, perhaps, or something much more sinister. "We have to do something," Teveran said, still trying to catch his breath. "My sister . . ."

Fex waved his hand across the orb, dismissing the star map. Then he turned and Teveran could feel his eyes judging him, weighing him. "Your sister is safe . . . for now. As for your father, and for your home, I cannot say the same. I'm sorry."

"Can't we go there? Maybe we can still stop it."

"There's nothing we can do."

"*You* can. You're strong, Fex. I've seen what you can do."

"Not even I can defeat the Council on my own." He began to creep closer, casually, the spots of darkness swimming across him in swirling black whorls.

Suddenly, Teveran saw again the chaos rip through the galaxy, saw the flames that it cast upon Etheron. It hurt, burned his blood. This was all the Council's doing. They were going to destroy everything in their blind rampage. They'd already begun.

But now Teveran had a chance to stop them.

"I . . . spoke with Korvis," Teveran said, though it was barely a whisper in the huge star chamber. "He told me everything, about your army, the magicians . . ."

Now Fex eyed him with renewed interest. "Did he?"

"I don't want to be Grand Highlord anymore. I want to *fight*. When are you going to teach me? Korvis has been taking lessons with Damian. So give me your alternative, Fex, the one you told me about when we first came here. I want to help."

Fex grumbled. "It is too early."

"But—"

"You must have patience."

"Korvis is already training—"

"*Teveran!*"

Teveran stopped, hands clenched in fists. Fex turned away from him and began pacing through the chamber. "You're not making much sense," Teveran said. "Do you want me or—"

"We *will* defeat the Council," Fex said, "but only in time. If it were so easy, I would've done it years ago. As for now, you must listen to your uncle. The pieces are not in place."

"The pieces . . ." Teveran muttered. "Fex, we don't *have* time."

"Why are you questioning my judgment? Do you think me a fool?"

Teveran grunted, folding his arms.

"Soon enough," Fex said, "this fleet will be yours, and we will use it to cripple our adversaries. In due time, the Forty-Ninth Council will join them. But that time has not yet arrived. It looms, yes, but it is still beyond our reach. Do you trust me, Teveran?"

Teveran reluctantly nodded—he *had* to trust him, because he had no other allies here, and this was *war*. Having powerful allies was the only way he was going to get through it alive, and possibly make it back to Elenah, and rid the galaxy of the Council's stain.

"Besides," Fex added, "you're not ready to handle this burden."

"Not ready?" Teveran blurted, striding up behind him. "I *am* ready! I came here myself, didn't I? You gave me an alternative and I just chose it!"

Fex spun and flicked his wrist. A lash of wind ripped Teveran off the floor and threw him up into the air. It trapped him, clutching his body like a thousand incorporeal hands. He could hardly breathe, could hardly move. Fex eyed him from beneath, cobalt eyes alight. "You're too *slow*," he hissed, then shouted something barely understandable and Teveran went sprawling backwards across the room. Then his body ignited with electric bolts. "Too *weak!*"

Teveran tried to cast some sort of defensive shield. A silvery mist rippled through the air in front of him. It lasted only a moment, before Fex was lifting him up by an invisible hand, latched around his throat, *choking* him.

"And most terribly of all," Fex said, veins pulsing in his face, "you're too *naïve!*" He slammed Teveran against the wall, knocking the breath from his lungs, then dropped to one knee himself, panting. Fex dragged a small vial out of his pocket, and downed some of the black ink-like liquid, so fast Teveran hardly saw it through his tears.

Teveran's head was spinning. "You bastard. What the hell was that for?"

"Blast it," Fex said. "I'm just trying to teach you a lesson."

"Teach me how to fight, Fex!"

Fex didn't bother standing up. He simply leaned back and

sat down, and eyed Teveran from across the room. "Very well."

Teveran nodded. "Okay. Then let's start." He crawled up off the floor and staggered towards Fex, pain still writhing all over him. "Let's start before my uncle destroys this fleet, before he destroys my home, and my sister, and the galaxy . . ."

A glint of light flashed across Fex's eye. "If you so desire it."

CHAPTER TWENTY-FOUR

THE VANGUARD

Founded in the year 43c01 by the revolutionary, Eva Barella, the Galactic Liberation Movement was originally a careful program designed to slowly bleed out the Forty-Ninth Council. A decade later, the movement was in pieces.

They were the rebel cell, Vanguard, of the Galactic Liberation Movement. Their meagre fleet of battered AT-Shuttles and other assorted models emerged from the dusty clouds of Devar, splitting through shades of yellow, orange and bronze. Streaks of golden sunlight trailed them, spinning through cracks in the haze.

Elenah clambered up to one of the shuttle's rattling portholes. Lurid crepuscular light flashed maniacally behind all the bronze and gold. In a flash, the clouds broke away and the brownish-yellow fields of the moon opened up before her. The wilted leaves of crooked trees snapped off their branches as the ship descended, then swiftly landed.

"Welcome back," said a dark-haired man outside the shuttle. He nodded to them all as they debarked, his bone necklace clattering. "Morning. Nolen, I do hope your leg is still working. Flair! I told you not to go with them; you're sick . . . Ah, Renar, here's your ointment."

Elenah followed the man with the crimson scarf and the skeleton hand. He leapt to the rugged dirt field and approached the man outside. "Levis, did your shipment arrive?"

Levis smiled, clapping his hands together. "Argus Kellier," he said. "Always good to see you in one piece. Yes. I should have no problem patching you all up. Did it go well? Is there anything I should be aware of? Anyone lose a finger?"

Argus chortled as he slapped Levis playfully on the shoulder and walked past him. "Not this time." He dragged up his scarf so that it shielded his mouth and nose, and then gazed across the fields as though seeing them for the first time.

Elenah avoided Levis's wary stare as she crept up behind Argus and took in the rebel base. Dead grass rolled in the wind. The other soldiers scurried about with their weapons close. The air here was stifling, and tasted bitter. The sound of dry leaves scraping the rough ground was grating. "This is everyone?" she asked, noting how quiet, how *sparse* it seemed.

"This is just Alpha Base," Argus said, his voice husky. He spun around and took her in. "We're the Vanguard unit. The cells are spread thin, times as they are. I know it isn't much, but . . ." His eyes flickered to the side as Hannah came striding up towards them. "It serves its purpose well. Follow me."

Elenah gazed in wonder as they crossed the shipyard. The various spacecraft looked ancient, battle-worn, like none she'd ever seen. Were they manufactured alongside the defunct Magicus-Class of ships, like their *Divinity*? Had the rebels commissioned them themselves? There were old warplanes lurking in the background, and all sorts of technology and equipment scattered across tables, piled in buckets and crates.

The base proper was an assortment of cubic wooden structures that seemed hastily strung together with nails and brute force. A tall, crooked hill stood behind it all, with a rickety farmstead at its foot. A wooden watchtower leaned against it; a sniper was perched at the top, gazing into the brown sky and not paying much attention to anything else.

Elenah wasn't sure what to make of this place yet. It was nothing like what Gilgan had said—though, surely she'd gotten used to this discrepancy by now. As was better expected, everything looked dead. The grass was brown and withered, the rivers had dried out, and were now all brown and muddy. The sky was bronze, laced with swirling storm clouds. She hoped this air wasn't toxic, but it certainly smelt like it. In the distance, men and women were up and about, humans and nonhumans alike.

So this is the Galactic Liberation Movement, she thought.

"Are you coming?" Argus asked. Elenah shook herself from her reverie, then looked at Hannah, who was watching her eagerly. Argus waved them forward with his skeletal hand, sunlight lacing his harsh features. "Time's wasting."

THEY MET THE CAPTAIN IN THE YARD outside the farmstead.

He stood with folded arms and beady eyes that were concealed behind the haze. He wore a close-fitting brown coat, with the crimson gear plastered across left shoulder and breast. A curly grey beard stretched across his jaw. His hair was matted black with dirt.

"We found them on Saecon IV," Argus told him, screwing the lid back onto his canteen. "But . . . We didn't find much else. Sorry, Cap. It was empty."

A despairing look crossed the captain's face, though it was as if he found the news unsurprising. "Then we were too late," he said, glancing at the girls. He seemed to weigh Elenah especially, pulling the hairs of his beard contemplatively. "Well?"

"I thought maybe they might know something," Argus said.

The captain raised his brows. "And . . . *do* they?" He seemed to pose that question to Elenah in particular, but it was Hannah who answered.

"No," she said. "Not really. It was the Troffren tribe, wasn't it, Elenah? That's what it was. They sent us there. I'd imagine they would've like to see us die there, too."

"Quite unremarkable," the captain said.

"If you were asking for my opinion," Argus said, "the place was attacked weeks ago—months, maybe. It was a massacre. No signs of life." Something in his words made Elenah feel uneasy, and she once again saw the man with his guts leaking on the dirt, his body sheared in half. Only a magician could do that—a very powerful one.

"I'm glad you got there *after* it happened," the captain said. He stepped forward, dropped his hands and rested them on two things strapped into his belt: a bulky pistol and a tarnished radio. In the light, he looked like one of the heroes Elenah had read about in Gilgan's stories. "I'm

Captain Jethre Hawkwind. If you would like to stay, we have room."

"More room than we would like," Argus grumbled.

Jethre seemed somewhat irked by Argus's comment. And, for a second, he reminded her of Gilgan. It made her heart race. The captain looked at her strangely, as if he knew something she didn't. "I wonder . . . Is it luck that brings the leaf back home, or the wind?"

Elenah had no idea what that meant. "Sorry?"

Jethre bowed his head and scratched his chin. "Just thinking out loud. Argus," he said, pulling a round chit from his pocket and tossing it to the soldier, "why don't you tell Makar to cook us a feast? I'm not placing an order, but I'm feeling like some stew."

Argus caught the chit. "Yes, Captain."

Jethre watched him go. "He's a good soldier, Argus. The others say he's blessed by the gods themselves. But what I think . . . He's just a good man. I wish we had more like him." He caught himself, anxiously rubbing his dry lips, and then put his hands on his hips and gazed at a distant point somewhere in the sky. "I didn't catch your name."

"It's Elenah," she said. "And this is Hannah."

Jethre's eyes lingered on Hannah longer, as though he were trying to decide whether or not she was actually a Felirean. Jethre seemed like the kind of man who knew what was happening in the galaxy, and the terrible state of it. "Elenah . . ." he muttered, then turned and started walking through the base, beneath the shade of wilting trees. Elenah followed on his heels, striding to keep up. Jethre smelt stale, like he'd not taken a shower in years. "So, are you going to tell me what led you to Saecon IV? Or to the *Troffren*, perhaps?"

Elenah bit her lip. Barely a week ago, she would've called the rebels traitors, terrorists and conspirators—like her father had. But these were the people fighting the Council, and now the Council was *her* enemy too. And, somehow, Elenah felt as though she could trust Jethre. She drew a deep breath and thought, maybe, with the luck of the gods, these people could help her find Teveran and save her homeworld.

"I was looking for someone," Elenah said. "A man. He lived in the castle on Saecon IV and . . ." She saw it again, a flash of the bodies strewn across the courtyard like newly laid grass, tangled in their own guts. And it worried *her* gut.

Jethre looked notably stiff. "Such are the times." He grunted, stopping outside a small hut, the door squealing on its hinges. "It would be unkind for me not to offer you hospitality. There are terrible times ahead. The days before the Council strikes, I can count on two hands. We have food and water, and you look like you could use some."

"I . . ." Elenah started.

Jethre cocked his head. And it all came out at once. She told him about the occupation of Etheron, and her brother, and the Council, and how she just *knew* he was in trouble.

The captain scratched his curly grey beard contemplatively, but he didn't look surprised. Did *anything* surprise him? All he said was, "It's dangerous out there. You should stay here. Though, I'm sure you will get your chance to rescue your brother, eventually."

Elenah nodded, hoping that time came sooner rather than later.

"As for now, let's get you two patched up, and fed. Gods,

you look atrocious." Elenah just nodded in acquiescence, unsure what to say or what to feel. *There's still time*, she told herself. *He's still out there. He's still alive.* She watched Jethre walk off, then her eyes wandered into an uncertain point, the browns and yellows all mixing into one.

"Hey," Hannah said. "This is good. This place . . . We might really have a chance."

"Do you think so?" Elenah asked. She walked over to a bench and sat down upon it, patting out the folds in her skirt. "I just feel like the galaxy is doing everything in its power to stop me from finding him. First Mokuura, then Saecon IV . . ."

"Yet here we are," Hannah said, sitting down beside her. Her cloak bristled about herself. It was tattered in places, and the cowl was hanging by mere threads now. The pink in her hair looked even more scattered, her natural brown becoming more prominent.

Elenah bit her lip. "I just can't wait around knowing he's out there. And not just him, but all of Etheron." She looked at Hannah. "And your home, too."

"I think it's too late for *my* home," Hannah said. "But yours . . . Well, it gives me something to fight for, at least. Knowing that, maybe, I can make a small difference somewhere."

Elenah considered it; she was beginning to realise how much she needed someone like Hannah, just to keep her focused, to have a friend to care about in terrible times like these. "Hannah?" she said, nervously wringing her hands. "Do you think we're safe here?"

"I hope so," Hannah said. "It *would* be nice."

"It would be, wouldn't it . . ."

ARGUS STRODE INTO THE COOKING TENT, which was pitched nearby the sparring fields, a simple structure of four walls and a single tarp for a ceiling. Makar was the only one inside, a tall balding man in a white apron, the little hair he had pulled back in a tail.

"The captain's ordered a feast," Argus said, slapping Jethre's silver chit upon one of Makar's benchtops beside a pile of dirty plates and bowls.

Makar laughed, busy stirring the chunky contents of a huge pot. "I knew there was something I liked about that man," he said, almost in a sing-song way. Argus couldn't help but feel happy when he saw Makar's beaming grin and smelt his cooking food. It reminded him that the war had not yet drained the passion from everybody. So, there was a certain spring in his step as Argus turned to leave the tent.

"Oh," he added. "He said he's in the mood for stew."

"Then stew it is!" Makar said, waving his stirring spoon. His booming laugh followed Argus back out into the dry, humid air of Alpha Base. He dragged his crimson scarf back up over his mouth and nose. Inhaling this stuff probably didn't help his breathing—which was already quite terrible at the best of times, a curse adopted from his mother.

"Argus, come over here." Jethre stood nearby, looking quite splendid in his captain's outfit—which, quite frankly, wasn't so much unlike all the others. What separated Jethre was not how he dressed, however, it was everything else. The way he stood. The hardened iron in his eyes. Jethre had been through hell and back, and now he was doing it all over again.

"What is it, Cap?" Argus asked, lowering his voice.

"It's the girl," Jethre said as he led him away from Makar's tent and the sparring fields, to a patch of several skeletal trees. As they approached, a single brown bird flocked from the branches of one, throwing dirt in their eyes.

Argus ducked his head. "The girl? Which one?"

"Elenah," Jethre said when they had stopped. "Come closer. She's important. I can't tell you how, or even why—hell, I hardly know myself—but if I don't make it—"

"Captain . . ."

"No, it's a possibility we must consider," Jethre snapped, clearly annoyed. "If I die before it's over, then I'm bestowing the duty of looking after her upon you. Do you understand?"

Truthfully, he didn't understand. The girl, Elenah . . . Hadn't she just arrived here? She was no one of any consequence, wasn't she? But he nodded despite this, because he trusted Jethre, and even though he could sometimes just be a cryptic old man, he was always right.

"I'll do it," Argus said.

Jethre grabbed his shoulder. "I appreciate it." Then he left in a hurry. Argus watched him, dirt flicking up in his tracks. He didn't know what made the girl so important but, at the end of all things, it didn't matter. He was a soldier, and so he followed the orders of his superiors.

That was the only way they could turn this into something bigger.

It was the only way to build his new empire.

Chapter Twenty-Five

Dark Magic

The Dark Lord's reign lasted five years, brought down by one fatal flaw and the perfect set of circumstances. I still wonder about the galaxy that might have been, had he not been thwarted.

They were going back down to the surface.

Teveran cursed as he sat in Fex's private shuttle, the cold of Kasnah already glazing up the viewports with a fine layer of ice. The planet was a death zone, abandoned for thousands of years, and the gods knew what creatures lurked within the snow. But that wasn't even the worst of it. The prospect of going out there in the pitch of night, alone with no one but Fex . . .

That was what really unnerved him.

"Do we have to do this here?" Teveran asked, feeling the shuttle sink through the bottom-most layer of atmosphere into the freezing, powerful winds.

"We must do it out of sight," Fex said from the cockpit.

"And the two of us taking a shuttle down in the pitch of night wasn't suspicious enough?" Teveran asked, rubbing his hands together, already feeling the bite of cold.

"I am a highlord," Fex said. "I've earned their trust."

A moment passed, ice scratching the windows.

Teveran sat up. "How did you do it then?"

"How did I convince your uncle to let me into the fleet?"

"Not just that. You're a *highlord*."

"It was not as exciting as you think," Fex said. The clouds stirred, then broke away, throwing them into the darkness of Kasnah. "I met him in a time of great need, a time before the *Subjugator*, when your uncle didn't have a ship at all."

"How's that?" Teveran asked.

Everything jolted as Fex landed the shuttle on a bank of ice, which cracked and groaned underneath the weight of it all. "I *saved* your uncle," he said, turning off the engines. All he left on were the lights, illuminating a huge chunk of the wastes.

"Saved him from who?" Teveran asked, his voice louder in the silence.

"The Architect had sentenced him to Area 664."

"Area 664?" Teveran whimpered. "What the hell did he do?"

"Pissed off the Architect," Fex said simply, stepping out of the shuttle and into the cold. "And the Architect . . . Well, he hasn't forgotten."

Teveran cursed as he followed Fex outside. The ice clutched his bones immediately, although he wasn't sure if it was entirely the wind, or thinking about being sentenced to Area 664. It was impossible to grow up without hearing its name.

It was in every scary story.

Teveran wrapped himself up tighter, trying to stave off the cold. He wore the same outfit he'd worn many times before, although the planet was so much colder now, in the night lit only by Fex's shuttle and the blue moon above.

"Come on," Fex said. "We don't have much time."

Teveran caught up with him and they walked abreast, away from the safety of the shuttle, into the great pit of darkness ahead. They'd landed at the gates of what looked like an abandoned town, with stone structures jutting from the ice and snow at extraordinary angles. As they walked through the rusted, black metal gates, Fex gestured with his hand and flames lit up across the buildings, burning restfully. Teveran tried to conceal his awe, but the white mist that left his mouth betrayed the gasp. Fex didn't seem to notice; he was walking briskly ahead.

"This place has been abandoned since the Battle of Haratheon," Fex said, taking him for a stroll through the town. "It is also a place *very* strong with magic."

"Why's that?" Teveran asked, eying a frozen statue that stood by the side of the road. It vaguely resembled a woman holding a sceptre, although it was difficult to tell.

"Who knows," Fex said, shrugging. "The touch of magic is simply more poignant in certain worlds, in certain parts of the galaxy. Kasnah was a holy land, once." As he said this, they passed a small shrine adorned with icicle flowers and frozen candles. Teveran tried to read who the shrine was dedicated to, but the inscriptions were not of any language he knew.

"Is there a connection between magic and all things holy?" Teveran asked.

"Magic is the gift of the gods," Fex said. "You should know this. Gilgan was a very holy man. Some, like himself, have even claimed to *speak* with the gods."

"Really?" He was certainly not aware of that happening before, but as he thought about it, he realised it *did* feel different here. There was magic in the air; he knew this even though he couldn't really see it. As Fex stopped by a frozen fountain, Teveran closed his eyes and drew a slow, deep breath. He felt something swelling inside him, something *pristine.*

He was also beginning to realise, merely within these past few days, that he knew hardly as much as he once thought. Gilgan's teachings had barely scraped the surface. But with Fex . . . With Fex he could continue his training and become the man they all needed him to be: a magician in their grand new order, with the strength to save the galaxy.

"Are you going to tell me why you brought me here?" Teveran asked, letting the sensation pass over him. He suddenly and distinctly became aware of the icy wind rushing over his bare skin, and the sound of snow swirling through the air. It was so quiet, so lifeless.

"We're waiting for someone," Fex said.

Teveran's heart leapt. "Waiting for who?"

Fex said nothing. Instead, he began rubbing his hands together as if he could possibly be human enough to feel this cold, and sat down on the edge of the fountain. He was lit by the blue moon and the fires he'd cast all about the town, ghost-like. "Speaking of Gilgan . . . Did he ever show you dark magic? Did he speak of it at all?"

Just hearing his name made Teveran bristle. A twinge of heat ran through him. "*Dark* magic?" He continued somewhat hesitantly, while simultaneously glancing around for this person they were waiting for. "He told me about it, but . . . he said it was dangerous."

"Gilgan never liked it very much," Fex said, almost ruefully.

"I suppose you think otherwise," Teveran said.

"Well, Gilgan was a very skilled magician, although he was scared of a lot of things. He was also too close-minded. He was afraid to venture into the unexplored, if you will. But I want you to understand that dark magic should not be considered a lesser form of magic, nor that it incites some sort of . . . evil deity like the old mages taught it. Dark magic is made up of three streams: Psychomancy, Summoning, and Necromancy. I am very confident in your abilities to learn at least one of these in the time we have together."

"And . . . which would that be?" Teveran asked nervously.

"Psychomancy," Fex said. Teveran nodded, not quite sure if he liked where this was going—but he'd asked for it, hadn't he? He needed Fex's help if he was going to escape his uncle's clutches and maybe get the chance to save his homeworld. "I say this because your connection to the source will be a great benefit in this particular stream. Secondly, understanding the laws of Psychomancy will assist you in other aspects, too."

"Do you really think I can be that strong?" Teveran asked.

"Stronger than you can imagine," Fex said. "Though keep in mind, some of the greatest magicians were not born any more gifted than yourself. It is what drove them, what they believed in, that gave them power. You already have so much magical talent, but that doesn't mean you won't have to work. You will need to work hard, and fast, times being as they are."

"Okay," Teveran said, nodding.

Suddenly, the air split open and a woman emerged, dressed in a white coat, with her short, ginger hair waving about uncontrollably. Teveran gasped, wondering how she'd gotten there so quickly, but it was Fex who spoke first, rising to his feet.

"This is Alice," he said. "She is one of the finest Spirit Magicians I have seen." Teveran contemplated her, wondering what position she was hiding in within the fleet. He didn't think she was a highlord. Maybe an officer? Somewhere in the military education department?

"Nice to meet you, Teveran," she said with a friendly smile. Her lips were bright red, brighter than the freckles that covered her face.

"You know who I am?" Teveran asked.

"Fex is very fond of you."

"Don't go telling him that," Fex said, walking in between them. "He might start getting ahead of himself, doing something stupid."

Teveran smirked.

Fex put his hands on his side and gazed up into the darkening sky. "Alice, I want you to help Teveran learn to control his own powers, and to influence the magical currents in others, as well. He's very powerful, very gifted . . . Though, it's often the untrained powerful who are the most in danger of harming themselves, or others. Understand?"

"Got it," Alice said. "What about you?"

"There's something else I must attend to," Fex said.

Alice didn't question him, and so Teveran felt like he was in no position to either. He knew it would be something related to the other magicians. He wasn't entirely sure how many there were on board the *Subjugator*, and certainly didn't know how many others were on Fex's side elsewhere in the galaxy, but he was one of them now.

Soon, they would come out.

"Take care of him for me," Fex said.

"I'll do my best," Alice said.

Fex nodded, then turned on his heel and departed through the snow.

"He's really going to end this war, isn't he?" Teveran said, more of a statement than a question. The more time he spent with Fex, the more he realised this was the *only* way to end the war. An army of magicians. Victory by the might of magic. The galaxy was built on it, after all. Forged in the debris of a magical explosion . . .

"We *all* will," Alice said, gliding closer to him.

"How many are there?"

It took her a couple of moments to consider this question, but when she finally answered, it was in a quiet voice. "At least nine that I know of, including yourself." She bit her crimson lip, and gazed at the fountain where Fex had been. "But there are many more, I've no doubt. Fex is keeping this a very secretive operation. He's got magicians all over the place. Dozens of connections." She didn't seem so certain of it all.

"And they're just like me," Teveran said. "I've always been so fascinated with magic, but my father didn't like it. He . . . They called him a heretic, you know? The kind of person who denies magical practices. He outlawed it in our world."

"Well, I suppose we're going to have to make up for all that lost time," Alice said, offering him a sneaky smile. She must have been seven or eight years his senior, but gods was she attractive. He wondered if beauty like this could be crafted with a kind of enchantment.

He smiled back. "Show me what I have to do."

Fex materialised in the sitting room within the royal palace of Etheron, silver particles of *Essence* shimmering in the air around him, gradually blinking out. He landed gracefully and immediately strode forward to meet Kloak, who was standing behind the couch, accompanied by four crimson-streaked soldiers from his own guard.

"A congratulations is in check," Fex said, standing roughly in the centre of the room. Outside, a thick grey mist rapped up against the windows, causing the light to take on a silvery hue. The lanterns on the walls had been ignited.

"Yes," Kloak said, although he didn't look too happy about it. Fex glanced at the blood that stained the highlord's austere clothing. "Mind fixing me up?" Kloak asked.

Fex cast a simple restoration spell upon Kloak, healing the wound, then said, "It might take a while before the pain goes away. Tell me: Is everything under control?"

"The city belongs to us now," Kloak said. "Though, I would have been more thrilled if we had managed to save the clock tower. They must have bombed it before we came."

"Yes, there were reports of open hostility following the High Prince's capture."

"There were magicians here," Kloak said grimly, walking to the back of the couch and leaning on the headrest. The effect of the firelight and the silver from outside on his burnt face was one of great fascination, like he was glowing with a robotic aura.

"Magicians? Did you find them?"

"I found their leader, guy called Morgan, but he was just a

pirate. I have reason to believe there was at least one magician among them, but he might have been killed."

"A shame," Fex said.

"There was likely another; he was using charms."

"No good," Fex said. He smirked as he turned away and walked to one of the windows, gazing out through the mist and onto the empty, wasteland-like roads. "I suppose there will always be those willing to defy their government. This was a Free World." Then he turned around and imagined Gilgan standing in this very room, with his walking stick and those mutant, silver eyes. He must have come here after the Dead Winter—that was when the Treaty of the Free Worlds was signed. He must have come here seeking to escape.

I wonder if he's still alive, Fex thought. He hadn't heard back from Pandion after Gilgan was relocated to the Tower. He was sure it was Volhous who would end up with him. Maybe he would be able to interrogate the right information from Gilgan, and do what Fex couldn't.

"Work on casting a protective spell on the city," Fex said. "We may need it soon."

"I will get that done imminently." A moment passed. Kloak looked troubled as he stepped away from the couch and folded his arms. His guards, troopers in immaculate armour, with crimson streaks on their plate, stood around him.

"What's on your mind?" Fex asked.

"I'm concerned about the boy."

"Everything is going according to plan," Fex assured him.

"His family ties will be very difficult to break. His father is dead and we killed him—"

"He does not need to know that."

"And what of his sister? She's still out there."

Fex had been considering this very carefully ever since he first learned of her existence. "She will be dealt with," he told him. "If it's his allegiance you're worried about, I assure you his hatred for the Council is only growing. He is beginning to realise he has friends among the magicians, and I don't see him betraying us anytime soon. He has nothing to go back to."

Kloak didn't look entirely convinced. "You're putting a lot of faith in the boy. What about this sickness, the one that took both his father and his uncle?"

This was the one flaw in the plan. Not even Fex had managed to understand what it was, or how to stop it, but the illness might cause a problem somewhere down the line.

"We will figure something out," Fex said.

"I hope we do, for your sake."

"For the sake of all of us."

Kloak nodded. Then, deciding there was nothing more to be said, Fex turned around and pulled out his glass vial of Essence, which would send him back to the *Subjugator*. He had more work to do. He uncorked the lid, channelled the waves of magic that connected all the worlds of the galaxy, and departed without a trace.

CHAPTER TWENTY-SIX

VISIONS

Where did it all begin? What is the root of all magic? And is magical ability tempered through bloodlines, or does it decay? I've searched countless years for the answers to these questions, yet I am no closer now than I was when I started.

"Their armies are preparing an attack," Argus said, punctuating each word with a shaking skeletal fist. "The longer we stay here, the better the odds we never get the chance to leave."

The rebels surrounded him, lounged on crooked wooden chairs, standing with folded arms. They were assembled inside the farmhouse beneath the hill, in a square room lit by the bronze sunlight. It shone through windows, illuminating twinkling motes of dust.

Elenah watched them from the edge. It was her second day here, and this place was ostensibly safer than any she'd been to before, yet she still felt tense, as though she stood on the precipice of disaster. Maybe it was knowing that things were finally in motion—and all that lay ahead of them was warfare, and even more bloodshed.

Graham, one of the more elite of the bunch, stepped into the circle, squeezing his fists and shifting from foot to foot. Graham intrigued Elenah; his skin often changed colour, depending on his surroundings. She guessed it was some sort of mutation, like Argus's hand. Graham's grim black eyes flickered about, seemingly searching for something. A candle gleamed upon a wooden table just outside the circle, although its light was diminished by the twinkling rays of mid-morning sun. Graham shook his head and said, "Argus, we're no better out there than we are pinned up in here."

This caused a ruckus from the soldiers.

Elenah's gut tightened. Hannah stood beside her. On the other side of the room stood Captain Jethre Hawkwind, notably stiff. Jethre scrubbed his beard, his lips moving but no words coming out. That man always looked on-edge.

Argus and Graham seemed to lead the debate. Occasionally, other soldiers chimed in. Humans, Taurans, amphibian Anthraks . . . She didn't know many of their names or even all of their species, but she was sure she'd read about them all before. People with furry skin, with red skin, pointed ears, and glowing eyes.

They don't know what they're doing, Elenah realised.

"It won't be safe here much longer," Argus said, turning on Graham. "Look around you! This place couldn't protect us from ten of their troopers, let alone their ships. We're not safe, not where we are."

"We have the advantage of territory," Graham said.

"They have an *empire,* blast it!"

"Then what do you say we do?"

"We have to leave, and strike *first.* Strike when they're unsuspecting."

"That won't work. Like you said, we're undermanned. Our only option is to wait and reconcile our defences. Dammit, Argus. The moment we leave, with all our troops in such disarray . . . I'm telling you, they'll tear us apart."

"Well, maybe if we actually fought together! Unite the rebellion! We're all fighting our own battles." He spun around, storming back to his seat. "Gods, we're back to where we began." He slumped down and the chair creaked beneath his frame. He arched his back, clasped his hands, and hung his head. Unruly brown hair fell across his face and he cursed it.

Graham turned to regard the others, hands on his hips. "We should try to make contact with Harth's cell. Our radios may be damaged, but they're still working. Send out a signal. Call—"

"No," Jethre quickly said.

"What do you mean?"

Jethre folded his arms. "I don't trust him."

Half the soldiers cursed and laughed all at the same time, and Jethre grew visibly taut. He looked like he was about to punch someone.

It all reminded Elenah of her father. As a child she'd seen him interact with other nobles, emissaries, and representatives from faraway systems. There were just too many different people with too many different ideas. She wondered if in the Council it was the same.

"Argus is right," Jethre said. "We have to leave, because whether we've got five hundred or five thousand men, the Council will *always* have more. But we can't go looking for Harth, either. That man's agenda will splinter from ours very, very soon."

This time it was Graham who grunted and strode away from the captain, sitting back down. Jethre finally walked into the circle, his footsteps almost *shaking* the ground, and he demanded a different kind of presence. The way he held himself, with a straight back and flared shoulders, made him look like a very powerful and influential man, someone who would've fit perfectly within the council on Etheron.

"We have to strike their flagship," Jethre said. "*Now.*" A chorus of complaints erupted from all the soldiers in the room. "We've come too far within their reach!" Jethre yelled. "The only way now is *forward.*" But nobody was listening.

"It's suicide!" snapped a lanky reptile.

"Their flagship is heavily defended!" grumbled a bearded stout fellow.

"It is impossible!"

"—stupid!"

"—foolish!"

"—madness!"

"*Enough!*" Jethre roared, and the room fell into silence. "Bloody hell." His face was tight with veins, the skin pulled back, sweat cracking his reddened forehead. "Have we become children again?" His eyebrow twitched, the muscles in his face twisting and turning. "If not us, who is it that will stand against the Council and rid this galaxy of their *genocide?* Who but us wields the courage to take back what was ours, and restore our freedom?" He paced back and forth before the soldiers, hands screwed into sweaty, blocky fists. "We are all there is now. Remember, they're hurting just as much as we are."

"We don't even know where their flagship is, Captain," Graham said, flopping his hand out in front of him. Elenah dropped her eyes to the floor. This wasn't what she'd expected of the rebellion. How could they ever hope to defeat the Council?

Jethre stopped pacing, resting his chin on his knuckle. He glanced around, then finally his eyes landed on Elenah, and her heart leapt, as if he was demanding something of her. She could see fire in those eyes, familiarity. But she'd never seen him before, had she?

Jethre grunted, shaking his head and striding out of the circle beneath the eyes of all his men. "Prepare the defences," he said. "Start limbering up. They're coming."

Then he walked out.

THE MEETING HAD GONE POORLY, even by Argus's standards. All it had done was highlight the frustration that had been boiling up in the soldiers over the last few years. No one knew what the hell was going on anymore, and more than half of them weren't willing to take action. As he walked through the training yard, he couldn't help but notice how despondent everyone looked. Tired faces stared back at him. Dawn had hardly broken but, like them, Argus felt like he'd been awake for a decade.

We're in trouble, he thought. *If we don't do something now, the Council will play their cards—and they'll play them quicker.* He kicked an empty can of rarebeer and watched it tumble down a loose shaft of dirt. *We need to move closer to the core, away from the Western Realm. They know we're here, dammit. They're going to find us.*

Eventually, he came upon the two girls who'd arrived the day before. They were standing outside a small shed with the armourer, Telek. Well, he *was* an armourer; now he was stuck fitting them clothes and making them uniforms. Argus wondered if the army would ever be as powerful as the Forty-Ninth Council. If that day ever came, he'd want Telek close by.

"That's no good," Telek said, watching Elenah shrug on one of the spare brown coats. It barely fit her—she had to roll the sleeves three times.

"I can make it work," Elenah said, patting down the folds and turning so that her friend, Hannah, could admire her. "Honestly, I'm not too fussed." Argus nodded and watched from a few paces afar. *She's important* . . . What did that mean? Why was Jethre so fond of keeping her around? Well, at least she looked like she wanted to be here. They were down so many soldiers already, and there was something refreshing about her desire to help.

"You look like a soldier," Hannah said. Argus studied her as he moved closer beneath a rotting, skeletal tree. He exchanged a furtive glance with Telek, who was now in the process of polishing two pairs of combat boots.

She's a Felirean, Argus thought as the girls exchanged several comments about their new attire. Hannah posed, her brown-pink hair flapping. To say the truth, Argus had hardly believed his eyes when he saw her amidst the storm on Saecon IV. If the tales spilling across the stars were anything to go on, she might have just been the last Felirean in the galaxy . . .

"Try these shoes on," Telek said, proffering them to Elenah first, and then to Hannah. "I know they might be big, but hopefully not too big. I don't want you breaking your ankles."

Argus moved out from the shade beneath the tree. "You're starting to look like soldiers," he said, studying them as they sat on two logs pulling on their shoes.

"Ha," Hannah said. "Well, I certainly feel like one." She fixed her laces and then stood up, patting down her sides and walking around a bit. "I only need a weapon."

Argus smiled. "I suppose you dream of liberating Feluria one day," he said, throwing his hands into his voluminous pockets and strolling towards them. "You must have been through so much. To lose everything . . . I know what it's like, but not to that extent."

A saddened look fell across Hannah's face and she grabbed her arm nervously. Argus cursed inwardly. *But these two aren't soldiers yet*, he had to remind himself. They were not yet impervious to the horrors of war. "Sorry," he said, rather abashedly. Elenah glanced at him curiously as she too stood up and tried her boots. "It's just that . . . to see a *Felirean*."

Hannah sighed. "Oh, it doesn't matter. I suppose running away from the fact is an unhealthy business and, well, maybe I've been running for too long." She looked at Argus, and Argus could read in her eyes the same feeling he'd read a hundred times before. Uncertainty.

"How are the boots?" Telek asked.

"Better than my old ones," Elenah said. Hannah agreed half-heartedly. She seemed to be lost in deep thought, and Argus felt truly sorry for her.

"I wish I could help you," he said.

"See, that's the thing," Hannah said, zipping up her coat and pacing away from the resupply hut. "Feluria's belonged to the Kerrean for eleven years now. The war we fight against them will be far bloodier than this one, I assure you."

Argus shrugged, following her. There were lots of people who thought this war was larger than just the Forty-Ninth Council and the Galactic Liberation Movement, but he didn't like to think of that. The troubles that would cause . . .

He waved for Elenah to join him, and she did so timidly. "If you look at it like that," he said, turning back to the Felirean, "then perhaps you're right. But once you understand that it's all just made up of tiny puzzle pieces . . . you begin to realise how flawed even the most brilliant design is." He puffed out a deep breath and looked up into the sky. "I always envisioned taking back Feluria. It would be something."

"How long have you been fighting?" Elenah asked.

"All my life," Argus said, focusing on the dirt crunching beneath his tight black boots. "Jethre's the one that brought me here, introduced me to the cause, showed me hope."

Elenah walked alongside him now, straight-backed and straight-necked, like she were gliding through the air. *Protect her*, came a voice inside his head. *She's important.*

"How long do you think this war is going to last?" she asked.

"The real fighting hasn't even begun," Argus said. "When it does, I hope there's enough of us left to stand a chance." He looked at her sidelong, then out across the fields. "Do either of you know how to use a gun?"

"No," Elenah said.

"And what about you?" he asked Hannah. She shook her head. Argus didn't believe her, but he was too tired to start another fight. Of course Hannah knew how to shoot. She had survived this long, eleven years after the Purge of Feluria. "Okay, well Jethre's told me to show you both—"

"Argus!" Graham came running up towards him, his skin

blending in and out of the surrounding environment. "I think you should go see Flair. She doesn't look good."

At the mention of her name, Argus was immediately overcome with a wave of dread. He must have looked visibly frightened, as Graham quickly said, "Don't worry. She hasn't died."

Argus forced some composure into himself. "Death's hardly the worst thing that can happen to *us*. I'll head there now. Would you mind taking over for me here? Captain's orders. Just show them how to defend themselves."

"No worries." Graham glanced at both Elenah and Hannah, and gave them a small wave. Argus strode past him and went to find Flair.

Behind him, Graham said, "I'll show you to the armoury."

SHE COULD FEEL IT AGAIN. The fire. The whispers . . . though they were of a language she had never heard.

Elenah lowered her pistol and found that her heart was beating faster than usual. A cold sweat had broken out across her body, spreading right to the tips of her fingers. No, not *cold*. It was the heat, so sweltering that it felt like ice.

It's happening again, she thought.

"Elenah," Graham called. "Are you all right?"

Elenah shook herself from her reverie and raised her pistol again. She tried to sight the targets set up twenty feet away across the training yard, gently squeezed the trigger, and the blast shook her hand, rippled up her arm, to her brain. The bullet flew astray.

Gods, she thought as the world began to spin. She squeezed her eyes shut and walked over to the nearby hut, where Hannah sat, awaiting her turn. Graham followed her, his boots crunching the loose dirt along the courtyard. Elenah tried to pass Hannah the pistol but it clattered on the ground between them, and the starfire cell fell out, leaking black unharnessed mist. She brushed up against the side of the hut and tried to stop the pounding in her head.

"I feel . . . cold." Was she cold or hot? And there was something clawing at her, pulling her soul towards some very distant point. Incomprehensible sensations flashed over her again, and Hannah urged her to sit.

"Are you okay?" Graham asked, running over to her.

Elenah wrapped her arms around herself, sitting there on the dirt with Hannah knelt over her. "Gods, I feel terrible," she muttered, though she couldn't hear much over the rumbling in her ears. Fear overcame her. She felt as if she were about to die. "I think . . . I think I need to lie down." But now her mind was going in circles. Distant screams resounded in her ears.

"Get help," Hannah gasped.

"Right," Graham said, running off.

"Elenah?" Hannah asked.

Elenah grit her teeth, clenched her fists. There were whispers in her ear, although she couldn't make out what they were saying. She couldn't even begin to guess what language it was.

Then, as suddenly as it had begun, the pounding in her head slowed down, and warmth returned to her body. The force that had been pulling on her emotions fled, and she was left with a hollow sensation in her stomach. As her vision began to reorient itself, she made out Hannah's pale-green face in the sunlight.

It was just a feeling, she told herself. But where had it come from? It was as if something was trying to . . . take her over . . . communicate to her . . .

"Are you okay?" Hannah asked.

Elenah tried to clasp her hands to stop them from shaking. Her breathing hissed a strange rhythm. "That was weird."

A burning pain lanced her forehead.

"*Ugh!*" She grasped her hair as it spilled across her face and she buckled forward. Hannah cried out. Elenah squeezed her eyes shut as her ears began to ring.

Elenah, came a breathless voice, like a demonic whisper. She felt completely weightless, as if she'd been flung out into the void of space. *Elenah . . .*

She forced her eyes wide open and was floating in blackness. She tried to scream, but failed to find her voice. She was floating towards a huge red star that seemed impossibly large. It loomed before her, growing larger still.

Let it in . . . let it consume you . . .

"Elenah!"

Then she fell, slamming the hard earthen ground on hands and knees. A battle was raging, footsteps thundering across the dirt. Heart pounding, she glanced up and tried to stand. People ran past her, dressed in black cloaks, several of them chanting indecipherable words.

Where am I? she wondered. A tall man with blazing emerald eyes sprinted towards her without really seeing. Elenah cried out, cowering, but the man went right *through* her. She twirled, watching him recede in the distance. There was fire ahead, and screaming, but there was nothing else save for endless stretches of land, and occasional clusters of ruin.

Then everything *shifted* and she was standing on a dark

beach. The ocean glimmered with a violet haze, and there were glowing purple crystals jutting out of the shallows.

Behind her came the voice of a little girl: "There's someone there!"

Elenah turned around to see a small hut built upon the sand, and the child standing out the front, pointing, with her hair in a braid. A woman walked out behind her. Even from this distance, Elenah could make out her bright blue eyes, shining in the starlight.

"Go back inside, Ilira," the woman said calmly, and the child obeyed.

As though no time had passed at all, the woman was standing in front of Elenah.

"Elenah," she said in a voice that felt like warmth and love. "When you face him, you will need to fight. Remember the spell, *Incantatum*, and use it to fend him off."

Elenah just stood there, not sure what to do.

Incantatum . . . The name of the spell reverberated inside her head. She had heard it somewhere before. It was an old spell, used by generations of magicians. She saw a black blade inside her mind, coalesced in mist, and felt a tingling in the palm of her hand. *Incantatum* . . .

"Who are you?" Elenah asked. "And where am I?"

"You are almost there."

The ground swallowed her up.

She opened her eyes again, and found herself sitting on a mattress. The doctor, Levis, stood over her. His face was slick with sweat, and Elenah felt that she was sweating too. She blinked out the muted sunlight, wondering where she was now.

"You're awake," Levis gasped. "Brilliant." He looked up

and raised his voice so that maybe the whole camp could hear him. "We have an all-clear in bay two!"

Argus came running over, his crimson scarf lowered around his upper chest, plastered with bronze dirt. He looked panicked, almost slipping over as he reached her. "You're okay . . ."

Elenah released a shuddering breath. "What happened?"

Levis stepped back and brushed himself off. "Whatever it was, it wasn't natural."

"Make sure you look after her," Argus said, patting Levis on the back.

Beside the doctor stood Hannah, with her hands against her chest, looking quite distraught. "You were out for almost ten minutes," she said. "How do you feel?"

Elenah rubbed her forehead. "I'm fine." But she was shaking, and her mouth was parched, and there was a sick stirring in her stomach, as though something terrible was about to happen—or already *had* happened. "I don't know what that was."

The battlefield . . . The violet beach . . .

The woman, and the girl called Ilira . . .

Incantatum . . . The soulblade . . .

"I'll get you something to drink," Levis said. "But you need to rest." He wasted no time running off to fetch something, and in his absence came Captain Jethre Hawkwind.

"Captain!" Argus said, but Jethre simply strode past him.

"What did you see?" Jethre asked.

Elenah just stared at him, not sure yet if she was fully awake. She climbed up out of the ruddy white sheets and looked at him. Jethre looked more haggard than usual, his greying brown hair all curled and frayed. "What did I . . . see?" Elenah asked.

"Hey," Hannah snapped. "Why don't you give her some space?"

"I need to know," Jethre persisted.

"Captain?" Argus asked, looking at him curiously.

"The woman is right," said Doctor Levis as he returned with a glass of water. "Elenah needs to rest. Come back later, Cap. I will try to administer some concoctions."

"Did you see anything at all?" Jethre persisted.

Levis turned on him. "*Captain!*"

Jethre pulled his hair, then wiped globs of sweat off his wrinkled forehead. He looked as if he might say something, but elected not to. Instead, he simply nodded to himself, slapped Levis on the shoulder, then grabbed Argus's arm and hurried with him back into the sunlight.

"What's *his* problem?" Hannah asked, folding her arms.

"He's been awfully uptight lately," Levis said. He proffered Elenah a glass of water and said, "You have to rest. Anything you need, come get me. And you . . ." He gestured for Hannah to leave, then followed her out of the hut, leaving Elenah by herself.

Chapter Twenty-Seven

BATTLE PLANS

Area 664, the Architect's famous death camp for political prisoners. Information being so scarce, I can only guess the number refers to its Eileptic Coordinates. Certain reports mention entire families being imprisoned there for the actions of just one.

The insurgents are coming at us from all angles," Thrakk said as Teveran followed him through the bridge of the *Subjugator*. Stars threw pale light at them. Officers worked and sometimes looked at him. Teveran just stared back and tried not to look so dreary. Playing with magic had given him an awful headache.

"We've identified rebel activity on Devar and Eriadu among other places, and I also have reason to believe an unauthorised transmission was sent from Malydor two days ago. In no due time at all, they'll be swarming across Tarthalus. And if they do, it will be on our heads." He walked with a cane now, his back refusing to remain straight, his breathing coarse and laboured. He didn't look good, and all Teveran could think of was his father. It made him anxious, because he knew this ship would be his soon, along with the fleet.

And he knew what he would have to do: finish the fight, stop playing mind games and switch to the counterattack, just like Fex said.

Teveran wanted to ask why they didn't just attack them now. After all, the Council had not hesitated to destroy the people of Etheron. But he couldn't trust himself not to shout.

They eventually stopped before a hologram that fizzled in rolling waves over a white disc. Teveran's nerves intensified, but he kept them under control, drew a steadying breath.

All of the highlords were here—well, *almost* all of them. Notably, Highlord Kloak, with the fiery hair and burnt face, was absent, as well as Fex—which wasn't too unexpected, for Fex's movements were always so mysterious. The others surrounded a holographic model of the Inner Realm, already trading whispers and utterances.

"Evening, officers," said Thrakk.

Teveran righted himself, swallowed hard and absorbed the imagery. It was a jagged chunk of space that looked puny even compared to the galactic star maps that Fex had shown him. There were several planets on display, occupying the space north and east of the core. He also saw dots and triangles that represented the Council's growing force, but it looked insignificant compared to the galaxy. And Teveran realised how small the Council really was.

What was I so afraid of? he wondered.

"We have new orders from the Architect," Thrakk said loudly, before he coughed into a pale, wilted fist. "The rebels are pushing too close to Tarthalus, and we've been tasked with sending them back." He waved his hand to rotate the star map. "What we know is they're running a scattered operation, with bases established at these locations." He effortlessly expanded the view of a single moon called Framus. "Here." He swiped to another one, then another, and another, planets and moons, although sometimes it was hard to tell: Eriadu. Devar. Draghelm. Aryos. Places Teveran had never even heard of, despite being so close to home.

Thrakk returned their focus to the coreward face of Framus, where the red clouds of a huge gas giant pelted it. "This is their largest base, where their forces will most likely fall back to. If we can drive them here, we can establish a blockade and besiege them. Then, we can *crush* them."

"Will they be so foolish?" a blue-eyed officer asked.

Another one added, "We're dealing with a military body here, not miscreants."

Thrakk's brows folded over his eyes, and he grit his yellow teeth. Teveran traced the star map with his eyes, drumming his fingers against his chin. *Does he expect me to say something?* he wondered as a brief silence fell over them. He looked around, searching for Fex, but the man was nowhere in sight. Thrakk stepped forward and said, "We cannot allow even one rebel cell to break through our wall. We have to push them back and lock them in."

"That won't work," said a red-haired officer.

"They'll just use the trade route," said another.

Thrakk reeled. The officers bickered, taking hold of the star map one after the other and barking contradictions. Thrakk said, "They know we're falling apart. They know we're vulnerable. And if we don't strike first, stop them before they manage to not only calculate but *execute* an attack, they'll finish us off. They'll *destroy* us!"

Teveran stepped forward. "Forget pushing them back. Let's *attack*."

The blue-eyed officer nodded. "They're hurting just as much as us, Grand Highlord. We still have time. They will surely be recovering from their defeats on Corion *and* Mokuura." Teveran caught the man's eyes, and received an approving nod. He caught his uncle's sidelong glance. Wrinkles tightened around the old man's mouth, his cheeks drooped. Thrakk was too timid, too apprehensive. That was why he failed.

"We have to strike first," Teveran said. "And that means *now*."

"Yes, but we need a contingency plan," said Fex. He came strolling in from the back of the room, wearing a tailored white suit and a high collar. "I apologise for being late," he said, joining them around the hologram. Then he promptly swung around to Thrakk and said, "On the contrary, Grand Highlord, we must ensure they *don't* flee backwards." Though he was decades older, Fex looked younger when he stood beside the ghostly Thrakk.

Teveran looked at him, and Fex looked back, and something ran between them that Teveran couldn't quite comprehend.

One of the officers began, "We could establish another—"

"No," Fex quickly said. "Teveran's right. A strike on Devar *will* put a dent in their forces. As our chief intelligence officer, Highlord Pandion will be able to track their movements and transmissions thereafter. The other cells will fall into place very, very soon." He eyed Thrakk darkly, as though they shared some long-broiling disdain. "There will be no chance of failure."

Thrakk grumbled. "Very well. Officer Hartwell will lead the assault, then."

"Hartwell, sir?" Teveran asked. *That's Snake . . .*

"I want you to inform him that this is now our highest priority. He can muster the battalions for imminent departure."

Teveran hesitated. "Yes . . . sir."

Fex cleared his throat, then clapped Teveran on the shoulder and led him a few long strides out of earshot of the dying fleet leader. "He doesn't have long left," Fex told him. "Once you inform Commander Hartwell, you should rest." He left the rest unsaid: *And then it's up to you. Finish the fight . . . and then I'll turn you into the man you're meant to be.* Without another word, Fex walked away, leaving Teveran all alone again.

He looked through the window and into the galaxy, standing in the middle of the bridge as officers ran past him, hurrying back and forth. *So this is it,* he thought. *This is where it ends.* Soon, Fex's grand plan would be unveiled.

He swallowed bile, and went looking for Snake.

THE HANGAR OF THE *SUBJUGATOR* was busy as always, with glowing white walls, an impossibly high ceiling, and a silvery force field that separated them from eternal space. Men and women hurried back and forth, performing last minute maintenance on their ships. The only sound in the chamber was of scurrying feet, voices, and the deep rumbling of engines.

Teveran watched them all prepare to face death.

This is cowardice, he thought bitterly. For him to simply

stand there and tell these people to go and die for the Council . . . It left a sour taste in his mouth. Thrakk made him do this.

There were three or four hundred troopers outbound, and who knew what they were going to find when they landed? Teveran watched them. He tried to hide the terror on his face, the guilt, the sickness. But he felt it all over. His gut was churning, the voices in his head—of Elenah and Gilgan and his father—all told him to stop this. But what other choice did he have?

This is what it takes.

"How are you, Teveran?" Snake strode up from one of the side doors, dressed in his gleaming armoured suit, the ivory plates scraping and sliding. His helmet, as always, had been clipped to his belt. Teveran had worn one, once. Gods, but the memory of it was so clear. A terrible slaughter upon Corion. Fex had sent him there . . . to show him the truth about the Council, to show him what terrible people they were, what hopeless fools . . .

"How can you do this?" Teveran asked.

"Hey," Snake said, gripping Teveran's shoulder. "Don't look so grim."

Teveran couldn't do much about it. He glimpsed the butt of Snake's rifle, which beamed in his eyes. He blinked. Snake dropped his hand and slapped Teveran's chest three times with the back of it. "Snake," Teveran said. "Thrakk's a *bad* person."

Snake sighed, and a sorry look crossed his face. His emerald eyes seemed to lose some of their light. "We're all bad people, Teveran. But that's the price we pay to restore order to the galaxy. Don't get me wrong, every damned night

I go to sleep and I hate myself. For the choices I've made, and some of those that I didn't. But you . . . You're not so bad. You still have so much left to do. You can make this galaxy a better place."

The brown hairs on Teveran's arms stood on end and he wished he could force them back down. "Thank you, Snake," he breathed. "Gods . . . thank you for everything."

"I know you'll make your family proud." He offered his hand, and Teveran grabbed it. "It's been an honour." Then, Snake turned and strode off towards the starfighters. Teveran could still see the man's emerald eyes when he blinked.

Those eyes reminded him of Rose, and the palace, and his father—who was probably dead. Gods, but they were *all* probably dead. The Council betrayed them.

And now, in the coming days, *he* was going to have to lead them. He was going to take Thrakk's place as Grand Highlord of this fleet, and he was going to destroy the scattered rebellion. He could see it all so clearly now.

He glanced across the hangar, to Snake's fleeing form, then through the docking bay doors and into the glittering starscape. He knew what he had to do.

All he had to do was execute it.

Korvis lay on his bunk, arms behind his head, staring at the bottom of the bed above him. He was trying to sleep, but the other guys were a rowdy bunch.

"The attack is happening now," List said. His bunk was on the other side of the room; however, the dorm was very small, and so he was barely a few paces away. "I heard the

Grand Highlord was sending out four battalions to finally crush the liberation movement."

"Well, it serves them right," said Graphs, who was the bespectacled man in the bed above Korvis's own. Altogether, there were seven of them.

There had been eight when Korvis arrived.

"I suppose," Risk said. "They *are* rebels, after all."

"What's wrong with you, Korvis?" Graphs asked. "You don't talk much, do you?"

Korvis grunted and rolled over. The truth was, he couldn't care less about the Council or these recruits. Soon, it would all be over. These boys would likely be dead, and Korvis would be somewhere far away with Teveran and Damian, and Fex's other magicians.

Unable to find a comfortable position, he sat up and yawned. Then he glanced across the room towards List, in the bed parallel his own. "Surely you guys realise that you won't be just sitting around forever," Korvis said. "Soon you're going to see battle."

"Bring it on," List said, grinning.

"The rebels are stronger than you think."

"What's the matter?" Graphs asked from above. "You scared?"

"No," Korvis said. He scooted himself around so that he was sitting on the edge of the bed, legs dangling over the edge. He was still dressed in his day's uniform, though he hadn't done more than deliver a couple of messages between various operating stations. He hadn't even done any training with Damian today. "I know what we are. We're pawns."

"Hell, what made you sign up anyway?" somebody else—

Bast, the oldest and most experienced of them by several years—asked. "Were you conscripted?"

"Something like that," Korvis said, thinking of how he'd met Fex as he tried to flee the planet, how he'd learned of the larger war, and the league of magicians. It was strange, looking around at his bunkmates, knowing how easy it would be to kill them . . . They thought he was weak, that he was just like them—only *lesser*. It was their greatest weakness.

"I don't know about you," Bast said, shooting him his auburn eyes. "You've been away an awful lot. You've been training with somebody, doing something suspicious."

Korvis felt a needle of heat. "That's not true."

Then, as if on cue, the door slid open and Fex was standing in the doorway. The room came alive with ruffling and hurried murmurs of "Highlord, sir!" as they realised who was standing before them. Everybody save for Korvis.

"Korvis," Fex said, gesturing for him to join him outside. Korvis got up quickly and tried not to make eye contact with any of the other soldiers. Gods, but could Fex have picked any worse time to speak to him? When they were standing together in the hall outside, and the door had closed behind them, Fex pulled Korvis close and slid something into his hand.

"What's this?" Korvis asked, opening his hand to see a torn piece of paper.

"It's a spell. I want you to learn it."

Korvis got a glimpse of its name: *Transfixis.*

"Our plan is about to be put into motion," Fex said, "though I fear that Teveran might not be capable of reliably fulfilling his part. I want you to stay close to him, and if

Teveran tries to flee or resist, then it is up to you to stop him. This spell will help you."

"How do I use it?" Korvis asked, beginning to sweat.

"You must speak it aloud. It is an offensive spell, one that requires immense concentration. Use it only on Teveran, but *do not kill him.*" As he spoke these last words, his voice was so hard, so intense, that Korvis melted slightly. "He may be accompanied by his sister. In fact, it is very likely. You will have to kill her, and anybody else who stands in our way. Understand?"

Elenah?

"I understand," he said, the taste of bile in his throat.

"I will be relying on you," Fex said. "Now, I have arranged your relocation to new sleeping quarters where you will be alone. Practise that spell. Do not let me down."

"Okay," Korvis said.

"Damian is waiting for you in the regular meeting place. Go find him, and tell him what you must do." Then he turned on his heel and walked away. Korvis watched him, still holding the torn piece of paper. It looked like it had been ripped out of something very old; the paper was harder than normal paper, but also more tarnished and bronzed.

Transfixis, he said inside his head. He told himself he might not have to use it at all. It was only to be used as a last resort, if Teveran resisted the plan, if Elenah interfered . . .

The prospect of seeing her again caused mixed emotions to well up inside him, and he wasn't sure if he was more excited or terrified because of it.

He pocketed the spell page and strode off to find Damian.

CHAPTER TWENTY-EIGHT

THE COUNCIL STRIKES

*The Theory of Subtly Sentient Technology was postulated
by the academic, Henry Eisenfort, and proposes that
starfire has sentient properties that work in service to the
user. I certainly support this theory; my pistol did seem to
have a mind of its own on many occasions.*

H elp me, Elenah.

She was standing on the bridge of a Leviathan,
surrounded by stars. Beneath them hung a striking
white planet, and she could almost hear the wail of the
wind from up here. *Kasnah.* Once, it had been a sprawling
metropolis of gods and dragons and the legendary Battle of
Haratheon. Now it was a wasteland. Officers hurried around
her, from station to station, as if she didn't even exist.
Hundreds of them.

Thousands.

And, among them, that voice.

Help me, Elenah.

She panicked, looking left and right. "Teveran . . ." she
gasped, but couldn't see him anywhere. The Leviathan
thrummed with the constant flow of starfire. Officers passed

her, running back and forth. She couldn't move; she was frozen in place.

Voices: "All hail the king!"

And then she saw him, stumbling forward with his hands bound and thick crimson blood dribbling down his face. The old man behind him kneed him in the back and sent him sprawling onto hands and knees. Around his neck was a metal choker.

Teveran's eyes widened, his mouth hung agape. "Help me . . ."

"Teveran!" Elenah screamed, and ran for him. But she wasn't moving anywhere. The old man gripped Teveran's chain with a single black glove. He grinned wickedly, then burst into mocking, mirthless laughter, and said, "Teveran's mine now."

"No!" Elenah screamed as a bright light struck her eyes.

SHE WOKE UP BENEATH THE VERY FIRST LIGHT OF DAWN, heart hammering.

Somehow, she had ended up on the ground. Brown windswept grass lay all around her, sticks and dirt tangled in her hair. The sun rose from beneath the edge of the world, entering its morning orbit, throwing golden streams across the brown-yellow plains of Devar.

Another vision, she thought. *Gods, what's happening to me?*

Slowly, Elenah found her way up, trembling. When she blinked, she could still see the last impression of the massive bridge, and Teveran, and the old man.

I'm running out of time.

She patted down her brown coat and pants, scrubbed dirt

from her arms. Black mud had plastered itself all across her body, and fell off in small flakes. She blinked, trying to break the painful needles of sunlight.

She saw the ice-planet Kasnah.

That's where they are.

That's where they're hiding.

Hurriedly, she scrambled to her feet and ran. She had to find Jethre fast. *Did you see anything at all?* he'd asked her.

What did he know? Who was he, really?

She traversed the uneven ground, jagged lumps of rock biting the bottom of her feet. She weaved between small huts, beneath twisted treetops with brown leaves that snapped and floated through the air. It was nothing like Etheron—although she could hardly remember what Etheron was like anymore.

She rounded a corner and saw the great shadow cast from the farmhouse beneath the hill. But then she stopped, and gasped, as she saw the group of soldiers within its shadow. Heart in her throat, Elenah crept towards them. She could make out individual voices in the tumult.

"They're all dead," a young man stammered. He looked like he could barely stand. His clothes were soaked in blood, his pale face all bruised and bleeding. "Gods, they're coming, Captain. We have to leave here *now!*"

Jethre grabbed the young man. He and Argus were all that was holding him up. "Where are they?" Jethre demanded, and when the young man didn't response, Jethre shook him. "Are you being followed?"

The blood-soaked man looked like he might be sick. "Yes," he mumbled, going deathly pale. "Yes . . . I think they followed us."

"You *think?*" Jethre hissed.

The man shook his head violently from side-to-side. "No, Captain," he hurriedly said. "I'm . . . I'm *certain* of it."

"Gods." Jethre broke away, then tossed the man into Argus's arms and rounded on all his men. "Prepare the ships for imminent departure," he said, veins throbbing in his temples.

"Captain?" Argus asked.

"We can't fight them, Argus," Jethre said, grabbing the side of his head and swiping greasy brown hair out of his face.

"We're just going to run away?"

"Yes," Jethre said firmly. "Yes we are."

"Where to?"

"Framus."

Suddenly, Doc Levis came bustling through the throng. "I'm here!" he announced, grabbing the man in Argus's arms. "Gods, you're a mess, son. What happened?"

"They ambushed us," he stammered.

Jethre grabbed Levis's shoulder and pushed him away. "No, Levis. There's no time. Take him to a ship and get him off-world as fast as you can. They've been followed. The Council will be here at any moment."

Levis hesitantly nodded, and then wheeled the young man off. Argus and Jethre exchanged tired, broken looks, and then Argus went off leaving the captain all alone.

"Jethre?" Elenah timidly said.

"Go with them," Jethre said without looking at her, and then he marched hurriedly from the spot. Elenah stumbled over a twig as she followed him to the twisted bole of a naked tree. Streams of bronze sunlight fell through the branches, casting crooked patterns along the ground.

She struggled to find her tongue. "Jethre, I *saw* it."

Jethre stopped beneath the tree, and narrowed his eyes at her. His eyebrow twitched. "What . . . What did you see?"

She averted her eyes and clasped her trembling hands. Her thoughts were racing. Behind her, she could hear Argus telling the other soldiers to pack up their supplies and get to the ships. *Avengers*, he called them. Those must have been the starfighters.

"Look at me," Jethre said, and she did. Somewhere deep within his left eye was a sliver of silver, almost surreal, that reminded her of Gilgan. She felt a heat in her chest, a shiver twisting the muscles down to the small of her back.

"I saw the flagship," she said.

Jethre hesitated. "Where?"

"It's over Kasnah."

For a moment, the captain looked unwell. He gripped her shoulders and struck her with a vehement gaze. "Are you sure?"

Elenah nodded. "We don't have much time."

Jethre let her go, then stepped away and whistled through crooked teeth. "I fear this attack is going to be relentless. Stay close to me. Do *not* go off on your own."

HANNAH SLID A SINGLE TWIG ACROSS THE DIRT, sketching another figure. The wind blew dirt across the ground, sending it rolling across her hand and clutching at the sweat.

She hummed a song to herself as she drew. It was a song her mother had taught her when she was very young. It felt like a lifetime ago. She couldn't remember much about her family—not since the Kerrean enslaved them—but she still remembered that song. She heard it in the silence, and in the waves, and in the wind that breathed gently against her ears.

> *Bygone towers of stone,*
> *Show me the way back home.*
> *Through misty worlds of glass and snow,*
> *To the lands I know.*
> *If we lose our way ahead,*
> *The path of light shall be re-tread.*
> *Bygone towers of stone . . .*

She let the twig drop and observed her drawing. It turned out to be a circle with three jagged lines protruding from the bottom arch: the insignia of her homeworld, Feluria. Was it actually possible that she might be able to save it? Was there even a chance that she could defeat the Kerrean and . . . *liberate* Feluria?

Thinking of what Argus had said lit a fire in her chest. The Council had done this. She knew there were Kerrean sympathisers in their ranks. She knew someone was funding their war crimes. If there *was* any chance in the galaxy, then she was going to make them *pay*.

"Excuse me."

The voice startled Hannah from her reverie, and she looked up to see a young man—no, just a boy—standing a dozen feet in front of her. He had ashen hair and a plump face, and made strange shapes with his fingers—a nervous habit, perhaps.

"Hello," Hannah said, her voice lilting.

The boy approached her unevenly on the cracked dirt ground. "I was just wondering . . ." he said. "Are you . . . *Felirean?*"

Hannah frowned at him, slowly rising to her feet. She clasped her hands, though found her old instincts kicking in. *They're out to get you,* something inside her said. *They're looking for you. They're hunting you down. Run, Hannah. Run!*

"Yes," she said. "Why?"

"I think . . . I think my father's friend was too."

Hannah just stared at him, her mouth falling agape. *There's another one,* she thought, but forced herself to stay composed. He was probably dead . . .

But what if he wasn't?

The boy anxiously wrung his hands. "He said there were no more Felireans. He said the Kerrean killed them all. But you . . . *You're* one. You . . . You have to go to him."

There's someone else out there, Hannah thought, over and over and over. *I'm not the last one.* Gods, it seemed impossible. "Do you know his name?" she gasped.

"Oi, Lirin!" shouted another man as he emerged from the haze. "Lirin, they're coming." This man didn't look much older than the boy, but his eyes were much more battle-worn.

Lirin turned around. "Who's coming?"

Suddenly the world began to shake. The familiar sound of low-rumbling engines filled the air. Hannah grabbed onto the ground as if it might prevent her from being shaken out of existence. "The Council," the man continued. "They followed Raz back on his—"

Shouts erupted from around the base. Hannah scrambled off the ground and saw the hurrying shapes of soldiers running for the ships. She'd hardly had a chance to move before the clouds cracked and silver shapes emerged. They were ships—*Ragnaroks*.

And they were coming closer.

"GET TO THE FIGHTERS!" Jethre roared, his voice cracking through the stale air. Elenah shuddered, glancing at him, then at the sky.

A contingent of silver ships approached. Their shadows laced the fields, flashing over faces. A bulb-like Banshee, spewing silver Ragnaroks with pointed noses and wide, blazing wings, descended from the pinnacle of the sky. Soldiers reached for their rifles, unbuckled their grenades. And then: impenetrable Manticore dropships emerged from the haze.

Gods, but nobody was listening to Jethre. The soldiers weren't running. They'd all drawn their weapons, and they'd left Elenah standing there with nothing. She glanced back into the sky, watching the clouds twist and turn, bronze sunlight slicing through.

She thought of Teveran, with the silver chain wrapped around his neck, and the man standing behind him. She saw his fear, *felt* it seeping off him like sweat. *Help me*, he'd said. Or had he really? It didn't matter. He was out there, and he was in trouble.

Whatever happened next, Elenah couldn't afford to die.

The rebels hurtled through the base of Devar, shouting, rapping against the wooden doors of the small huts. It reminded her of Mokuura, but this time she couldn't run, she couldn't let her fear overwhelm her. Regardless of their strength, the Vanguard was all she had now. She needed them. They might be her only chance of getting to Teveran.

"They're here!" shouted a man. *"The Council is here!"*

The Council's Ragnaroks ripped through the clouds alongside the Manticores, circling the base, and slowly descending. Fear rushed through the air in pulsating waves. Elenah's blood burned, her gut tightened, and the breath in her chest grew hoarse. Somebody grabbed her arm, and she turned to see Jethre again. A tempest shone in his eyes.

"Go," he said.

Elenah froze. "No," she said without thinking. She couldn't just abandon them, just run away like she always did. She had to help them, because these people were her only hope . . .

"Let me help," she said.

"It's too dangerous."

"*Captain*," Elenah snapped.

"You don't even know how to use a gun!"

"I do! Graham taught me."

"And you passed out!"

"You know that's not true."

Jethre grunted. He pressed a pistol firmly into Elenah's hand. She looked down at the glistening metal. The weapon felt odd there, as if it didn't quite belong. She wanted to throw it away, to give it back and head for the ships.

But she couldn't.

Jethre rolled his rifle into his hands and backed away from Elenah. She watched him, nerves shaking. He said nothing else, just turned and marched through the base, shouting orders. Elenah curled her finger around the trigger.

She glanced at the silver ships controlling the airspace.

Chaos erupted around her, a tumult of shouting and stamping. Men, women, Taurans, Kasnans . . . They roared and screamed and established a single line of defence. Death stared them in the eyes.

"The Avengers!" came a nearby roar. "Get to the Avengers! Fly away!"

"Target their dropships!" another voice commanded.

The Manticores roared as their landing ramps flipped out. They broke through the brown and orange clouds of dawn. Everything was rammed up a hundredfold.

"Form defensive ranks!" Jethre shouted.

There are so many of them, Elenah thought. Ragnaroks laced the sky like a twisted kind of patchwork, shooting back and forth before the sun. She tried not to panic, wrapped her hand around the pistol, raised her eyes, and ran.

All she could hear was her own rapid breathing and the crunch of her boots as she ripped up the dirt. She tore dead grass from its roots, slid down a hill, tripped over and over and over. "Hannah!" she cried, slewing a corner. One of the Manticores crashed down, its landing ramp slamming the dirt ground. Elenah saw the white glint of trooper armour, their bold black rifles. Two Ragnaroks attacked the farmhouse beneath the hill, drowning it in relentless bulletfire. "Hannah!" She stopped to catch her breath, spinning left and right.

She wandered between the huts. Everything became a blur. Her breathing grew ragged and burdensome. Her eyes darted back and forth. She collapsed against the wooden wall of one of the huts. A woman shouted, "Bets, they're on your flank!"

"Get down!" Argus grabbed her coat, throwing her to the side and into his arms. He wrapped her up, then whipped out a pistol and stabbed it through the air. Elenah managed a glance at him. His auburn eyes were alight, sweaty locks of wavy hair all messy and unkempt. He shoved her off him.

And then, gunfire.

Elenah yelped. She raised her pistol in trembling hands and threw herself against the wall. Bullets ripped through the base, shredding flesh, cutting wood. She crumpled to her knees. Argus rose and emptied rounds at the armoured troopers.

"What the hell are you doing?" Argus yelled.

"I'm helping," Elenah snapped.

"Gods! *Get to the ships!*"

But she couldn't. She sucked in a deep breath, peered around the hut and tried to aim at the troopers. *I can do this*, she told herself, metal grip slipping in her sweaty hands. Another Manticore landed, and two dozen more troopers emerged from its guts. She grit her teeth, held her breath, and sighted them.

Heartbeats flickered past.

She screamed as she pulled the trigger. A single bullet hissed through the air. It seemed to disappear, *warp* several feet, before striking the trooper in the chest. It ricocheted into the dirt. He recovered quickly, levelled his rifle on her. Elenah pumped off as many as she could, her pistol jerking up and down, the bullets going wide and too high. She managed four more hits, finally breaking his armour and biting into flesh. He screamed, flying back.

"Got him," she muttered, adrenaline pumping through her body.

A Ragnarok soared overhead. She spun back behind the

hut and glanced at Argus. Sweat streaked his face as he reloaded, the starfire cell rattling.

"Fall back!" somebody yelled.

"They've got us pinned!"

"We don't stand a chance!"

Elenah rounded the hut and sprinted across the battlefield, bullets rasping all around her. Argus shouted behind her, but she didn't break stride. Dropships descended, throwing off streams of white clouds. She slid to her knees behind one of the huts as bullets whacked the wood. Glancing over her shoulder, she saw Jethre stride through the ranks. He unloaded bullets across the troopers, like a warrior from Gilgan's stories.

"To the ships!" Jethre barked at her, and this time she ran. The shipyard lay ahead. She tripped, her foot sliding across a loose shaft of dirt. Sunlight streamed before her, breaking through the parting clouds, forcing Elenah to squint. Hills rose up around her, and the ground was split by twisting gullies. To her left was but the faintest sliver of light as it bounced off a silver Manticore. It landed, billowing dirt and haze of dust.

"Elenah, keep running!" Argus yelled from behind.

She watched the landing ramp unfold, and then troopers spewed out. They raised their blazing rifles, set their aims across the base, and Elenah felt them all over her.

"Ignore them! *Run!*"

One of them emerged from the convolution, his armour sizzling with a hazy blue outline, like some sort of electric shield. Elenah's heart leapt. She froze. The trooper flipped a switch on his helmet and the visor shot up, revealing gleaming emerald eyes.

The eyes of a snake.

"*Princess*," he gasped.

Elenah raised her pistol, aim unsteady. She blinked away tears, and pulled the trigger. She got him in the shoulder, and the bullet bounced off.

Gods!

"Move!" Argus shrieked, taking her hand and pulling her across the plains, alongside two dozen other soldiers. The officer's emerald eyes were printed upon her vision. *Princess*, he had called her. Yet, she'd never seen him in her life.

I must be imagining things. Gunfire roared all around her. There was a ringing in her ears. Argus was fast. She was almost at the ships when two Avengers of gunmetal grey streaked across the sky, shooting off streams of golden sunrays.

Elenah froze, tripping, stumbling, then composed herself and raised her pistol, shooting at the troopers that were still converging upon them. There seemed to be hundreds of them, a never-ending supply. Her first bullet went astray, the second struck a trooper's chest plate; it sprayed into the ground. Another bullet lodged between two plates. The next *cracked* it.

"*Everybody get down!*" someone screamed.

And then something slammed the ground barely three feet away from her, throwing up chunks of rock and fire and choking her in a cloud of dirt. Elenah slammed her back hard; it knocked the breath from her. The explosion deafened her. She was unsure which way was which. The sounds beyond the cloud were muffled. She could see flames and blood and not much else.

"What was that?" she gasped, everything going black.

The bulletfire continued around her, but each time she

blinked the sounds grew deeper, until it was as though the entire moon was shaking. She closed her eyes, her strength availing her. Something exploded nearby; it racked her brain. There was shouting, but she could no longer distinguish what they were saying. Another blast. Another.

And then it was gone.

Chapter Twenty-Nine

LEGACY

It's like a song composed by the gods. If we could only predict the next beat, the next lyric . . . then perhaps we could also prevent the next catastrophe. Unless it is already happening.

Thrakk lay on his deathbed.

Teveran watched him, standing by the smelly white coverlets that drooped onto the floor, hands behind his back. The room was stained by the familiar, sickening stench of rot and death. For once, Fex wasn't there. Thrakk's only guests were the last of the highest ranking officers, those Teveran had seen constantly roaming the bridge. They came and went, ghost-like figures roaming back and forth. The last of them was Highlord Cadus, a tall man who didn't look much older than Teveran, save for his white moustache and scarred jaw.

"My salutations," Cadus said.

Teveran shook his head. "I never really knew him."

"He was a brave man. I met him on the battlefield. He was a true fighter. I suppose if anything were to kill him, it'd be something like this, something . . ."

"Something you can't defend," Teveran offered.

Cadus seemed to consider that a moment, and then nodded in agreement. "Yes. Truly tragic." A moment passed in silence. Teveran wondered if Cadus was allied with Fex's league of magicians, or if he was just another highlord. "I suppose you're his natural heir."

"You make it sound more noble than it really is."

"It's noble work, leading a fleet."

"I'm sure."

"You don't seem very enthused. Though, it isn't often you can change the natural order of things. As is such, I'd like to be the first to make your acquaintance." He turned and offered Teveran his hand; a white glove, not unlike Fex's, covered it. "I'm Vorin Cadus."

Teveran looked him up and down, then hesitantly shook his hand. *They're already trying to win me over,* he thought with disgust. *I've already become a prize in their political games . . .*

Cadus was not a magician.

"I look forward to working with you," Cadus said, turning abruptly and leaving the room. Teveran watched him go, and he felt the room become much, much smaller.

"My boy," Thrakk said. It startled Teveran, who thought for sure he would never hear his uncle's voice again. All that kept him alive now was the flashing lights and machinery. The man, once the revered Grand Highlord, could hardly move, for the sickness had all but paralysed his body. He now resorted mostly to flicking his eyeballs left and right. Teveran supposed his own father was spared from such a cowardly fate. Thrakk breathed steadily, but it sounded more like a croak. He gestured with his wrinkled hand and said, "Come closer."

Teveran simply knelt and stared into his uncle's eyes.

"We have faced no greater threat," Thrakk said, "than what we do now." He spoke so quietly that Teveran had to lean closer just so he could hear. "I'm sorry for giving you this burden. But it is up to you now to carry on our family's legacy."

Teveran eyed him grimly. This was where it all ended. All he had to do was face his uncle one last time, and inherit the bloodline, and be proud of it, and lead this fleet against the rebellion. It would all be over soon. He would be *free* of these chains.

"You will be one of the best," Thrakk said. "I can see it inside you, the same fire that once made me so cherished by my own men." He coughed and hacked, and Teveran shuffled away, avoiding his sickness. Was it possibly contagious? Or was it *programmed?*

"Look at me, boy."

Teveran moved nothing but his eyes, shifted them no more than an inch. Anger burned inside him now, causing his thoughts to reverberate inside his own mind. It was an anger that felt . . . *invigorating,* like he could challenge the galaxy.

"If only your father was half the man you will become," Thrakk said with a crooked smile.

"You *killed* my father."

Thrakk's smile vanished like a silenced flame. His face grew notably stiff, his wrinkles tightened like strings pulled too tight, and he spoke through hoarse breaths. "He was killed by his own arrogance."

Teveran shook his head but said nothing. He almost started laughing. Thrakk gripped his wrist, and the strength in that hand surprised him. Now he faced him directly, and Thrakk's eyes were cold, and angry, and hungry for more war. Through his eyes Teveran could see hundreds of battles, could see friends torn apart, and the galaxy in turmoil.

And he could see himself.

Teveran realised he was clutching the cord to his uncle's life support. He felt it between his fingers, like ice, thrumming with whatever kind of magic they used to keep Thrakk alive. He stared into his uncle's eyes as he twisted the cord around his hands, secretly.

"You're a tyrant, Thrakk," Teveran said, barely containing his anger. "I should've seen it sooner. This army, and what it stands for, and what *you* are really. You're scared."

"What are you talking about?" Thrakk rasped.

"Scared of the Architect. Scared of the rebels. You were scared of my father, too, and the power he had as the chancellor of the Free Worlds. That's why you killed him. Well, let me tell you this: You should have been scared of *me*, because I'm better than my father. I'm a magician."

"Teveran . . . But you were the High Prince."

Teveran clutched the cord. "That name died with Etheron."

And then he *jerked* it.

Thrakk gasped. His eyes dilated. One final breath scraped from his lungs. Realisation struck him, but it was too late. All he could do was gape, as slowly he died.

It was over too soon.

Teveran basked in the silence. And then he threw the cord onto the floor and stood up, drawing steady deep breaths. He felt a huge weight drop off his shoulders, but, at the same time, something stronger and heavier fell upon him. The huge burden of leading this fleet. *I'm Grand Highlord now*, he realised, but it didn't bother him as much as he thought it might.

After all, it was only temporary. The Forty-Ninth Council was falling apart. Fex knew that, and Thrakk himself knew it. Soon the war would enter a new dawn, a new phase, and things would get a whole lot worse.

"Congratulations." Fex's wise voice rang from the back of the room, but this time Teveran didn't turn to face it. He just stood there and raised his head a fraction, as if he might see Fex approaching in the reflections on the walls. He didn't, for the room was empty . . . but he heard his footsteps ringing. Coming closer . . . *closer* . . .

"It's over," Teveran said.

Fex eventually stopped, perhaps five strides behind him. The ringing of his footsteps remained. "It's over, Fex. My uncle's dead." He spun around to face him—only, there was no one there. He panicked, looking in every direction, but he was alone in the infirmary now, alone save for his uncle's rotting dead body.

"*Then go*," came Fex's chilling voice.

Teveran nodded, and strode through the infirmary. *I'll go, then*, he thought, and felt it flowing through him again. *But first, there's a battle I've got to finish.*

He left the infirmary, entered the silent lift, and shut the doors, locking himself in. He would play his part in destroying the rebellion, then let the Forty-Ninth Council slowly crumble in the absence of their greatest fleets.

"I'm ready," he told himself, and when the lift reached its final destination, Teveran strode from its bright white lights, into the darkness beyond.

AN UNCERTAIN MOOD HAD FALLEN across the bridge of the *Subjugator*. It was filled with mutters, and tense discussions, with officers staring into space, praying at their stations. Ensign Kyle Beret was among them, standing where he always stood.

He was trembling, and he found it hard to concentrate on anything but his impending death. The war was getting worse, the blasted rebels were retaliating, and now that the Grand Highlord was dead, who was going to lead them? Who was going to *save* them?

There were rumours, of course. Maybe old Yuir Ren. That old man knew a few things about winning a war, but maybe he was just too old, as many of them believed—including Kyle himself. There was always the younger yet intelligent Brin Tepper. Kyle thought that young Brin might do alright, but he was no Grand Highlord.

They all turned towards the sound of the opening doors. There was a figure standing in the doorway. Kyle had never seen him before, but from this distance who could tell? *Always jumping to conclusions*, his mother had told him. *Just wait a blasted moment.* Still, he tensed.

A deep black cape billowed behind the figure as he walked into the room. *This is him.* He wore the same massive cloak that Thrakk had worn before him. Except, the clothes looked too big on him. *What's going on? He's just a child!*

But as the figure entered the bridge, everybody stopped and waited. *That . . . That's the boy who's been training with Fex.* He found that someone else echoed his thoughts. *Gods no.* Kyle walked forward to meet their new leader. His hair was a princely shade of brown, and he had burnished hazel eyes, which reminded him of the colour of wood after it burned.

"Grand Highlord—" Kyle began. He glanced at the old man standing on the Grand Highlord's left shoulder and Kyle realised he had seen that man before. *Oh, hell.*

There were rumours. Rumours that the old man was a very powerful magician. When he wasn't around, word was he played with dark arts, participated in rituals and rites among other dark magicians. Gods, it was Fex. It was bloody *Fex.*

Kyle swallowed, and faced the Grand Highlord again. "Sir, the longer we stay here—"

"Don't wait," he said, looking at him with those icy cold eyes. There was a tremor in his voice, which made Kyle settle somewhat. The new Grand Highlord stepped forward and raised his chin, scanning the entire bridge all at once. It was as if he'd never been here before.

"I want you to muster the fleet," said the Grand Highlord, "and destroy the rebellion."

CHAPTER THIRTY

HOPE FAILS

Nine . . . Nine . . . Nine . . . Nine . . . Nine . . .

Elenah opened her eyes and was surprised she wasn't dead.

Black thunderclouds swirled through the sky, cracking with thunder and lighting, throwing harsh rain upon the dead fields of Devar. The winds curled around her sodden body, pinning her to the ground. This was it. This was where it ended.

"Teveran . . ." she muttered, her cheek buried in the mires. The mud drew her downwards, sucking her deep into the core of the moon. Lightning flashed, accompanied by a symphony of thunder that made her whole body feel weightless. "I'm . . . I'm sorry." Her voice cracked. She drew herself up onto all fours, wondering where everyone was. "I . . ."

Lightning crashed. She raised her eyes toward the storm, and pleaded for it all to stop, but the storm ignored her pleas and only beat her further. She tried to curl her hands into fists, but they were frozen stiff from all the mud. She could feel nothing but the rain. A fork of frantic lightning lit up the night sky. Shards of white light pelted her skin. She clenched her jaw, clawed at the mud and balled it up in her fists.

Gods, but things had been going so well! She glanced about for a sign of life, but she could hardly make out anything. Where was Hannah? Argus? Jethre . . . Where had they gone? Flashes of lightning cast white lights across dead bodies: hundreds of them, thousands, all posing with frozen limbs and bloodied mouths hanging open.

You're only going to get yourself killed.

Voices swirled through her head, making her dizzy, even louder than the tempest. It angered her, realising how right he'd been. Gilgan knew so much more than herself; how could she ever turn her back on him, or think she knew better?

She squeezed her eyes shut, trying to forget it all. But in the darkness she saw Gilgan's face: long, drawn and dead. But he couldn't be dead . . . could he? Not *Gilgan.* The dead face of the man opened his mouth and said, "If you go out there, you are putting yourself in grave danger. You're not *trained.*" She opened her eyes and dragged herself onto hands and knees.

Help me, Elenah . . .

She could see them all. Oswald and Hannah and Eukaloo. Were they all dead? Were they all just victims of the Council's death march? What of her father?

She saw Teveran on his knees, all alone.

"I tried," she croaked, dragging her nails through the mud, searching for her pistol. It was gone. She thumped her fists against the mud. *Dammit!*

Elenah raised her eyes and saw someone standing among the fury of the storm: a black figure silhouetted against the silver storm clouds. He was tall, standing about fifteen feet away, holding something short, black and jagged towards the ground. Elenah's heart hammered. She tried to scramble up, but the mud clung to her. He turned to her, and suddenly the weapon was gone. Then he approached, squelching through the mud.

"Stay back!" Elenah screamed, flicking out a soaked hand, but the figure didn't stop. The lightning flashed; his black cloak caught the light and threw it off in different directions. It flared open down the middle. He came into proximity and Elenah felt a warm hum rip through the air. This man seemed familiar—he emitted the same sort of aura as Jethre, and even Gilgan . . .

"Please," Elenah pleaded. "Just leave me alone."

The man knelt in the mud before her. His angular face was clean-shaven. "Look at me." His voice carried an incongruous warmth, and each word seemed to carry a large weight of its own. In the darkness, she couldn't guess his age. "I've been looking for you."

It took Elenah a moment to process what he was saying. *He's been looking for me?* None of it made sense. She didn't even know who this man was. He offered her his hand, and she regarded the black leather glove, pulled tight. "I . . ." Her mouth went dry.

"Come with me," said the man, and he grabbed her hand.

He led her inside one of the square huts as the storm beat outside. Thunder bellowed in the grim skies, rattling the walls. A small damp pallet lay in the corner, reverberating, and a single window dragged in the harsh lightning blasts.

The walls were so thin she could hear the rain as though it slapped her skin. She heard the thunderclaps and it shook her bones.

A single lamp hung from the ceiling, swaying side-to-side.

The man paced around the room, exercising his hands. Rain dripped down his leather coat. His skin was awful pale, like a ghost. His age was difficult to tell, though he couldn't be younger than sixty. "Sit down," he said, gesturing to the bed. Elenah just looked at it, not quite sure what she should do. Her head was still thumping.

She remembered the bodies outside, melting in the storm, and realised she'd seen it before—on Saecon IV, outside the ancient black castle. She glanced through the fogging window, and saw the bodies all lined up haphazardly. "Did you do that?" she asked. "Did you kill those people outside?" Her voice trembled. She felt bile burning her throat.

"They died long ago," the man said. "The Council killed them, and turned them into monsters." He grinded his throat, balled his hands, then unravelled his fingers and flicked droplets of blood and rain onto the ground. "You should sit down."

The bed creaked as she followed his instruction. The air reeked of death. A tattered uniform draped the ground, soggy cards were scattered in the corner.

"Are you a magician?" Elenah timidly asked.

The man chuckled weakly. He was pacing back and forth, the light swimming across him. His head almost brushed the ceiling, silvery black hair soaked from the rain, falling across his shoulders like chains. "Yes. But I'm one of the good ones. I'm not here to hurt you."

Elenah frowned. "Gilgan was one, too."

"*Gilgan.*" She wasn't sure if was a statement or question, or just a simple observance. He hummed. "I fear the worst for him."

Elenah started. "You knew him?"

"We fought together, once." There was a tone of reverence in his voice, as if he was talking about some long-dead god. "He was my friend." He looked up and said, "That's why I'm here, to do what we should've done years ago."

"Who are you?" Elenah asked quietly.

"They called me Lothar." He developed a distant gaze as the name drifted across the room. Elenah found that her heart was racing. Before she could press him further, Lothar said, "There is a dark force gathering. Take this." He reached down behind him, flicking back a fold in his coat to reveal a small glass vial filled with silver dust.

He proffered it to her. "They already have your brother. There was nothing I could do for him, but maybe you still can. There's a great power in you, Daughter of Etheron. Even untrained, I feel it strongly. This will help you get him out of there."

Elenah took the vial in shaking hands. She had no clue what it was, but that was not what occupied her thoughts now. "My brother . . . Have you seen him?"

"No."

Elenah's heart sank. She dropped her eyes to the vial. The silver particles seemed to *float* inside it. She turned it this way and that, and the dust seemed to fall at the wrong angles.

"That's an Essence," Lothar said. "You can use it to travel between worlds. All you need to do is grab a pinch and channel the spell, *Transcendius.* It doesn't take much magic.

Whatever Gilgan taught you . . . That will be enough. It will *have* to be enough, I'm afraid."

"Where will it take me?" Elenah asked.

"Somewhere safe." However, he seemed to hesitate for a second, as if there were some kind of chance that it might not send her to this place at all.

Elenah tucked away the vial and looked up at him. "Is my brother okay?"

"I'm afraid not," Lothar said, folding his arms as he leaned casually against the wall. Elenah struggled to draw breath. A wave of dread rocked her.

"What do you mean?"

He lowered his head, said nothing.

"*What happened to him?*" Elenah demanded.

Shadows bathed the man. "They've corrupted him, turned him into their secret weapon. But there is still a chance we can save him. I still believe you can bring him back." He dropped his stern eyes to the ground, then wandered toward the window.

"But . . ." she managed, tears drowning her words. "That's not true. He can't be. He . . ." She felt it again, the icy sensation swimming across her body. "But I've felt him out there!"

"Of course you have," Lothar said. "That is why you're in such danger." He strolled into the centre of the room, one hand resting on his belt. "A terrible thing has happened," Lothar continued, as if to himself. "The Dark Lord has returned, and . . . I'm afraid war is coming."

"The Dark Lord . . ." she muttered, her mind revolving in circles. "War . . ." She felt sick with frustration and anger and confusion. "No . . . War's here already!" she blurted.

"I'm afraid not," said the man. "This is hardly the beginning."

Elenah felt a pit of terror open up inside her heart. She realised Amohria had spoken of the same thing: *This war is not about the Council,* she'd said. *Soon they will be gone, yes . . . but there is more to it. Soon, it will take a much darker turn, and from there . . .*

She looked back at Lothar. "What's going to happen?"

"We're going to have to fight. You and I, and others of our kind." He seemed troubled by something, then withdrew a glowing red stone from his pocket. He held it in his outstretched hand. "Did Gilgan ever give you one of these? You know . . . Before he left?"

"No." Elenah shook her head. She felt winded, tried to breathe but found she couldn't. "What is it?" she uttered, her voice rattling.

Lothar pocketed the stone. "It's been infused with a very dark kind of magic. The Dark Lord's power has infected this stone, as well as eight others. We must protect them at all costs to ensure our enemies do not restore the Dark Lord his power."

Elenah had so many questions, but couldn't speak.

"There isn't long left," Lothar said, turning back around. "You must go to your brother and bring him back . . ." He trailed off, then slumped down in the corner. "Your brother is in great danger. He's been taken by a man called Fex."

"Fex." Elenah tested the name on her lips.

"I knew him once. I couldn't save him. But you can still save your brother." His gaze was firm, his voice like steel. "You have its gift. And you have that Essence. *Use it.*"

Elenah stared at him, trying to find the right thing to say.

"There's something else." Lothar eyed her warily, gradually beginning to scratch his chin. "Gilgan gifted me his shade." Yet it had not saved her. It hadn't helped her flee with the others.

Lothar smiled. "Of course he did," he said, as though it were obvious. "Gilgan's a very smart man. He sees far deeper and further than anybody else I've ever met. If he truly gifted you his shade—the Sandred, if I recall correctly—then you are in very safe hands."

"But it didn't work!" Elenah blurted.

"It will come," Lothar said calmly. "It will come."

Elenah could only hope he was right.

"Is there anything else you would like to ask?"

"I . . ." She wetted her lips. "How do you know who I am?"

"I don't. Not really." He swept back folds in his coat, revealing some kind of ruby charm, but only for the briefest moment. "But I know *what* you are."

"What am I?" she asked.

"A very powerful magician." He gave her his hand. "Come. I should take you back."

"Where?"

"Back to your friends, of course."

HANNAH WAS ALONE AGAIN, though she wasn't surprised. It always ended like this. It had been like this ever since she was a child on Feluria, when the Kerrean came . . .

But she was far from Feluria now. She was standing in the grey haze of Framus, a moon in some grim pocket of the galaxy she didn't know. The fortress was much larger than the one on Devar, with stone buildings pockmarked across the uneven wastes, scattered like the teeth of some giant. Watchtowers of crooked stone slabs scraped the dull skies. Soldiers with packs of rations hurried about, loading rifles with new starfire cells and bullet cartridges.

Mountains rose in the distance. They were obscured behind the mists, but she could see their bold outlines, like an artist's unfinished painting. And, beyond the mountains, lay the ever-present swirls of red gas thrown off by Atrea.

They're all gone . . .

Hannah couldn't remember much of what had happened. They'd been attacked; it was a slaughter, relentless and fast. They'd barely managed to escape, and she was sure she'd only escaped on luck. Somehow the Forty-Ninth Council had found them, and she was beginning to realise those bastards would find them wherever they were in the galaxy.

In the chaos she'd lost sight of Elenah, and had taken a bullet in her shoulder. She remembered stumbling about, half-dazed . . . Then one of the soldiers had grabbed her, flown her to this other cell. He'd looked vaguely Tauran, and he'd probably saved her life.

She rubbed at the bandages they'd strapped across her shoulder. She could still feel the blood streaming down her arm as they'd pulled the bullet free. Doctor Levis had attended to her; he'd nearly killed his assistant when the young wolf-like Kyubo almost set her arm on fire trying to stave the bleeding. Why did they care about her so much? They hardly knew who she was.

"The *Subjugator* is currently in orbit over Kasnah," Jethre said, pacing back and forth around the dockyard of ships. There were so many of them, even though there weren't many soldiers left. Of the survivors, so many were wounded.

She could see that look of despair in their eyes. She'd seen it before, each time she looked in a mirror.

But for now these soldiers looked like they were going to keep fighting. They hurried about, prepping the custom-built Avengers for take-off, for one last strike against the Council's flagship. Most of them were probably going to die but, if they cared, none of them showed it.

Hannah just stood there, watching. She couldn't run; there was nowhere to go. She couldn't just go off and fly away, because the Kerrean wanted her dead. So, she just listened.

Jethre went on: "The Council knows where we are, and they're targeting our cells, one at a time, slowly chipping us away." He stopped and eyed each soldier, singling them out with those eyes that were hardened from so much violence. He curled his hand into a fist, blood trickling out from his palm. "If we wait here any longer, I'm afraid it will be too late."

The soldiers returned his gaze with hunger in their eyes. This time, nobody argued. Hannah looked at the starfighters, which had been painted various colours.

"We have to strike them down *today*," Jethre said, "otherwise it will be too late. We'll burn their flagship, bring down their Grand Highlord, and save this rebellion." He glanced at Hannah, his brown irises swirling with passion. "Then, the galaxy."

She felt the pistol tucked into her belt. A young blonde-haired soldier had given it to her, as if he'd expected her to be able to use it. She wasn't sure if she could. She'd survived this long by running, and hiding in the shadows, and staying out of trouble.

But I can't die, she told herself. *There's another Felirean out there somewhere, perhaps the only other Felirean in the galaxy . . . I have to find him.* It was that thought that rooted her feet upon the dry dirt ground, that kept her heart beating, that kept her wanting not to die.

"For too long have we been their victims," Jethre said. "But the time now is to strike back! We are all that stands in their way of tearing this galaxy apart!" He spluttered as he shouted, and Hannah felt herself trembling. She glanced about, searching for the young boy whose name was Lirin. He'd been the one who told her about the Felirean.

"Hey." Argus stood beside her. His crimson scarf circled his neck and drooped across his chest. He wore the same brown coat with the blood-red gear painted on the shoulder. His messy brown hair waved and curled around his head. In his belt was a pistol, across his shoulder an intimidating black rifle. He also carried a fully-stuffed backpack. And his right hand . . . She could barely refrain from looking at it. An exoskeleton completely engulfed the skin. It must have been some sort of mutation. It unsettled her.

"You all right?" he asked.

Hannah averted her eyes.

"I'm sorry about what happened to your friend." He looked pale, sick. There were deep bags beneath his eyes, and he had a nasty gash underneath his jaw.

"It's okay," Hannah said. "We'll be all right."

"I failed," Argus said, shaking his head. "But you know what? You're right." He stepped closer, trudging through the dirt. "This is our chance to change the galaxy. As long as we keep moving forward, keep fighting, one battle after another, we'll get there."

Hannah turned towards him. "How do you know?"

"Because they can't keep fighting forever."

"And what happens if we *do* win? I can't imagine a galaxy with no one in charge."

Argus frowned and opened his mouth, but was brought up short by a rumbling in the air. Hannah spun around and saw a massive black shuttle descending through the haze. Wisps of cloud outlined it, spraying off in great bursts. A wave of sickness overcame her. *Not again,* she thought. *They don't stop coming . . .* She reached for the pistol in her belt, but Argus grabbed her arm and sternly shook his head.

A crowd gathered as the black shuttle touched down. It had a sharp nose, a square viewscreen, and two wings jutting left and right. It couldn't have been much larger than the starfighters down here, but it looked incredible. Soldiers hurried to surround it. Jethre, with a disgruntled look on his face, charged to the fore, waving the others away. He rested his hand on his pistol, but made no move to draw it.

The door slid open.

Elenah stepped out, her raven hair a mess. Hannah's heart leapt and she ran towards her. Jethre tried to catch her, but she slipped from his grasp and threw her arms around Elenah. "You're alive!" Hannah gasped.

"I'm alive," Elenah breathed, as if she needed to convince herself. She stepped away from her, hazel eyes glimmering, reflecting the stars. She looked different, stronger. Her gaze darkened as she took in the fortress, and the soldiers, and the shipyard. "Look at this place." She wandered around, and somehow seemed awed by it. "We're so close. Are you ready?"

Hannah nodded firmly. "Yes."

Jethre strode past them as a tall, lanky man disembarked the shuttle. He had black hair and a black coat, marmoreal skin and a ruffled, grey shirt. Judging by the wrinkles and folds in his skin he was sixty or maybe seventy. "Gods," Jethre said. "You came back."

"Hmm," said the other man, hands dug deep in the pockets of his black coat.

"Who is he?" Hannah whispered.

"An ally," Elenah said.

The man in black stepped past Jethre and examined the wastes of Framus. Soldiers climbed into the cockpits, carrying supplies back and forth, praying to the gods that they weren't all killed. The man turned around and looked at Jethre. Hannah wondered how they knew each other. "Do you still have the stone?" asked the man in black.

Jethre nodded.

The other man leaned in and whispered something that caused veins to burst across Jethre's forehead. Jethre stepped back and said, "Stay safe out there."

"You too, Jethre." However, he lingered. "If you see Fex, give him my regards. Tell him I wish I could be there. Tell him . . . Tell him that he has to stop this *right now*."

Jethre nodded sternly.

Without another word, the man in black returned to his shuttle and disappeared into the stars. Jethre strode back across the shipyard. "We don't have much time," he said. "Get your asses in those fighters." He reached them, and stared regretfully at Elenah. "I'm sorry for leaving you there. I should've known."

"Did you know Gilgan?" Elenah asked.

Jethre paused. "Yes. We . . . worked together on occasion."

Elenah gave him a soft smile.

"He would've wanted you to go through with this," Jethre said. "You're the only one who can." He stepped up towards her and touched her shoulder. "Are you ready?"

"It doesn't matter," Elenah said. "We're running out of time."

"Enough talking, then," Hannah said, trying to bolster her voice with confidence. Of course she was scared, and anxious—but she always was. That feeling never went away, so the most she could do was suppress it and focus on the end goal. Today she was going to have to stare down the eyes of death and deny it. She couldn't keep running, for somewhere out there was a distant hope that she was not alone in this galaxy.

"They can come with me," Argus said, stepping up towards them.

Jethre eyed him speculatively, then gave a crooked smile. "You're ever the gentleman. I suppose you've finally started to take Flair's advice to heart."

"Just want to help out, Cap."

"I'm afraid they won't both *fit* with you, Argus."

"Are you calling me fat?"

"I'm calling you too noble for your own good."

"I can fly," Hannah said, even if she wasn't the best pilot in the galaxy.

Jethre seemed pleased by that. "Come with me and I'll get you sorted. Argus, take good care of Elenah. Anything happens to her, I'll have your head."

Argus grinned. "This time I won't let you down."

"Don't take any chances with her life," Jethre said, then walked back to the ships.

"Hannah," Elenah said, turning to her. "You don't have to do this."

"I want to," Hannah replied, then leaned up and kissed her on the cheek. It was just the smallest peck, the softest brush of the lips.

Elenah stared. "What was that for?"

"For luck." And then she turned and hurriedly followed Jethre.

Chapter Thirty-One

FLIGHT OF THE REBELLION

The Magician's Code:
1. *The Soulblade, to duel;*
2. *The Shade, to command;*
3. *The Essence, to transcend.*

Nineteen rebel Avengers spiralled through the tunnels of space.

Elenah sat in the co-pilot's seat beside Argus. Lights flashed all around them, starlight reflected off the cockpit window. The hydraulics beneath the seat softened every jerk, every bump, and every jolt. It reminded her of Gilgan's Starsinger.

Stars striated and mystical objects darted in and out of view. Elenah watched them pass by as she and Argus cut through the endless starscape. Silver lights flashed across the window. She felt the gentle thrum of starfire, like a constant reminder of where she was.

They ventured in the custom Avenger farther and farther from safety, into territory that lay firmly within the Council's grip, to the worlds at the heart of the Inner Realm.

Jethre's voice crackled through the radio. "*We're coming up on the* Subjugator."

A spike of fear ran through her body, but she convinced herself that she was ready. She *had* to be ready, because getting there was just one part of the rescue. The second was getting inside. The next was locating Teveran. And then she needed to get him out.

And . . . there was the man called *Fex*.

The more she thought about it, the worst things looked.

Lothar's vial of Essence hung at her belt. *Your brother's been taken,* he'd told her. *There was nothing I could do for him, but maybe you still can.*

There's a great power in you, Daughter of Etheron.

His words reminded her that she was not only doing this for Teveran, but for all of Etheron, and for her father . . . She *was* Etheron's daughter. She was all that remained of it.

And she also had Gilgan's own power, his shade, the Sandred: king of dragons. This was where he wanted her to be. Gilgan certainly thought she was capable of saving Teveran, so now she just needed to borrow some of his own confidence and get the job done.

Argus leaned in to the microphone and said, "I'm moving in." He bent the steering yoke forward, sending their fighter spearing ahead of the others. Graham's fighter and four others burst off after them, silver starfire crackling about the thrusters. "You ready, Elenah?"

Elenah nodded.

Argus flipped an overhead switch with his skeletal hand. "Graham," he said. "Take my left. Cellis, I've got your flank. Bets. Nolen. Erith." Their various responses crackled through the radio. Elenah gazed out the cockpit's canopy and saw their starfighters break away, white lightning bursting from the aft thrusters. A green fighter, slashed by a white streak of paint. A blue one covered with scratches. Elenah could see the young men inside.

"You look nervous," Argus said, his flesh-knuckle turning white as he gripped the steering yoke and mechanically flicked switches. Elenah saw sweat beading on his forehead, glittering beneath the hundreds of lights flashing all around. Lights from the Avenger, the blue and white streams that shone from Kasnah. The canopy began to grow *icy*.

"Nervous?" Elenah said, the shaking fighter causing her voice to rattle. "I'm fine." She focused on her breathing. *We're almost there,* she thought. Music in the cockpit alerted her senses, causing her to jump. A smirk crawled across Argus's lips.

"Music?" Elenah asked.

"Ludenberg's final symphony," Argus said.

Elenah frowned, shooting him a sideward glance. The music strobed through the cockpit. Strings. *Keening* strings. "Well it's not really helping," she said, then puffed out a breath and tried to calm herself. She squeezed her eyes shut and saw Teveran's face. She saw Gilgan. Her father. Suddenly she was back on Etheron.

"Gods," Argus muttered. "There it is."

Elenah opened her eyes and saw the *Subjugator*. It loomed above them, glowing in the lights from Kasnah. A Leviathan. Elenah's heart started racing. The music dissolved into the background, and she couldn't tell if it was still playing.

"Teveran." She breathed his name.

I'm coming.

TEVERAN STOOD ON THE BRIDGE of the *Subjugator*, surveying the vast expanse of stars. He was finally here, where he was always meant to be. Not that it really mattered; soon, it would all be over.

They were steadily creeping away from Kasnah, but the icy planet still lay beneath them, desolate and secluded—like Etheron. Fex stood beside him with a datapad, making notes. The officers reported to Fex, too, but they also feared him.

Teveran grabbed the ends of his black leather gloves and pulled them on tighter. The uniform fit him well; it was far superior to those armoured suits the troopers had to wear. But what made it more fitting was that he no longer had to worry about what he'd been, or where he'd come from. He was the High Prince no longer. To these men he was nothing but their Grand Highlord, their leader. It gave him the confidence to do what needed to be done.

Fex watched him from the corner of his eye.

Fex *always* watched him.

"My lord . . ."

Teveran turned to see a young officer. His hair was close-cropped and he had blue eyes that reflected the endless starscape like mirrors.

"Sir, we have detected movement."

Teveran saw it too. Through the large window upon the bridge of the *Subjugator*, he saw the starfighters approaching. They came from below, leaking streams of eclectic starfire. He felt something, a strong surge of . . . *anger*. He watched the fighters, and was suddenly glad Thrakk was no longer at his side. He felt free now, no longer held back by anyone.

Not Thrakk, not his father, not Elenah, or Gilgan . . .

He blew a deep, trembling breath, and turned back to the starfighters, approaching from below. A ripple of sweat cracked his forehead.

For the greater good, he thought.

"My lord?"

"Destroy them," Teveran said.

ELENAH ONLY SAW THE FLASH of distant starfire, and the whir of a missile, before one of the nearby Avengers exploded and debris flung out in all directions.

She didn't even have time to scream.

"Cellis!" Argus roared.

Jethre's voice rumbled through the radio: *"Forward!"*

Argus slammed forward the steering yoke. The music cut off abruptly, plunging them into silence. Elenah's stomach gushed up into her throat and a menacing force drove her back into the seat. The Avenger lurched forward, then pitched downwards as another missile split the endless void of space with a soundless shriek.

Then, from the underside of the *Subjugator* hurtled silver enemy Ragnaroks. A massive Banshee floated into view, radiating a sound like endless thunder and releasing hundreds more enemy fighters. Their thrusters came alive, bright starfire billowing out, and they roared forward, buzzing like insects coming out to defend their nest.

"Graham!" Argus snapped. "Dive!"

Graham's fighter plummeted down below Argus's as a storm of bullets hissed in their direction. Silver blasts ripped through space. Elenah could smell it from within the cockpit, could feel the searing heat. Argus sent their fighter surging after Graham's, following in his twirling streams of starfire.

Argus threw them to port as bullets rattled against the viewscreen. They gnawed at the shields, bouncing off at seemingly random trajectories. Elenah's seat kicked her up. Voices crackled through the radio, battle and attack formations shouted out by Jethre and others. Seven Avengers closed in from their left, another half-dozen from their right. There was one above them, slightly damaged, and it might have been Hannah's.

Bulletfire streaked both ways.

"Return fire," Argus said. Then he flipped a switch, slammed down a trigger on the yoke, and berserk bullets surged from their front cannons. It was *deafening.* Elenah gasped, clutching her seat straps as Argus brought them back up. They careened left. Graham broke right. Two other Avengers emerged into the battle overhead, and one of the Council's Ragnaroks exploded in a dazzling display of lights.

Argus barrelled as a missile cut beside them. He hadn't even levelled yet when he jerked the trigger and brought down another Ragnarok. Sweat sprayed off his forehead and onto Elenah. She groaned, flicking it off. Argus grinned as green and white lights danced across his face. "You okay there?" he asked, a smirk drawing up the ends of his lips.

"I'm doing just—"

An Avenger exploded ahead of them. Argus screamed, "*Erith!*" He shoved the yoke forward. The fighter dropped, just briefly, and when it popped back up she could see the entire rebel force converging on the *Subjugator*. There were fighters buzzing in all directions, Avengers and Ragnaroks, engaged in a dozen dogfights.

Like the endings of Gilgan's stories.

They were so close now. The *Subjugator* was right there, waiting for her. Into the radio, Argus said, "I'm going in," and a crackly response sent him affirmative. Argus glanced at Elenah as the hangar's ingress loomed before them. Steel was all she could see. The huge Leviathan filled her vision, blocked out the light of Kasnah, of the sun. "We're going in."

"GODS, IT'S HER," Teveran gasped. He wasn't sure how he knew; he just *did.* For a split second he felt like he was back on Etheron, with Gilgan and Elenah at his side, laughing and singing and—

Fex stepped up beside him. "She is brave."

"No. She *shouldn't have come.*"

"How did she find you?"

Teveran grinded his teeth, curling his hands into fists. "I don't know." He watched the colourful fighters converge upon the *Subjugator.*

Why are you doing this to me? he asked her. *I can't go back now.*

He turned away from the glass. "Just get rid of her."

"No," Fex said.

Teveran eyed him darkly. Fex's eyes glinted. Bright lights from explosions crossed the bridge back and forth. "What do you mean?" Teveran asked.

"You must confront her."

"Fex . . . I can't."

"Prove to yourself that you're no longer the child you were. Prove to me that you are ready. Make me believe that you can do what must be done."

"I *can't!*" Teveran yelled. "Gods, but she's my *sister.*" He felt sick. Slowly, his eyes rolled and then his body turned to follow. The rebels were targeting the flagship now, not that it would matter because they had the best shields in the galaxy.

This galaxy needs a hero, Fex had said in the star chamber so many days back. *A chance to be a part of something larger than the sum of us both,* in the icy temple of Kasnah. *A chance to escape the Council, and maybe even end this war . . .*

His head was spinning.

You're too slow! Fex had told him. *Too weak.*

What you have to do, what you have to become . . . I don't think you understand yet. How could you? You're only a child. His voice became all that Teveran could hear, as clear as if he were speaking right now. *You need someone who can teach you how to fight. Not just to stay alive, not simply to resist—but to act, to win, to do what must be done.*

Opening his mouth felt like pulling apart strings. He tasted blood and fire. He curled his hands into fists. "Bring her to me, then." He faced Fex again, and Fex nodded approval.

Teveran's trembling fingers curled around the handle of his pistol. It weighed a hundred pounds. *I'm sorry,* he thought. *I'm so sorry it has to end like this.*

"Entry in three . . . two—"

The Avenger ran through the gateway into the hangar of the *Subjugator,* slamming the metal ground. Elenah jerked in her seat. The starfighter grinded along the floor, sending up crackling sparks and a loud, droning wail. Argus grunted as they spun, jamming the brakes. They slammed into a dormant Ragnarok, and finally stopped.

The glass canopy flipped open, throwing off flakes of ice that quickly melted. For a while, Elenah just sat there, trying to catch her breath. The second fighter came in faster, scraping the floor, then slamming a wall and causing all the lights to flicker.

Argus slapped their belts off and grabbed Elenah's arm, hauling her out of the cockpit. She hit the ground and reeled. Argus pulled out a pistol. From the other fighter emerged Graham. He teetered, uneasy on his feet. A long trail of blood rolled down his face, over his chin, and onto his jacket. If it worried him, he didn't show it.

"Blast it, I'm getting rusty," Graham grunted. Elenah stayed close beside Argus, her hands and knees trembling, her stomach rolling, the pistol tucked behind her back weighing her down.

Another Avenger roared through the force-field. Jethre hopped out, rifle cradled in his arms. The next ship came in slower than the others, but landed gracefully. The pale lights swam across Hannah's milky-green face as she also debarked, pistol in hand.

Jethre strode out before them, ripping the radio from his belt and pressing it to his lips. "Bets!" he barked, then dragged it away and puffed out a long, ragged breath.

"*Roger. Approaching the aft terminal.*"

"And Sim? Levis?"

"*They're en route. Give us a minute.*"

The captain nodded and stuffed the device back inside his belt. Long barrelled rifle cradled in his arms, he turned to the others and said, "Stay together. Stay on point." He looked at Elenah, and she hurriedly dragged out her pistol. She gripped it tight, steadied her nervous breathing. She glanced at Hannah. The young Felirean nodded firmly.

Jethre swung around and marched forward. "Let's give these bastards—"

A wide door at the back of the hangar screamed open, and troopers piled out, raising gleaming black rifles. Their lieutenant, a full-clad trooper with cobalt stripes along his shoulder plate, stepped ahead of them and said, "Stand down and surrender."

"Bastards," Graham cursed. He raised his rifle and put a hole through one of the troopers. The lieutenant ducked as another bullet was fired. A couple more troopers went down, their armour glowing red.

Jethre threw himself in front of Elenah and continued to fire into the troopers. More were piling into the hangar. The lieutenant flipped out a pistol and fired back at them.

Graham went down first.

"No!" Argus yelled.

"Hold your fire!" the lieutenant barked as he fired blindly at the group. Bullets whacked his armour and bounced off, exposing a sizzling blue body shield. Jethre and Argus continued past Graham's dead body, firing until the last trooper fell and the lieutenant was pinned against the rear wall, firing his last bullets at them. "*Hold your fire!*" he cried out again.

Jethre moved like a blizzard, kicking the pistol out of the lieutenant's hand and kneeing his jaw out of its socket. Then he slammed the guy into the wall with blood dribbling out of his mouth. With the efficiency of a master soldier, he replaced his rifle with a pistol and aimed it at the poor guy's sweaty forehead.

"The girl," choked the lieutenant. "She's been summoned to the bridge . . ."

"What do you want with her?" Jethre snarled.

"Not us . . . The Grand Highlord."

Elenah's chest burned as she slowly approached them, tucking away her pistol. "It's Teveran," she said. "Teveran's the Grand Highlord now. It's him, Jethre. I have to go there."

"Wait," Jethre hissed.

Elenah broke to the front of the group, looking down upon the lieutenant, whose face was turning purple. "Take me to him," she said. "I'll go alone. Just take me to my brother."

"Right," Jethre said, though he didn't take his aim off the man.

The lieutenant nodded hurriedly, then stood up. He was still looking at Jethre, eagerly. "You're the rebels, aren't you? You've come here to take the ship . . . or destroy it." Jethre barely twitched. "There's a way to shut it all down . . . but you will need the key." He retrieved a red keycard from his suit and proffered it to him shakily. "Um . . . I heard somebody left the doors to the main operations bay unlocked . . . That's where you will need to go."

Jethre snatched the keycard from the lieutenant and nodded to him graciously. "Take the girl to her brother. If there are others like you, tell them to get off the ship."

"Okay," the lieutenant said, then looked at Elenah. "Come with me."

THE BRIDGE OF THE *SUBJUGATOR* WAS COLD. Two troopers

led Elenah inside, into a quiet stillness that not even the rumbling engines could disrupt. She gazed through the four large windows into the galaxy beyond. She'd always dreamed of being among the stars, and now she was.

All she had to do was save Teveran.

They carried her into the centre, then stopped, and the man standing fifteen paces away ordered them to leave her there. People watched her. Officers, highlords . . . *So this is the Council,* she thought. *These are the ones who have taken you away.*

Silence. A man with a black cape: the Grand Highlord.

Elenah's heart leapt up into her throat.

They've corrupted him, Lothar had told her. *Turned him into their secret weapon.*

Her breath snared, disbelief and denial overcoming her all at once. Although the man on Devar had already told her, seeing it was a whole different thing. It was worse.

"Clear the bridge," Teveran said, his voice familiar yet . . . different. Harder. Like iron. It *hurt* to see him like this, to just think about what could have led him here. She hesitantly half-reached towards the vial of Essence hanging from her belt, concealed beneath her coat.

Soon, they were all alone.

"Teveran," Elenah said. "It's time to go home."

For a while, he just stood there. That onyx cape fluttered behind him. His brown hair was all ruffled and unkempt, laying across his shoulders. His bright, hazel eyes watched her apprehensively. He breathed coarsely, shakily. He was afraid.

Elenah stepped forward. "Teveran . . . Come on." She tried to hide the fact there were tears welling behind her eyes. "You're being silly." Her timid steps became paces, then strides, and she split the middle of the bridge. "I've come to take you back."

"Don't come any closer." His voice wavered. He also stood clearly on the verge of tears. Elenah stopped, maybe out of instinct, or out of fear, or just uncertainty. She couldn't leave him here. Not him. She'd come all this way, and she wasn't leaving without Teveran.

"What do you mean?" she asked.

"You have to go, Elenah."

"Sorry?"

"I'm staying here."

"Why would you want to *stay*? It's the *Council*, Teveran! They betrayed us. They've ruined everything." She felt anger rush through her, swelling like a sore bruise. "I am *not* leaving here without you."

"You're mistaken," Teveran said, walking towards her. "I'm not doing this for the Council. This is larger than that. Elenah . . . I've *seen* what's going to happen if we don't do anything. But you . . . You can't be here." His eyes were glowing with some kind of frightening awe. It made Elenah feel sick. It twisted her gut and she almost ran away.

"I am *not* going anywhere."

"Don't be a fool!" he yelled. His voice echoed through the chamber. The stars outside strobed across the room. It had become a field of metal and bodies now. Elenah could feel the gentle thrum of starfire keeping the Leviathan running through space.

"Teveran . . ." she stammered. "Please don't yell."

He pulled a pistol on her. Elenah gasped and drew her

own in a trembling grip. She couldn't shoot him. Sweat slithered across her palms. "You're forcing me to do this!" Elenah cried.

"I'm not forcing you to do anything. We're not enemies. Just leave. Go back."

"Put down the gun. *Please*, Teveran." She gripped it in two hands, but still she couldn't keep a level aim. Teveran held his pistol with one, and he looked so calm with it. But Elenah felt his fear, and she knew he was still in there. "Come back," she whispered. Behind him, an elderly man appeared with his gloved hands clasped together. *Fex.*

It was the same man from her vision, the man who held the chain around Teveran's neck. He was the one who did this to her. He was the very thing Amohria and Lothar had spoken about, the one thing that was worse than the Council . . .

The old man calmly said, "Do it, Teveran."

Elenah shook her head, but she didn't dare peel her aim from him. "He's tricked you," she said, taking a step closer—just one. If she could get close enough, she could use the Essence to get them both out, get them far away from here. "There's still so much beauty and majesty left in this galaxy. Come with me, and we can see it all together." She felt anger fuel her again, and when she blinked, tears crossed her vision. "What . . . What would Gilgan say?"

"Gilgan?" Teveran said weakly.

"He never meant for any of this to happen."

Teveran grit his teeth. "Don't you see? Gilgan failed us. Our *family* failed us. They were liars. The galaxy is falling apart, Elenah. We've both seen it. Besides . . . This is who I am now. This is *what* I am. A hero, like I was always meant to be." But he was no hero. Had he become so unhappy with himself that he would rather become a slave to the man called Fex, than Teveran Lockwood, the High Prince of Etheron?

"This isn't you!"

"*Go back home, Elenah!*"

She whipped out the vial of Essence and threw herself at Teveran.

A blast of energy smashed her from the front and flicked her across the bridge. She slammed the metallic floor on all fours. The glass vial shattered and silver dust-like particles sprayed out all over her. She gasped. When she looked up, she saw Fex with his hand outstretched. The old man stepped in front of Teveran. He loomed over her, like the villains in Gilgan's greatest stories. "A vial of Essence," he snarled. "How did a girl like yourself come across one?"

Elenah glanced up at him. "What have you done to him, you *bastard?*"

"I asked you a *question!*" He cast another spell which sent her spinning into the wall. She slammed it hard, the breath hurtling out of her lungs. She collapsed on all fours, but managed to keep herself from falling flat on her face. "Go, Teveran," Fex said. "Get out of here."

"Don't listen to him!" Elenah croaked.

"Go!" Fex spat. "Find an escape pod and get as far from here as possible. I'll find you."

Teveran hesitated, and somewhere in those lost, cold eyes, Elenah saw him. He was still in there. She could still save him. She just needed to show him the way, as Gilgan had shown her. She mouthed, *You don't have to go,* but Teveran wasn't listening. He looked from her, to Fex, then quickly spun around and strode from the chamber.

"No!" Elenah yelled.

Fex cast a spell that sent her barrelling across the floor, flicking up particles of Essence. "Teveran is not the man you think he is," Fex said. "He's stronger. He's like a black cloud of unharnessed starfire, broiling, *broiling*, just waiting to be unleashed . . ." A semblance of a smirk crossed his lips, but Elenah felt nothing but raw anger.

"You're insane," she grunted.

"Who gave you the Essence?"

"I won't tell you anything!"

Fex cackled, threw his hand to the side. "Then I will simply have to *force* it out of you." His arm went taut, and then the entire galaxy seemed to tilt on its side as a short, jagged blade, pitch black and emitting inconceivable power, flared into existence within his grasp. Nearly imperceptible crackles of black light flourished around it.

"A soulblade . . ." Elenah whispered. Her whole body throbbed, pain shooting through her chest. Fex's menacing figure filled her vision, bright lights spinning above his head. Time stood still. The old man, with the magical sword. A sinister energy surged around him. His eyes shone like black obsidian. He looked larger, more intimidating.

Fex: the man who had taken her brother.

Elenah snarled as she dragged herself up, clutching a handful of Lothar's silver Essence. *There's a great power in you, Daughter of Etheron*, he had told her. *You have its gift.* Elenah drew a long, deep breath. Fex's smile grew, his crooked teeth like tombstones in the starlight. Elenah felt something calling her. Incredible anger. Pain. Untapped fury.

"Will you fight, child?" Fex taunted, testing his blade. "Show me what Gilgan taught you. Show me your power!"

His words became meaningless as Elenah took a wobbly step in his direction. "Come! I know what you are! Face me!"

When you face him, the woman in her vision had said, *you will need to fight.*

Remember the spell, she had told her.

Incantatum.

Incantatum, Elenah thought. *Incantatum . . .*

She strode forward and *summoned* it.

The blade clapped into existence and she grabbed it. Fex's eyes widened. A strange kind of power surged through Elenah's body, twisting and bending her emotions. She felt invincible, a thousand years of magic burning in her blood. She felt like she could bring down the galaxy. She sprang forward and engaged him with insurmountable force, but Fex parried it and stepped swiftly aside. "You have strength," Fex gasped, sliding back on his heels, "but no skill. You have potential, but you have no control!"

"I don't need it."

And then the Sandred burst free. It was a huge dragon-like beast almost twice the size of a starfighter, spreading its obsidian wings and roaring incredibly as it charged Fex. Huge black spikes covered its body, concealing a lurid, violet glow underneath. Its eyes were the precise colour of the red star she'd seen in her vision . . . Fex cried out, hurtling backwards as he attempted to avoid it, his sword shattering mid-air.

Elenah stumbled, but she only had a split second to move. So she picked herself up and sprinted across the chamber, clutching the Essence, her body pulsing with power.

"You fool!" Fex roared, rising unsteadily to his feet. "*Fool girl!*" He tried to strike her but she dodged. She began to hear gunshots and shouting resounding through the ship, but she didn't let them distract her. Fex's voice rumbled behind her, but she was no longer listening. She fled through a series of passages. *Where are you, Teveran?*

She emerged in a long, straight corridor. The lights overhead were flickering, the doors along the walls were sealed shut. But she could hear voices all around her, and footfalls echoing across the metal floors, and screams, and shouts, and frantic gunfire.

And the distant chime of *magic.*

Elenah channelled the hot anger rushing through her body into the magic around her. Several lights blacked out, the walls began to rattle. The melody grew more sinister, but it still bellowed strongly. She gently closed her eyes, tightening her grip around the Essence. *I'm not going to hurt you, Teveran.* He was somewhere up ahead.

She sprinted through the corridor.

I just want to help you . . .

She rounded a corner, skidding maladroitly into the wall.

Teveran . . . What has he done to you?

She emerged at the mouth of yet another corridor, just as the distant form of her brother rounded the corner. He was somehow trailing blood, which glistened under the lights. Elenah's heartbeat quickened as she ran faster and pursued him.

"Teveran!" she cried.

"Stay away from me!" he yelled.

Another corridor.

Teveran collapsed halfway through, sliding in his own puddle of blood. Elenah dived at him. Teveran elbowed her in the head and she rolled off him. He tried to scramble back up, every sharp breath bouncing off the walls, but Elenah lurched up and wrestled him back down. She opened her hand, sprayed Essence across them both and channelled the spell.

Transcendius.

The galaxy fragmented, crumbling piece by piece . . .

And then they *fell.*

CHAPTER THIRTY-TWO

THE MOONSHRINE

The name Ezellegar, I believe, was derived from a language so old that I struggled to find more than a handful of words from it. This language predates Asmorean settlement, predates all historical records. It should not exist. Ezellegar means death, and this language is of it.

They emerged in a world that was black.

A cloud of silver Essence puffed out around them, then began to blink out of existence before touching the ground. Elenah clambered off Teveran and looked around. The land was flat, broken only by long, jagged cracks that emanated some sort of azure haze. Stars littered the sky. In the distance lay nothing but endless plains.

This isn't right, she thought. They seemed to be in the middle of nowhere. The air was chilly, and turned her breath into a diaphanous white mist. She tried to catch the particles of Essence as they floated through the air, but they fizzled before she could touch them.

Teveran lay several feet away, splayed out on his back, staring up into the sky. "Elenah," he whispered, grimacing with pain. He reached out to her in a disorientated way.

Elenah crawled across the cold, rocky ground towards him. "You have to run," he rasped.

She clutched the front of his uniform. There was blood everywhere, although it was difficult to tell where he'd been struck—or if he'd been struck at all. "Who did this to you?" was all she could say, despite where they were, despite the fact something had clearly gone wrong.

"Leave me here," Teveran said. "They're going to kill you."

"I'm not going to leave you," Elenah said, determined.

"They're stronger than both of us." His face went taut and he grabbed reflexively for his wound. Blood was soaking his uniform red. "Elenah . . ." He looked at her with an expression that caused Elenah's heart to ache. He'd gone pale, like a ghost. His brown hair was unruly and hanging off in all the wrong places. "I'm sorry for getting you into this . . . But everything is about to change. You have to go far from here."

"No," she persisted.

There was a crack like lightning somewhere in the distance. Elenah jerked her head up, but couldn't see anything. The sky was still. The stars were motionless.

"I made a mistake," Teveran said. "A terrible mistake. And I don't want you to get hurt because of me. *Please.*" He gripped her arm and dragged himself up. "That way." He pointed through the darkness. "Go that way."

"Well come on, then," Elenah said, grabbing his arm and hauling him to his feet. She propped him up beneath the arms and they stumbled forward through the dark.

There was another loud crack, and then another.

"They were among us all along," Teveran groaned,

struggling to walk. "In the *Subjugator* . . . I don't know how many, but one of them attacked me as I was trying to leave."

"Who are they?" Elenah asked.

"They're with Fex. *Magicians*."

Elenah grunted. She'd read about all sorts of magicians, good ones and bad ones, and the many forms of magic they studied. "You're not going with them," she told him. "Teveran, they're only using you. They know how powerful you are. They want your *power*."

Teveran hesitated, but did not say anything.

"Well," she said, "I haven't come all this way to lose you now."

"If you think you can fight Fex, you're wrong. You can't win this, Elenah. You're better off leaving me here and saving yourself. Go. You made it this far. I believe in you."

"Gilgan would have wanted us to fight," Elenah said.

"Gilgan's not here, though, is he," Teveran said.

Elenah huffed, struggling beneath Teveran's weight. However, soon she could make out a dim blue glow in the distance, which became a shrine of sorts, and they scrambled inside. The shrine was a dome in shape, ringed by steps and marble columns that emanated a faint sapphire glow. Elenah slipped on the polished floor, causing both her and Teveran to collapse.

Her radio fell out of her pocket and scattered across the floor. She watched it recede into the dark, and her eyes ended up on a tall goblet wrought of humming black stone. As suddenly as she looked at it, she heard a voice shriek through her ears: *Ezellegar* . . .

"I don't think we should be here," Teveran said.

Elenah rose to her feet, half a dozen strides from the

goblet, which stood in the centre of the shrine. She glanced along the colonnaded walls, upon which strange black markings were written, completely encircling them. She hurried towards the radio and swiped it up. "Jethre," she said frantically, but there was only static on the other end. "Jethre, are you there?"

"Who's Jethre?" Teveran asked, his footsteps ringing behind her.

Elenah just tucked the radio back inside her pocket and rose to her feet. Teveran stood beside her now, gazing at the black water swirling within the goblet. "Jethre was a friend of Gilgan's." There were four of them: Gilgan, Fex, Lothar, Jethre . . .

Somehow, everything that was happening involved them.

"And what do you think *that* is?"

Elenah took a closer step towards the goblet, feeling a surge of magic within. It was the same thing she'd felt on the bridge of the *Subjugator*, when she'd fought Fex . . .

Teveran took her hand. It was cold, like the chill air of this strange planet. Elenah turned around and met his frightened eyes. "Don't go near it," he told her, voice rattling. Gods, but Teveran had changed. He was no longer the brave, young man she'd seen on Etheron. Her brother looked decades older now, and his eyes were unfocused. They'd both gotten themselves into so much trouble. Elenah let him pull her away from the goblet.

"Step away from him!" The voice came from behind. Elenah spun around, instinctively reaching for a weapon, but she had nothing on her. A tall woman stepped out from behind a column, a black duster twirling around her. She wore a top hat and a pin-stripe shirt beneath the duster. She casually folded out her arm and a frenetic firebolt erupted over her palm.

Elenah grabbed Teveran and rotated her gaze. Another black-clad magician stepped out from behind another column, and a third from another. There was another loud crack, like the ones from before, and a fourth, lanky man materialised from the air, ahead of the others.

He strode up towards them and didn't look like stopping.

"*Stand back!*" Elenah cried, yanking Teveran closer and backing towards the goblet. She could feel its power against her back as she pulled Teveran closer and closer towards it. The magicians by the edges of the shrine closed in. The man at the front exhaled an audible breath, stopping outside the faint blue ambit given off by the mysterious source inside the goblet.

"Hand over Teveran and leave," said the man.

In the light, Elenah recognised him.

"Korvis?" The boy who'd chased her around the city so long ago . . .

Korvis's eyes darted wildly from Elenah to Teveran and to their dark, ancient surroundings. He steeled himself, then bared his glowing white teeth and hissed, "Hand him over!"

"No," Elenah retorted, shaking her head. She clutched Teveran's hand and arm, but could feel him trying to resist her. She only gripped him tighter, relentlessly.

"Come on, Teveran." Korvis extended a hand towards him. "This is where you belong. You're a magician. You're one of *us* now. Remember?"

"Don't go," Elenah whispered, trying to hold him closer— but there was only so much she could do. "Korvis, stop!" Teveran shook himself out of her clutches, until all that held them together was Elenah's grip around his cold, lifeless hand.

Korvis gestured Teveran towards him. Elenah felt herself weaken, and Teveran slipped out of her grip. He began to walk slowly towards him. Beyond, the three other magicians approached from the shadows, sinister expressions on their faces.

"Teveran," Elenah pleaded.

"What are you going to do, Korvis?" Teveran asked.

"I'm taking you back by Fex's request," Korvis said. "We shouldn't delay. He . . . He's not in a very good mood." Then he turned around, walking back towards his three companions, who watched with spells boiling on their lips. Elenah took a step towards Teveran, but then a sharp gaze from the woman with the top hat stilled her feet.

Suddenly, there was a sharp *shift* of magic in the shrine.

Teveran cast a sudden spell.

Korvis spun and lashed out in defence.

A black light pulsed through the shrine and then the woman behind was staggering on the spot, clasping her smoking chest. "Oh, hell," she gasped as she crumpled to her knees. Her top hat fell off, hurtling away. Elenah looked at her, feeling her heart begin to burn.

"A . . . killing curse," Korvis said, then eyed Teveran darkly.

Elenah lunged for Teveran.

Teveran thrust a bolt of light at Korvis.

"*Transfixis!*" Korvis screamed as the bolt hit his shoulder, throwing him around. As he slammed the ground on one knee, his spell—a black coil of light—streaked through the air and struck Teveran in the hip. A shallow shriek escaped him as he recoiled there on the spot. He let out a shaky, misty breath. It was as if he'd been impaled by a large, invisible spear. His eyes were wide. Sweat cracked his face.

"Stop!" Elenah cried.

"Get away from him!" Korvis roared, dragging himself up, but the spell had rattled him and he fell back down. "*Teveran!*" he screamed, then clenched his hand into a fist. He lunged upwards, approaching with light footsteps that became stomping. "We have to go *back!*"

"Elenah . . ." Teveran gasped, slumping to his knees.

"Gods, Teveran, get up!" Elenah cried as she ran forward to grab him.

"I told you to get away!" Korvis barked, blasting her with a spell that sent her flying back across the slippery stone floor. She landed on her back, the breath lashed from her lungs. As she glanced back up, she saw Teveran try to climb to his feet, but he fell forward instead.

Motionless.

Dead.

"NO!" Elenah screamed.

"But the spell . . ." Korvis muttered. "But the spell . . ."

The air cracked behind him and Fex emerged in a flash of silver Essence. He staggered a couple of paces, then regained his composure just as Korvis turned and spotted him there. "*Korvis!*" Fex roared. "What have you done? I wanted him *alive!*"

"Fex . . ." Korvis choked.

Fex knocked him aside and knelt down at Teveran's lifeless body. "You idiot," he snarled, looking perplexed at the blood that was pooling across the shrine's stone floor. He looked up at Elenah, but she could hardly make sense of anything anymore. She couldn't move, couldn't draw breath; all she could do was watch, with the goblet's fury behind her. And she began to wonder: *What kind of spell requires verbal casting?*

Fex stood up unsteadily, eying Elenah like she'd gone mad. His eyes were bulging, his wrinkled skin was plastered with sweat. And Elenah recognised this look.

Fex was *afraid.*

He turned around to regard the three dark magicians who stood before him. They were each silenced by his gaze. They no longer had any spells brewing on their tongues. "Go!" Fex spat, gesturing through the icy air. "Go back to the Tower!"

All three of them disappeared.

"What do you want?" Elenah whimpered. "Why are you here?"

Fex looked at her, fury in his eyes. Then, he started walking towards her, his feet clapping the stone floor. Elenah backed away from him.

"Don't *touch* her."

Fex froze. Behind him stood Jethre. The shadows were still slithering off his haggard frame as he walked into the light with a pistol poised at the back of Fex's head.

"How . . . How did you get here?" Fex growled.

"The same way you all did. You took something that did not belong to you. That Essence is Lothar's. I assume that name sounds familiar, old friend."

Fex hesitated.

"He told me to give you his regards."

Fex swung around and cast a lightning bolt at Jethre.

Jethre whipped his hand upwards and the electric bolts sprayed outwards, fizzling almost instantaneously. Fex looked rattled. Jethre didn't move from the spot. "Leave, Fex. Go back to where you came from. But if you touch the girl, I will follow you and I will kill you all."

"You always were such an angry man," Fex jibed.

"*Don't make me kill you!*" Jethre barked, then cast a flame up above his palm. It was hatred like Elenah had never seen. Fex eyed him hotly, then twisted round in an instant, pulled out a vial of Essence, grabbed Teveran by the arm and departed in a flash of white light.

"Stop!" Elenah cried, but it was too late; they were gone. "Jethre . . ."

"Don't talk," Jethre told her, expelling his fire. He rushed to her side as he withdrew his own vial of Essence. It was sapphire, and emitted a light that flashed in his eyes. "Take my hand."

Elenah took it.

"Everything is going to be okay," Jethre whispered.

And they got away.

Chapter Thirty-Three

THE DARK LORD

Somebody has reawakened the Dark Lord. I must find them.

A red star ripped through space.

Elenah watched it hurtle across the sky, then vanish in the distance. It left nothing behind but a crimson trail of light, like a furious bloodstain on the galaxy.

She stepped forward and placed a hand against the dirty window of this cramped little hilltop house. Beyond the glass, she saw rolling hills and moonlit fields. And, reflected on the night, she saw herself, with raven hair washed yet too long, and pale cheeks cleaned yet scarred and bruised. It was three days since the battle at the shrine, but she couldn't stop thinking about it.

Below her, on the second or third storey, the others were fighting again.

"You told me you searched the castle," Jethre said. His voice resounded through the house; these walls were thinner than slabs of paper. The floor and the ceiling creaked. She could hear the rebels overhead, and in the rooms beside her. There were a dozen of them.

"The castle was empty," Argus assured him. "Whoever lived there . . . They were long gone when we arrived. And they left a bloody *graveyard* in their garden, too."

"Then Ithrial's still alive," Lothar said—who had recently arrived.

"You really believe that?" Jethre asked.

"Who's Ithrial?" Argus asked.

"He's the one who taught us everything we know," Lothar said. "He's still out there. We have to find him." He lowered his voice, but barely enough to escape Elenah's listening ears. "The gods know if Fex is already looking. And maybe Ithrial can help us find Gilgan—"

"I don't think Gilgan's coming back," Jethre said.

Elenah felt a needle of heat streak through her, and she stepped away from the window. A wind rushed by, rattling it in its frame. Where did she go from here? Etheron was gone, and her father along with it. Gilgan was somewhere far away, if not already dead. And Teveran . . .

Transfixis!

She could still hear the spell echoing in her mind. The vibrations of the tune bounced around inside her body. It was a verbal spell, like none she'd ever read or heard of. Was it dark magic, or was it something completely different?

Anger swelled inside her. Fury, and hatred, and pain. Fex and his magicians had taken Teveran from her, and the gods knew *where* they'd taken him. *Why?* she asked herself. *Where are they taking him? Why can't I just see him one more time . . .*

The door creaked open.

She turned. Hannah stood in the doorway, still dressed in her shabby brown coat, with the crimson gear plastered across the shoulder and breast. She walked forward and the wooden door squealed shut behind her. Elenah could feel her apprehension. "What is it?" she asked.

"I want to talk to you about something," Hannah said.

Elenah nodded, then crossed the room and sat on the bed. It squealed. The bedroom was far from the kind of room she'd grown up inside. The desk drawer was locked with a key that was no longer there. The floorboards were splintered. The lamp flickered occasionally, and the light that it emitted was so dim that the starlight outside was brighter by tenfold.

Hannah sat beside her. "There's another Felirean out there."

"What makes you think that?"

"One of the soldiers told me on Devar." She swallowed, and glanced at Elenah anxiously. "I have to go," she finally said. "If there's even a chance that I might be able to free Feluria . . . Then I'm not going to hang around. I'm done running. You understand, don't you?"

"Wasn't there a prophecy?"

"There's no such thing."

Elenah rested a hand on Hannah's pale green one. "Be careful."

"We're leaving in the morning," Hannah said. "I . . . I feel so bad. You've just lost your brother, and your home, and . . ."

"I haven't lost as much as you have."

Hannah nodded and stood up, then started for the door. "I hope I see you again, Elenah. Whatever happens, be careful and please take care of yourself."

"You too, Hannah."

Hannah smiled back at her, then walked out the door. Elenah watched it fall shut with a clap. Dust and dirt sprayed out from underneath it, and began coiling and writhing within the rays of light. Elenah eyed the swaying lamp. She turned her palm towards it, inhaled a long, shaky breath, and the light blacked out. For a moment, she simply sat there in the darkness.

Then, she began to cry.

FEX SHOVED OPEN THE HUGE, STONE DOOR of an obsidian tower. Silvery light flowed out like water, undulating across the glossy ground. He squinted, for the lights burned his weary eyes. Blood rushing through his body like a storm, he stepped through the doorway and into the Tower.

"Korvis," he snapped.

"Fex, I'm sorry—"

"Stand aside." Fex brushed past him and into the circular room beyond. He'd sent away the body of Teveran with the magician, Rivas, but he would be returning to him shortly.

The spell . . . The spell had *killed* him!

No, it was not meant to be used against him in the first place!

Small alcoves were hollowed out in the tower walls. Red and white light streamed around him as he ventured to the stairwell in the centre and ascended the steps two at a time.

His breath rang in his ears, restless and hoarse. This tower was ancient. The walls were falling apart. The stairwell, wrought of crooked stone slabs, was eroding even now. It wasn't long now before they relocated to Etheron. Kloak's most recent report was encouraging.

He reached the highest level and emerged inside a domed chamber. Everything stilled, and the sudden stillness accentuated the silver and red wisps of light, which flitted about, bouncing off corners and constructs. There was only one other person in the chamber, a silver-haired magician by the name of Arathelle, who stood with her hands cradled before her and some sort of metallic object within it. Fex eyed her, then righted his shoulders, and stepped deeper into the chamber.

He swallowed, then called out, "My lord!" It echoed through the chamber, bouncing off the glittering stone walls, off panels of cracked and mouldy glass. Ringing the chamber were twisted obsidian pillars, which seemed to curl as they stretched impossibly upwards. There was no starlight, for the sky was shrewd and ashen tonight. There was only the pale aura that surrounded the figure ahead, standing in his livid shroud of darkness.

"Where is the boy?" asked the Dark Lord. His voice was withered and cracked, like a stone that had fallen from the highest tower and had weathered a thousand storms. In the shadows, Fex couldn't make out much save for his thin, wiry frame swallowed by a frail black cloak.

"The boy is dead," Fex said bluntly. "Korvis killed him."

"A shame," the Dark Lord said, almost voicelessly.

"But I promise I will find those stones and—"

"I am growing tired of your failure, *Fexer Anteris*."

"Forgive me, my lord." Fex fell to one knee and bowed. He raised his head and tried to catch a glimpse of the Dark Lord through the shadows. He failed.

"My lord," interrupted Arathelle. "If I'm not mistaken, Fex has not yet succeeded in reclaiming *any* of the stones. If I were you, I might start questioning his . . . *loyalty*."

"I don't suppose *you've* come bearing gifts?" Fex hissed.

"In fact, I *have.*" Arathelle stepped in front of Fex and fell so elegantly to one knee. She proffered a silver sphere. "This is an Asmorean galaxy map."

The Dark Lord stepped forward, yet he remained cloaked in shadow. He took the sphere from Arathelle, holding it in his skeletal, deathly hands. "Where did you get this?"

"I took it from a *Troff,*" Arathelle said with a joyful tone. "Cut off her head and put it on a steel pike." She cackled, then lowered her hands as the Dark Lord observed the Asmorean map. "We can use it to find the stones, my lord."

"I can *tell* you where they are," Fex said, determined to please the Dark Lord. He raised his head and could almost see the Dark Lord's ghostly, emaciated face. "My old master, Ithrial . . . We failed to capture him, yes, but I know where he has gone. And Gilgan . . ."

"Yes." The Dark Lord vanished in the darkness. "Gilgan proved *very* useful."

"Then Pandion delivered him in one piece?" Fex asked hopefully.

His answer was cold, rough cackling from the shadows at the back of the chamber. Fex turned around and rose to his feet as another dark magician, Volhous, emerged. He was still fastening the buckles of his black coat, trying to stifle his raging laughter—which was accompanied by the grinding of metal chains. "Gilgan doesn't look so good," Volhous said. He dragged Gilgan into the light. There was blood all over him, his clothes were charred and tattered. His mutated leg was completely shattered now, and his eyes . . .

He no longer had them.

"What did you do to him?" Fex gasped.

Volhous swung Gilgan's limp body forward, and the chain

slammed the ground with a loud crash. "Loosened him up a little." Volhous's bald head seemed to glow for an instant. "E4 Station," he announced. "It's over Tannis II. There are a couple of stones there."

Threpe, Fex realised. *Gilgan must have given him his own stone.*

Suddenly, Gilgan coughed out a bloody tooth.

Arathelle cackled as she joined them around the body. "He's not dead."

"No," Volhous grumbled. "What would be the fun in that?"

Fex eyed his old friend for one moment longer, then spun on his heel and crossed the chamber back towards the stairwell. He glanced to where the Dark Lord had been standing, but now all that remained was a deep, spellbinding darkness. He descended the steps two at a time, brushed past Korvis at the bottom, then drifted through the door and out of the tower.

Read on for an excerpt from the first novella
in the Magicus Eye expanded universe:
REBEL AND THE AEONSEER

which takes place eighteen years before the
events of Daughter of Etheron

CHAPTER ONE

SKORWICH CAMP

A storm blew through the mountains of Skorwich.

Eva Barella pulled her coat tighter around herself as she wrestled through the narrow, slick roads. The wind wailed, throwing up clouds of snow and shaking ice from the white fir trees. Snow and rain pelted her jacket, rumbling against her skin. Her chapped lips glowed, and the hole in her left glove made the storm feel like fire as it whacked her bare skin.

Dawne had gone quiet, cradled in her arms, wrapped within layers of rough-hewn cloth. Eva tried to shield her from the worst of the storm, but it was coming right at them. "It's okay," she muttered, trying to console the five-year-old. "We're almost there."

"Mama . . ." Dawne croaked. Gods, she was shivering *bad*.

Lanterns shook wildly from the eaves of various wooden structures, the bulbs of starfire within flickering up against the mouldy glass. Eva glanced hurriedly to the side as a tall Kyubo with wolf-like features brought down his massive steel axe and split a log with a loud *crack*. A knot of other assorted species surrounded him, trying to fix the frozen machinery.

Eva ducked her head and quickened her pace against the belting winds. She needed to get out of this cold; Dawne needed warmth. The rattle and squeal of wood constantly reminded her of how close to disaster they'd built this place. The Skorwich refugee camp was nestled on the rugged shafts of the Steel Mountains. The road she was on ran jaggedly up the middle, and the architecture was uneven, pinned up in a hurry.

"Mama . . . Where are we going?" Dawne asked in a weak voice.

"I'm going to make you better," Eva said, stroking her daughter's fine black hair—quite unlike her own, which was auburn, short and wavy. She could barely control the panic in her voice. "It's going to be okay, Dawne. Just close your eyes. You need some medicine." But what if it didn't work? What if she wasn't fast enough? What if there was nothing she *could* do?

She threw her shoulder into the wet, wooden door of a small hut and tumbled inside.

The storm followed her in, whipping about various bottles and flasks and puffing out the candles set about the tables. Eva spun around and pulled the door shut. Silence. Darkness. And then a single flame was lit nearby, and Levis appeared beside it. Clean-shaven and with a fresh cut of slick black hair, he looked a decade younger than thirty.

"I need your help," Eva gasped, flinging off her hood and striding through the room. It was a cramped dwelling that served both as Levis's home and the camp's sole medical bay.

Levis took one glance at the shivering form of Eva's daughter, then cursed. He turned his back on them, racing to the potion racks on the other side of the room. "Put her down on the bench," he said as he absentmindedly put a flame to another candle.

Eva did exactly as he said. "It's the *parasite* . . ."

"Yes, I conjectured," Levis muttered, returning to her with several misshapen vials filled with funny-looking colours. Luckily, Levis had been trained in the natural arts of healing from a very young age, and he knew how to deal with such things. It was a synergic contrast to Eva, who had grown up with the most complex technology, mending broken codes.

"Will she be okay?" Eva asked.

"Yes," Levis said, though he barely made eye contact.

"*Levis—*"

He tossed the coverlets off her daughter, revealing the burning red glow underneath Dawne's pallid skin. Eva cursed and covered her mouth, fighting the urge to go and wrap her back up. Levis slapped the potions on the bench and unstoppered the lids. Sweet, bitter and citric smells filled the room. "You did well," Levis said, wiping sweat from his jet-black hair. "It hasn't spread."

"Oh god . . ." Her heart was racing. She felt like she was going to be sick.

Levis bent in towards Dawne and gave her a sip of a pink, bubbly concoction. Then he tossed back that one, yanked off her cloth wrapping and brandished a steel syringe. Before Eva could blink, it was glowing with another potion's essence. Levis inserted it into the soft skin concealing the red parasite. He waited several heartbeats, then exhaled sharply. Turning back to Eva, he said, "Keep her here tonight, maybe?"

"Thank you, Levis."

"My pleasure." Keeping his potions handy, he crossed the room and began to wash out his various tools inside a wooden basin. "Please, sit. Can I get you anything?"

"No, I couldn't possibly take your food . . ."

"Water, perhaps? We'll have no shortage of it after this blizzard." He chuckled to himself, skin glowing with the candlelight's amber.

"Thank you," Eva said. She didn't sit; instead, she touched her daughter's forehead, feeling the warmth return, and gently kissed her. "How do you feel?"

"Better," Dawne breathed.

"Just close your eyes and try to get some rest."

"Okay, Mama."

Levis hummed to himself as he returned to her with two flagons of water, handing one to Eva. He stood a few paces away, leaning crookedly on one of the benches as he sipped his water. The storm continued to beat outside, relentless, shaking the ground beneath their feet. "I gave her a shot of Stormweed Essence," he said. "It's actually a very strong poisonous decoction, rating quite high on Professor Grimward's potency scale. During the Jiaran Spike . . ."

"Wasn't Grimward a god?" Eva asked sceptically.

"Well, some historians also claimed he was immortal, and that would give a man plenty of time to diversify his interests . . . wouldn't you agree?"

Eva smirked.

"Typically, Stormweed Essence is used to kill cotylmongers, but paired with *this* serum of luran blood, your daughter will be well-protected against its effects. *Hopefully*."

"Hopefully!" Eva cried.

Levis chuckled, spilling some of his water. "Sorry, I just couldn't resist. No, Dawne will have a swift recovery. Just keep an eye on her."

Eva let out a shaky breath. "Oh, where in the stars do you learn this stuff?"

"Books, mostly," Levis said, turning his eyes towards Dawne, now resting peacefully, her chest moving up and down in calm, controlled motions. "So I heard Andis managed to link a couple of our routers to one of the network hotlinks over Tannis."

"Yes, although I told him not to. It's dangerous, too easy for hackers to get inside and feed viruses into our system. Those men over Tannis *are* hackers, might I add. They have quite the reputation. Anyway, I couldn't imagine the signal would be very strong here."

Levis nodded as he sipped his water, then set it down on the bench beside him. "I suppose you have a point." Then he looked out one of the frosted windows, frowning. "Do you think this will ever end? This winter? It's lasted five years. It's as old as your daughter now."

"It's just another movement in the turning of the Eternal Cog," Eva said. "When the magicians return, everything will go back to normal."

Levis looked at her uncertainly. "You seem quite convinced."

"Well, surely you don't think they're gone forever, do you?"

"Whatever caused this thing—"

There was a loud *thunderclap* in the sky. The wooden door was flung open and Eva saw a bright light shining amidst the diaphanous storm clouds.

A huge *Leviathan* emerged from hyperspace.

Time seemed to freeze just for an instant. The huge obsidian warship hung there ominously for a few moments, large enough to cover the faraway sun. And then something left it, the smallest bead of silver, sinking into the planet's atmosphere.

"What are they doing here?" Levis whispered.

The door slammed back shut, plunging them into silence. Eva looked towards Levis and Levis looked towards her, and the room was significantly darker than before.

"They're not going to attack us," Eva told herself. The uneasy look in Levis's eyes did not comfort her very much. But any contradiction would be a lie.

It was the Forty-Ninth Council, empire of the galaxy, and though they were heralded across the stars, they seemed to care little for protecting it. Memories of the skies during the Wiskan Revolt came to her in a flash. The world had never been so black. After only one day of fighting, the Council had abandoned them. And now Eva had been thrown here, alongside her daughter, in these blasted mountains, sequestered from everything.

"I'm going," Eva said, already shrugging back on her coat and throwing up the hood. "I imagine they will want to speak with me. Please take care of Dawne for me."

Levis didn't object; he knew her well enough. *Besides*, Eva thought as she put her hand against the door and began to heave against the wind, *I'm the one who brought us here.* And if the Council had a problem, they would need to take it up with her.

She stepped out into the storm as a crowd began to gather. Despite the cold, people were piling out of their homes, workers were staring up into the sky, clutching their steel weapons. So they should. The Forty-Ninth Council was not welcome here.

Eva hurried up towards Venrau: her friend and also a tall female Tauran who happened to be about twice as bulky and three-times as strong as the average Tauran woman. Her pale skin, with a vague hue of blue, burned a slight-blistered red in the heart of the storm.

"They're here for Andis," Venrau said, pulling anxiously at her dark, braided hair. Venrau's little son was nagging at her dress.

"What did Andis do?" Eva asked sternly.

"I . . ." Her once-calm voice faltered. "It's just what I've heard . . . He's been using the hotlinks to transmit messages . . . propaganda and such. Anti-Council messages."

Eva frowned. "No way is the signal strong enough—"

"Apparently it's stronger than we thought," Venrau said.

"That's not possible," Eva growled.

"Doesn't matter what's possible; it's what I've heard."

"Oh, goddammit." Eva took off, winding through the snow-slick roads. Everything seemed *off*. The buildings were crooked, even more so after this storm. Ice glittered off the mountainside, and the tempestuous winds made everything seem distorted. She glanced at the Leviathan in the sky, obscured by snow and cloud. She could no longer see the shuttle that had left it. She cursed under her breath and turned onto another road.

The place they had named the main courtyard was completely deserted save for the silver shuttle and the man that had emerged from it. People were watching from their houses and from the sides of the road. There was a well in the middle of the courtyard, and a small stone statue that had been carved by Temet: another deformed-looking bird. A river ran down from the top of the mountain and passed through here, although it was completely frozen.

Eva had not seen many officers of the Council so far, but she did recognise the large white coats they wore in the winter, and she noticed their simple-yet-effective insignia: a phoenix, black as pitch, standing out in stark contrast to everything else.

Snow blew up around him, whipping about the tassels of his coat. Eva pushed her way through the crowds—there must have been a dozen people gathered here, which was quite a large portion of the collective number here at the camp. From the darkness behind the officer came four white-clad troopers with snow-covered rifles in their arms. Unlike the officer, the troopers wore full body armour, which appeared to be modified for the cold. Narrow slits in their helmets and chests emitted a fiery red light, and their helmets had some kind of exhaust at the fronts, expelling pale breath vapour. Up in the sky, a second transport shuttle was descending in an array of blinking lights.

"Officer," Eva said, clutching her coat about herself.

The officer regarded her first, and then the crowd that had gathered. There were almost as many species as there were individuals, many of them with battle wounds, others still clutching the tools they'd been using to keep the camp running. Eva's heart was racing as the troopers stepped forward, straying from the officer and gazing about the place. All Eva could think of was her daughter, with Levis . . .

She hoped this didn't escalate.

"What is this?" the officer snarled.

"We're just trying to survive the winter," Eva said in her softest tone of voice. The officer scrutinised her words, as though trying to decide how far they were from the truth. He walked forward, snow and ice cracking underneath his heavy black boots. This man looked like he'd been serving for many years; his skin was wrinkled and his eyes were cupped by deep black marks. He also had stitching across his cheek, and auburn hair peppered with grey and white.

"Our intelligence has intercepted several illegal transmissions," the officer said, "all of which have been traced back to this very location." He turned on his heel, tracing his jawline as the troopers scattered far enough apart to occupy the entire courtyard. "It would seem that somebody here has been spreading lies across multiple star systems."

"I wasn't aware of it," Eva said.

"Oh, of course not," he snarled.

Eva eyed him down, feeling anger well up inside her.

"Kill someone," the officer said.

There was a blast and a flash of light and then a body *whacked* the ground.

Eva gasped, her body kicking into overdrive. She scrambled from the source of the sound, swirled on her heel and saw the crowd scatter from the body. *Merri's* body, a proficient cook. A narrow river of blood ran down from the slight incline, zigzagging towards her and causing steam to rise from the snow. Eva glanced back at the officer, who had not moved from the spot.

"I don't think you understand the severity of this offense," the officer said, his chin raised towards the mountain peak, as though the murder had empowered him.

"We haven't done anything wrong," Eva said.

"Are you trying to start some kind of insurgency?"

"No," Eva gasped. The officer pulled out his own pistol and fired three shots into the air. Eva flinched but managed to hold herself. This place was all they had. Where would they go? How would she raise her daughter in all this chaos?

"This mountain now belongs to the Forty-Ninth Council,"

the officer said, striding past Eva towards the others, who tried to cower as far away from him as they could. "And you are all property of Highlord Vicera." Eva felt herself grow tense, her blood boiling with every word this man uttered. "So, let's do away with the formalities." He pointed his pistol at a woman in the crowd. She shrieked and he shot her in the knee, sending her into the snow.

"Lara!" a man shouted.

"*Get away from her*," the officer scowled, his pistol aimed directly on her head. "Nobody move. Nobody speak." He adjusted his gloved grip around the pistol. "Just the one who's been sending those messages. Step forward."

Not a person moved.

Eva looked into the crowd. They were all going to die if Andis did not step forward. But did *Andis* deserve to die, or to be taken to one of the Council's prisons? She was itching to do something. She *had* to do something. What was it her uncle used to say? *I'm not a mathematician, but two lives are always worth more than one.* It didn't even make sense.

But what did she really want? For the Council to leave them alone? For her daughter to be safe? For Levis to be safe? For Venrau to be safe?

And wasn't Andis jeopardising their safety?

"Just do as he says!" she cried. "Who did it?"

Andis, she thought. *Andis, just come out . . .*

"Take aim," the officer said, not moving. The four troopers raised their rifles upon the crowd. A rumble came from behind them as the second shuttle set down on the ice and two more officers came out alongside a contingent of troopers.

Eva couldn't breathe. She could barely process what was

happening anymore. Her instincts told her to run and find her daughter. But these people . . .

Andis . . .

"I will not bow down," the officer said. Eva scanned the crowds for Andis, but he was nowhere to be seen. She glanced at the troopers, their rifles, *glinting . . .*

"Wait . . ." Eva muttered.

"I'm here." The voice came not from the restless crowd, but from the mountain slopes. Andis took the crooked stone stairway to the courtyard, his comically-large coat trailing behind him. Raising his arms to the side, he said, "I'm here, but I won't kneel to your oppression. *We* won't kneel."

The officer scowled.

"We'll *fight*," Andis said, stopping on the final step.

"Some might call you terrorists," the officer said.

"You have them fooled."

"Get him." Three troopers hurriedly stormed through the snow and grappled Andis beneath the arms. Andis struggled, but he was a small man who was often too distracted by his work to eat. The other officers converged upon them with their hands unsteadily on their holstered pistols. "Inform the Architect of this victory," the officer said to the others.

The Architect . . . The name went through her head too fast for her to make much meaning of it. The officer snatched her arm with a strength that betrayed his haggard frame.

"We'll take this one to trial before the Prime Court," he said.

"No!" Eva struggled, trying to break out of his grip but failing. She collapsed to her knees but the officer only dragged her further through the snow, drenching her trousers. He couldn't do this. Eva had to get back to Dawne. She tried, and tried, but the officer was unbending.

"I know who you are," he said. "You're a Barella. *Dissidents*, the lot of you."

Eva didn't question *how*, or *why*, but she looked at Andis, filled with so much anger she could barely control herself. This was all his fault.

"Surely you don't think this victory was yours, Brickam," said one of the other officers, a man who stood several paces back with his hands on his hips.

Officer Brickam gripped Eva's coat tighter as he swung around. "I am the commanding officer here. Start clearing out the rest of the camp. Eliminate all hostility and ensure they don't send out another signal. Keep it *clean*, men."

They followed begrudgingly.

Brickam threw Eva towards another trooper and said, "Restrain them and load them into the ships." Then, looking towards the Leviathan in orbit, he brushed off his hands: satisfied.

Halfway to the ships, something detonated.

There was a *rumble* on the higher mountain shafts.

"What the hell was that?" Brickam growled.

Then there was an explosion, throwing everyone to the snow. Flames ripped through the stormy sky and Brickam's private shuttle splintered apart like glass, embers and debris flicking across the courtyard. Eva rolled out of Brickam's grasp, the snow burning her.

"Get out of here, Eva!" Andis roared.

Without thinking twice, Eva scrambled away from the chaos as the shouts came nearer and successive blasts consumed the night. Bombs? Where in damnation did they get *bombs?*

The troopers and officers returned fire and dead bodies wet the ground.

Eva shot to her feet and left the courtyard. She sprinted through the roads of the encampment proper where people were going crazy. "Stay inside your houses!" she cried, although she wasn't sure if any sound came from her lips. "Stay hidden!" She slipped on a loose shaft of ice and crashed to her knees. The ice threw her onwards until she whacked a frosted fir tree, cracking the weakened bole. She grunted, then climbed unsteadily to her feet.

"Dawne," she muttered. "Oh, gods . . ."

Another explosion rocked her back into reality. Fire spiralled into the sky over the courtyard. Her eyes kept moving, up and up into the highest clouds where the Council's warship, a Leviathan of their famous Legacy-Class, hung ominously, so imposing . . .

They're watching us, she thought. *Always watching . . .*

"Eva!" came a nearby scream. She turned and saw the hazy outline of Levis. He had Dawne in his arms, wrapped in sheets and sodden cloths. "Eva, we have to leave!"

She glanced back at the Leviathan, back at Levis and her daughter.

"*Orbital strike!*" somebody yelled.

A flash of light cracked by the warship and ten heartbeats later there was an explosion near the mountain peaks, which resonated straight down to the camp. It knocked the breath from Eva's lungs, threw her off-balance, slipping on the ice.

She lunged forward and swiped Dawne out of Levis's arms, stamping her feet down in the snow to lodge herself on steady ground. Another blast sounded, shaking the entire planet, and white snow was tumbling from the mountain peaks.

A familiar face emerged from the tumult.

"I know a way," Venrau said, holding her own child by the hand.

Eva nodded, willing to follow anyone under these disastrous circumstances. The Tauran, dressed in her warrior-like native Tauran clothing, turned on her heel and began following a path leading down the rumbling mountainside.

They diverged from the path, descending the snowy incline between frosted shrubbery and bushes, trying not to slip over and tumble down, winding between trees.

Then there was a brilliant flash in the sky, a mighty crack that sounded like bones breaking, and a brief second of *silence*. They kept running, Eva's heartbeat pounding in her ears, her breath coming in loud, hoarse gasps. *Keep running,* she thought. *Keep running . . .*

Then a huge crack ran up the side of the mountain, from the bottom to the top, splintering out a thousand ways. Eva stopped, but gravity propelled her downwards. Her legs went out from underneath her and she slammed down on her back, clutching Dawne with everything she had. A blast sounded. Dawne tumbled from her grasp.

Eva managed to regain her vision just in time to see the crack form right beneath her. The ground shifted. The mountainside swayed back and forth.

And then it swallowed her.

To continue the saga, explore the extensive Magicus Database, see exclusive behind-the-scenes details, and view news and updates regarding further instalments in the series, visit: www.themagicuseye.com

ACKNOWLEDGEMENTS

The most special of thanks must go out to all those who helped in the creation of this novel. Asher Blake, who read it first; and Annabella, who read it second. To Zoe (one of my first readers *ever*) and Jun, who knew these characters when they were starring in worse novels. My beta readers: Baelen, Delaney, Elisabeth, Max, Owen, Spencer, and Tazz, for helping to refine the story and fix all the broken threads. And Liz Kemp, my manuscript assessor from Writers Victoria, who made the novel even better.

And finally to you, the reader, for trusting the unknown writer and coming along for the ride.

ABOUT THE AUTHOR

BRANDON YOUNG is the debut author of the *Saga of the Magicus Eye*. He's also a musician, gamer, and avid Star Wars fan living in Melbourne, Australia.

@BrandonYoung400